THE COUNT OF CASTELFINO

BY
CHRISTINA HOLLIS

Christina Hollis was born in Somerset, and now lives in the idyllic Wye valley. She was born reading, and her childhood dream was to become a writer. This was realised when she became a successful journalist and lecturer in organic horticulture. Then she gave it all up to become a full-time mother of two and run half an acre of productive country garden.

Writing Mills & Boon® romances is another ambition realised. It fills most of her time, between complicated rural school runs. The rest of her life is divided between garden and kitchen, either growing fruit and vegetables or cooking with them. Her daughter's cat always closely supervises everything she does around the home, from typing to picking strawberries!

You can learn more about Christina and her writing at www.christinahollis.com.

To Martyn, for all his help and support

PROLOGUE

Meg could hardly believe her luck. Charity Gala Night at the world-famous Chelsea Flower Show, and she was part of it! The rich and famous jetted in from all over the world for this exclusive preview. Her display of tropical flowers attracted them all, so she was getting a grandstand view of their wealth and beauty. When she heaved a sigh now, it was only to experience the fragrance of a million flowers and acres of crushed grass. Her career might be on hold, but this experience was taking her mind off her pain.

Suddenly, a strangely determined movement caught her eye. A gorgeous man was threading his way between the tycoons and movie stars. Patting a shoulder here, kissing a woman there, he looked as though he owned the place. Tall, athletic and moving with natural grace, he was born to wear a tuxedo. Meg couldn't help following him with her eyes. His dark good looks were illuminated every few seconds by a flashing smile as yet another person tried to catch his eye. Meg wondered what it would be like to be part of his charmed circle. Watching him was her window into another world. When the crowd closed around him, hiding him from view, a light definitely went out of her evening. She dropped her gaze to the reality of her job on the Imsey Plant Centre stand again, wondering what it would have been like to sample some of his charm for herself.

The expression froze on her face as she realised her day-dream was about to come true. Her ideal man was walking straight towards her display stand, and smiling. He obviously wanted to attract her attention. He got it—instantly.

'*Buona sera, signorina!*' He twinkled, his voice rippling with Italian delight. 'I need beautiful presents for some…*special* people. I've been told this sort of plant is foolproof…' he continued, looking down at an open note-book in his hands. Frowning briefly, he raised his eyes to hers again with a particularly devastating smile. 'Mmm…I wonder—can *you* read this handwriting?'

He made no move to hold the little book out to her. Meg couldn't reach it from where she stood. She might never get a better chance to approach a man like this. Glancing apprehensively all around, she nipped around the end of the Imsey stand and went to his side. She felt unbelievably shy, but it was worth it. The closer she got, the more darkly handsome he became. He wasn't just lovely, he had everything. His designer suit was so crisp and new, a gold Rolex shone against his flawless tan, and when he moved she was engulfed in a waft of expensively discreet aftershave.

'This is the first chance I've had to get out from behind this display all day, sir!'

'Don't worry. I'll make sure it's worth your while.'

With a flutter of pleasure, Meg heard all sorts of un-spoken promises in his voice. It didn't take a mind reader to know that was exactly what he intended. Smiling down at her indulgently, he showed her his notebook. The first thing she noticed was the way his fingers curled around its leather-bound cover. They were long, strong and a shade of brown more usually seen on the men who worked beside her in the greenhouses at home. There was only one difference. Unlike them, this man had fingernails that were neat and clean. Meg found herself wondering if the rest of him was equally smooth and perfect…

Her handsome customer cleared his throat. It was a soft, polite sound but Meg's guilt made her jump. She looked back at his notebook. Most of the page was covered in staccato Italian written in a strong, clear hand. Then an expansive, old-fashioned script had added something. Meg leaned close to her visitor, trying to make out what it said. The warm night released another tantalising hint of his expensive cologne into the air. She inhaled, trying to make it sound as though she were concentrating. This was a once-in-a-lifetime moment for her. When she had served him, this stunning man would be gone from her life for ever. Meg made sure she stretched out the moment for as long as she could.

'It's an Imseyii hybrid, sir. They're exclusive to my family's nursery,' she announced, leaning back from him with regret. She was rewarded with a look that made everything worthwhile. His dark brown eyes glittered with pleasure. Meg gazed into them, and was lost. His teasing smile was as irresistible as the rest of him and she felt herself getting warmer by the minute.

He leaned toward her with a wicked grin. 'What I want to know is: *do women like them*?'

'They can't resist them, sir!' Meg giggled, surprising herself. She had never found anything remotely funny about her work before. 'Our orchids are the perfect impulse gift to give a lady.'

'Or perhaps *several* ladies?'

Meg let his remark pass. There were too many people relying on her, back at home, for a flirtation to lead her astray. Turning away from the influence of his beautiful eyes, she spread her hand towards her display, inviting him to admire the carefully crafted arrangement she had made of the nursery's best plants. Dozens of them nestled in a bed of soft green moss. Hundreds of arching stems as fine as florist's wire trembled in the slightest movement of air. Each was set with dozens of perfect little flowers, some plain, some patterned, and in almost every colour of the rainbow. Meg was so proud of them she allowed herself another smile.

'They're often called "dancing delights". Are you tempted, sir?'

Her handsome customer put his head on one side and looked at her mischievously. 'That depends. Do you dance?'

Meg giggled again. At any other time, in any other circumstances she would have cursed herself for being so unprofessional. Tonight, it felt *right*. Simply looking at this man lightened her heart. There was something about the glitter in his sloe-dark eyes, and the life burning in his expression.

'I don't suppose you need to dance, with a smile like that.'

Magically, the gap between them closed. Meg couldn't see him moving, but it was definitely happening. Confused, she looked at her plants. 'I don't have time for dancing, sir—or anything other than nursery work, really. Looking after all these is more than a full-time job...'

'Then you must do it very well. Everything is looking lovely.' He tilted his head again, and there was no mistaking his expression.

'Thank you!' Meg responded with a delight that over-came her shyness. And then she realised he wasn't concen-trating on the plants, but on her. Immediately a molten core of heat threatened to melt every square inch of her skin. It erupted in a blush as he trained a knowing look straight at her.

'I'll take a dozen. Send them around to my Mayfair apartment. That should keep my current string of beauties quiet for a day or two. My name is Gianni Bellini. Here's my card, and thank you—these last few minutes have been a real pleasure.' His smile was roguish, and told Meg that plants definitely took second place with him. 'Now, I must pay.' He pulled out a sleek leather wallet and extracted a sheaf of banknotes along with his business card. As he passed them over to her a smile animated his beautiful lips and suggestive eyes. Her blushes flared again as he took her hand in his warm, sure grip. Raising it to his lips for the soft sensuality of a kiss, he reduced her legs to jelly.

'And so, until the next time we meet, *mio dolce…*'

Dark eyes flashing, he nodded a discreet farewell. Then before Meg could gasp or laugh or speak, he withdrew his touch, turned and vanished into the crowds…

CHAPTER ONE

MEG woke with a jolt and realised she was back in her aircraft seat. Her heart tumbled thirty thousand feet. A lot had happened since the Chelsea Flower Show, but the image of Gianni Bellini still haunted her. Only the thrill of starting work full-time at the Villa Castelfino could take her mind off him. She had been commuting to Tuscany regularly over the past few weeks, but from today she could properly call herself the Count di Castelfino's Curator of Exotic plants. It was the official start of her new job with her grand Italian employer. Although she was looking forward to it, Meg was very nervous. It was the first time she had lived so far away from her parents, and she didn't like leaving them to cope with their business alone. It didn't help that after sleeping on the plane she had a head full of cotton wool, and all the most uncomfortable bits of her aircraft seat imprinted on her body.

Shuffling off the plane along with everyone else, she comforted herself with the thought someone would be waiting for her in Arrivals. Once she left airside, Franco the chauffeur would be there to help with her luggage, as usual.

Meg's budding self-assurance lasted for as long as it

took her to glance around the waiting area. Franco was nowhere to be seen. With a flicker of fear she wondered if this meant there was trouble at the Villa Castelfino. She had picked up enough from working alongside the Count di Castelfino to know that the old man did not get on with his son. Meg had never seen *il ragazzo*, as her aristocratic employer scornfully called his heir, but she had learned enough to dislike him. The Count di Castelfino loved the varied landscape of his estate with its olive groves, gnarled oaks and wildflower meadows. His son wanted to transform it into a monoculture—nothing but ordered rows of vines as far as the eye could see. As for the count's beloved plant collection—Meg smiled ruefully to herself. Life at the Villa Castelfino sounded like a continuous struggle between beauty and business. The old man's hobby was always in danger of losing out to his son's ambition.

She waited and waited, but no one arrived to collect her. It was a bad start for someone with half a ton of luggage. Time crawled past. Looking up and down the concourse, she spotted an arrow pointing towards a taxi rank. Rather than wait and worry, Meg swung into action. Pushing her trolley towards it, she waited nervously for a vacant cab, glancing in every direction. Neither help nor trouble arrived, but by the time she could scramble into the safety of a taxi she was in a state of nervous collapse.

The driver recognised the address she gave him, and let fly a delighted stream of Italian. Meg went weak with relief. At last something was going right. She tried to explain her situation, but soon used up her tiny vocabulary of halting holiday phrases. Her driver found the whole thing hilarious. Unable to understand and feeling totally isolated, Meg sank back in her seat.

I wonder what gorgeous Gianni is doing right now. Not being stood up at an airport terminal, that's for sure! she thought, imagining him shouldering aside his flock of girlfriends to rescue her. She sighed, wondering if she would ever see him again. It didn't seem very likely. Her only hope would be to persuade the Count di Castelfino to stage an exhibit of his plants at one of the big London flower shows. In her dreams, the gorgeous Gianni Bellini haunted them in search of more treats for his harem.

She spent the taxi ride imagining what it must be like to be seduced by such a charmer. *It's no wonder he's got so many girls in tow,* she thought. His smile had warmed her in a way she hadn't experienced for a long time. She was strictly a one-man girl, so common sense always told her to put a lot of distance between herself and men like Signor Bellini. But a wisp of wicked excitement curled through her daydreams like smoke. In her fantasies, she could do what she liked.

And so could Gianni…

While Meg simmered, the man of her dreams stared down the barrel of a gun. It might look like the neck of a crystal decanter, but it was equally deadly. Gianni Bellini knew full well that alcohol solved nothing. It would only slow him down. Going for so long without sleep was bad enough, and drinking would only make it worse. It would have a knock-on effect on him, and all his newly inherited staff, for the rest of the day. He decided against it.

'Shall I fetch you some champagne instead, Count?' A uniformed waiter bowed obsequiously. All he got in reply was a grunt and a dismissive wave of his new master's hand.

Barely twenty-four hours into his life sentence, Gianni was still coming to terms with what had happened. He had known this would be his destiny for as long as he could remember. Reacting by developing a strong streak of independence, he had made sure he didn't have to rely on his inherited wealth. Instead he had forged a brilliant career for himself. While his father was alive, Gianni's Castelfino vineyard had been relegated to a distant corner of the estate. That was about to change. Now Gianni was in total control, his business would take centre stage. Despite his exhaustion, he smiled. That would stop the questions, for a while at least. People knew he was obsessed with the idea of making Castelfino wines a luxury with an international reputation. They would think he was simply shelving any quest for an heir while he expanded his empire.

Now he had inherited all his father's land and property, there would be no stopping him. Every suitable inch of the Castelfino estate would be turned over to growing grapes. Production would rocket, and so would Gianni's sense of satisfaction. He enjoyed playing the part of self-made millionaire, although his playboy image was a pretty intangible asset. It was good to have a new girl every night, but they were nothing more than a perk of the job. While celebrity spotters tried to guess which one of his beautiful companions would be chosen to produce the Bellini heir, Gianni kept his real love a secret. The Castelfino vineyard was his baby. When it came to children…Gianni didn't want anything to do with them. His own childhood had been made an absolute hell by his warring parents. He couldn't stomach the idea of inflicting that on an innocent infant.

A movement outside the summer dining room caught

his eye. In the far distance a dust devil spiralled along the line of the drive. It was heading for the villa. Gianni's eyes narrowed with annoyance. He really didn't need visitors right now. With an exclamation, he slid his palms back across the white linen of the tablecloth and cranked himself to his feet. His sleep-deprived brain was still functioning, but his limbs were set in concrete. Crossing the room, he went out through the open French doors and onto the terrace. However he felt, he had a duty to those arriving to pay their respects to his late father. He shut his eyes, concentrating on what he would say.

The Tuscan countryside sounded as only an afternoon in high summer could. In the still, hot air not a leaf moved. A single bird called, with the monotonous *chip-chip* of two parched stones tapping together. The only other sound was that single car engine, making a tunnel through the dense air as it tore towards him. Everything else held its breath.

Gianni heard the car swing around in an extravagant semicircle to stop in front of the villa's main door. Puzzled, he opened his eyes and saw—not some grand limousine, but a simple radio cab. There wasn't time to be shocked before its driver bellowed a hearty greeting and leapt out to open the car's boot.

The cabbie began hauling out suitcases and piling them on the dusty ground, while keeping up a cheerful conversation with his still invisible passenger. Gianni stared at the scene with disbelief. All the time the car radio chattered away. No one at the Villa Castelfino had raised their voice above a whisper for days. Until that moment, the vast face of the house had been blank with shutters closed against the sunshine. Now flickers of movement ran along behind many of them. This unexpected racket was mobilising

Gianni's staff. Sure enough, one of the kitchen lads raced out from a side door to tackle the new arrivals. While he was busy silencing the cab driver, the brand new count got another shock.

The rear door of the taxi opened and the most beautiful woman in the world struggled out. Her skirt, already short, had ridden up during her journey exposing long, beautifully shaped legs. Her dark blonde hair moved loosely around her shoulders, shining in the sunlight. She looked dazed. As she straightened up she staggered slightly, as though pushed back against the security of the car. Gianni realised she had been caught off guard by the sudden contrast between the air-conditioned taxi and the sun-baked amphitheatre in front of the Villa Castelfino. *Is it any wonder,* he observed, *when she's wearing tights?*

With a curse, he turned away. His body had sprung to life as it always did at the sight of a pretty girl. How could it possibly play a tasteless trick on him like that, today of all days? A keen interest in all things feminine was only natural, but noticing such fine detail at a time like this was grotesque. Gianni dropped his gaze to his feet. And then he heard her laugh. It was as captivating as a charm of goldfinches.

'Signor Bellini! What a surprise! I never expected to see you again, let alone here! What a lovely surprise!'

He heard her take long, confident strides toward him across the gritty forecourt. From his vantage point on the terrace he could look down on her with the mere flick of a glance. As she noticed his bitter, twisted expression she stopped smiling. In half a dozen steps she went from delight, through puzzlement, to concern. Her steps became hesitant, and when she spoke again her voice was halting and uncertain.

'You *are* the man I met at the Chelsea Flower Show, aren't you?'

'*Sì*. I am Gianni Bellini.'

He dropped the words like icicles, but then recognition swept over him. This was the flower girl. Gianni never forgot a pretty face—or a curvaceous body like hers. Manufacturing a smile, he nodded a brief welcome. Details slowly came back to him. This one was not only beautiful, she was clever, too. That was enough of a novelty for her to have made a special impact on Gianni at the time, but he had never dreamed of seeing her a second time.

The force of his reply didn't stop her. She advanced with another laugh and stuck out her hand in greeting.

'Good grief, I never would have believed it. You've changed—all those girlfriends must be running you ragged, *signor*!'

'What are you doing here?' he enquired in a voice like cut glass. As he spoke he looked down at her outstretched hand as though he would rather shake a viper by the tail.

She frowned, looking into his face as though searching for recognition.

'I work for the Count di Castelfino. I'm moving into the Garden Cottage today. Someone usually meets me at the airport, but for some reason the chauffeur didn't turn up today.'

'That is because my father is dead. I'm the Count di Castelfino now,' he announced with crisp formality.

Her smile vanished, and she stared at him in growing horror.

'Oh…I'm so sorry.' Helplessly she looked from the taxi, to her heap of suitcases and then back to him. 'How crass of me to arrive in such a flurry like this… C-can I ask what happened?'

'He suffered a stroke some days ago, in Paris. He died yesterday—*no*, the day before—'

Shaking his head, Gianni raised one hand and dragged it wearily down over his face. The rasp of stubble under his palm was loud and intrusive in the horrible, thick silence.

'I—I'm so sorry…' she repeated, her voice soft and insubstantial.

Exactly like her, Gianni thought instinctively, before silently cursing his reactions again.

'You weren't to know. I didn't know you were expected. That's why no one was sent to meet you. I was only driven back here an hour ago.' Distracted, he looked across at the taxi and pulled out his wallet. 'I'm afraid you've had a wasted journey. You'll have to go back to wherever you came from. How did you get past my security guards at the gate, in any case?'

Her eyes opened wider and wider as he spoke until they looked like two clear reflections of the cobalt sky.

'They were expecting me…my name is on today's visitor list…so they just waved my taxi straight through…' Her voice was faint. As it faltered still further he had to lean closer to hear what she was saying. 'But I can't go back…all the plants here will need someone to look after them. The count—the *old* count—would have wanted them cared for properly…'

Gianni shook his head. 'I'm the Count di Castelfino now, and I have my own plans. It's the start of a new regime. There's no room here for anything that doesn't pay its way. Whatever projects my father may have had in mind won't be going ahead. I'm in charge now, and my interests are much more practical.'

As he spoke he saw the heaven of her eyes become cloudy and misted with tears. She shrank visibly, and when she spoke her voice was barely more than a whisper.

'You can't mean that, *signor*?'

'I'm afraid so. The Castelfino vineyard is my only concern. I'm interested in practical projects, not hobbies.'

Springing lightly down from the terrace, he started to walk towards the taxi. Because old habits couldn't be shaken off, he put a comforting arm around her shoulder to lead her in the same direction. 'Don't worry, *signorina*. I'll pay your taxi fare back to the airport. By the time you get there, my staff will have phoned through and arranged a return ticket for you. Where did you fly from, by the way?'

'Heathrow—but—'

As they reached the open passenger door of the taxi Gianni took his arm away from her. After pressing far too much money into the taxi driver's hand, he swivelled on his heel and walked off. As he headed back to the villa he threw a few disjointed words over his shoulder at her.

'I'm sorry you've had a wasted journey, *signorina*. Goodbye.'

Closing a mental door firmly in her face, he forced himself to push thoughts of her inviting full lips and big blue eyes right to the back of his mind. He ought to be concentrating on his plans for Castelfino Wines, not distractions like her.

And then a voice interrupted his thoughts, ringing out through the hot, still air.

'No, thank you, Signor Bellini.'

He stopped and frowned. That wasn't supposed to happen. If the girl was going to say anything at all, it should have been a diffident 'yes'. That was the way things worked in Gianni's universe. People did what he told them to do. While he stood wondering how she could possibly have misunderstood his instructions, he heard a muffled bang. It was followed by the sound of light footsteps in the dust. That made him look back, over his shoulder. What he saw puzzled him still more. The girl had dropped her hand luggage and was running to catch him up.

Gianni Bellini, Conte di Castelfino, thought of all the staff members who would be watching this fiasco from behind the Villa Castelfino's shutters. They all knew his reputation. The old place must be alive with gossip already. Playboy he might be, but Gianni knew what to do. It wouldn't hurt to reinforce his authority. When this girl launched her screaming, hysterical scene, he would silence it with a single roar of his own.

He snatched a deep breath, but never got to use it.

'With all due respect, *signor*, I think I ought to stay.'

She skidded to a halt, almost within his reach. Her voice had been little more than a whisper. He hadn't expected that. When she glanced nervously at the front of the house before speaking again she surprised him a second time.

'For a little while, at least. Please?'

Totally wrong-footed, Gianni was stunned into silence. Not by what she said, but by the way she said it. An arrow of thought shot through his brain. *It's almost as though she's as concerned for the staff as I am...but, no, she couldn't be...*

Words hissed through his clenched teeth like a November blast.

'You have the nerve to speak to *me* of respect? A woman who bursts in on a house in crisis with laughter?'

Meg was so close she could hear the breath labouring in and out through his parted lips. She was petrified, but desperation kept her standing firm. She had to hope that she could make her new boss see reason and keep her on. It was vital.

'I meant no harm, *signor*. I would never have made such a fuss if I'd known the circumstances. Can't we draw a line under all this and start again?'

Within seconds she realised her mistake. Gianni Bellini had no reverse gear.

From the moment she'd arrived, she had realised this was going to be difficult. Now it looked close to impossible. She felt weak with terror, but couldn't let him see that. She needed this job. Too many people were relying on her to simply roll over and accept what this strangely changed Gianni said.

With nothing to lose but her dignity, Meg pressed on. She lowered her lids. It was a slow, methodical gesture like that of a diver standing on the topmost board. To her surprise, he reacted by giving her time to speak.

'When your father was alive, he specifically wanted me to come and work here,' she said with measured calm. 'I was the most highly qualified applicant for the post, and without my skill his plants will soon suffer. He had all sorts of plans in mind for the Castelfino Estate. Now he's…well, let's just say he'll need a fitting memorial. He was always worrying about the future, and a lot of his ideas were practical. He spoke about throwing open his plant collection to the public one day, as a way of encouraging tourism in the area. I'm sure you'll be carrying on all his other good works, *signor*,' she added, and was relieved to see her innocent remark seemed to impress him. 'Any man would be proud to leave such a legacy. Believe me, I know.'

His attitude hardened. 'How do you know? Because you have a fistful of paper qualifications?' he scoffed, clearly unimpressed.

'No, I can say it because my father was exactly the same,' she said evenly. 'When he was taken seriously ill, he spent so much time worrying about what he would leave behind, he couldn't rest. He was his own worst enemy. Your father was a good, kind man, *signor*. He deserves a living tribute. I worked with him closely on his new project here. He was so keen for it to go ahead, I really think it would be a mistake for you to cancel it just yet.'

Gianni stared at her for a long time. Then the corners of his mouth lifted in the slow, devastating smile that had been haunting all her dreams since their first meeting. He took a step forward, and held out his hand. 'Allow me to congratulate you, Miss—?'

'Imsey. Megan Imsey.'

His fingers felt deliciously warm as he enfolded her hand. It was a heat reflected in the colour of her cheeks.

'Well done, Miss Imsey. I'm lost for words—something that has never happened to me before!'

Meg smiled back. She was a fast learner. In the last few minutes Gianni Bellini had morphed from her dream man into a living, breathing human being. Someone she could reach out and touch. To her surprise she realised they had at least two things in common. Work was everything to him—and he was as good at hiding his real feelings as she was. He might have started off as her fantasy lover, but Meg recognised a realist when she met one. Brought up on the breadline by devoted parents, she had become ultra ambitious to try to cushion them from poverty. She needed this job, for their sake. If that wasn't reason enough to make a stand, Gianni Bellini was so magnetic. His playboy side had entranced her at Chelsea. He was so much more glamorous than anyone she had met before. Now he had been catapulted into a position of power, she wanted to see what his ambitions would make of her careful plans.

'Surely you don't need to make a snap decision about something as insignificant to you as my job, *signor*? Right now, you must have a thousand and one other things to think about.'

That at least was uncontroversial. He might be practised in the art of blocking his emotions, but for a split second Meg saw pain in his eyes. Anyone else would have missed it, but she'd been in some cold, dark places herself. She remembered how it had felt when her own father was hovering between life and death. With a pang she put her hand out to her new employer, but couldn't quite manage the intimacy of a touch. Instead she withdrew, and let her words convey her sympathy. 'And top of that list should be *you*.'

Her feelings were totally genuine, but they weren't welcome. Gianni frowned.

'No…I'm all right.'

'You look as though you've been out all night,' Meg said, torn between sympathy and adding the judgemental word *again*. It was hard not to remember all those plants she had gift-wrapped for his string of girlfriends.

'I wasn't there when it happened,' he muttered, almost to himself. 'I was in a nightclub with a thousand other people, none of whom would have cared if I dropped dead in front of them. I went straight to the hospital and sat beside him, trying as hard as I could to feel something. There was nothing…but then—'

He stopped.

'It's OK,' Meg said softly, reaching out again. This time her dreams didn't come into it. She laid her hand lightly on his sleeve, but taking a step backward he quickly put himself out of her reach again.

'Then I came straight back here because this place won't run itself…' Gianni's words began briskly enough but the lids of his olive-dark eyes were growing heavier all the time. He checked his watch. '*Dio!* I haven't been to bed for days…' he finished with weary disbelief.

'I can see that,' Meg said softly. He looked as though he had been sleeping in his beautiful designer clothes. As she watched he put a clenched fist up to his brow and scrubbed at it roughly. Meg knew how he felt. She had fretted for days and nights about her own father, when he was lying in Intensive Care.

Her memories were still too raw, and suddenly they overwhelmed her. Rushing forward, she put her arms out to him. She couldn't help herself. His reaction was equally instinctive as he threw up his hands to stop her.

'No! It's fine. Please—don't.'

Meg stopped. Forced to resist the urge to comfort him, she mirrored his gesture with one of peace.

'All right—all right—you're concerned that we're being watched by your staff. I know. But you aren't doing yourself or anybody else any favours by going beyond the point of exhaustion, *signor*. You need rest, and unless you get some *you'll* be in hospital, too! Who will take care of the Villa Castelfino and all your staff then?'

He looked at her steadily for a long time. As he did so

his dark, enigmatic expression began to stir a transformation deep within her body. Meg reacted to his scrutiny like a bud growing beneath snow. Gianni Bellini was unshaven and exhausted, yet he still looked totally irresistible. All the wicked fantasies she had dared to dream about him filtered back into her mind. She had spent so many long, lonely nights remembering his face, his smile, all his easy charm. Now here he was, right here in front of her. She began to blush. Something that began as heat rising from her breasts to her cheeks blossomed into the colour of a guinée rose, and silenced her.

'Why are you doing this, Megan Imsey? You've only just got here. Why should you care about me? I'm a cold, unfeeling taskmaster. You'll hear that from anyone outside the clubs and beaches. When I shelve all my father's wild ideas, there'll be no job here for you.'

Meg raised her eyebrows. The old count's plans had all seemed perfectly sensible to her. This was her dream job, but there was definitely no place for daydreams in Gianni's new regime. It was time to tell him some of her hard home truths.

'I can't afford *not* to care,' she said in a careful, matter-of-fact voice. If he wouldn't recognise simple compassion, that must mean he didn't want any. 'I'm on the Villa Castelfino payroll, but so far you're the only person here who knows I've turned up for duty. To put it bluntly, it's in my interests to take great care of you if I ever want to be reimbursed for this pointless jaunt, Signor Bellini. And there's always an outside chance you might see reason, and stick with the old count's plans as I suggest,' she finished boldly.

It took some time, but Gianni's expression gradually moved from resignation to distaste. 'I might have guessed. With women, it all comes down to money in the end. And people wonder why I keep them all at arm's length!' He grimaced at last.

His reply was a final wake-up call for Meg. In real life, he was turning out to be quite a different prospect from the ideal man she wanted. With regret, she recognised he was as practical and down-to-earth as she was. It was beginning to feel as though work was the only certainty in her life. With no illusions left about Gianni, all she could hope to do was to secure her future. Apart from all the pressing practical reasons, her parents had waved her off at the airport with such high hopes for her. She couldn't bear to disappoint them by returning home without achieving anything.

'It isn't simply money, *signor*. Common sense and practicality come into it, too. My family back home are relying on me as a backstop. I've put their business back on an even keel. They're doing really well at the moment but we all know from bitter experience how circumstances can change overnight.'

When she said that, Gianni briefly made eye contact with her. He nodded, but didn't speak.

'That's why I need this job, *signor*. Your father arranged for me to live in the Garden Cottage here on the Villa Castelfino estate. I've visited before, so I know where it is. There's no need to worry about me,' she said, in the unlikely event Gianni Bellini ever worried about anyone but himself. 'I can sort myself out. I'll be absolutely no trouble. We can talk about all this later. You just see about getting yourself some rest.'

'No. I need to be alert.'

He looked as belligerent as only a sleep-deprived man could look.

'Of course you do, *signor*.' Meg smiled as he played

straight into her hands. 'That's why you must get some sleep. Don't worry; I've already had some experience of how this house works. They'll keep you informed. You won't miss a thing,' she said soothingly. 'The previous count was always telling me he was careful to employ only the very best staff.'

Gianni locked eyes with her for a long time. Then unexpectedly he took her hand again and raised it to his lips for another heart-stopping kiss. It brought back every spine-tingling sensation he had ever evoked in her, and left her gasping. When he looked at her now his expression overflowed with all the dark promise she remembered from their first meeting.

Then he said slowly, 'Yes. He was. I can see that now.'

CHAPTER TWO

GIANNI followed Meg's instructions only by default. He was so tired his body took complete control of his mind. Leaving the new arrival to fend for herself, he trudged up to his suite. Working entirely on autopilot, he kicked off his shoes and fell into bed.

The next thing he knew, he was waking up with the sun in his eyes and hunger gnawing a hole in his stomach. Grabbing his bedside phone, he rang Housekeeping to order some food. Megan was right, he told himself. He *had* needed sleep. He must have been out of action for hours.

Twenty minutes later, shaved, showered and feeling slightly more human, he walked into the dining room of his suite. A meal was being laid out on its central table. His body clock told him it should be dinner. It didn't look like it. In fact, it didn't look like anything that had appeared on the Villa Castelfino's menu in all his thirty-two years.

'That food looks delicious,' he said suspiciously, picking up the neatly folded copy of *La Repubblica* lying on his tray.

'It is, *signor*. Some of us were invited to lunch over at the Garden Cottage today, and the head gardener gave us this to eat, too.'

Before Gianni could question the man further, he noticed something.

'This is Monday's newspaper. What happened to Sunday, Rodolfo?'

'The indoor staff had strict instructions not to disturb you, *signor*.'

The man put such an odd emphasis on the word 'indoor' that Gianni's mind filled instantly with suspicion. He walked around the table, surveying his unlikely meal from every angle. There were cheese palmiers with half a dozen different sorts of salads and a cut glass dish of something brightly coloured.

'This looks like English trifle. I haven't seen that since I was at school. Where did it come from?'

'The head gardener suggested some amendments to your menu, *signor*.'

Gianni stopped pacing. Frowning, he shook a finger in the air. '*That* was what I was going to ask you a moment ago. I didn't know we *had* a head gardener,' he said slowly, suspecting he already knew what had happened. The girl who had invited herself into his estate had become a cuckoo in the nest the moment he turned his back.

'Miss Imsey has only recently arrived, *signor*.'

'Oh…*her*,' Gianni said with the airy exhaustion of a man who had a million employees, all of them more trouble than they were worth. 'Well, don't worry. She won't be here for long. I'm more interested in practical skills than paper qualifications. People who hide from life by studying are always afraid of hard work.' He was quite confident in his views, but the look on Rodolfo's face instantly made him suspicious again. 'Oh, now *don't* say you've been taken in by that face, or those legs…her smile, that rivulet of hair or those baby blue eyes…'

Gianni's tone began to waver along with his conviction. Straightening his jacket like a prosecuting counsel, he brought himself briskly back to the ancestral line. No member of staff could be allowed to run riot around the place. It didn't matter how pretty and distracting she was.

'Or anything else, for that matter!' He added sharply. 'That girl is only interested in one thing—collecting her wages. She told me so herself, the moment she arrived.'

Gianni's waiter was in no hurry to leave. It was obvious he had something more to say. Reaching for a second cheese palmier, Gianni gave him a stare calculated to squeeze tears from a commando.

'You look like you've got something else to tell me, Rodolfo.'

The man coughed politely. 'You may like to know that Cook is currently wearing a face like an old lemon, *signor*.'

Gianni was bringing the serving tongs from the silver salver to his plate. When he heard those words, he stopped. The thought that Meg had been nice to him only so she could get paid was irritating. News that she could manage to annoy his staid old cook brought a grudging smile back to his face.

'This wouldn't have anything to do with the new head gardener, would it?' he asked innocently.

'*Sì*, Count.'

'And…morale in the kitchens is…?' Gianni probed, brushing pastry crumbs from his fingertips.

'On the way up.'

'I always said the Bellini family lets good staff have its head,' Gianni said in a warm glow of self-satisfaction.

Dismissing the waiter, he settled down to enjoy his meal. He was ravenous, and ate himself to a standstill. It was the first time he could ever remember sitting in the Villa Castelfino and pushing away a plate because he was full, rather than nauseous. It was then he realised he was beginning to feel better than he had done in years. As well as the improved diet, in one day he had managed to get more sleep than he normally did in a week. Then reality kicked in again. His father was dead. The future of hundreds of hectares of real estate and thousands of staff across the globe relied on him, in his capacity as the new Count di Castelfino. His business could expand now, exactly as planned.

Walking over to his sound system, he put on some music. Then he went out onto the balcony leading from his private dining room. From there he could survey the scene at his leisure. All the land below him, right out as far as the sheltering hills, was now his responsibility. Until a few days ago, his vineyard had occupied fewer than a hundred hectares of the vast estate. That was set to change. Gianni had his gaze fixed firmly on the future. His nights of excess were behind him. From now on, improving his wine business would absorb all his waking moments. It saved him having to think about the one aspect of aristocratic life that loomed over him like a cloud of volcanic ash. He didn't want to be the last man to bear his name and title—but neither did he want to see a child suffer by being born into the Bellini family. The taste of that was still bitter in his own mouth.

He sat down to reflect on the view, trying to avoid thinking about the inevitable. It was quite a distraction. He had never really looked at the landscape outside his suite before. It had simply always been there. Now every vine, olive tree and cypress belonged to him. He relaxed in his seat contentedly.

And then Megan Imsey walked into view, pushing a wheelbarrow loaded with tools. A broad brimmed straw hat shaded her expression, but Gianni could see she was enjoying herself in the sunshine. As he watched she turned her head this way and that, looking at the desiccated grasses sprawling over the weedy path. She must be heading for the walled garden, he realised. Work was already well under way there, on his father's last project. It was an extravagance of greenhouses, wild enough to bankrupt the Bellini coffers. His study of her became critical. Why was she going there when he had already told her what he thought of his father's plans? And what sort of person worked when they didn't have to, in any case?

With that, Gianni's scorn slipped into a smile. He only had to think of the times he'd rolled home at first light, still on a champagne-fuelled high. He'd stopped off at his vineyard many times, to work off his excess energy. An attitude like that had carved him a spectacular career as a wine producer in only a few years. He had done it by applying the same guidelines he used in his private life— if you want something done properly, do it yourself.

He wondered if Miss Megan Imsey had a similar interest in quality control. This might be the perfect moment to find out. It was a beautiful day, and he was feeling lucky…

The Tuscan sun clung to Meg like a second skin. To call it hot was an understatement. Beneath her long sleeved white shirt, baggy overalls, shady straw hat and sunglasses she was coated in sunscreen. It might be safe, but it felt totally suffocating. Despite the heat she bowled along through the gardens at a good pace. She was always eager to get to work, but the Villa Castelfino had one big novelty that made it really special. A hundred years ago, an earlier count had built his aristocratic young English wife a walled kitchen garden to stop her feeling homesick. Nothing had been done with it for years, until Gianni's father had hatched this scheme for a grand range of state-of-the-art greenhouses. The new complex was almost finished, but on this sunny morning Meg was more interested in the un-developed parts of the garden. Its faded melancholy really appealed to her. Smiling, she unlocked the garden door and let herself into one whole hectare of heaven.

She stood for a moment and relished her achievement. This was what she had spent the last few months planning and supervising on her trips to Italy. A glass palace took centre stage in the secret garden. There were still a few cosmetic touches to add, but the main building was pretty much complete. This morning the entire roof was open to catch every available breeze. It looked like a stately galleon in full sail. Flushed with success, Meg wondered how Gianni could possibly dislike such a lovely thing. With a pang of fear, she wondered how she could persuade him to keep her on. She couldn't bear to think of anyone tampering with her beautiful greenhouses. This success had given her a welcome boost, on top of saving her parents' business from bankruptcy. The possibility they might slip back while she was away was enough to worry about. Her fragile self-confidence didn't need this project to founder as well.

To cheer herself up, Meg turned her attention to the rest

of the garden. Once upon a time it had produced all the food for the villa. Decades of neglect meant it was now nothing more than an area of infrequently mown grass and overgrown fruit trees. Without regular care their long, lissom branches grew in all directions, throwing welcome pools of shade throughout the day. She parked her barrow in one of these slightly cooler spots, beside an ancient dipping pool. Then she went back and locked the garden door. That would ensure she wasn't disturbed. Returning to her barrow full of tools and provisions, she tied one end of a length of twine around the neck of her water bottle. Lowering it into the dipping pool would keep the contents chilled. Then she started work.

The structural work of repairing the hard landscaping was complete, so it was left to Meg to begin the best job of all. She was about to mark out new flowerbeds, and couldn't wait to get started. There would be borders at the foot of the encircling wall, designed to complement the new garden buildings. Meg's mind had been turning over ideas for a long time. Now she needed to see them marked out on the ground, to get a feel for how they might work in reality. Once she had the details right, work could start. That meant there would be something worth seeing by the end of the week. The bigger the impact she could make on Gianni Bellini, the more likely he was to let her stay. Or so she hoped.

She began measuring up and marking out, but soon felt overdressed. The first things to go were her sandals. The short, prickly grass beneath her bare feet made her laugh with the excitement of it all. She was making the closest possible contact with this grand estate, and it was fun! Curling her toes into the hot turf she carried on, hammer-

ing in pegs and laying out string to plan the new flowerbeds. There was so little air movement that soon her hat
and shirt began to cling uncomfortably in the heat. She
hesitated for a moment, wondering if she was brave enough
to strip off completely. Glancing around, she came to a
decision. The garden wasn't overlooked. Working in her
underwear was no worse than wearing a bikini, and she had
worked in one of those often enough at home. The door into
her sanctuary was locked. No one would see. If she was
careful to avoid getting sunburned, no one would ever
know.

Impulsively, she tore off her outer clothes and went
back to work. When the sun parched her skin too fiercely,
she dodged back into the shade and enjoyed a drink of
pool-cooled water from her bottle. She was straightening
up to assess how the outline was developing when a frighteningly familiar voice almost sent her into orbit.

'Is this how all English gardeners dress, Megan?'

Meg whirled around and her heart stood still. It was
Gianni: the *real* one, not the exhausted version who had
tried to send her away the day before. Today he looked
every inch as seductive as he had done at the Chelsea
Flower Show. That alarmed her as much as his anger had
done.

'What are you doing here?' she burst out, her hands
trying ineffectually to cover all the bits her scanty underwear was failing to hide.

He nodded towards the villa. 'I live here, remember?'

Meg was caught completely off guard. 'I'm sorry—
how could I possibly forget?' She gasped. A blush was no
defence against him. He continued looking at her with undisguised interest.

'You certainly seemed to have done.'

'I never dreamed anyone would disturb me in here. The door was locked. I have the only key. How did you get in?' she blustered, embarrassment mixed up with growing anger.

One hand in his pocket, Gianni strolled over to the old medlar tree where Meg had hung her hat and shirt. Plucking them from the branches like particularly desirable fruit, he made his way over to her. He took his time. It was painfully obvious to Meg that he was making her wait for her clothes. She wasn't in the mood to be toyed with. As soon as he got close enough she snatched her things from his hands and pulled them on. He watched with something close to amusement. Then he drew a second key from his pocket with a flourish.

'As I said—I live here. I have a copy of every key in the place.'

Barefoot but otherwise decent, Meg rallied.

'That doesn't explain why you felt the need to come in here.'

'It wasn't a need. It was a want. I wanted to see you, Megan.'

There was a haunting look in his dark eyes. It was so delicious she could hardly meet his gaze. Nervous that he might be able to read all sorts of things from her own expression, she looked down at the coarse wiry grass at her feet. All sorts of hope were beginning to stir deep within her, but there was only one she could put into words.

'I hope you're feeling better, Count.'

His smile widened, bright as pearl against the golden warmth of his skin. 'Yes, I am—but call me Gianni, please.'

Meg's heart did a little skip—until she realised he probably gave that bonus to all his staff.

'Part of the reason I came out here was to thank you,' he went on. 'You were right. I was overtired when you arrived. All I've done since then is sleep—and enjoy an excellent late lunch.'

'That's good,' Meg said with genuine relief.

'Afterwards I went down to the kitchens, where they told me that the meal I so enjoyed was your idea. What made you challenge Cook?'

She looked up quickly to find out exactly how much trouble she was in. In response Gianni smiled, raising his eyebrows in silent approval. It was an expression that made her shiver, despite the heat.

'You looked so distracted. I knew eating would be way down on your list of priorities. When I saw steak on today's menu I thought it sounded far too heavy for this weather. I decided to cater for myself, and guessed you might like something light and familiar too. I'd already discovered from chatting with the other staff that you attended boarding school in England. It just so happens my aunt is now Head Chef at the same place. I rang and asked her what dishes would be most popular at your old school on a day like today.'

Meg didn't add that everyone loved comfort food in times of trouble, but could see he knew that already. The softening around his eyes proved it to her.

'That shows real initiative, Megan,' he said with conviction. 'Especially in view of what happened when you suggested it to my cook. I've come straight from the kitchens. As soon as she has finished the larder inventory, she'll be coming out to apologise to you for the things she said.'

Meg blinked at him. An apology was the very last thing she expected, in the circumstances.

'Pardon?'

'The staff said she tried to pull rank, but you stood your ground. Well done. You're the first member of staff who's done that to her.'

'Are you saying you don't mind?' Meg said warily. People grand enough to employ gardeners never usually bothered to praise their staff.

'I'm delighted, Megan.' His voice lilted slowly over her name, trying it out for size.

'Are you *sure* you don't mind?' She asked uncertainly. 'I mean, I hadn't been here for more than two minutes before picking a blazing row with your cook. She's an old family faithful; I'm the new arrival—and you're taking *my* side?'

Gianni searched her face, mystified that she seemed incapable of taking in what he had said. 'But of course. It's the only stance to take. She was wrong, you were right. One of my first duties as the new count was going to be to go through all the menus. You got there before me, that's all.' He saw her face flush deeply. Instantly concerned, he reached out to her. His strong brown hands grasped her elbows to give support. 'Megan? What's the matter? It must be the sun. Here—I'll help you to a seat.'

She looked down at his fingers. They slid over her skin and closed around her with exactly the same relish she had conjured up in all her fantasies. It was wonderful.

'There's no need...I'm fine.' She gasped, barely able to raise her voice above a whisper. The sheer delight of feeling his touch was breathtaking. 'I've just had a bit of a surprise, that's all. I—I thought the only men who weren't afraid of cooks were head gardeners,' she improvised quickly.

Gianni let go of her, offended. '*I* make the rules here.

All of them. And that includes whether or not we employ a female head gardener,' he finished with slow, devastating meaning.

Meg was alert immediately. 'What do you mean?'

She bounced the question straight at him, but could see he wasn't fooled for a minute. Gianni wouldn't be taking any chances with her. Anyone who could put a cook on the back foot as she had done would need to be watched carefully.

He looked down at her for a few seconds longer than was strictly necessary before giving her a meaningful shrug.

'That rather depends.'

'Thank goodness for that, as my original title was Curator of Exotic Plants. I'm no Head Gardener—though I'm more than qualified to do it,' she added quickly, 'But when I saw how things were here, I knew the staff wouldn't take kindly to a newcomer's suggestions so I took a chance and borrowed the title for a minute. The whole kitchen staff fell for it.' She finished with a nervous little laugh.

To her amazement Gianni's devastating smile burst into life, but he was careful to quash it almost straight away.

'That's what I call insight. A girl who shows insight *and* initiative? You'll go far, *ragazza insolente*!'

Tiny muscles quivered all around his lips. Meg could see he was trying not to laugh. What made it worse was that he knew *she* knew. It wasn't the sort of position she wanted to put her new boss in. Especially when that boss was Gianni Bellini, a man guaranteed to have any girl he wanted.

Dutifully, she looked down at the grass again to hide her own smile, but wasn't about to stifle her ambition.

'I already have, *signor*,' she said, careful to hide any hint of humour. 'I graduated top of my intake, I saved my parents' business from ruin, then I landed the top job here. And I haven't finished yet.'

'I'm beginning to realise that,' he said quietly. 'So, Miss Curator of Exotic Plants—what are your plans for my new garden?'

Meg sensed he was trying to lighten the tone. Despite the twinkle in his eyes, she decided to tread carefully until she was certain where she stood with him.

'I'm here to implement the old count's plans, not my own,' she said carefully. 'At the moment, his collection of tropical plants is restricted to that old lemon house at the far end of the kitchen garden. They were all going to be moved and the collection expanded into this new glass-house range as soon as it was finished.'

She began walking off toward a long, low building set against a distant wall. Gianni did not follow her immediately. When he did, he lingered a few steps behind.

'Am I walking too fast for you, Gianni?'

'Not at all,' he said airily. 'It's a beautiful day, and I have a beautiful view. Why hurry?'

She looked back over her shoulder and realised what he was watching.

'*Signor!*'

'I've told you before—my name is Gianni.'

'Not when you're looking at my bottom like that, it isn't,' Meg said, desperately reminding herself how many plants he had bought from her stand at the Chelsea Flower Show. He had done it to keep all the women in his life happy. She had no intention of becoming one among many. Even though her limbs turned to water whenever he looked at her in that deep, meaningful way…

The original lemon house had been built with an open front. Later on, its graceful stone arches had been glazed to create a greenhouse. Meg opened the door on its riot of damp, lush leaves and exotic flowers.

'Isn't this wonderful?' She took in a leisurely lungful of the warm, moist air. It was rich with the fragrance of bark and tropical flowers.

'As a twenty-first century woman, I hope you're being ironic,' Gianni observed drily, following her into the building. 'Keeping these plants in luxury must cost the earth, both in money and resources. Air conditioning isn't in vogue, Megan—especially for flowers,' he finished severely.

'Oh, I know it's extravagant and old fashioned.' Meg ran her hand lovingly over one of the crumbling stone pillars. 'That's why the count wanted me to build him a dedicated range of greenhouses, to give his plants ideal growing conditions. That means computer-controlled atmospheres. He wanted to include the latest equipment and ideas, so that everything will be perfect. He intended his estate to be a showcase. His idea was that this part of the Val di Castelfino should become an extra special tourist attraction, and an example of best practice.'

'How does this steam-filled white elephant qualify?' Gianni was haughty. 'Had my father never heard of climate change? I'm surprised someone as well qualified as you didn't put him right, Megan. My father always lived in the past. An educated woman like you must be well briefed in all the drawbacks.'

Meg knew it wasn't her place to comment, but a point of honour was at stake. She tried to pin a bold stare on him, but it was difficult when he could out-stare her so easily. 'You don't seem impressed by my qualifications, *signor*.'

Though outwardly calm, she was trembling too much to say any more. His penetrating gaze made her too light headed for words. Instead she raised her eyebrows, simply inviting more comment.

'In my experience, the more exam success someone has, the less likely they are to get their hands dirty. I'd rather someone had worked their way to the top of the tree, in the same way I've done.'

'With no help from your family name, your position in life or your father?'

There was an ironic lilt in Meg's voice. She regretted it instantly, but Gianni hardly seemed to notice.

'Exactly!' He dropped one hand onto the greenhouse staging with a resounding thump. 'The Castelfino vineyard is my baby, from conception right through to international prize-winning status. I've earned every penny—there's no job on the land I'm not happy to do myself, and I've never had a cent from my father. As you must know,' he finished gruffly.

'I never discussed you with the late count, Gianni. I had no idea you were related to him until a few hours ago, remember.'

His eyes narrowed into channels of suspicion. 'You mean to say he never complained to you about the way I only wanted money spent on cost-effective projects, not his hobbies? I've been studying the work you did for him. All of it—and that includes the dummy sets of figures forwarded to my accountants. Do you deny that they were prepared to stop me discovering exactly how much money my father was frittering away on this…this…?' Exasperated, he waved his hand towards the exotic display of orchids and coloured foliage.

'It was all perfectly legal. The late count's own financial advisors always submitted the correct figures for audit. It was thought you would object to his budget, so he had a separate set made up in case you wanted to inspect them. We didn't want to worry you, that's all.' Meg threw up her head to challenge him with a glare, but something happened. Their eyes met, and for Meg it was the point of no return. She had always thought Gianni was stunning. Now, with the sun lighting a bronze shimmer in his devastating eyes, words didn't do him justice. The breath caught in her throat, stifling all sound. He knew only too well what power lay behind his eyes. As she watched he lowered his lids a fraction, tempting an unconscious sound to escape from her all too self-conscious lips.

'I hope my father didn't lead you to believe that I'm mean.' Gianni's voice was a drawl, as lazy as the air moving through the lemon house. 'On the contrary: I can be the most generous of men if the circumstances—and the woman—are right,' he said, leaving the suggestion in his final words hanging in the air.

'I know. When you were in London I supplied you with all those flowers for your girlfriends, remember?' Meg breathed, trying to keep her voice steady. She was getting dizzy, but it wasn't only the lack of oxygen. The nearness of Gianni in this small, sun-soaked space sent her senses reeling. The light citrus fragrance of his aftershave was so clean and fresh in an atmosphere charged with the heavy hints of bark and mosses. It sent a charge of electricity fizzing down her spine. Without realising it she moved slightly towards him, hungry for contact.

'Then you'll know what I'm going to say next?'

Meg's lips moved, but no sound came out. She knew

what she wanted to hear, but moved her head slowly from side to side.

'I've decided this new range of greenhouses would be a great memorial to my father, after all. You were right to suggest it—very clever, and very provocative. There aren't many women who would think of pampering mere greenery like this.' His voice was as low and inviting as a cool river in the enveloping heat of the tropical house. Meg sighed as his expression softened. The greenhouse she already thought of as hers was working its magic. It was beautiful, and she could make it even better. He could sense that, and she was spellbound.

He was gazing at the wonderful display of brightly coloured flowers and trailing foliage around them, but at any second he might turn that wonderful look on her...at least, that was her dream.

'You're going to cost me a fortune,' he murmured, when she could hardly breathe for suspense.

'That depends on what you want. This is Tuscany. Everything's ripe for enchantment.' Her voice was husky.

'And it all has its price.' He watched her carefully, gauging the effect of his words.

Meg suppressed another sigh. 'Do you agonise like this over your women?' she asked, giving him a knowing look.

'I'm not agonising. It's merely an observation. The price of this new construction is a minor consideration to me. Women are a far more serious matter. There's a lot more than mere money at stake when it comes to the future of my family. The Bellinis haven't lasted this long without being able to pick winners. That's why my father never re-married after my mother died, thank goodness.'

Meg said nothing. The way she fidgeted uncomfortably

within her clothes said it all. She was becoming unbearably hot, but her rising temperature had nothing to do with the tropical house.

'It may sound a harsh judgement to you, Megan, but I know what I'm talking about. When it came to matters of the heart, my father knew his judgement couldn't be trusted.' Gianni continued to gaze at the soft sea of butterfly-bright foliage surrounding them. A playful breeze blew in through the open greenhouse door. It ruffled his dark curls over his brow, giving him a dangerously piratical look. Meg laughed, a little nervously.

'Your father certainly got one thing right,' she said quietly. 'He would be proud of you, Gianni.'

He turned to face her slowly. When Meg got the full benefit of his dark, restless eyes she felt her heart respond. From that moment on she knew that if he ever made a move on her she would be powerless to resist. It was a perfect dream, but something she couldn't dare risk in reality. This job meant a lot to her, and her family. She wasn't about to throw it away for a boss's whim. Even if that boss was gorgeous Gianni...

'I hope he would be proud of me. That's exactly what I intend. I gave him a lot of grief when he was alive, Megan. The least I can do is respect his wishes now. Let's hope I never have to make a choice between my heart and my heritage.' His brow creased as though with the effort of fighting some inner demon.

'Why should you?' Meg asked innocently, not knowing what she was letting herself in for.

'Any number of local "princesses" are desperate to become my wife,' he sighed. 'The Bellini family blueprint says I should choose one of them. She should be installed in one of my town houses as my official partner and mother of my heir. There she'll enjoy a life of pleasure. But that way of life went out with the Middle Ages! Life has moved on. It's all so different now. Marriage isn't simply a matter of duty and honour. It's all pre-nups and making watertight arrangements to secure every stick and stone of my assets for the inevitable divorce.'

To hear him talk about marriage as nothing more than another agreement to be crossed off his list of 'things to do' disappointed Meg.

'There shouldn't be anything inevitable about divorce! No one should marry for anything less than love,' she said firmly, stroking her fingers down the long, leathery leaf of a miltonia. Meg was the last person to contradict an employer, but some things ought to be set in stone. 'Women usually have their own careers nowadays. Marriage isn't seen as the only life for them. And they aren't all grasping parasites.'

'I love women. Don't get me wrong,' Gianni said quickly. 'It's just that the Italian thoroughbred model holds no interest for me.'

'Then you'll have to find someone else.'

'There *is* no one else. All the women I meet are out for everything they can get—believe me.'

Meg was busy adjusting the ties securing a budding flower stem and replied without thinking. 'I'm not.'

Gianni sighed. 'That's what you say now. But I wonder…'

His voice was heavy with regret. It was such a heartfelt comment that she looked up sharply. In that instant all trace of a smile vanished from his face. He was deadly serious— and all Meg's wildest, most wanton fantasies were reflected in his eyes.

She caught her breath. She could not look away—and didn't want to.

And then suddenly she was in his arms.

CHAPTER THREE

THEY kissed with a passion that was totally consuming. His hands held her close to his body. Her fingers tangled in his hair, desperate for him. It was everything she had ever dreamed about, all she wanted and would ever need, and more than was right. But…this was wrong in so many ways. Pitched through passion on a tidal surge of excitement, Meg took precious seconds to catch her breath and call a halt.

'No! Gianni, stop!'

Alarmed, he let her go. 'What's the matter?'

'Nothing…not now…'

'That's all right, then!' His hold on her tightened and he chuckled with a sound as irresistible as chocolate.

'No!' she yelled, all her conviction boiling up again. 'Don't you have *any* morals?'

'Not when it comes to a girl as beautiful as you…' He dropped his face to her hair and began nuzzling it playfully.

Meg had to act fast, and totally against instinct. Her fantasies had primed her to find him irresistible. Now she was actually feeling his touch for herself, she was almost at the point of no return. Fighting against the urge to melt into his coiling embrace, she braced her hands against his shoulders and levered herself out of his grasp.

'Oh, no, how could I forget? Of course you don't have any morals!' she retorted, trying to shock him into retreat. 'After all, you're Gianni Bellini, international ladies' man, aren't you?'

Gianni wasn't shocked by anything, especially a girl barely half his size. He was flushed and breathing fast but did not release her straight away. Despite that, Meg sensed she was out of danger. The smile returned to his face. His irresistible charm should have made him more dangerous, not less, but in a strange way she realised he was no longer a threat to her—for the moment at least. She already knew Gianni Bellini had a highly developed sense of family loyalty. He wasn't the sort of man to risk a scandal by forcing himself on an unwilling member of staff—especially a new member of the team. They were likely to run straight to the press.

'I came here to work at the Villa Castelfino, not to become a source of entertainment for you,' she said firmly, in case he was still in any doubt.

Gianni said nothing, but let his hands slide reluctantly away from her body. She looked down to see him bury them deeply in his pockets.

'I'll take that as your agreement, Gianni.'

He paused before replying. 'Think of it more as a qualified acceptance, binding on neither side,' he said with a flash of roguish humour.

The nerve of the man took her breath away.

'There really is no arguing with you, is there?'

'No. As you will soon discover from the rest of my staff, Megan, when it comes to work, it's my way or the highway. I wanted to find out exactly how keen you are to keep this job.'

Despite the lightness of his tone, Meg detected a sinister meaning behind his words. From feeling flushed and excited, she went hot and cold with dread.

'Does that mean…you're going to sack me after what's just happened?'

Gianni looked genuinely shocked. 'Of course not! That would be illegal. But, *far* more importantly as far as I'm concerned, it would be immoral. This is the twenty-first century. I may be your employer, but that doesn't mean I can force myself on you, against your will. What *do* you think I am?'

Meg's eyes opened wider than she thought physically possible. Gianni looked as innocent as a priest as he stood in front of her, his hands now outstretched in a gesture of disbelief. Yet only a moment ago he had treated her to a ten-second burst of absolute temptation.

When she didn't answer, he clicked his tongue in exasperation. Then he reached out and touched a wayward lock of her hair gently back from her forehead.

'I'm interested in having a good time, but pleasing women is a big part of my enjoyment, Megan.' His fingers trailed from her brow, lingering around the smooth curve of her cheek before falling away with obvious regret. 'Blackmail and bullying have no place in my life. If you're not scared off by what just happened, but you don't want to sleep with me, then that's fine. It's your problem, not mine. '

He gave her a crooked smile of rueful acceptance. Meg was lost all over again. She desperately wanted to throw herself back into his arms, but found she couldn't move. The look in his eyes riveted her to the spot. Then he spoke again, and burst her bubble of temptation.

'Originally, I came out here to warn you that Cook will be arriving in peace. She won't expect you to declare Round Two, so be careful not to take your sexual frustration out on her, won't you?'

With that, he strolled away.

As Meg watched him walk nonchalantly along the greenhouse path a terrifying truth surged through her body. She *did* want to sleep with Gianni Bellini.

She wanted it more than anything she had ever wanted in her entire life.

From that moment on, Meg's excitement at working in a totally alien environment took a back seat. Thoughts of Gianni Bellini coloured her days and haunted her nights. He had totally bewitched her at their first meeting. As a fantasy lover he was ideal. With those devastating looks and charm, he had no drawbacks. The spell he held over her refused to be broken. Despite her dream becoming reality, his power over her increased rather than dimmed. Although their paths rarely crossed, from that moment on Meg was in heaven. All she dreamed about was their torrid kiss, but as far as Gianni was concerned it might never have happened. He showed no signs of wanting to repeat their wonderful experience. He spent most of each day shut away in the Castelfino estate office. Meg spent virtually all her time out in the gardens and grounds. That meant her chances of catching sight of him were remote. That didn't stop her keeping a keen lookout for him. His words circled her mind in a torrent of temptation. '...*pleasing women is a big part of my enjoyment...*' Her mind continually played with everything that might mean. Gianni had accused her of being sexually frustrated. If she was, it was because of him. With only one long-term relationship in her life, Meg was no expert when it came to romance. She used study to save her having to mix with people. Until her first meeting with Gianni, Meg hadn't realised how much she was missing. He had set light to the fuse of her desire. Now everything about him made her desperate to find out more.

Gavin, her only serious boyfriend, had been too heavy-handed. He was fine as a friend, but he had kept trying to push Meg further than she had wanted to go. On top of that, he had tried to monopolise every second of her free time while she had wanted to study. Meg had resented that. After watching her parents struggle to pick things up by experience, she knew the value of gaining proper qualifications. She was in no hurry to curtail her career by making a serious romantic commitment, either. Or so she had always thought in the past...

Gianni Bellini had come into her life and thrown all her careful plans into chaos. He was like no other man she had met before. Always in her thoughts, he wasn't often in her sight. Once or twice she saw him pacing around the cypress walk, deep in conversation on his mobile phone. While he was totally absorbed like that, she watched him. It was wonderful. She indulged herself, gazing at him for seconds on end. That was so much more satisfying than the quick glimpses she got when he strode out to inspect the estate with one of his tenants or managers.

Evenings presented Meg with some of her greatest pleasures, and her worst tortures. Her new home stood not far from the villa's driveway. She always knew when Gianni was going out for the evening. His frighteningly fast Ferrari was just getting into its stride as it accelerated past Garden Cottage. The first time she heard it, the unexpected roar made her drop a plate of freshly baked cookies. The sudden noise was more terrifying than the RAF's low-flying exercises at home in England. She soon got used to it, but it was a different matter whenever Gianni returned in the not-so-early hours of the morning. There was never any chance of getting back to sleep after being woken like that at three a.m. Guiltily, she would slide out of bed and creep to her window. Then she hid in the shadows, hoping for a glimpse of him. There was always a tiny window of opportunity, between the moments when he sprang from his car, leapt up the front steps and dived into the main house. Each night Meg held her breath, fearing the worst. Gianni had the villa to himself, so she expected him to bring a whole harem back home, every night. It never happened. He always returned alone.

Meg would have been relieved, if it hadn't been for one disturbing fact. Gianni always looked up at her bedroom window before he disappeared into the villa. She was careful to stand well back, and tried everything to avoid being seen. It was no good. His last gesture was always a quick glance at her house. It seemed to be directed straight at her. Meg was mystified. Something must alert him, yet he never confronted her about spying on him. That was stranger still. She knew enough about him by now to sense he wouldn't keep a concern like that bottled up. He would have sought her out at work and said something. It didn't happen. Meg suffered in silence, but it was no hardship compared to the alternative. That would be to give up her nightly vigils, which she would never—*could* never—do.

Lying in bed listening to Gianni's footsteps would be no substitute for watching the living, breathing reality of her fantasy man.

* * *

Meg lived on in an agony of suspense for several more days. She supervised the last adjustments to the magnificent range of greenhouses she had designed without any more visits from Gianni. It was only when she was putting the finishing touches to the planting plan inside the greenhouse that the axe fell. Her mobile phone interrupted her while she was wiring some young orchid plants to an artistic arrangement of tree branches in the new tropical section.

'Miss Imsey? The Count di Castelfino wants to see you in his office.' It was one of Gianni's personal assistants. Meg's heart bounced like a ball at the request.

'OK—when?'

There was a shocked silence. Meg realised this must be the first time anyone had ever tried to keep Gianni Bellini waiting. The reply was terse, and to the point.

'*Immediatamente*, if not sooner!'

Meg didn't need any more of a warning. She ran to obey. Covering the distance between the old kitchen garden and the villa at top speed, she was still brushing chipped bark from the knees of her jeans as she dashed into the estate office. Its noisy hubbub fell silent in an instant. The eyes of every secretary and PA followed the journey of each small brown fleck of bark raining down from Meg's clothes and boots. One woman, as beautiful as a bird of paradise, moved swiftly to sweep up all the bits with a dustpan and brush. A second secretary stepped forward holding a roll of perforated plastic. Chivvying Meg toward an impressive mahogany door labelled 'Strictly No Admittance', she knocked on it loudly.

'Come in!'

Meg had thought she was nervous. Hearing the rich,

smooth sound of Gianni's voice added an extra frisson to her fear. She froze.

How the secretary threw open the door and bowled the roll of perforated plastic inside so casually, Meg had no idea. It uncoiled as an eighteen-inch-wide strip, protecting the highly polished wood floor of Gianni's office.

Meg was desperate to break the tension of her ordeal. 'No red carpet for me, then?' She giggled nervously to the secretary.

'No, only a carpet protector,' the woman snapped, shooing her along.

Meg walked forward. Gianni was sitting behind a vast workstation at the far side of the room. With his back to the windows, head down and engrossed in his work, he presented an imposing figure. Meg wasn't sure what to do. She looked back the way she had come. As she did so the door slammed shut. That cut off any hope of escape. Edging forward, she stopped a respectful distance before the end of the silver plastic road. There she knotted her hands together in an agony of guilt, and waited. It felt as though one end of her nerves were nailed to the tip of Gianni's fountain pen. The further across the page his hand moved, the further they stretched.

He was writing an extremely long sentence.

Outside, swifts screamed across the sky. Dust motes spiralled up the shafts of sunlight thrown across the glassy floor of his office. The heat increased. Meg's temperature rose. Outside, a dog barked down in the village. A clock ticked. The dog barked a second time. Beneath his desk, Gianni shuffled his feet.

He was testing Meg's nerves beyond endurance. Suddenly, she couldn't stand it any more.

'I'm sorry I've been spying on you out of my window at night but it's just that your car always wakes me up when you drive past and I can never get back to sleep after that and it's become a sort of habit that I have to get up and look out to make sure everything's all right and you always happen to look up at the wrong time and—'

Her first word stopped his pen. The rest of them lifted both it, and his head. By the time her voice trickled into silence he was staring at her with naked curiosity.

'That's interesting, Megan. That's *extremely* interesting,' he murmured at last, with a drawl that made her squirm. Throwing his pen down on the blotter, he sat back in his chair. Then he put the tips of his fingers together and looked at her keenly over the top of them.

'Do you know, I had absolutely *no* idea you were doing that, Megan?'

She squirmed some more.

'I actually called you in to my office for a completely different reason. I wanted to find out how you're settling in—nothing more exciting than that. Perhaps you would like to go out, come back in and we'll start this interview all over again?'

She threw another hunted look over her shoulder at the door. It was the only thing standing between her and the complete destruction of her self-esteem.

'Do I have to?'

He gave a low, throaty chuckle. It was calculated to snatch her attention straight back to him, and worked like a charm.

'I wasn't being entirely serious.' His expression had all the delicious amusement she had enjoyed at the Chelsea Flower Show. It had the same effect, too, soothing her nerves just enough to let a little smile escape.

'You might be on to something, Gianni. Running the gauntlet of your beautiful office staff without having had time to take a shower, change my clothes and put on a bit of make-up was a real challenge!'

'There's nothing wrong with the way you look.' His eyes roamed over her body, giving weight to his words.

'They seemed to think so,' she said nervously. 'That's why they rolled this out for me.' She pointed at the carpet protector. Once again he chuckled.

'Don't take it personally. It's done for every visit from a member of my outdoor staff. As well as my own vineyard, I've inherited olive and citrus plantations and any number of farms. A lot of it would end up in here, scattered all over my office floor if they didn't take precautions like that.'

'Your indoor staff aren't like the people who work in the grounds,' Meg said, still stinging from the scornful looks she had been given.

'My domestic staff are all fine, but it's a jungle out there.' He nodded towards the outer room before adding quickly, 'But don't worry—you're of absolutely no interest to my office staff. They don't see *you* as any sort of threat at all.'

Meg wasn't remotely reassured.

'Is that supposed to cheer me up?' she asked faintly.

'Of course. Now—to business. How are you getting on here, Megan? I've been meaning to check up on you for the past few days, but no sooner do I spot you in the garden than you vanish. That's why I've called you in here. I want to talk to you properly.'

'And I wanted to do the same, Gianni,' Meg said before she could stop herself. He was interested straight away.

'That sounds promising. Take a seat.' He indicated a

deeply buttoned visitor's chair drawn up before his workstation.

To reach it she would have to step off the carpet protector. He saw her glance from one to the other and back again, and laughed.

'Don't bother about the floor. I never normally give my cleaning staff anything to do. Your little footprints won't kill them.'

She walked over and sat down in the chair. Elbows on his desk, Gianni leaned forward, his grin growing predatory. After all her fantasies, all the hours spent wondering what to say and how to act the next time they met, Meg froze again. Her wild confession might turn out to have been a fatal mistake. If he tried anything now, she could put up no resistance. Trembling, she waited for his next move. Forcing herself to sit back in her chair, she looked down at her hands. They were twisting nervously in her lap.

'While I've got the opportunity, Gianni, I'd like to ask if you could possibly—that is, if you don't mind—if there's some way…if perhaps you could be a bit quieter when you return from your nights out?' She finished in a rush, crimson with embarrassment. Cringing at the way she had told Gianni everything about her night-time vigils, she waited for him to laugh.

All she heard was the sound of him sitting back in his chair. There was an agonisingly long pause. And then he said distantly, 'I've been thinking about that since the moment you mentioned it. You're the first person to say I've woken them up. Nobody else has ever complained.'

Meg tried to make a joke of it. 'Perhaps they're afraid of you!'

'And you aren't?' He sounded curious, rather than cross.

Meg risked glancing up. He looked calm enough, and his beautiful eyes were dark with questions.

'I-I'll have to think about that,' Meg said eventually. It was true. Gianni Bellini could be terrifying. He could also be warm and funny, but Meg wasn't sure how deep or genuine any of his emotions were.

'Don't take too long making up your mind, will you?'

She heard the laughter in his voice and couldn't resist looking up again. Gianni smiled at her over his clasped hands.

'So I've been costing you your beauty sleep, have I? If it's any consolation, it's impossible to tell. Nobody would ever know. Have you thought that, while you're watching me, you could be in bed, getting more rest?'

'There's no point at that time in the morning. I don't bother. I might as well get up, do some paperwork and then go out to work.'

'I know,' he said, quite unrepentant. 'By the time I'm stripped and ready for bed, you're out and about, heading for the gardens.'

She frowned at him quizzically. 'How do you know that?'

All he did was smile as he waited for Meg to work out what he meant. It didn't take long. The footpath from her cottage to the old kitchen gardens passed straight along one side of the villa. His suite must overlook her route. Meg had a sudden, delicious vision of him standing stark naked on the balcony of his bedroom, watching her. At any time over the past days she might have glanced up and caught sight of him in all his glory. But she hadn't. Her shift from puzzlement to disappointment must have been obvious. Gianni responded with a slow, teasing smile that filled her mind with all sorts of possibilities.

'Don't worry. Now I am Count, I shall be partying less and entertaining here at the villa a lot more. You won't be troubled by me during the night too often in the future,' he said with sly humour, as though he knew she always would be. 'I'll be too busy working—and your job is another reason I've asked you here. Something you said on the day you arrived stuck in my mind. I got my staff to check you out, Miss Megan Imsey. Did you ever tell my father you were so grand and so well qualified you turned down a job with the English royal family?'

'No! I'd never say a thing like that, even if it was true!' Meg flapped her hands in embarrassment. 'I didn't turn them down—I couldn't take the job. There's a difference. My father had his heart attack the day after I was offered the position. I'd already accepted, but couldn't take it up. My parents needed me, and all the help I could give them. I knew there would always be another job beyond the palace gardens, but my mum and dad are the only family I've got. People are more important than careers.'

He ignored her. 'I've decided you're wasted here, Megan.'

The breath caught in her throat. What could he mean?

'That title, Curator of Exotic Plants, confines you in those glass prisons behind the ten-foot-high walls of my kitchen garden. I want to set you free, Megan. You're going to take on the role of my Head Gardener, here at the Villa Castelfino. If you live up to my very high expectations, there could well be a promotion to Co-ordinator of Horticulture for all my properties—Barbados, Diamond Isle, Manhattan, and the rest.'

Meg could hardly take it in. Gianni was speaking so casually, and yet the job he was talking about would mean the world to her.

He stood up and pushed back his chair. Strolling around his desk, he perched on the corner, one leg swinging. The toe of his handmade leather shoe was only inches from her knee. Looking down on her from his vantage point, he tried to reassure her. It had exactly the opposite effect.

'There will, of course, be all sorts of fringe benefits.' His beautiful face was slowly lit by a meaningful smile.

Meg gazed up at him. Her future career lay in the hands of this bewitching, desirable man. From the look in those haunting dark eyes, she was only a heartbeat away from a still more torrid destiny.

'First on the list is a dress allowance,' he announced.

Meg looked down at what she was wearing. Her simple white T-shirt showed off her new tan beautifully, but neither it nor her jeans were new. On the other hand, they were comfortable.

'But these clothes are best for my job,' she murmured.

Gianni grimaced. 'They may be in England, but here you are part of my new Villa Castelfino Project. I have decided my vineyard and my father's plans for increased tourism will complement each other. Instead of appealing only to wine connoisseurs, a visitor centre that leads people on from my vineyard to other attractions will bring in a wider, though still discerning audience. I intend all my staff to be my ambassadors, and that means they must look the part. When I host my first banquet here as Count, the head of every one of my departments will attend. It's going to be a prestigious evening, so you will all be expected to look as good as these surroundings.' He looked around his stylish office with satisfaction. 'Particularly you, Meg, as you will be showing my guests that tropical wonderland you're developing.'

Meg began to relax. If all his staff were to be treated alike, she could accept something as simple as a dress allowance with no qualms.

'I got the idea from some background research I did, after my people handed me the file they'd opened on you,' Gianni went on. 'A hundred years ago, English aristocrats used to give their grandest guests a tour of the kitchen garden. Did you know that?'

'Yes…' Meg said uncertainly, not sure where this was leading. 'But this is modern Italy,' she added, remembering how keen Gianni was on looking forward rather than back.

'I know. I've spent my whole life trying to escape from the old-fashioned image of the Bellinis. Now I've shouldered all my ancient responsibilities, I'm looking for ways to make life here more bearable for myself. The old counts never simply sat around on the foothills of their wealth. They all scaled the heights, and I'm no exception. I've turned a few dozen hectares of run-down vineyard into the nucleus of a multimillion-pound business. I did it to make myself independent from my family's wealth. I've got nothing to prove in that direction. Now I've started looking into the idea of producing other local specialities. The Castelfino estate also produces top quality local food and olive oil. I want to make this villa into a beautiful place to do business with my friends and associates. They can all come and see how it's done, and help local trade at the same time. That's why I've started targeting my social life so ruthlessly. After my trophy head gardener has shown my guests around the grounds, they will be treated to a lavish banquet. Everything that can possibly be supplied by the Castelfino estate will be on display: food, wine, your flowers…everything I'm most proud of is going to be shown to its best advantage. So I want you to make as spectacular an impression on my guests as my house and grounds, Megan.'

CHAPTER FOUR

MEG loved his idea, in theory. In practice, she felt the sort of parties thrown by a social butterfly like Gianni would be as nerve-racking for her as a week at the Chelsea Flower Show.

'I can't argue with that,' she said tactfully.

'I'm *so* glad, Megan.' He gave her a knowing smile. 'In which case, you can take the rest of the day off to go and find something suitable to wear.'

Meg moved uneasily in her seat. She didn't have much experience of clothes-buying. Money had always been in short supply at home so she tended to buy things with an eye to durability rather than fashion.

'There's no need to waste a lovely afternoon shopping. I'll go into town on my next day off.'

Gianni looked pleasantly surprised at this, but Meg's next words definitely didn't impress him.

'Or…I can make do with the skirt and jacket I arrived in,' she said with a flash of relief at the thought she might avoid shopping altogether. 'It looks nice and official.'

Gianni gasped. 'Megan! It's *black*!' he said incredulously. 'That's fine for meetings, but I'm organising a banquet. And *nobody* on my staff "makes do". You'll need something new and spectacular…hmm, in the same shade of blue as your eyes, I think. Yes—that would set off the rest of your colouring perfectly. As for the style—the skirt you wore the day you arrived was good. *Very* good,' he repeated with relish. 'It showed off your legs to great effect.'

'Neither you, nor your visitors should be interested in my legs,' Meg said stiffly.

'I'm a man. But, then, you noticed that a long time ago, didn't you?' Gianni countered her disapproving expression with a winning smile. 'You are my only female head of department. I must have some small consolations in my life. To see you holding court dressed like a princess will make up for leaving the clubs of Florence behind me, and filling my home with overweight, boring businessmen, Megan.'

When he said that, Meg's common sense almost flew out of the window. It took every ounce of her will-power not to fall for his line. She knew he must spin similar stories to a new girl every night. But that was so hard to remember when his words, and the way he looked directly into her eyes as he spoke them, combined with those richly Mediterranean looks. She had to keep reminding herself that it was all part of a devastating plot. Gianni was putting her at her ease, softening her up before he moved in for the kill…

Meg knew she would have to try and turn his interest to her advantage. With a supreme effort, she forced out a few coherent words.

'Acting as an ambassador for you will be a great opportunity to show my skills to a wider audience. I'll be able to network with people who can be useful to us both. I think it's a great idea, Gianni. Do you have any other suggestions about what I should wear?'

For the second time in as many minutes he was visibly

surprised by her words. His scrutiny became slightly less seductive, but much more wary.

'Hmm…I'm beginning to think I may have misjudged you, Megan. If you're so uncertain about clothes, you need specialist advice. I'm not running the risk of you turning up in chain-store chic, no matter how *chic* that can be. A girl like you may be able to make a potato sack look sexy, but that's not the point. When I hold a party, the Villa Castelfino is out to impress. The extra sheen designer labels can give you will be well worth seeing.'

He stood up and went around to sit behind his desk again. After making a quick request through his intercom, he folded his hands on his desk. In that position he looked every inch the successful businessman. Meg could only marvel at the transformation from seducer to tycoon, but nothing could stop his true spirit gleaming through his patina of ruthless efficiency for long.

'There—I've had the best shops in Florence put on standby. I've got accounts with all these…' opening a drawer in his desk, he pulled out an indexed folder and dropped it onto his blotter '…and I send women in there all the time to treat themselves to pretty things,' he said airily.

Meg hoped he meant business-wear for the girls from his outer office. The secret smile playing around his lips as he peeled the top copy from a pile of papers made her doubt that very much.

'Any one of these places will soon fix you up with something sexy but suitable.'

He slid a single sheet of paper across the desk towards her. Meg picked it up and looked at the neatly printed list of designer names. The only place she had seen them before was in glossy magazines in the dentist's waiting room back in England. She stared at it, wondering how she would have the nerve to cross the threshold of any of the shops on his list.

'Any thoughts?' he said nonchalantly.

Meg didn't know how to put them into words. Her parents' debts had indirectly cost her the job of her dreams. Now she had worked her way up to an even better career, was it going to bankrupt her?

'All these places sound pretty...exclusive,' she said carefully.

'You don't think I'd bother opening accounts with anywhere less than perfect?'

Meg pursed her lips. She had managed to persuade Gianni not to sack her once. If she disagreed with him over this, he might change his mind. Her fear of snooty shop assistants looking down on her fought with her terror of poverty. She had seen how that could wreck lives. It wasn't something she could face a second time. Her wages for working on the Castelfino estate meant she would be able to send impressive amounts of money home each month. Although the Imsey family's plant centre was thriving now, Meg knew how narrow the line was between comfort and disaster. Her mother and father had teetered along that tightrope for too long in the past. She wanted to make sure they had plenty of funds to withstand whatever life might throw at them in the future. This job was a magnificent opportunity to build up a nest egg for them. That way, she could be sure bankruptcy wasn't lurking around every corner.

'Of course not—and that's what worries me,' she confessed. 'I need every penny of my wages. Shops like the ones on this list probably charge a fee for looking in their windows!'

Gianni leaned across his desk toward her, wrinkling his brow. 'That's what accounts are for, Megan. Everything will be charged to me. You won't pay a cent.' He used the slow, carefully enunciated speech usually reserved for speaking to small children.

She almost collapsed with relief. Then she realised she might be walking straight into a trap. The bait was sweet as honey, but she had one exceptionally good reason not to take it. Exactly how thankful would Gianni expect her to be? Her body wanted to get closer to him, there was no denying that. This would give him the ideal opportunity to tempt her further. That was why her mind was determined to hold her back. Her experiences with ex-boyfriend Gavin had given her a taste of what some men were like. She knew from experience that a man who spent money on a woman thought he had a say in her life. Accepting Gianni's generosity might lead to all sorts of things…

She looked once again into the deep, dark pools of sensuality that were his eyes. There wouldn't be any harm in accepting his generosity, her body cooed. A smile was already warming her face as she raised her eyes from the list in her hand.

'That's more than I ever expected, and very kind of you, Gianni,' she said, and was rewarded with a laugh that enclosed her in a warm, protective force field. It gave her enough courage to face the curiosity of his fearsomely glamorous assistants in the outer office again. Assuming her audience with him was finished, she stood up. As she turned to go he checked his watch.

'Wait—I'm about to leave for the Florence office. I can

give you a lift. While I'm busy, you can shop. We'll meet up again afterwards, and I'll bring you home.'

Meg stopped. Those few words sent her into total meltdown. Time alone with Gianni in his office was one thing. Travelling with him was something else.

'Fine, b-but I'll need to change first!' she stammered, already halfway to the door.

'There's no time. You look great as you are,' he announced, although Meg noticed he didn't actually look at her as he said it.

'And then there's my work—I can't just disappear without telling my staff what's happening, Gianni! Why don't you arrange a car, while I go back and leave some instructions for the men?'

He grinned and pulled a jangling collection of keys from his pocket. 'Oh, no, you don't! I know all there is to know about women. If I don't keep my eyes on you, you'll head straight for Garden Cottage and spend the next two hours delaying me while you get ready. I'll come with you, every step of the way.'

Meg wasn't about to stop him. His presence at her shoulder kept her nerves singing with anticipation. He shadowed her as she went back to the kitchen garden and completed all her meticulous checks. All the time, Meg knew he was watching. She felt his gaze running over her like quicksilver. It only slid away whenever she tried to catch his eye.

'What is happening to Imsey's Plant Centre while you are enjoying yourself here in Italy?' he said as they walked out through the garden gates and went to find his car.

'I ring home every day to find out. On my mobile, of course,' Meg added hurriedly so he wouldn't think she was running up a bill on the estate account. 'Mum and Dad say they are coping, but I'm still worried. I'm afraid they don't tell me everything. That's what happened last time.' She bit her lip.

'It seems strange to take a job far away from home when you're so devoted to them.' Gianni snapped off a tall stem of ornamental grass in passing and rubbed the embryo grains between his fingers.

'I had to.' Meg stared at the seed head in his hands, re-membering. 'When your father offered me this job, it was the perfect opportunity. Helping them so successfully gave me the confidence to look for another challenge. I could strike out on my own, and begin building my career afresh.'

Her words slowed as she thought back to the one thing that had really kick started her new life. It was the night at Chelsea, when she had first met Gianni. For weeks after-wards she had fantasised about him. Then her life had turned upside down with the offer of this job, and now she was walking through a Tuscan estate beside him. It was a dream come true...almost. She tried not to notice the sunshine glittering over his raven-dark hair, or the beauti-ful cast of his features. It was becoming really difficult to keep work at the forefront of her mind.

'I'd secured Mum and Dad's business, and it was my time to shine again,' she added, dragging herself back to reality.

'And then out of the blue I received your father's letter, giving me the chance to pitch for the position of his Curator of Exotic Plants. He'd been impressed with me. We spent a very long time talking together at the flower show. I never dreamed you were related, but, thinking about it, that must have been his handwriting in your notebook.'

'That's right. He sent me to seek you out, so he must have been impressed.' Gianni nodded.

'Mum and Dad said they didn't need my help any more at the nursery, so here I am.'

They reached his car. The sleek black Ferrari crouched on the gravel like a wild cat. It was a great distraction from her problems, and she couldn't resist smiling.

'I'd never been close to anything like this until I came to Italy,' she breathed.

'Why? What do you drive?'

'I don't—not in this country. I'd be petrified of driving on the wrong side—I mean on the *opposite* side of the road.' She corrected herself quickly in response to the scornful look Gianni shot at her.

'Then it's time you got some practice.'

Without another word he tossed his jangling set of keys and passes at her. Meg bent to pick them up. He leaned against the passenger door with a knowing look on his face.

'You want me to drive your car?' She gasped.

'Everyone who lives in the country must drive. It's best if you start right now. And I'm only going to let you pilot her the few kilometres across my estate to the public road. I'm not completely insane.'

'But what happens if I crash it?'

He looked at her as though she were the mad one. 'I'll get the factory to send me another, of course. There's an inexhaustible supply, or so they told me the last time. And don't change the subject. We were talking about you. I thought you said you were happy at home?' he mocked, as though exposing some hypocrisy in the way she had left England. 'It didn't take much to set you on the path to fame and fortune again, did it?'

'If you had been listening carefully, you would have understood what I meant.' Meg's cheeks flared as she got into his car and tried to find a comfortable driving position. He looked puzzled. Then understanding brought his smile out of the shadows.

'You were *quite* happy, but not *completely*.' He nodded. 'Something was missing from your life.'

Someone…Meg thought. There was a pain beneath her ribs, interfering with her breathing. It was the same feeling she had endured back in England, every time she spotted someone in the distance who might have been Gianni, or thought she heard his laughter. Her heart rode a roller coaster each time it happened. She had thought no disappointment could have been greater than never seeing him a second time. But meeting him again had been more agonising than any mistake made in a shopping mall. She sensed that deep down he was suspicious of her motives.

'I wanted to make a success of my life on my own terms…' she said with difficulty.

'I can relate to that.'

His reply held such feeling Meg instantly needed to know more. Before she could ask, Gianni launched a list of instructions at her for starting his car and coaxing it toward the road.

She didn't have a hope. It was her very first driving lesson all over again, scary and embarrassing all at once. She clung onto the leather bound steering wheel in grim determination as they kangaroo-hopped down the drive. That was more than Gianni could bear. After thirty seconds he slapped both hands down on the dashboard.

'No, no—stop!'

Meg was so relieved, her emergency stop would have

passed any driving test with distinction. Gianni jumped out the second she braked. Rounding the bonnet at high speed, he opened the driver's door for her to get out.

'I'll get my office to arrange a few driving lessons to get you used to the local conditions, and then organize a car for you.' He said succinctly as he slipped into the driving seat.

Meg walked around and got in beside him. He was already caressing the steering wheel with both hands. Meg thought nothing of it, imagining he was waiting for her to fasten her seat belt, but he continued for some seconds after she was settled. Then he did all the things he had told her to do, faultlessly and in exactly the right order.

'Have I done any damage?' she risked as the upholstery surged forward against the small of her back.

'Only to my nerves.' Gianni glanced at her before checking his rear-view mirror. 'Cars are like women. They must be treated with care and respect.'

'I'm sorry,' she said in a small voice. 'I'll pay for anything that needs to be fixed.'

He laughed, loosening up as his Ferrari hit the *autostrada*. 'I think working for the Bellini family will extract a high enough price!'

'I liked your father. He was a good employer,' Meg said, filling every word with meaning.

'And you're hoping I'll carry on the family tradition, *bambola*?' Gianni slipped the words slyly across at her. 'I doubt that. I'm entirely different from my father. For one thing, he had been desperate to marry. It turned out to be the worst mistake he ever made, and I've learned from it. When my mother died in childbirth it was the ultimate irony. The whole experience damaged him so badly he spent thirty years licking his wounds. I intend to take my time choosing a bride. Not for me the flighty socialite, ready to bleed me dry in the name of marriage,' he finished darkly.

'I think you're very wise.'

'Really?' he drawled, grinning across the car's interior at her. 'And is that the only reason you accepted this lift? It wouldn't be because you were thinking of renegotiating your terms of employment, would it?'

The look he gave Meg then told her exactly what he meant by that. His mind, like hers, was savouring their kiss all over again. The warmth of his expression spoke to the deepest, darkest parts of her. She reacted with a furious blush, and the knowledge that she would never be free from the temptation of Gianni for as long as she lived.

'While I'm living at the Villa Castelfino, I'm not remotely interested in anything other than work,' she announced, being careful to stare at the countryside rather than look at him. 'When I mentioned about getting paid for turning up ready for work you looked at me as though I was a gold digger. What illusions could I possibly have about a man who treats an employee like that on her first day?'

The taboo subject of money had been mentioned again. Every muscle in Meg's body tensed. For an awful minute she thought Gianni might throw her out of the car for being hard-hearted and interested only in her bank balance. When he didn't, she began pulling her fingers through the wind-whipped tangle of her hair. It was easier to worry about her appearance than to apologise.

Out of the corner of her eye she saw Gianni shrug. 'It's a shame more women don't think like you do. All the girls

I meet are out for everything they can get. I'm definitely *not* looking for the same kind of woman who ruined my father's life, and mine. So far, I've been proud to say I'm not the marrying kind.'

'I hope you never used that phrase on any woman when you lived in England. It has a meaning there you wouldn't like,' Meg warned.

He winced. 'Of course I didn't. In any case, once a woman is with me, she knows I'm one hundred per cent male.'

At that moment he turned another unmistakeable look on her. It was rich with lingering meaning. Meg had to fight the urge to reach right out and touch him. Then she saw the juggernaut thundering towards them and snatched at her seat instead.

'Gianni! Look out!'

'*Inferno*, woman! Do you think I would risk an accident now? In my new car, I mean?' he added quickly, before she could read any more temptation in his words.

Gianni was careful to drop her off at the nearest possible point to the first shop on her list. Ignoring all the blaring horns around them, he parked his car, got out and opened the passenger door for her.

'How much would you like for a tip?' she asked mischievously as she unfolded herself from the front seat.

'I'll let you have it on account.'

Meg's heart almost stopped as she saw his watchful expression. When he caught up her hand and kissed it, she was speechless. If he hadn't leapt straight back into his car and roared away, she would have thrown herself into his arms then and there. Breathless with amazement, she stood on the pavement and stared, long after his car had turned a corner and disappeared from view. An afternoon off to take her pick of clothes from some of the world's most decadent shops was one thing. For Gianni to kiss her hand the same way he had done at Chelsea was a dream beyond anything Meg had ever imagined. She felt inches taller, and even began to look forward to her shopping expedition. The man was a miracle worker.

Meg usually looked on shopping as a torture. This was a different outing altogether. Today she was under Gianni's instructions to buy something she really liked, while he picked up the bill. She usually bustled through crowds, head down and hurrying. Today she strolled, taking time to enjoy her afternoon off in the sun. The touch of his lips still tingled on her fingers. Only one tiny cloud lingered on her horizon. It was the thought of what embarrassments might lay in wait for her inside the beautiful shops she would be visiting.

It took her quite some time to pluck up the courage to put her hand to the door of the first boutique on her list. After that, things happened in such a blur she didn't have time to lose her nerve. The door flew open as a tall, stick-thin woman decorated with twenty-four carat jewellery strode out. Meg was bundled aside in the rush but a voice from inside the shop was quick to apologise.

'Miss Imsey?'

She looked up in amazement to see an exquisitely turned out Florentine matron holding the door open for her.

'H-how did you know it was me?' Meg stammered.

'The Count di Castelfino himself rang to tell us to expect you. Now come inside out of this heat!'

Meg was made to feel at home instantly, despite all the designer labels. She was almost disappointed to find the perfect dress within minutes. It was a close fitting sheath of sky-blue moiré. Sleeveless and low cut with a matching jacket, it would make the most of her newly acquired tan. The assistant helped her choose an outrageously high pair of silk slingbacks to complement the outfit, and promised they would be dyed to match in time for Gianni's party. Strutting through a gallery of full-length mirrors, Meg marvelled at her transformation. She felt like a million dollars, and the effect on her was obvious. She glowed. It was amazing—this outfit took pounds off her, and gave her so much confidence! She had never dreamed she could look so good. For the first time she revelled in her own reflection. Instead of seeing Gianni's coming banquet as a terrifying ordeal, she actually began to look forward to the experience. Expansive with self-confidence, she cheerfully announced that she would take the dress and the shoes, which should all be charged to the Count di Castelfino's account.

The manageress shook her head gravely.

'Not yet, madam. I was instructed to ask how many shops you have visited so far before agreeing to sell you anything.'

'This is the first,' Meg answered honestly, but soon wished she hadn't. A second assistant gently lifted the beautiful blue outfit from her hands and whisked it away to a back room.

'Don't worry. We'll keep it safe for you. But knowing the new count, it is as well to follow his instructions to the letter.'

Meg could believe it. Her heart sank. All she wanted to do was get back to her little house on the Villa Castelfino estate. It was the only place in this foreign land she felt truly comfortable. She understood all there was to know about plants, but shopping was a mystery she'd never had enough money to investigate before. It was made only slightly less nerve-racking by the fact that Gianni would be paying.

'Oh, no…does that mean I have to do this all over again, from top to bottom of the city?' She stared at the sheet of paper Gianni had given her. Her face was as long as his list.

'It may not be so bad, madam. Try to put a brave face on it,' the assistant sympathised. Her words brought Meg straight back to her senses.

'Good grief, to hear me talk anyone would think this was hard work! If all I've got to do to please him is to rifle through a few clothes racks, I'll be finished in no time!' she announced.

Things didn't go quite according to Meg's master plan. She swept in and out of the next shop at high speed, but as she progressed down the list each visit became longer, and more leisurely. Although she never found anything that suited her taste and Gianni's instructions as perfectly as the blue sheath and jacket, she actually began to enjoy herself. All the shop assistants fawned around her as though she were royalty. She was offered drinks, sweets and snacks everywhere she went. Trying on clothes became a delight rather than a chore. She learned that rich fabrics needed to be enjoyed and lingered over, not pulled on and off at speed. When she got to the final establishment on her list, she was amazed to find it was a real wrench to leave. But at last, awash with coffee and stuffed with cantuccini, she returned to seal the deal on her ideal outfit.

* * *

She had arranged to meet Gianni near the Ponte Vecchio. He was already there, laughing into his mobile. The moment the weight of his gaze fell on her, he ended the call. Walking towards her with a smile, he pulled out his car keys.

'You haven't taken as long as I thought you would!' His gaze ran over her, and Meg's mouth went dry. The afternoon was so hot she'd been convinced her temperature couldn't possibly climb any higher. She was wrong. He looked magnificent. The contrast between his olive colouring and the brilliant white shirts he favoured was one she always admired. Today she was in for an extra treat. Gianni had not only turned back his cuffs so they exposed his smooth tanned forearms, he had also taken off his tie, and there were enough buttons open at his neck to expose a dark shadow of hair. Meg's pulse began to race away with her manners. It was all she could do to keep either under control.

'Don't worry, Gianni. I've got everything for the business banquet, exactly as you instructed. Thank you so much. And would you believe it—I got most of it only after I ended up back at the *very first shop* I visited! They're going to deliver it as soon as all the alterations have been made. Now—let's get back to the villa. I can't wait to get home, kick off my shoes and—'

She stopped, painfully aware she was gabbling. Gianni raised his eyes to heaven and clicked his tongue.

'Women! If they're at home they want to be out shopping. If they're out and about, they want to get back home! They're all the same!' he said in a voice full of Italian indulgence.

I'm not. How I'd love to linger here with you. Oh, if only you knew… Meg thought, but bit her tongue. It wasn't the first time, and it wouldn't be the last.

The days before Gianni's first formal banquet passed in a whirl of preparations.

'I knew I made the right decision in employing a female head gardener,' he announced innocently as Meg knelt on a hearth, working at a flower arrangement. When he said that she sat back on her heels.

'So you weren't the man who threatened me with redundancy the moment I arrived?' she mocked, without looking at him.

Gianni ignored her comment. He was too busy surveying the floral decorations draped around the summer dining hall. 'I ask you—what man could have done this so beautifully?'

'My great-great-grandfather and his contemporaries, for a start,' Meg said, adding an extra spray of tiny orchid flowers to the display of lichen- and moss-encrusted logs set in the fireplace. She had designed everything, from the colour schemes to the hand-tied bouquets. It had given her so much pleasure. Gianni's praise more than doubled her satisfaction, and she smiled as she put the finishing touches to the floral fire in the empty hearth. It was a sparkling mass of red and gold flowers, all cosseted in the perfect environment of the estate's brand-new greenhouses. That was an extra source of pride for Meg. She had done it all herself.

'Years ago floral art was part of every head gardener's job description, no matter how tough and manly he was,' she continued. 'Going even further back, it was a prized skill among samurai swordsmen in Japan.'

'I'd prefer geishas myself.'

'I'm sure you would.' Meg half turned to shoot the remark over her shoulder. The sight that met her eyes brought her up short. Although there was still some time to go before his guests were due to arrive, Gianni was already in full evening dress. He looked magnificent. Every inch the tenth generation aristocrat, he surveyed her work with pride. Meg couldn't help staring up at him in barely concealed wonder. He grinned.

'Flattering though your expression is, you don't have time to crouch in the hearth, Cinderella! Your big moment starts in under an hour, and I want all my staff ready on time.'

Meg got to her feet slowly. It wasn't often she had the chance to get so close to Gianni. She relished this rare excuse. Brushing the creases from her clothes added a few moments to her time in his presence. She was in no hurry to leave. He soon noticed.

'I get the impression you aren't looking forward to this.'

Meg made a face. Her mind had been full of all sorts of things but he had picked up on a particular worry. She decided there was nothing to lose by being frank.

'I'm dreading it, to be perfectly honest.'

'So am I.'

She stopped dead and stared at him, incredulous. There were only three other words this man was less likely to say, and they were *I love you*. His response had been so unexpected, she almost laughed.

'But you're the original socialite! How can you be dreading a party?' she mocked. 'I don't believe it!'

Gianni was engrossed in removing a stray thread from his sleeve. When he heard the amusement in her voice he looked up.

'This isn't a party. This is work, Megan. To my mind

the two things don't go together at all. Once upon a time I could afford to relax. Now I'm responsible for the whole of the Castelfino estate and its employees, I can't miss any opportunity to push the brand forward.'

He sounded so grim, Meg shivered.

'Then thank goodness I have a job I love!' she said with such feeling he laughed. The next moment he had closed the gap between them. Patting her shoulder, he gave a reassuring smile especially for her.

'Don't worry, Megan. It'll be fine. You'll see.'

Meg couldn't share Gianni's confidence. It took her no time at all to shower and change into her party clothes, but then her worries began in earnest. She dithered over which perfume to choose, and whether or not to wear lipstick. It was a classic case of putting off the moment when she would have to leave home. Only the memory of Gianni's smile and his comforting words drew her out of her sanctuary. By the time she left her cottage the first vehicle was already visible in the distance, coming through the estate's main gates.

'*Bravissimo*—you look stunning.'

A warmly welcome voice descended on Meg from above, making her jump.

'Gianni!'

Looking up, she saw him leaning over the wrought-iron balustrade of an upstairs balcony. Her stomach leapt as she remembered what he had said about watching her from his window. The darkness behind him must be his bedroom. Still warm and fragrant from her shower, Meg's body began fizzing with unusual excitement.

'W-what are you doing up there?' she said, trying to disguise the depth of her need to know.

'Waiting for you to appear, of course. Another ten seconds, and I would have sent out a search party.'

His admiring look made her bold.

'You're such a devoted employer, Gianni, I thought you'd be only too keen to take on the job yourself.'

He wrinkled his nose in disdain at the idea. 'No, certainly not. Any visit to Garden Cottage would deserve time I don't have at the moment. If I undertake a task, I follow it right through to the end.'

His voice was slow and deep with meaning. Until that moment Meg had been convinced her desire for him would never be allowed to come to anything. Now she saw her destiny. It was written in his eyes, and her temperature went off the scale. Only one thing would satisfy her now, and he knew. She saw it in his stance and his confident attitude. He was totally at home, and at ease with himself. It was the best aphrodisiac Meg could wish for.

A hot breeze rustled among the ornamental bamboos. It carried the sound of expensive engines prowling closer by the second.

'I—I must get to my place in the greenhouse.' She backed away towards the kitchen garden, wanting to keep eye contact with him until the last possible moment. His lips parted in the famous Bellini smile, an inheritance that surely must have spelled disaster for dozens of girls.

'Don't worry, *mio dolce*,' he said with leisurely confidence. 'I won't be starting without you.'

CHAPTER FIVE

MEG had been on pins all day. It was her job to show Gianni's guests around the restored kitchen garden and the new greenhouses, before the banquet. How to keep calm among dozens of wealthy and glamorous guests was the last thing on her mind now. As she waited to welcome the first visitors into her workplace, her mind was feverish with possibilities. Other aristocrats and billionaires meant nothing to her. All she could think about was their host.

While she was stuck out here in the grounds, Gianni was inside greeting his guests. He was within forty metres of her, but she wouldn't be able to catch so much as a glimpse of him yet. She shut her eyes and imagined what was going on inside the house. Every inch the rich, pampered playboy, Gianni would be charming everyone. She knew exactly how he would look, the warmth of those fathomless dark eyes, the perfection of his skin, and the contrast with his even white teeth. Her body lurched with desire for him, and her eyes flew open with the sensation.

In desperation she tried to focus on the ordeal ahead. All the time she was counting down the seconds until she could see Gianni again. She already knew the dining hall's seating plan off by heart. She had been placed opposite him, and between two of the most important local business-men. It was her job, along with all the other heads of de-partment employed by the Castelfino estate, to persuade them to join Gianni's local suppliers' scheme. He would be working his own particular brand of magic on two other dignitaries on the other side of the table. One of them was a Signora Ricci. Without knowing a thing about the woman, Meg's instinct was to hate her. To deserve an in-vitation to Gianni's stellar event the woman had to be rich and well connected. What if she was beautiful and charm-ing as well? Already green with jealousy, Meg retreated to the place where she felt safest. Roaming restlessly through the glasshouses, she checked her watch. There was an hour to wait until they were summoned in to dinner. Meg didn't know how she was going to stand the suspense.

She need not have worried. When the first visitors strag-gled in through the gate to her kitchen garden, pride over-whelmed her. She was so busy trying to give everyone a glowing account of the work in progress the time flew past. It was in everyone's interests that the evening went well. Gianni had a lot of money riding on the result. Meg's job might well be at stake too, and she was determined to make a success of her life. She didn't intend disappoint-ing herself, or anyone else.

To her relief, no one shared Gianni's opinion of green-houses as an expensive, outdated luxury. Not one of them mentioned the words 'carbon footprint'. They all loved the exotic displays she had built and the luxurious feeling of walking through a rainforest. Meg felt vindicated, and relieved. When the time came to shepherd the last few guests in towards dinner, she had an extra reason for need-ing to see Gianni. She couldn't wait to tell him how well everything had gone. The hot summer evening and that vision of him on his balcony had sent all her fears of making another mistake into a black hole of desire. Her body now hungered for him more than any food. She was glowing with arousal as well as success.

The ground floor of the villa teemed with hundreds of people. Meg scanned the crowds, searching for that one unmistakeable figure. When she saw him, she smiled with recognition at the image. He was working the room, and looked effortlessly impressive. Uniformed waiters moved smoothly through the crowds, ensuring the champagne flowed like water. Huge silver salvers of canapés were circulating, and no one was allowed to stand around empty-handed. Gianni was the most generous host, and his famous charm kept the party mood buoyant. Meg had all of five seconds to watch him doing what he did best before her ordeal began. The dinner gong sounded, and the waiters began showing everyone towards the lofty splendour of the summer dining room. Although everyone smiled at her and many men gestured for her to go ahead of them, Meg shook her head. She hung back, careful to let all the grand guests go in to dinner before her.

Suddenly Gianni was at her side. 'What's the matter?'

It was such a relief to stop smiling for the guests, Meg couldn't help letting her true feelings show.

'I feel so awkward! I don't know anyone!' she muttered. He dismissed her attitude with a wave of his hand.

'You know *me*, and that's all that matters.'

He flipped the edges of his jacket, momentarily showing off his expertly fitted waistcoat and snowy white shirt beneath. Meg's heart jumped. All the polite, charming and witty things she had been planning to say to him fled from her mind. She was left gazing at him in wonder. His crisp shirt accentuated the fine colour of his skin and the darkness of his eyes. He smiled at her, showing his beautifully white, even teeth. Meg felt a tingle of anticipation. Then with a jolt she saw she wasn't the only one. Behind Gianni's politely formal expression she sensed something very different. It was raw, naked desire. Her senses spun out of control. Suddenly she wanted to stride forward, push her fingers through his unruly tousle of curls and experience his kisses again, no questions asked.

Instead she blushed, dropped her gaze, and shuffled uncertainly on the spot. Gianni knew exactly how to reward such touching allure. He took a few lazy steps forward and cupped her chin with his hand.

Meg raised her head. Their eyes connected in a look that was totally out of place in such a high-class setting. But Gianni Bellini thought nothing of convention. He levelled a look at Meg that dared her to move. She could not. Instead she relished the touch of his fingers as they slid along the line of her jaw. His touch was strong, yet cool. If it had been any other man she would have pulled away. This was different. She smiled, and so did he.

'I've never seen a lovelier woman,' he purred. 'Or one so beautifully dressed.'

Meg opened her mouth to say something, but those words turned her mind to jelly. Brushing her free hand over the silken folds of her new clothes, she tried another smile. Luckily, those muscles were still working despite the effect Gianni was having on the rest of her body. She could only hope her expression spoke for her.

She smiled at the idea.

'That's better! You don't need anything more than a

smile to make you the loveliest woman in the universe, Megan.'

Her heart sank as his touch left her, but he could not keep his hands off her for long. He took her arm, his fingers running slowly over her sleeve until they reached her hand. Then he inclined his head towards the summer dining room. 'And now, Miss Imsey, shall we...?'

'I'd be delighted, Signor Bellini.' Meg smiled, and meant it.

Her mind was in a whirl as Gianni led her towards the banquet. The nearness of him acted on her like a drug. How was she supposed to make polite conversation over dinner when she felt like this? She was so nervous she could barely glance at him, but tried to look on the bright side. Her shyness was because he was so gorgeous. He was the most handsome man she had ever seen. *And it feels as though he's pretty impressed with me tonight, too,* she thought, and blushed. What would he think if he knew that, despite her determined stand against his liquid eyes and irresistible hands, his gaze and touch still filled her mind? She was already fantasising about kissing him again. As she did so she coloured guiltily, and he noticed.

'Don't hang back! What's the matter? I hope none of my male guests tried to distract you while you were show-ing them around your tropical empire?'

Her heartbeat increased. There was only one person in the world who could distract her, and that was him.

'Don't tell me that old dog Alterra has been up to his tricks again?' Gianni said with sudden vigour.

'No! Everyone has treated me very well. I was a bit

worried that Italy would be full of bottom-pinching Don
Giovannis, but luckily that turned out to be nothing but
a—'

She stopped with a squeal, her eyes wide with surprise.
Gianni's hand had slithered over her rump and delivered
an intimate squeeze. In between smiling and nodding at his
guests as they passed on their way in to dinner, he leaned
in close and whispered in Meg's ear.

'It would be *such* a shame if every single man here
tonight let the side down, *mio dolce*!' he murmured. With
a mischievous wink he detached himself from her, ready
to take his place at the main table.

Meg couldn't help herself.

'Don't leave me, Gianni!' The cry escaped before she
could stifle it. 'I'm not cut out for this!'

'Of course you are!' His hand darted out to her again,
but this time he gave her nothing more than a friendly pat
of reassurance. 'Come and sit down. Remember how impressed I was by you at the Chelsea Flower Show? Think
about your spectacular triumph there. Concentrate on your
achievements, not your doubts. If all else fails, count your
qualifications,' he finished with dry humour. Suddenly he
leaned forward until his breath was whispering right into
her ear. 'You've got more to be proud of than all these
celebrità put together!' he murmured. Then he squeezed
her elbow, and was gone.

Meg's mouth fell open. Could that possibly be true?
Her mind reeled through everything Gianni had ever said
to her. Her body had burned for him from that first meeting
at Chelsea. Now she was fired up for quite another reason.
She had a job to do, and it was one full of purpose. By
helping Gianni push forward with his plans for the

Castelfino Estate, she would be securing her own future here at the villa. She might even earn some special thanks from him…

His flattery worked. Meg walked through the banqueting hall with her head held high, full of his encouragement. As she scanned the crowds of Europe's most influential people only one man could hold her gaze. Gianni was in his element. Tall and suave, he stood behind his chair at the centre of the fifteen-metre long dining table, chatting with everyone. Meg hungered for another taste of his skill at putting people at their ease. She could not wait to take the empty place opposite him, but the crowd in front of her moved with agonising slowness. They were more interested in the life-sized Bellini family portraits ranged around the walls. Meg had to content herself with watching Gianni from a distance as he entertained his audience like the professional he was. She didn't have long to savour his skill. He must have felt her watching him because suddenly he stopped, and shot a smile straight at her.

'Ladies and Gentlemen—please give a special vote of thanks to the Villa Castelfino's head gardener—Miss Megan Imsey. On top of her usual duties, she is responsible for all the wonderful floral art you see around you tonight!' With that, he began to clap. His audience joined in. They all turned patronising smiles on Meg as she stood in the spotlight, shimmering with nerves.

She could have died from embarrassment, but cringing wasn't an option tonight. *Gianni likes my work so much he's telling everyone. Perhaps I'm as good as he says I am, after all!* She told herself. Nailing on a broad smile, she stood up as tall as she could and flung back her shoulders.

The gaggle of guests blocking her way parted like magic. That gave her the confidence to stride straight towards the table. A footman pulled out her chair as she arrived. As she sat down he took the starched napkin from her side plate. Shaking out its folds, he settled it on her lap. Gianni watched the whole performance with undisguised pleasure.

'I said you would be the star of my show, Megan,' he murmured.

A portly, florid-faced couple waddled up to take their seats at the table, interrupting before Meg could respond with anything more than a nervous laugh.

'Can't you leave the girls alone for a single minute, Gianni?' the man wheezed cheerfully.

'When are you going to settle down under a mountain of debt and responsibility, like us?' the woman added as she took the seat next to Gianni. This must be the Signora Ricci whom Meg had imagined to be a teenaged supermodel. Instead, she was an elderly woman wearing inches of make-up and weighing close to twenty stone. Meg heaved a huge sigh of relief. Despite Signora Ricci's supercilious expression, Meg gave her a particularly warm smile. Gianni cleared his throat. Always glad of an excuse to look at him, Meg glanced across the table. He fixed her with an amused smile, but the look in his eyes was penetrating. 'Never, if I have any say in the matter!'

His expression almost took Meg's breath away. There could be no doubt about it—he meant what he said. This was a stark reminder. Giving her a conspiratorial wink, he greeted the newcomers with his special brand of charm. Meg tried not to look. But she couldn't help listening in to the conversation, and was soon overwhelmed with a mixture of shock and admiration. Gianni could make all his words sound as convincing as his flirtation. She had to admire him for it. If only she could charm people so easily! She might have bounced Imsey's Plant Centre out of trouble in minutes, rather than months. That would have left her free to concentrate on her own career. She could have taken that job with the royal family...but then, if she had done that, maybe she would never have met Gianni...

'Aren't you going to introduce your latest "friend" to us properly, Gianni?' Signora Ricci boomed suddenly. She refused to be deflected from inspecting Meg, and looked at her as though she were something usually found in a spa drain. 'Though how we're expected to remember the names of all your women I really don't know. You'll have found yourself another before the evening's over, I'll bet!'

Meg didn't know what to do. She wished she could think of a stinging reply, but this company was far too important to upset. She blushed and shrank in her seat, but Gianni came straight to her rescue. He drew himself up to his full impressive height. Everyone around them gasped. At well over six feet tall, he towered over his audience. Right now he was using every inch of his powerful build to drive his message home.

'That's what you think, Signora Ricci,' he murmured, his seductive dark eyes hard as jet. 'Now I am in charge here, the Castelfino estate is my priority. Everything else takes second place. And I mean everything. When I misbehave these days, I do it in private.'

This didn't satisfy his tormentors. They guffawed loudly. 'No, you'll never change, Gianni! It's a pity your father never saw through you, and recognised the truth. Someone should have told him. All your fast living will wreck this beautiful land, and you couldn't even be bothered to give him a grandson to carry on the family name while he was alive!' Signora Ricci cackled.

Until this point Gianni had merely looked annoyed. Now Meg saw a change come over him. At the mention of his father he drew in a long, exasperated breath and raised his granite chin in defiance. A nerve pulsed in his neck. Danger flashed in the glitter of his eyes. This guest had definitely found a chink in his armour of suave sophistication. He looked down his aristocratic nose at her as he delivered a damning retort.

'That's all in hand,' He said coldly. 'As soon as my plans for the Castelfino Estate are up and running, I shall marry. And I would be grateful if you would show my head gardener a little more respect, *signora*.'

His manners were perfect, and his smile as polite as ever. Despite that, Meg saw that his body was rigid, and his knuckles were white as he gripped the back of his chair. A cocktail of alarm and dread rushed through her veins. Signora Ricci had no such fears. She laughed out loud.

'You're going to get *married*, Gianni? *You*?'

'*Naturalmente*. Tradition means everything to my family. I must have a child, whatever the cost.'

In a flash Meg saw that the price to him would be astronomical. His words were darts of barely concealed anger, puncturing Signora Ricci like a balloon. Meg wilted at his tone, even though his rage was not directed at her. The moment he noticed her reaction, he took his seat and called for wine to be poured. It was enough of a distraction to allow him to shoot a few words across the table to her without anyone else noticing.

'It's OK, Megan. Cheer up—this evening is supposed to be a chance for people to enjoy themselves, don't forget!'

When Gianni saw her smile, his temper improved in a flash. This might not be the nightclubs of Rome or New York, but it was a party, for all that. He was in his element. There was gourmet food, vintage wine and he had the most intriguing girl in the world seated opposite him. And every time he spoke to her, Meg's lovely face lit up with a promise that was reflected all through her body. Candlelight rippled over the caramel waves of her hair, making it glitter with gold. She moved like a gentle breeze, tempting him with thoughts of possible pleasures to come. His eyes were drawn back to her time and again.

She's some girl, he thought appreciatively, *and tonight she's acting the part of gracious lady to perfection.* He smiled again as she was thrown into a momentary panic. Her napkin had slithered over the slippery surface of her dress, and fallen to the floor. Lifting the damask square from his own lap, he flourished it across the table towards her in a crackle of starched linen.

'Don't worry, Megan. You can take mine.' He glittered at her. She responded with a flurry of blushes and thanks. He liked that. He never had to try when it came to impressing women, but his mind had seized on an intriguing idea. He felt the urge to turn this banquet into the equivalent of their first date. At times like this, it never hurt to go the extra mile.

That's progress! he thought, taking note of the way Meg thanked him. Dancing shadows thrown by the candlelight accentuated the tempting depths of her cleavage.

Although the room was warm, her nipples were already obvious through the silk of her dress. Gianni's temperature rose. A new idea was forming in his restless mind. She was ambitious. He wanted her body. There might be a way to satisfy them both. His polite, public smile took on considerable inner warmth. This staid business banquet had given him a very good idea. Turning from playboy to patrician was shaping up to be the best sacrifice he had made in his life.

CHAPTER SIX

MORE wine was poured. Meg looked doubtfully at the mildewed peeling label on the bottle before her. She questioned Gianni across the table with her eyes.

'It's the villa's tignanello reserve, kept for extra special occasions,' Gianni explained, skimming his spoon across the bowl of soup in front of him. 'Don't let your consommé get cold, Megan. It's too delicious to miss.' He shot a look across the table at her. His meaning was as clear as the crystal carafe of water standing between them. It said: *And so are you…*

Gianni was a dedicated playboy, and while he might not yet be interested in marriage it did seem that for now he had his sights set on an affair with her, making it clear he was hers for the taking! *He blew into my life like a tornado and wiped every other thought clean out of my mind. It's the perfect excuse. Why shouldn't I go mad, just this once? Heaven knows I deserve it. Up until now, I've sacrificed everything for the sake of my career. Surely it's time to find out exactly what I've been missing!*

She lifted her eyes and looked at Gianni across the table.

No woman can possibly be safe from him. So no one in the universe could blame me for falling under his spell…

She wavered. Then Gianni suddenly switched his attention to the pretty little waitress who had come to take his empty soup plate. The same irresistible smile was turned on her. In that instant Meg almost came to her senses. A voice in her head told her that this tiger would never settle down. She had heard it from his own lips, only a moment ago. Where did that leave her misty dreams of true love? But screams of reason, no matter how shrill, never had a chance. Meg's whole body, mind and spirit had been taken over by thoughts of Gianni. Common sense dissolved. Everything about him overwhelmed her, from the delicious fragrance of his aftershave to the lilt of his voice. She wanted him, even if he slipped away through her fingers like a sunbeam. Whatever heartbreak the future might hold, she would be sure of at least one brief moment of happiness.

In that instant, Gianni's expression changed. His eyes narrowed. A triumphant smile teased his lips. He became as watchful as a panther. Instead of being caressed by his gaze, Meg now felt invisible hands bending her to his will. The more certainty there was in Gianni's expression, the more unstable she felt. *I'm way out of my depth!* she realised desperately. *I can't allow myself to fall into the hands of a man who'll drop me in an instant! What will he think of me?*

Even as she cringed at the thought, that wicked voice of temptation called to her again. *This could be the most spectacular night of my life. If I never take a risk, I'll never know. As long as we're both discreet, where's the problem?* it said, loud and clear. The sudden rush of bravado raised her head and lowered her lashes. When she gazed across the table at Gianni now, it was with new eyes.

Delicious courses of the finest organic produce the Castelfino estate could produce came and went. Meg barely noticed. The conversation washed over her like a gentle tide. Finally, when the last pudding dish had been spirited away, more champagne arrived. Gianni pushed back his chair and stood up to give his speech. He spoke to the whole room, like the seasoned professional he was, but Meg felt every word of thanks and praise directed straight at her. He was laid-back, and delighted them all. She followed his every movement, every gesture. His gaze ranged right across the assembly but he never once made eye contact with her, however much she lusted after his attention. He announced many toasts, but barely touched his own foaming glass of Taittinger. In her nervousness, Meg emptied her glass twice. As Gianni sat down a waiter moved in to fill her glass again. The host was equally swift. Reaching across the table, he removed the crystal flute from her fingers.

'That's quite enough for tonight, don't you think? You'll need to keep your wits about you on the dance floor.'

His words wiped the smile straight from her face. 'I'd forgotten that. I was looking forward to escaping to my greenhouses,' she muttered, watching the glittering assembly with a hunted expression.

'*Whose* greenhouse?' Gianni's supercilious expression was only slightly softened when he raised his eyebrows. 'Don't worry. A couple more hours of dancing to my tune, then you'll get your reward. You promised me a deluxe tour of the new empire you've created for me out in the grounds, remember? I'm the only person who hasn't inspected Castelfino's new exotic plant ranges, ladies and gentlemen,' he explained to all the guests seated within earshot. 'This evening has been such a success I'll need some time to wind down afterwards. Would you mind if I took full advantage of your tropical paradise later on, Megan?'

His voice was as seductive as his expression. The promise in it was dark, dangerous and totally irresistible. She could only nod in reply. He smiled, his eyes flashing something that might have been triumph. Meg was on fire, but that look warned her she would have to be patient. This was Gianni's evening. His cool confidence would keep him in control—until the moment they were alone together…

Meg yearned for a touch, or a look. It was a long time in coming. She had to watch him working the room in the same way he had charmed everyone at the Chelsea Flower Show. He had a smile and a friendly word for everyone—except Meg. She developed a way of flicking glances around the ballroom while still appearing to keep her full attention on the guest who was talking to her. Meg wasn't one of life's minglers, but she could do it when necessary. Gianni was an expert, and tonight he was conducting a masterclass. By the time his circuit of the room brought him back to her, she was burning with anticipation.

'Thank goodness you're back, Gianni! I'm running out of things to say!'

'Oh, I doubt that.' He chuckled. 'You're a natural at this, Megan. I've been watching you. You've missed your vocation in life. You would have been a great addition to the English royal family.'

Blushing furiously, Meg opened her mouth to protest at his joke but Gianni waved her worries aside.

'Don't disagree with me, Meg. I don't have time for any of this "English reserve" nonsense. Diffidence never won any sales.' All the time he was speaking, Gianni was casting an eye around the ballroom. He was the perfect host to his fingertips. Although concentrating on his guests, he noticed something the moment he began guiding Meg onto the dance floor.

'It's good to know you haven't been trampling all over my clients' feet. Not many girls can dance as well as you, Meg.'

Remembering his earlier words, she accepted the compliment gracefully. 'Thank you, Gianni. It's a useful social skill.'

'And you have plenty of those. Thank you for being such a help to me this evening.' He stopped studying his guests and looked down at her. His smile was too calculating to warm his eyes, but she couldn't help reacting. Warmth flowed through her limbs like melting chocolate, slow and sweet. All the compliments she had been given about her work in the kitchen garden finally made sense. Gianni appreciated her efforts. His guests liked her work. They couldn't all be saying nice things simply to be polite. They must mean them. All the compliments on top of two glasses of champagne made it a night for bravery.

'It's all an act,' she admitted.

'*Mai!*' he laughed. 'I don't believe you. For instance, if I were to take you in my arms properly, and sweep you across the floor like this—'

With one bold movement he drew her into his body and propelled her towards the centre of the room. Other dancers melted away before them. Breathless with amazement, Meg was carried along by his expertise, held as though she were precious porcelain. Her beautiful new gown shimmered like a peacock's feathers in the glow of a thousand candles. Caught up in the moment, she looked up into his eyes and saw the chandeliers were reflected in the darkness of his eyes, too.

'Gianni…I never thought anything could feel like this…' she gasped. His smile broadened. Meg knew instinctively she had said the wrong thing. This was Gianni Bellini. His silence had led to her spilling her soul in his office. Now his firm grasp and sure footsteps were dancing her into more danger. Her mind whirled in waltz-time. Only silence could have saved her. Telling him how she felt had only confirmed his already high opinion of himself as a ladykiller. She had played right into his hands. Hating herself for melting so completely against his body, Meg still could not stop. His touch was light but so assured she was powerless to resist. While his left hand clasped hers, the fingers of his right hand spread out in a protective cage across her back. He kept up the pressure, her breasts held secure against the broad expanse of his chest as they made turn after turn around the room. Meg shone in his arms, shown to her best advantage as she followed his lead. When the final strains of Strauss died away, Meg felt her face fall with disappointment. Then the applause began. Looking around with the confusion of a sleepwalker, she realised everyone was clapping—including Gianni.

'Ladies and gentlemen: I give you the best qualified, the most nimble and the most beautiful head gardener in the history of horticulture!' he announced.

Meg threw her hands up to her face, trying to cover her embarrassment. The crowd cooed its approval, and Gianni reached out to her. Meg looked at him with shining eyes. All he did was pat her shoulder in a parting gesture.

'There—I said you could cope with anything!' he said with a wink as his adoring crowd absorbed him again.

'Gianni—' Meg began, but it was hopeless. He had moved on. Guests began reclaiming the dance floor. Soon she was enveloped by a tide of couples. They all smiled and nodded knowingly at her, as though she were a marked woman from that moment on. As the band played on Meg forced herself to walk steadily away from the dance floor, head held high. Gianni might have taken her to paradise, but she could not afford to have her head in the clouds. No good ever came of mixing work with pleasure. As a student her studies had faltered when she had allowed Gavin to distract her. She was not going to make the same mistake again. She couldn't afford to—in any sense of the word. This was the best job anyone in her position could wish for. *And it has the best employer too,* she thought wistfully, before she could think of a more politically correct reason. *I can't afford to mess up this one chance of making a success in a job that really matters to me.*

The rest of Meg's evening passed in an agony of suspense. Simmering with the promise Gianni had shown her, she was petrified the guests might notice something. She felt feverish. Catching sight of a reflection in one of the huge antique mirrors set around the summer dining hall, it was a few seconds before she recognised herself. She was used to seeing a dowdy little country mouse peering back at her. Tonight she saw quite a different creature. Her new dress and high heels made her look tall and sleek, but they were only window dressing. Meg had blossomed to complement their designer chic. Her eyes were large and luminous, her cheeks flushed and her hair coiled around her shoulders with a life of its own.

Gianni looked as though he didn't have a care in the world. Cool and composed, he was totally absorbed by his guests. None of them was in any hurry to leave such a brilliant gathering, and he showed no signs of evicting them. Brought to fever pitch and now abandoned, Meg grew increasingly restless. Finally, she couldn't stand it any longer. If he was so busy with his guests, he obviously wasn't that bothered about her. In a flurry of indignation she set off towards the door. She had taken no more than three determined steps when Gianni appeared from nowhere and put a hand on her arm.

'And where do you think you're going, *mio tesoro*?'

His dark brows were raised. No answer was needed. The touch of his fingers on her sleeve was light, but inescapable. 'None of my staff leaves before I dismiss them personally. Your time has not yet come, Megan. You are going to show me around your famous greenhouses, remember?'

She hesitated, not knowing what to think. How could he talk about work when he must know how her mind, body and soul ached for his touch?

'If you insist,' she said, but any attempt at dignity was completely foiled by what Gianni did next. His fingers closed on her. Then he slid his hand down her arm until he could grip her hand. He held it for half a heartbeat. In those blissful seconds she was touched by unmistakeable promise, and then released. This was going to be no ordinary meeting between employer and employee.

* * *

Gianni took his time in saying goodnight to his guests. He knew he could afford to. Megan Imsey was *so* hot for him. He wanted to savour the sweet anticipation of her supple little body for as long as possible. As the crowds thinned he began dismissing his staff. Finally, when the night shift moved in to clear away the remains of the dinner, Gianni strolled over to one of the refreshment tables. There he poured two espressos. Meg had been shadowing him closer by the minute. Turning, he held one cup of coffee out to her. The look on her face told him all he wanted to know. Sleeping with her was simply a matter of time. It was entirely up to him when, where and how. That feeling of power was unbeatable. His body hardened with delight, and he smiled. Megan was a smart girl. He had absolutely no doubt she would agree to his terms. He foresaw no trouble at all. Hadn't she told him on her first day that she was only interested in getting paid? That direct approach deserved respect, of a sort. Gianni knew exactly where he stood with women like that. His mother had been a good teacher in that way.

Meg would be all over him from the moment he made his move. Women always were, but the divine Miss Imsey represented something a little different. He watched her concentrating on her tiny cup of coffee. If he hadn't been so practised in the art of seduction he would have thought she was shy. Instead, he identified only the sly upward glances of an experienced seductress, and sighed. Women never gave him a moment's peace. The only respite he'd ever had in the presence of a beautiful woman was Meg's excitement when she talked about those blasted greenhouses. She was as bad as his father had been in that respect. Gianni felt many emotions when thinking about his late father, but pity was the only one he could put into words. He had spent too much time trying to avoid his father's fate to feel anything more. He played the field, determined never to risk falling in love with a woman. Love had driven the old count to live the life of a virtual recluse for nearly thirty years. No way was Gianni going to allow himself to be bewitched like that.

He reached out and pulled an alpine strawberry from one of the floral decorations lined along the refreshment table. A tiny bud hung against the rosy cheek of the ripe fruit. Its stem was as fine as embroidery thread. Scrutinising it with the air of an expert, he saw a perfect flower in miniature, severed from its parent too early. It would never get the chance to flourish and fulfil its promise now. He held it out to Meg.

She shook her head. 'There weren't many ripe fruits available—you have it.'

'No. I've had my fill of perfection. This strawberry may taste as good as it looks, but that isn't always the way,' he said at last, thinking back over his life. 'It's yours.'

He raised the berry to Meg's lips. Obediently, she bit into it. The effect was magical. It was softly, sweetly, fragrant, and everything a strawberry should be. She sighed.

'I can't believe anything could be better than that.'

Gianni felt seduction warming his smile. Unwilling to betray everything that was going through his mind, he soon put a stop to it.

'Oh, no? But I have a second treat in store for you, *cara*. Don't say you've forgotten?'

Everything about his voice told her he was no longer talking about fruit. In a visible agony of anticipation, Meg waited. Gianni began to stroll away, throwing her a few words over his shoulder.

'Come on, Eve. Let's go and find your Garden of Eden.'

The gardens around the Villa Castelfino were a magical place at night. Lanterns fuelled with perfumed wax had been hung from every tree. In their soft light the flowers Meg tended so carefully took on an ethereal quality. Airy canopies of verbena and tobacco plants shimmered in the gloom. As Gianni led her into the new greenhouse complex their shadows danced in the light cast by thousands of fairy lights threaded through the plants. Without realising what she was doing, Meg pressed a button to override the ventilation system and put on some more air.

'I didn't bring you out here to work,' Gianni said severely. 'My father's plans showed fully automatic systems throughout this entire crystal palace.'

'In my opinion there's no substitute for the human touch.'

She spoke without thinking, and instantly wondered if he would pick up on her words. When he said nothing, she began talking quickly to fill the silence. 'What do you think of your father's memorial? You need the proper greenhouse lighting to appreciate the plants. I'll switch it on, and turn these coloured ones off—'

'No—stop. The effect is perfect for what I have to say, Megan.'

She was already walking on into the first bay of the greenhouse. Gianni followed her. She stopped. He came to a halt only when he was close enough for his breath to ruffle the crown of her head.

'I have a proposition to put to you,' he added softly.

Meg whirled around. He smiled down at her in a way

that answered all the questions she would never be able to ask.

'What sort of proposition?' Meg said when she could manage to speak.

'The very best sort.' Tearing his gaze from her, he cast a critical look around the high, airy structure of the greenhouse. Meg's design was so perfect it looked like a tropical glade. Branches hung with orchids and bromeliads rose from a soft mossy bed studded with tiny bright flowers in every shade of amber, ruby and rose opal. The sound of water trickling over a rock face into a shallow pool completed the lush effect. Locked in behind the safety of the kitchen garden walls, Meg and Gianni were alone in her idea of paradise.

'Are you as hot as I am?' He passed one hand over his brow, his breath escaping in a hiss. Meg couldn't bear to think of dark patches ruining the effect of her new designer dress. Slipping off her jacket, she laid it over the nearest branch.

'Before the banquet you tried to tell me you were nervous, but now you're stripping off!' he teased her gently. 'Don't say my delicate little English Rose is turning into a man eater!'

'Lovely as this is, it's still my place of work,' she said with uncomfortable, shy embarrassment. 'I feel overdressed.'

'So do I. May I take off my jacket, too?'

'Of course.'

Once he had removed it, he released the knot of his tie and let it fall loose.

'I can't apologise enough for the way Signora Ricci treated you tonight, Megan. It was unforgivable, even though she has good reason to be bitter. She wants me,' he explained without a flicker of embarrassment.

Every woman must want you, Meg thought, *especially me…*

'I could see that by the way she spent all evening eyeing you up,' she told him. 'I could also see she didn't think much of me.'

'That's why I want to make it up to you, Megan. You're already my ideal employee, hard-working, discreet, and with perfect manners. You put on such a spectacular display tonight, both with your flowers and with the way you coped under pressure. I'd like to offer you an enhanced position, shall we say?' His words were serious, but his beautiful eyes were laughing. 'The fact is, I'd like you to take on a much more hands-on role in my household, *carissima…*'

His final word was a caress as intimate as his touch. He laid his hands lightly on her silk-clad shoulders. When she didn't move, he allowed the tip of one finger to stray beneath the material of her sleeveless dress.

'I'm still not quite sure what you're saying…' she ventured, and then tried to make a nervous joke out of the situation. 'I mean, it's not as though you're about to pull out an engagement ring, is it?' As she looked up at him her gaze was steady, totally unlike the unruly thunder of her heart.

'Of course not—but you're on the right track. You must know what I'm about to propose?' Gianni looked at her closely. Beneath the dozens of tiny coloured lights his eyes were as bright as polished jet, but they dimmed as he realised she had no idea what he was talking about. 'So…you're telling me you have no idea what's on offer?' he said slowly.

Meg shook her head. Watching him, it became obvious

that his natural good manners were fighting a losing battle with something wild and untameable. He looked up and down the shadowy greenhouse. As he did so he rolled his lower lip over his bottom teeth, holding back some remark. Meg watched him suffer until she couldn't stand it any longer.

'What is it, Gianni?' she asked softly.

'I want you to be perfectly clear what I have in mind for you, Megan. It isn't marriage. That is an entirely different contract. And don't even *think* about love. I'm incapable of that.'

Meg's heart began to race so fast she could hear it. She ought to run—hide, do anything but stay with a man who was about to tempt her beyond all endurance. Whatever Gianni said now, she was lost. One way or another, she was about to surrender her whole future to him. She looked up at him in spellbound fascination, not knowing whether to smile or escape while she still could.

He carried on in a low, level voice. 'In my world, marriage is a dry legal process: it's entirely about inheritance and money. It's nothing to do with the way a man needs a woman. It deals only in cold, hard common sense. When I marry, Megan, it will be for the sake of dynasty and ambition. I shall marry an Italian woman who can bring even more wealth and status into the Bellini fold. A man like me finds his pleasures outside that old institution.' His voice dwindled to a whisper. Meg leaned forward, trying to catch his words. Gianni moved in to meet her. His right hand now strayed up to stroke her cheek with a touch as light as thistledown. 'On the other hand, when it comes to choosing a mistress I can afford to look much further afield. And I've chosen you, Megan.'

She had to be dreaming. Gianni's hand idled up to her hair, and then down again, revelling in its silken smoothness. Afraid he might stop if she moved, she stood as still as a statue. Only when he continued his downward exploration, reaching her waist and drawing her in towards his body, did she dare to think it might really be happening. Moulding into the warm, solid power of him felt like the most natural thing in the world.

'You showed me when you first arrived that you're a woman who can stand up for herself,' he went on, 'and I respect that. But if you're going to try and resist me, Megan, I should warn you that no woman has ever succeeded.'

Meg gazed up at him, unblinking. She could believe it. She waited, and then realised he was waiting, too. It was an invitation for her to try and defy his words. She couldn't do it. For long, agonising seconds she floated in the dark depths of Gianni's gaze. They both knew that once the tiny distance between them was breached, there could be no going back.

'There's a first time for everything,' Meg managed eventually. Her voice was nothing more than a breathless whisper.

Gianni lowered his long dark lashes and slowly nodded his head. 'And forbidden fruits taste sweetest,' he reminded her.

She looked up sharply. It sounded as though he had guessed her secret, and with it the real meaning behind her words. The wicked smile dancing around his lips suggested that discovery would make her all the more desirable.

'I want you, Megan,' he whispered.

His honeyed words trickled through her body like warm

water. Her hands gripped his arms. In that instant his mouth clamped over hers. It was firm and possessive, a reassurance that took away all her fears and common sense at the same time. Meg knew this was mad, dangerous and totally wrong, but for once in her life she didn't care. She simply relaxed into his embrace and let his passion engulf her. It was far too wonderful to resist, but she knew she had to make a token effort.

'We can't, Gianni. *I* can't.'

Sliding one hand beneath her chin, he lifted her face. First he placed a kiss on the tip of her nose. Then the need to kiss her properly again overwhelmed him. Meg was powerless to stop him, but when he lifted his lips gently from hers a second time he murmured, 'Of course we can. When I show you how good it can be you'll never want another man.'

'I know…oh, how I know…' Her voice was drifting away with the last of her self-control but there was something he had to know. 'But, Gianni…I can't, really. I don't know how. I've only had one serious relationship, and that ended because he tried to come between me and my work. What I'm trying to say is…I don't know how to love.' She finished in a rush. Gianni froze, and began to pull away from her. When her hands clenched convulsively on his sleeves, he stopped.

'Are you saying you're scared, Megan? That I'm frightening you?'

'No! Nothing could be further from the truth.'

Gianni took her gently in his arms again. This time he cradled her as though she were crafted from finest porcelain.

'Then what is to stop us having the very best of times?

You have no need to worry about love where I'm concerned. I don't know what the word means, either. Certainly, I've never seen it in action.'

She pressed her face against the crisp white warmth of his shirt, desperate to hide her embarrassment. Kissing him felt so right, but in all the wrong ways. She was a virgin, with nothing to offer an experienced man of the world. She wasn't qualified for making love with him once, let alone agreeing to be his mistress! 'This is wonderful, Gianni, but as for taking it any further…I've got no experience…'

'Ah-h-h…' he murmured, his hands beginning a slow dance over the smooth silk of her dress. 'So you're a virgin?'

'It's a bit old-fashioned, I know, but s-sex has never happened for me.' She had difficulty saying the word. 'I was always too busy…I did have a long-term boyfriend, but every time he threatened to come between me and my studies, I backed off,' she whispered into the warm confessional of his arms.

'Then that is what I must do now, *mio dolce*,' he said softly.

That was a shock; it hurt desperately to hear his rejection. 'No! Why?' She looked up at him in anguish.

'You mustn't take a life changing decision in the space of a few seconds,' he warned, but she was determined.

'If only you knew, Gianni. I've waited so long for this experience, and passed up so many opportunities. My focus was always on something else, but now it's my turn to make a decision. I want experience. I want to know what it's like to live as other people do. When I watch you with women, you all seem to be members of some wonderful secret society. I'm sentenced always to be an outsider. I need a taste of real life, Gianni. I've spent years concentrating on my work. Now I want you to be the man who shows me what I've been missing!'

He was quiet for a moment, while his fingertips danced delicately over her back.

'Are you sure?' he said at last.

'I've never been more sure of anything in my life, Gianni. Take me,' she whispered simply.

Outside in the dusk a nightingale poured out its heart in an ecstasy of song. Acting on visceral instinct, Gianni dipped his head and touched his lips to her neck. Meg gasped, revelling in the experience. It was an invitation he couldn't refuse. He wanted to go on enjoying the anticipation of what was to come, but the temptation was too great. Suddenly he was kissing her with more power and passion than she had experienced in her whole life. His tongue urged into her mouth. She let him explore with a relish that had been building since the moment they first met. This felt so right. For the first time in months—years—she was free to put herself first. She had been waiting for so long. Her needs and desires surged in a tumble of excitement. Her hands went up to his head, clawing at his hair to pull him closer. Hungry for his kisses, she was desperate for his attention. His fingertips felt hot through the thin silk of her dress. They circled over her back, ran up and down over her ribs with the sweet certainty of possession. Meg undulated beneath him until the soft pale skin of her inner thigh was rubbing against his leg. It brought back all the turmoil his caresses had as they danced. Now they could release all that pent up passion in one wild moment. She threw back her head with a gasp.

'Oh, Gianni…' she called out, and he was there to answer her cry.

'Good, isn't it?' he purred. The low resonance of his voice was so delicious she could almost taste him.

'Don't stop…please, don't stop…'

'Don't worry, *mio tesoro*, I'm not going to…' His hands roamed over her willing body. His kisses worked their way up from her cleavage and over her neck.

'And now…to make sure you really are as eager as you say, undress me.' The words were growled into her hair. Tentatively, Meg's hands went to the tiny pearl buttons of his shirt. As it fell open, the warm fragrance of his body tantalised her into diving her hands inside, encircling his waist with her hands. Leaning her head against his chest, she pressed her cheek against the soft fur covering it. For longer than either of them realised they clung together in the dappled darkness. Then Gianni's hands stroked her dress up until he could reach the hem. From there he peeled it off over her head in one fluid movement. With it went her last inhibition. She stood before him proudly wearing nothing more than a few scraps of silk and lace.

He smiled.

'You are lovely,' he breathed.

Meg closed her mind to thoughts of how many other women he had spoken to like this. Tonight, he was hers. None of his yesterdays mattered. She could only focus on this moment, suspended in time among bowers of tropical luxury. She didn't care about the shadows. For now a thousand tiny coloured lights illuminated her life.

'This is going to be the best ever…' Gianni whispered, in his element. 'You will be totally mine.'

His gaze now went deeper than mere sexual gratification. He had taken plenty of women in his life, but none had given themselves to him so freely and so willingly. He smiled to himself, fuelled by more than a hint of pride. The experiences she shared with him tonight would colour the rest of her life. She would measure any other man against him—

All of a sudden a frown flitted across his face. For some strange reason, he found the idea of Meg in the arms of any other man unthinkable.

'You can never be anything more than a mistress to me, remember,' he reminded her, caressing the sleek beauty of her hair. 'There can be no strings on either side.'

'I can't think of anything more unlikely than a tethered Gianni.' She chuckled, her voice rich with meaning.

Excitement burned in her eyes. His body sprang to life at the sight of it.

'You'd better believe it,' he growled, rising to the challenge.

Teasing her mouth with his lips, he fed her hunger with his own. She wrapped herself around his body, eager for the penetration of his tongue. The questing point thrust into the accepting softness of her mouth, blocking her moans of pleasure. As Gianni kissed her his hands roamed over the back of her head, twining into her thick silky mane of hair. Meg felt a rising pulse throbbing between them. It was him, it was her, it was both of them, melding in a frisson of excitement. Light-headed with arousal, she ground herself against his body in an ecstasy of anticipation. Gianni responded by trailing his touch down around the curve of her shoulder to mould her breasts with his hands. As his thumbs brushed her nipples a tightening low in her belly pulled breath deep into her lungs. She needed him. Reaching down, she returned his caresses by tracing the shape of his maleness through the soft fabric of his clothes.

Taking her hand, he drew her down gently to the soft mossy bed among the flowers. 'This will be like making love in heaven,' he murmured, his voice thick and low as he released her from his embrace. 'And I shall make it heaven for you.'

Dragging off his shirt, he threw it aside. The sudden movement stirred the soft darkness of his curls into a tousle that Meg could not resist. She stretched out her hand to it. Gianni instantly buried his cheek against her palm, covering the inside of her wrist with a flutter of butterfly kisses. Pleasure danced in her eyes as he stripped off the rest of his clothes and she saw his arousal springing from the soft luxuriance of his body hair.

'Now you're the one who is overdressed, *carissima*!' he purred softly. Meg trembled from head to foot. Her fingers stumbled to help him, but he stopped her. 'No—this pleasure will be mine.'

With a teasing smile, he slid his strong brown fingers between her skin and the thin straps of her bra. Pulling them down over her shoulders, he exposed the glory of her breasts. Meg blossomed under his appreciative gaze. When he closed in on her lips again she moved forward, eager for his touch. As his fingers strayed down to the waistband of her panties she gasped. With infinite gentleness he traced the lace around her waist and over her hips. When his fingers finally insinuated themselves between the wisp of fabric and her skin, she gasped again. A throb of excitement was building up between her thighs. With a moan she felt him ease her panties down, leaving her naked before him.

'And now the teasing has to stop…'

Every inch of her skin was alight with desire for him.

Liquid longing spilled from her body as his fingers spread over her flanks and swept around to caress the sweet soft cleft of her sex. Meg's breath locked in her chest. Driven by an instinct so basic she barely realised what she was doing, she reached out to encircle his erection. Hand over hand she caressed him until he shuddered with a life force as irresistible as her own.

'Not yet,' he growled, pulling her hands away. She moulded her body against his, half delirious with desire. In reply he pressed the length of his body to her nakedness and she gasped in a tumult of longing.

'You must be quite sure—there can be no regrets,' he warned.

'No. As long as this is what you want, too, Gianni.'

He drew back a little, the usual teasing amusement dancing in his eyes.

'Can't you tell? Perhaps I should be asking you the same question!' His touch danced over her erect nipples. 'Although the reactions of your body tell me all I need to know…'

She cried out with pleasure as his fingers swooped down to slide along the crease of her femininity. A million stars exploded over her delicate rose-pink flesh as he sought her clitoris and rolled its tiny bead beneath his fingers with expert delicacy. Her body rose to meet him, pressing upwards against his touch. She was trapped in the promise of his eyes. With tigerish concentration he drew his hand up and over her belly again, resting it there as his other hand drew her face towards his for another long, lingering kiss. She wriggled still closer to him, so eager for the touch of his body against every inch of her skin. He drew shudders of pleasure from her again and again as his kisses traced a line over her throat and across the creamy softness of her breasts. Desire bubbled in her throat and powered through her veins until she felt weak with longing. As his tongue rolled over her nipple, teasing it to a peak of perfection, she locked her fingers in his hair and cradled his head closer to her breasts. The warm glide of his hand swam over her body and she felt her legs part, enticing him further. The dense, soft curls hiding her sex nestled beneath his hand, filling it with warmth. She had known desire before, but never like this. No temptation had brought her to such heights, submerging everything beneath her naked desires. Gianni's thumb nuzzled against the point of her clitoris again and she cried out with longing. His eyes were alight with a fire that burned as brightly as her passion. Mewing wordless arousal, she vibrated with the touch of his fingers. She was desperate with need. It sent her rolling over the bed of flowers with wild abandon.

Gianni was on fire. Meg was unlike any other woman he had ever known. She was so pure, and yet he could inspire all these feral reactions in her. It made her perfect in his eyes, and beneath his body, too. His finger sought out the tender tip of her femininity, circling it until she glistened with pleasure.

'I need to see you—every part of you...' he said thickly, lifting her thighs to rest on his shoulders. As the roughness of his stubble grazed her thin skin he tasted her arousal. It was indescribably good. He had to experience her with all his senses, her rich perfume powering him to still greater heights. He bent his head, running the tip of his tongue the whole length of her swollen creases. Plump with desire, her body spread eagerly beneath his touch. Impassioned cries tore from her throat as she begged and pleaded with him to bring her to a climax. The desire to penetrate her overwhelmed him in a rush of male need. Easing his finger into her, he felt spasms of pleasure grip him again and again. His whole body reverberated with the thought that soon, very soon, she would seize the most sensitive part of his body with the same powerful movements. His heart went into overdrive and a slick of sweat broke out all over his body but he wanted to take his time. Drawing his long, lean finger back even as she clenched down on him, he insinuated a second finger into her willing body. Never had a woman responded to him so eagerly. Her hips thrust against his penetration in a rhythmic dance he longed to complete. Squealing with excitement, she arched her body, working her way beneath him as he pulled her closer. His muscles throbbed with the pressure of restraint as he forced himself to go slowly, extending the pleasure for them both. As the proud swell of his erection finally sought out her yielding warmth he felt her muscles open around him and then close with the pressure of ultimate pleasure. Suddenly, madly, penetration wasn't enough. He wanted all she could give him and more. She was worthy of everything he could give her. In a wild ecstasy of realisation he filled her with every passion he was capable of experiencing. She responded with a primeval cry of pleasure that excited him beyond endurance. This was it, and as he held her in his arms he knew she realised it too.

CHAPTER SEVEN

IN THAT moment, Gianni's life began again. He was used to having the world. Now, with Meg as his mistress, nothing in the universe was out of his reach. The lovely little virgin he had lusted after was now his mistress. The responsibility gave him satisfaction as welcome as his physical release. The moment she went limp in his arms, he picked her up and carried her back through the garden. Taking her through the silent, watchful villa, he laid her gently in his own bed. There they entwined again and again until dawn coloured the skies.

Meg became his consuming interest. No woman had cast such a spell over him before. Her body was sheer magic. From then on, he made love to her at every opportunity. He took her into his bed each night, although it meant he got virtually no sleep. Even when she slept he woke a dozen times a night, simply for the pleasure of reaching out and touching her as she lay beside him. When the praise and orders flowed in after his magnificent banquet, Gianni let his army of personal assistants deal with everything. For the first time in his working life, routine was forgotten. Nothing was allowed to get between Gianni and his ultimate pleasure.

* * *

One morning they were lying in bed together, entwined in the warm afterglow of lovemaking. Gianni's fingers were describing lazy circles on Meg's shoulder as she gazed across to the open French doors. The warming dawn air gently moved the white gauzes draped on either side, giving tantalising glimpses of the blue, misty hillside beyond. The twitter of swallows clustering on sagging, swinging power lines was the only sound in the dreamy warmth of his arms. Meg sighed.

'What's the matter, *tesoro*?'

'Nothing, really… I was only thinking that what you've told me about your life makes you sound like one of those birds. They're always on the move. Until I came here to the Villa Castelfino I'd never been outside of England. My feet were always firmly rooted in my home patch, either waiting for the first swallow to arrive in spring or watching them all getting ready to leave in autumn, like they are today.'

Gianni stopped stroking her. Raising his head, he looked at her quizzically. 'You mean to tell me that my new International Co-ordinator of Horticulture hasn't been anywhere more exotic than Tuscany?'

Meg shook her head. With a smile of perfect bliss she closed her eyes and wrapped her arms more tightly around the expanse of his chest. 'I don't need to, either. I've got everything I want, right here.'

'Yes…'

Gianni sounded thoughtful. Meg opened her eyes. That single word had a worrying note of qualification about it. From the first heady moment of his kiss, her mind had spun fantasies, possibilities and now the fantastic reality of being his mistress. But Meg was painfully aware that her position came with a rigid sell-by date. No matter how lost in luxury she might be, she could not afford to miss the signs that her time was running out. Walking the line between delight and disaster made her sensitive to his every mood.

'That is…for as long as this arrangement suits us both,' she said, careful to sound as unsentimental as Gianni always did. 'I get to network with your international clientele and show off my skills to them—'

'While I get you,' he said succinctly, delivering a loud kiss to the top of her head.

Meg smiled—almost. She had noticed that Gianni was only spontaneous when she couldn't see his expression. He was always more passionate in darkness than in daylight. When, as now, her face was pressed against his chest she had to rely on the vibration of his diaphragm to discover when he was laughing silently. She raised her head quickly, but he was an expert in hiding his feelings. His face showed nothing but the warm satisfaction that had become his trademark since their first night among the tropical flowers.

'Were you laughing at me?'

'Never,' he said in a way that did not convince her for a second. 'Although you must admit, *mio dolce*, an expert on tropical plants—no matter *how* well qualified—who has done all her learning from textbooks ought to spread her wings before she can call herself truly experienced…' he stretched out the syllables with a relish that didn't need explaining. As he smoothed away her frown with kisses she couldn't help smiling despite her private fears.

Outside a hawk streaked into the flock of swallows, sending them screaming in all directions. Meg started at the noise, but Gianni's hand gently stroked away her fears.

'That was why I was going to take you away from all this
for a while. Madeira has everything we need. Luxury and
opportunities, all set in a sea of flowers. What do you say?'

A paradise island, with the chance to have Gianni all to
herself for a while without the daily distraction of his work?
There was only one thing she could say. Tipping back her
head, she gave him a long, lingering kiss before murmuring:

'That's fantastic. When do we leave?'

Her delight lasted only a few hours. While Gianni was in
the shower she borrowed his laptop, ready to surf the
Internet. The first page she opened on Madeira fluttered
with a banner announcing it to be 'the perfect honeymoon
isle'. That headline meant only one thing to her—disaster.
She slumped back in her seat, staring at the screen. With
an advertising line like that, the place was sure to be full
of couples. *Married* couples. That would be the last thing
he would want to see. Closing down the computer, she
walked slowly across the bedroom, towards the en suite.
Gianni was in the wet room. Instead of slipping into the
shower with him, she paused outside, deep in thought. It
was only when he turned off the monsoon downpour they
both loved so much that he realised she was watching him.
He chuckled. The sound was low with testosterone. It
fuelled her own arousal as he murmured, 'Can't you wait,
pretty one?'

Stepping forward, he took her in his arms. Pressing his
wet body against her filmy, sheer negligee, he soaked her
in seconds. Feeling his manhood spring impressively to life
against the smooth plane of her belly, Meg wavered. It would
be so easy, so lovely to suspend real life and let him carry
her off to bed again, but she felt bound to question him first.

'Gianni…have you ever been to Madeira?' she asked between kisses.

'Mmm…loads of times,' he muttered through the filter of her hair.

'And you like it there?'

'Mmm.' His reply was indistinct, but his caresses were full of meaning. She melted as he lifted her into his arms. 'You'll be perfectly at home, *tesoro*. For you it will be like living in a greenhouse, complete with warm, English-style rain.'

'There's nothing about the place that…worries you at all?' she pressed on, thinking of all those legally happy couples. Gianni was concentrating on carrying her carefully back to his bed.

'No. Not at all. If rain stops play outdoors, then we'll simply have to find some way to enjoy ourselves indoors…'

For a long, leisurely time he showed her exactly what he meant. Meg soon forgot all her misgivings, and surrendered totally to the luxury of his caresses. When eventually she fell asleep in his arms, she was the happiest woman in the world.

Waking later to hear the movement of staff in the dining room beyond his bedroom, Meg reached out for him—and found herself alone. Hearing voices in the main body of the suite, she padded barefoot to the bedroom door. An empty breakfast trolley was being wheeled away, out into the upstairs hall. Gianni was on the far side of the room, his back to the door. Silhouetted on the sunlit balcony, he was chuckling into his mobile phone.

'As I'm quite sure she'll tell you herself—she graduated top of her intake,' Meg heard him telling someone on the other end of the line.

'There's no stopping her. Yet look at me—I've never taken an exam in my life. It's never done me any harm. My father's obsession with these things has led to all this. He's to blame. Yes, I know, I know! Unbelievable, isn't it?'

She could hardly believe it—hardly bear to believe it. Gianni was laughing at her. Worse, he was laughing at her qualifications, behind her back, with a stranger.

Fury surged along Meg's veins with all the power of a tidal wave. From their first kiss she had been bracing herself, ready to lose Gianni to another woman. This was a totally unexpected betrayal. He didn't respect her career. He was humouring her over her work.

That was it. This was the end.

Meg stormed out to confront him. Hearing a disturbance, he swung around, smiling broadly.

'Ah—*scusi*, Chico, something's come up…something very important…' he purred meaningfully, rippling an appreciative gaze all the way up Meg's body as she advanced—until he reached her face. When her expression registered with him he stopped smiling.

'*Ciao.*' Barking the single word into his phone, he snapped it shut and threw it aside. '*Cara mia*—what is it? What's the trouble?'

'You are! I heard you, patronising me!' Meg blazed.

'When?'

'On the phone—just then!'

'Oh, *that*.' He smiled easily, shrugging it off. He moved to take her in his arms, but Meg was having none of it. She backed off. Rigid with rage, she clenched her fists in impotent fury.

'How *dare* you dismiss my work like that?'

Gianni had no intention of arguing with her. He began moving back towards the balcony. 'My staff have set up a table out here. Come and have breakfast in the sunshine.'

His conciliatory tone only enraged her further.

'Don't change the subject! I'm responsible for everything that's been achieved in the kitchen garden since I arrived. Do you always speak to other people about my job as though it's nothing?'

His eyes became points of laser light. 'You're the one who's so quick to say it isn't work to you. I was only repeating what you have said yourself, so often in the past.'

Meg tried to take a couple of deep, steadying breaths. It was no good. Her words, when they came, shuddered with suppressed anger.

'I didn't spend all those years at college for nothing.'

'No, as you're always so keen to remind me you did it to gain a clutch of qualifications and a string of letters after your name,' he responded evenly.

'They got me this job!'

Gianni's expression was unforgiving as he shook his head. 'No, you got this job because you impressed my father. You knew what you were talking about. You had a clear vision of what could be achieved. That was the only thing that secured you this job, Megan. You could have been as under-qualified as I am. We share the same objective, you and I. It's to see the Castelfino estate become as productive and cost-effective as possible. I wanted to do it by expanding the wine business. You came at it from a different angle. I hadn't thought of developing the amenity and visitor side of things until you started the job of restyling the gardens here. A job, I would remind you, that should have died with my father and would have done, if it wasn't for me indulging you to begin with.'

'So you admit it!' she raged. 'You've got no respect for me at all! You're humouring me, every minute of every day! I'm your trophy mistress in the bedroom, then let out to play in your toy garden. It's all for show, isn't it? The moment it suits you to get a wife, I'll be nothing more than one of your outdoor staff again—and an expensive, unwanted one at that!'

She shoved past him blindly and started snatching up her clothes and shoes from where they had been discarded during their lovemaking of the night before. Gianni held up his hands, trying to calm her as she dressed in a fury.

'You need to calm down, Megan. We both need to take some time out before we say something we regret. I'll run us a bath, and light some of your special rose and lavender candles—'

'Don't bother. You won't get the chance to sweet talk me back into your bed, Gianni. This is it. I'm leaving!'

He stared at her, incredulous. 'You want to leave the Villa Castelfino, and all we have?'

As she dashed past, heading for the door, his hand shot out and grabbed her by the arm.

'Then you're mad.'

She pulled herself out of his grasp, desperate to escape. She wanted to get away from him before her memories of this glorious time together could seep in and change her mind.

'What *is* your problem, *donna*?'

Flinging himself away from her with a curse, he began pacing the room, glaring at her. His fury wasn't a thing to be roused lightly. The desperate need to make a clean break for the sake of her sanity pushed her into a confession.

'My problem is the same as it's always been!' she announced defiantly. 'I came here to work, and not to become your mistress. I don't want to be a second-rank player in the di Castelfino historical pageant!'

'I don't understand. What could be better than life here with me, with money no object?' Gianni hunched his shoulders. 'Women! They're all the same! When it comes down to it, none of you are any better than *her*!'

He stabbed a finger in the direction of a life-sized portrait hanging on one wall of his suite. It was a picture of Gianni's father as a young man, standing beside the most beautiful woman Meg had ever seen. She combined Gianni's come-to-bed eyes and a raven tumble of hair. Her voluptuous figure sparkled beneath a waterfall of gold and diamonds. 'Draped in Dior, weighed down with the priceless Bellini hoard, pregnant with me…yet it *still* wasn't enough for her! My father gave her everything any woman could want, and more besides. In return she made a fool of him, drove him mad, broke his health and his spirit—so why the hell did I think *you'd* be any different? Go on, tell me! What more could you possibly want from me, Megan Imsey?'

Meg felt a pulse throbbing in her head. 'The only things you will never give me,' she said quietly. 'And that's respect. Respect and commitment.'

'Oh, for goodness' sake! This is the twenty-first century, woman!' Gianni threw himself away from the confrontation again. Standing before the great windows of his suite, he seethed visibly. 'Women want it all. With me, they are certain to get it. You've got my body, whenever and wherever you want it. Nothing else was ever on offer. I made that clear to you, right from the start. What's so wrong with the arrangement? You're a seasoned businesswoman, Meg. You must be able to see you're throwing away a better life than you could hope for anywhere else in the world. As my mistress, I can give you everything. Believe me.'

No, not everything! she cried out silently, her heart breaking. *I want you to stay exactly as you are, while becoming the one thing you will never agree to be—mine, and mine alone!*

That thought tore words from her like thorns. 'There's more to life than having a good time, Gianni!'

'Good times like those we share?' Realising anger would not change her mind, Gianni let his voice become a low, slow river of regret. Instead of pacing, he now approached her obliquely. 'I don't think so, and neither do you, in your heart of hearts. You are my mistress, Meg. That's been a prize many women have wanted. Grab this chance of happiness while you can!'

'No…no…I need security. I'm not like you—I can't afford to think only of myself,' she said, trembling with the effort of keeping her voice steady. 'Others depend on me, back at home. I can't let them down, Gianni. They're proud of me, and the way I've worked. You aren't—no, don't try and laugh it off. I heard you talking to your friend as though my work was nothing more than a hobby to keep me occupied when I'm not warming your bed. I can't stay here, knowing you think like that. I'll lose all my self respect.'

Her glance slid away from him in a multitude of emotions. After a pause, Gianni looped one arm around her shoulders and gave her a reassuring squeeze. It was too much. Rigid with anger, she burst into tears of rage and shame.

Gianni softened his tone to a seductive purr. 'No, that's not so. We work well together, Meg. Our aims and methods complement each other. They fit together like pieces in a jigsaw. I'll do everything in my power to keep you happy, and keep you here. Name your price—anything. I don't want to lose you.' His hands went to her shoulders and he gave her a tiny shake to emphasise his words. There was no doubting the earnestness in his eyes. It was such a shock to Meg she mastered her tears and stared at him.

'You don't?'

'Of course not! You're the best employee the Castelfino Estate has ever had.' Her spirits rose again. The elation lasted only as long as it took him to add smugly: 'And you come with so very many benefits, *tesoro*!'

She froze, growing up and out from beneath his protective hands. 'Star employee and stellar mistress, in that order?'

'That rather depends…' he said with a lascivious smile. When she still did not nestle into him as she should have done, he encouraged her with a tug. Then he delivered a kiss to the top of her head.

'I don't want to lose you,' he repeated gently.

'In which capacity?' Her reply was clipped and dangerously businesslike.

'Now let me think…'

His fingers trailed over her cheek and down her neck, insinuating their way casually between the neckline of her negligee and her skin. With equal offhandedness Meg moved slightly, away from him and the shelter of his arm.

'While you're thinking, Gianni, I'm going to get

dressed. Then I'm off to tell everyone of my decision to leave.' Her voice was cool and strangely emotionless.

He let her go, instantly on the alert. 'What's your hurry?'

'Because, Gianni, if I stay here, you'll keep trying to change my mind. I don't want that. I want witnesses to the fact I'm going, and as soon as possible.'

'Oh, you know me so well!' He laughed.

In that instant Meg knew there could be no going back. She had touched him for the final time, and could never allow herself to get this close to him again. If she once let him back inside her defences, she would be lost for ever. She could not afford to let that happen.

'Goodbye, Gianni,' she said, her hand already on the handle of the door.

He crossed the room in two strides. Pushing his palm against it, he stopped her opening it.

'No. You must stay.'

Something snapped inside Meg. How could he drag out her torture like this? He was no better than a cat with a mouse, giving her hope then snatching it away again.

'I'm doing this for your own good, Gianni.'

His laughter rumbled around the room. 'Don't be so old-fashioned, *tesoro*! And I hope you aren't expecting life back home with your parents to be the same as before. You're always telling me their sales are increasing by the day. Their success must mean they're still following the business plan you drew up for them. But they don't need you on the spot any more. Stay here with me, Meg. Things will have changed back in England. Your parents are grown people who managed without you, before you were born. They will resent having to make room for you again when they thought you had made a new life here!'

His shocking announcement overshadowed Meg's dread of parting from him. She stared at him in horror.

'How can you say that?' Her voice was a whisper of ice. 'It's no wonder you were so keen to act the playboy if you think parenting is something that ends when children can fend for themselves! Hearing that would have made your poor father despair for his descendants.'

'Leave my father out of this!' he snapped. 'He's got nothing to do with it. His only interest in me was whether or not I would find a reliable, loyal wife. One who was the complete opposite of the woman he chose for himself. But in my experience all women are out for what they can get.'

His last words were a bitter announcement of defiance. Once upon a time his tone would have frightened Meg, but not any longer. She shook her head slowly.

'Then I feel sorry for you, Gianni. It's no wonder you're so dead set against making any sort of commitment to a woman. You must have been damaged in some way, a long time ago.' She gazed at him, desperately trying to strengthen her conviction that she would be better off without the uncertainty of life with him.

His voice was full of the bitterness of unripe olives as he shot a poisonous stare at the family portrait. 'My upbringing took away any capacity I might have had to love, and be loved in return.'

He was quite deliberately twisting the knife in her conscience. 'I'm going, Gianni,' she said, almost managing to keep the tremor from her voice.

'Then you're making a big mistake.'

She hardened her heart and put her hand to the door handle. 'So you say—but I'd rather be free to make my own mistakes in the real world, than locked in a barren paradise like this.'

'Megan—Meg…'

The regret in his voice was so alien, she had to see if it was genuine. Looking at him was almost her downfall. Something glimmered in his eyes just long enough for her to identify it as anguish. Then he stood back from the door with a sigh of exasperation.

'Fine. Go. Do what you like, only never say goodbye to me, Meg.' His eyes were dark with meaning. 'Because between us it can only ever be *au revoir.* We are meant to be together. Apart, we are two halves. Only when together can we be whole.'

'In your mind, maybe,' she said quietly, adding to herself, *but not in your heart…*

'Isn't that the best place?' Leaning negligently against the wall, he watched her open the door. 'That secret refuge where life is as sweet as we can make it, as often as we like?'

Meg put her head down and ran. She headed for her cottage, not caring who saw her. She did not dare stop, because the rip tide of her emotions would drag her straight back into his arms.

'Don't worry, Meg. You'll always have a position here.' His voice followed her out into the upper hall and down the marble staircase. 'You'll be back—and I'll be here. Waiting…'

His chuckle was so delicious. The knowledge she could never afford to hear it again cut Meg to the bone. Squeezing her eyes tight shut against the pain, she refused to weaken, and ran on.

CHAPTER EIGHT

MEG had to keep telling herself she had done the right thing, because it went against every instinct. She knew her spell as Gianni's lover had been doomed from the start. It was bound to end, the moment he found himself a wife. Taking fate into her own hands hadn't made her feel any better. She wrote a resignation letter the moment she got back to the Garden Cottage. As far as she was concerned, it wasn't merely her job but her whole life that was over. Losing Gianni would have been unbearable, until she had heard how little he thought of her. That made it easier—but only slightly.

Though she wanted to leave straight away she was too conscientious to leave her colleagues in the lurch. She did her best to work out her notice without seeing him. It was almost impossible. He had transferred most of his business interests to the office in the villa, so he rarely left the Castelfino estate these days. Until her resignation, he had taken delight in staying at home with Meg rather than roaming the world. If business concerns hadn't started dragging him away again, she would have been in utter despair. Meg knew his future could not possibly lie with her. She prayed he had accepted she would not weaken and tried her best to avoid him whenever she could. Turning aside or hurrying away whenever she heard his footsteps was bad enough. But each time she did it, Meg then tortured herself by watching him secretly until long after he disappeared from sight.

The twelfth of November was to be her last day at work. Meg marked it with a big red circle on every calendar she could find. It sat on the page like a spider waiting to pounce. She tried to see it as the first day of a whole new life. It didn't work. All it signified was the end of her brief, joyous affair with Gianni. That thought made the time pass faster still. And all the time her body was distracting her. She lived in a perpetual state of arousal, needing Gianni, but scared of the consequences. Things came to a head one day when she was cutting flowers for the house. Thoughts of him had kept her awake for half the night. She was tired, and her guard was down. He sauntered up behind her while she was unaware. The first thing Meg knew was the glorious sensation of his hand slipping around her waist.

'Megan—'

'No!' She leapt aside like a gazelle. Avoiding his touch called for drastic action. Thanking her lucky stars that her arms were full of *Monte Cassino* asters, she thrust the airy mass between them quickly.

'What's wrong?' Offended at her reaction, he frowned. It could do nothing to spoil the rising tide of need in her.

'N-nothing. You made me jump, that's all.'

'Does that mean we can be friends again?'

A slow, predatory smile tantalised his lips. He began moving towards her.

'No! I'm sorry—that is…please don't, Gianni…'

Fighting every instinct to throw herself into his arms, Meg shuffled backwards and away from him. For the sake of her peace of mind she could not afford to be seduced by him, ever again. Although he projected the image of an ideal modern man, every fibre of his being was stiff with heritage and aristocracy. The moment Gianni decided the time was right to provide himself with an heir, Meg knew he would see *her* as nothing more than an inconvenience.

'It doesn't have to be like this, Megan,' he said, disappointment clouding his eyes.

'No—thank you. Things have changed. You made it crystal clear how you feel about me and my role here, and in any case it's time I went home to visit my parents. My father is due to go into hospital again soon, so my mum will be glad of company. They need me. Think how you would have felt if you hadn't been able to see your father when he was in hospital!'

She threw out one last desperate excuse, and saw it connect. Instantly the light went out of his expression and he took a step back from her.

'Yes, of course.'

She tried to view her situation through his eyes. From the gossip she had picked up, it was practically standard practice among aristocrats to have affairs among their employees. Gianni had only humoured her over the kitchen garden project because he had wanted to get her into bed. She could see that now. The realisation hurt her more than his anger would have done. That was why she needed to escape back to England as soon as possible.

Autumn blew in with the second week of November. Gianni stood with his back to his desk, hands on hips, watching the sky. It was a wild day. Watercolour clouds billowed over the ridge of di Castelfino land far beyond his window. For centuries his ancestors had watched and waited for attack from the north. Gianni, Count di Castelfino had never feared anything in his life. Now the thought of winter chilled his heart. The bitter wind sweeping down from the Alps wasn't the only thing on his mind.

He strolled back to look at the sheet of notepaper lying open on his desk. Meg's clear, well-rounded handwriting flowed across the page. It was her resignation letter. Reading it again, he almost smiled. Instead of a stiff farewell, she had added thanks for all the help and support she had received, and for the wonderful experience working at the villa had been.

Gianni glanced towards the telephones on his desk, automatically reaching forward. Then he reconsidered, and subsided into his office chair. He was deep in thought.

All his other staff were happy, and none of them had experienced the bonus of his constant physical attention. Why the hell couldn't Meg see when she was well off? He'd offered to do whatever it took to keep her at his side. No inducement worked. Instead she had done her best to disappear off the face of the earth, while still working as hard for the estate as ever. Her influence was everywhere: in the floral art gracing every room of his house, and in the cold empty space beside him in his bed at night.

He had been forced to go around to the kitchen garden several times, trying to find her. He told the staff it was because he needed to make sure she had suitable plans in place for her successor. Not that he had the heart to advertise the post. He already knew Meg was one of a kind. The gardens of the Castelfino estates could sicken and die for all he cared. The greenhouses and flower borders would be too painful a reminder of her, once she was gone. On the few occasions he managed to track her down, she was never alone. She refused to dismiss her staff, and made sure he never got within arm's length. Each time, she went through an emotionless ritual of showing him all the records and computer updates. Gianni couldn't break down the barriers she had raised against him, and he couldn't catch her out on anything. She was impossible to distract. Whether he tried to slip in a sly comment or lifted a quizzical eyebrow expecting a smile, he got the same response. Meg had become a stone-faced company girl to her icy fingertips.

The wind tossed a blizzard of white doves across the autumn-gold slopes of the hillside outside his office window. Gianni barely noticed them. Right now he should be busy on the phone, oiling the wheels of commerce and loving every minute of it. Instead he was wasting time over a letter that took seconds to write and could be binned with equal ease. Snatching it up, he swept Meg's note towards the shredder—but something stopped him dropping it in.

He needed closure. It wasn't something that could be put into words on a featureless white page. There was a need deep inside him to clean out the wound Meg had caused to his pride. It mustn't be allowed to fester. Within twenty-four hours he would be heading across the Atlantic, and the moment would be lost.

He stood up again, roaming around his office like a fury. Not even the display shelves lined with their tasteful objets d'art could distract his attention for long. He lifted a millefiori paperweight, and dragged his finger across the sinuous folds of a modern bronze, but none of these beautiful things made any impression on him. All he could think about was the hole Meg would leave in his life when she left him.

His intercom clicked. He killed it stone dead. Then he dropped his hands onto his desk in exasperation. Meg was wreaking almost as much havoc as his mother had done. But Meg was an intelligent woman. Why couldn't she see that a secure job here with the benefit of his lovemaking was worth a lifetime of scratching a living anywhere else? For the sake of some outdated notion of commitment she would throw it all away and simply because...

He stood up, letting his hands fall to his sides with a smack of infuriation. One minute his life had been running smoothly. The next, Meg had demolished the statue of his pride and left the remains strewn all over the place. It was one thing to accuse him of being incapable of commitment, but to accuse him of being damaged had torn away all his layers of resilience. She hadn't even given him the right of reply. Each time he had cornered her since then, the moment was never right. He always came away with her assurance that everything was under control. That included his reactions. He felt manipulated, without knowing exactly how she was doing it.

The reassurance of her constant presence at his side had been a bittersweet pleasure that had never failed. He frowned, unable to understand how this girl had found something so soft and yielding within him. It was a quality he had never suspected that he possessed. For once in his life, Gianni had stopped looking for his next great conquest.

He wanted the one he hadn't finished with.

Living the perfect modern life with unlimited money

and an intelligent, career-minded woman gave Gianni the best of both worlds. He was in no hurry to relinquish his hold on either.

He set out for the airport next day determined to drive straight there with absolutely no distractions of any kind. He lasted twenty yards. Grabbing the Ferrari's handbrake on with a twang that sent pigeons flying from the trees, he crossed the drive towards the Garden Cottage in a rattle of gravel. No woman had ever walked away from him in the heat of a relationship before. Megan Imsey wasn't going to carve a first on his spirit.

Her little hire car was parked outside. Resisting the temptation to check it for dents, he went straight to the front door. Lifting the heavy black knocker, he dropped it with a bang.

There was no reply. Gianni felt the back of his neck burn with the curiosity of a dozen pairs of eyes, watching secretly from the house and grounds. He didn't care. It didn't matter how many members of his staff saw this. The story would be all around the villa in seconds anyway, whatever he did. That was something else to add to Miss Megan Imsey's list of triumphs.

He was about to lift the knocker again for a second thunderous report when the door jerked right out of his hand. Meg scowled up at him from the doorway. She had one hand cradled in the other.

'You should be on your way to California by now, Gianni.'

Her face was white as paper. It made quite a contrast with the thin red seams of blood running between her fingers.

'You've cut yourself!' He stared down at her, the gyroscope of his anger unable to get a purchase on the slippery slope of circumstance.

'Thank you. I know. I would have had it cleaned by now if I hadn't had to stop and answer the door.'

Meg's crisp defiance was in total contrast with her feelings. The relief at finding Gianni on her doorstep was tempered by the suspicion he was expecting her to faint at his feet like a Victorian heroine. The sight of blood—especially her own—always made her feel wobbly. She felt herself growing into the part of feeble woman by the second, but gritted her teeth. Fainting was most definitely *not* part of her job description.

Gianni clearly agreed with her. Taking charge of the situation, he bundled her into the house and slammed the front door behind him.

'You should be sitting down.' He guided her into the kitchen with a firm hand under her elbow. 'Take a seat while we have another talk about this.' Pulling out her letter of resignation, he brandished it triumphantly.

'Oh, Gianni, I haven't got time for that right now! Look at this mess…' She spread her fingers in a hopeless gesture. Beads of blood were blossoming across the ball of her thumb.

'I'll talk and you can listen while I see to your cut,' he said firmly, grasping her hand and pulling it towards him.

She flinched.

'I'm not going to hurt you.'

'You might. And an argument isn't going to make you feel particularly caring.'

'This cut has got nothing to do with you or me. This is a simple health and safety issue.' He glanced at the scatter of plant material arranged over her worktops. 'What have you been doing?'

'I wanted to take home some mementoes of my stay here. I was preparing some cuttings when the knife slipped.'

He picked her penknife up from the kitchen counter and tested the blade carefully against his skin.

'When was the last time you sharpened this knife? Really sharp knives are always less dangerous.'

Meg looked away. 'I was trying to be quick.'

'Yes, and look where it's got you.'

'All I wanted was some souvenirs,' she muttered.

Gianni dropped the penknife and stared at her.

'You wouldn't need any souvenirs if you simply agreed to carry on working here. You don't have to go, Megan! How often must I tell you? If I said anything I shouldn't, then I'm sorry. You see? This hell is all of your own making,' he finished triumphantly.

'Your memory is painfully short, Gianni. You didn't want to employ me at all to begin with. Now you want my contract to include being your mistress, without giving me any loyalty when you talk about me to your friends. Or any assurance of how long it will last—and we aren't talking only of my career. I need my future to provide a lot more security than you're offering me, Gianni.'

Her voice rang with the resignation of someone who knew exactly what she was up against. This time Gianni couldn't stare her out. The first-aid box was open on the table, so she pushed it towards him. He dropped his gaze to her hand. She stared at the top of his head as he bent over the cut on her thumb.

'It's been hopeless, trying to dress my right hand with my left,' she said, suddenly glad that he was here and taking control. She felt more faint than she wanted him to know.

'I wonder if you might need a stitch or two in this…'

'What?' Meg roused as though from a dream. She stopped, unable to carry on. He wasn't listening to her, but concentrating on her thumb.

'It'll be fine,' she said, trying to convince herself.

'Are you up to date with your tetanus shots?'

'It's practically inscribed in my job description.'

He cleaned the crime scene with all the skill of a surgeon.

'Are you quite sure you don't want me to run you into town to get this looked at? You're very pale.' He searched her face. Meg looked away.

'Thanks, but I mustn't delay you any longer. It's time you weren't here,' she said with chilling certainty.

'Sit there.' He indicated tersely. Meg did as she was told as he began organising scissors, tape and bandage. She watched him, but neither spoke.

She felt she had drawn a line under their affair and said enough: no more. But to her irritation Gianni couldn't leave it at that. He had a pathological need to have the last word, and to always be in the right. Meg had presented him with a wrinkle in his smoothly ordered life. He couldn't leave it alone. He'd had to visit, expecting her to roll over and pander to him eventually, as everyone else always did. She pursed her lips. How could he call himself forward thinking, while keeping a mistress as all his ancestors would have done? If she gave in to her instincts and threw herself into his arms, she would be right back where she'd started. The clock would be counting down the days until he started clearing the way for a wife and legitimate family to replace her. That would spoil any last illusions she had about him. *I'm not falling in with his plans just to salve his guilty conscience,* she thought. As that thought crossed her mind Meg had a flashback. She was in the greenhouse with Gianni. He had played on the sensuality of his caresses all that evening, and made her wildest fantasy into a dreamlike reality. On that first precious evening he had carved his name deep into her heart.

I want you to be perfectly clear what I have in mind for you, Megan. It isn't marriage.

With those few words he had drawn her into a way of life that could only mean heartbreak. She looked down at him as he bent over her hand. It was all she could do not to dive the fingers of her good hand into the thick darkness of his curls. But that would plunge her straight back into his arms and his bed. Meg moved restlessly in her seat. She only felt truly alive with the touch of his fingers and the bliss of his kisses, but she could never risk leaving herself open to the pain and misery of seeing him marry another woman. She couldn't expose her heart to the sort of damage losing Gianni a second time would inflict.

'I've stopped the bleeding. How does that feel, *mio dolce*?'

'Much better, thanks.'

To her horror, Meg realised she was smiling. She had gone into this with her eyes wide open, yet Gianni had still managed to get the better of her. His seductive skills were irresistible. She knew he could sweep her up on wings of desire and take her to indescribable heights. They always shared something way beyond lust or heat. It had been a melding of two spirits…but one of them had resolutely kept a foot on solid ground at all times. Gianni was too keen on watching his back to give himself to her completely. She knew he would never let himself suffer by being led astray.

She watched him as he finished bandaging her hand. Part of her was praying he would leave straight away. Every other fragment of her body desperately wanted him to stay.

'I'd feel happier if you got it looked at the moment you finish work today.'

'Always the thoughtful employer.' Meg sighed. 'It's going to be some homecoming for me, sporting this.' She raised her bandaged hand, because anything was easier than having to look Gianni in the face. He leaned forward, trying to catch her eye.

'How about some strong, sweet tea for the shock?'

His dark eyes were dancing. Meg felt her heart begin to melt, and had to look away. Once he had filled the kettle and switched it on, he picked up her penknife again.

'A blunt blade is dangerous,' he repeated, picking up the pocket steel she had been in too much of a hurry to use. Working quickly he whetted the knife across each side of the file until it was razor sharp.

'That's very impressive,' she acknowledged. 'Although I hope you realise I could have done it myself.'

'But you didn't, did you?' Gianni cross-examined her with one of his unanswerable looks. 'And that's how accidents happen.'

Meg put a hand to her forehead. She had wanted to get on with the work and so hadn't bothered with breakfast, although hunger wasn't the reason why she was feeling light-headed. She was trying so hard to be adult about the situation, yet Gianni was still patronising her. It was impossible to stomach.

'How are you feeling?'

'I'll be great the minute I know you're safely on your way, Gianni.'

'I'm not going anywhere until you've had something to eat.'

Gianni swung around the kitchen counter and opened the fridge. He didn't intend leaving her before he had the answers to a few questions, either. From the way she did her best to resist the temptation to look at him, he knew their shared memories were as fresh in her mind as they were in his. Gianni was accustomed to women falling at his feet, not avoiding his eyes. He was beginning to get the faint suspicion she might have been using him to fill in the gaps in her work schedule. That was an affront to his machismo. He ought to turn his back on her for ever. Somehow he simply couldn't. He told himself it was nothing more than the sight of this blood-stained and bedraggled little *bambola*, her eyes as big as saucers in her white face. It didn't work.

This is impossible, Meg thought. Gianni was looking at her as if trying to decide which part to devour first. She glanced away, wondering if he was doing it to spite her or whether his face had a naturally insatiable cast.

'You'll have to go, Gianni. The Napa Valley is a long way away.'

'I know, but they won't dare start the meeting without me.'

Her mouth gave a wry twist. He reacted like lightning. 'What is it?'

'This cut is aching a bit, that's all. It's in such an awkward place, right on the ball of my thumb.'

'Then perhaps you'll take more care next time.' He grunted, flipping open the first-aid box again to find her a couple of paracetamols. Returning to her side with a glass of water and the tablets, he glanced away quickly when she trained a look on him.

'Yes. Of course. Thanks for everything, Gianni.' She took the tablets from him, feeling his palm warm and smooth beneath her fingertips. 'It's the first time I've ever cut myself like this.'

He turned his back on her and made himself busy in her tiny kitchen. While he carved a slice of focaccia with laser-like accuracy, Meg took the paracetamols and drank the water. Moving around the room as though he had done similar things a hundred times, Gianni flipped the bread onto a plate for her, and added some flakes of ham.

'Eat that. You'll need to keep your strength up. You're getting much too thin,' he observed unasked.

Meg took a fork from the table drawer. As Gianni's hand dived in to pull out some cutlery for himself they might have touched if she had not been so quick to withdraw.

'You're staying for breakfast?' The words leapt out before Meg realised they could be open to misinterpretation.

'I can't resist this Castelfino ham,' he said with real relish, before his eyes became pinpoints of accusation again. 'Besides, I want to make sure you're going to eat what I've given you, rather than feeding it straight into your Bokashi bin.'

He took a seat on the wide, low sill of the kitchen window. Silhouetted against the glass, he looked every inch the man of her dreams. Meg looked away quickly. She couldn't afford to be distracted. Gianni was as determined to get his own way as she was, and this sudden concern of his was all part of the softening-up process. Demanding that he get out of her home would only provoke a showdown. Meg felt too morally weak to risk that. So instead she kept the conversation light and insubstantial.

'It will be a relief to get back home to England after all this rich food and easy living,' she joked.

Gianni's brow contracted and his jaw tightened.

'Only the English can turn the good things of life into a disadvantage,' he said in an offhand fashion, watching the scarlet claws of autumnal ivy tap against the window-pane. Time stretched between them, elastic yet brittle. Either one could snap the silence and end everything. Meg waited, listening to her heartbeat but deliberately shutting out what it was trying to tell her.

'Stay...'

When Gianni spoke that single word out loud, it was almost too much to bear.

'I can't...I can't!' Dropping her fork, she scrubbed her hand back and forth across her eyes, distracted. 'I don't want to be your mistress any more, Gianni! I'm so used to being in control—I wouldn't be capable of standing by and watching you marry another woman! That would mean giving up all claim to you!'

'So that's what all this is about!' Chuckling, Gianni went to her side and tried to slip his arm around her shoulders. 'Don't be silly—'

'For the last time, stop patronising me!' she blazed.

Realising he had miscalculated, he reined back.

'I came to the Villa Castelfino to work for you—how can I be expected to do a proper job when I'm distracted by being your mistress? I'm torn between two universes, Gianni! Do you really expect me to be satisfied with life on the extreme edge of your orbit? One day soon you'll have the inner circle of your own little family, and I'll be out in the cold. I'll be nothing more than an occasionally useful bystander! That may be your idea of a fulfilled and happy life, but it's not mine! I don't have to be a bit-player in the family Bellini. From now on, my *own* family will be the only thing I'm interested in!'

'Your parents' firm is going from strength to strength. As I said, *they* don't need you now,' he said with feeling.

'Of course they do. How else will they manage while Dad's in hospital?'

He glowered. 'I'll have my people send someone in to cover for them both. I want you. Stay here. With me.'

'I can't. I must go home. I can't stay here!'

He snorted with derision. 'Back to Mama and Papa? When you've tasted life with me? After this, home life will be nothing but a burden, *tesoro*. Your parents have moved on—why can't you? The restrictions of your old life back in England will drive you insane. You won't be able to take quick shopping trips into Florence whenever you feel like it. You won't be your own boss any more. How is that going to feel, when you've thrown away freedom with me?'

The freedom to have my heart broken every time I see you with your new wife? Meg raged inwardly. Concentrating all her pain into her next words, she tried not to dwell on how true they would be.

'You've got absolutely no idea what my life is going to be like once I walk away from here, Gianni.'

'I can guess what life beyond the walls of my estate will be like for you. I feel supremely qualified to judge everything against the life you might have had here. It will never satisfy you. You've had introductions to all the top land-owners in the world, and they've had a chance to see your work. You'll never have such an impressive network of contacts again!'

Meg's face burned, but she wasn't about to back down. 'I'll have something far more important back in England. A real home, and a family that loves and supports me. I can't say the same for this place.'

Gianni's voice was emotionless as he crossed to the door. 'Don't blame me if things aren't quite as exciting with your parents as you remember. You left when you were the driving force behind Imsey's Plant Centre. The business has carried on without you, and has kept on getting better.'

Meg had been trying everything to take her mind off her broken heart. Gianni managed to distract her completely with those few words.

'How do you know? Have your "people" been keeping you informed?' She became a seething mass of indignation. It was made worse by Gianni's outward calm, especially when she saw in his eyes that he was struggling with inner tensions, too.

'In a manner of speaking.' His words were full of meaning. 'How could you think I was like other men, not paying attention when you read to me from your parents' letters, or told me about their phone calls? I heard everything you were telling me. Stop looking back. Start concentrating on the future. Walk away from me now, and you will lose everything. When you arrive back home, believe me, you will find you've become a mermaid in an English village duck pond.'

Meg could hardly believe what she was hearing. Of all the arrogant, high-handed attitudes to take, Gianni's was the most outrageous. Anything less than life as his mistress was clearly second best to him. As far as he was concerned, only he could make something of her. To suggest she might manage to have a life outside his charmed circle was beyond his comprehension. Raising her chin to mirror his own determination, she smiled.

'Then I'll just have to carve myself out a bigger duck pond, won't I?'

Without a word, Gianni turned on his heel and walked straight out of her life.

CHAPTER NINE

MEG stood and watched him go. Only one thing stopped her throwing herself at his feet, begging him not to leave. Pride, pure and simple. Pressing both hands against her face she squeezed her eyes tight shut, willing herself not to scream Gianni's name out loud. He was the only man she would ever love. She couldn't tell him, because he couldn't love her.

She heard his Ferrari roar off down the drive in a squeal of wheels and a scatter of grit. Rushing to the open front door, she was met by a smokescreen of dust. It covered his tracks, but Meg couldn't have seen him anyway. Her eyes were too full of tears. Slamming the cottage door, she ran upstairs and threw herself face down on her lonely single bed. Telling herself a clean break would be the best way was so easy. Experiencing the actual agony of losing him was hell.

She cried until the shadows lengthened. Only the pressing need to pack and escape got her through the next few hours. All the time her hand throbbed against the bandage Gianni had tied. How ironic that the last memento she would have of him was a tight binding. Wild ideas about never taking it off swam in and out of Meg's mind as she tried to cling onto Gianni's memory. All she had was this dressing to remind her. The cut on her thumb might not even carry a scar.

Unlike her heart.

Meg travelled back to England in a daze. She got off the bus outside the local pub and completed the last few hundred yards of her journey on foot. It was time to clear her head and get a grip. She needed to work out some coping strategies—for losing Gianni, and for telling her parents she had thrown away the best job she was ever likely to get. Walking up the lane towards home, she decided work would have to come to her rescue, yet again. She smiled for the first time in days. It was a weak, watery expression, but it was progress. She began to look forward to her mum making a fuss of her. After they had shared a nice pot of tea and some comfort food, Meg would retreat to the greenhouses and immerse herself in the million and one odd jobs that must have piled up since she left.

The once-potholed country lane leading to her old home was now a smooth, well-made road. Meg was too full of her own thoughts to notice. It was only when she rounded the final bend she realised Gianni had been right. Things certainly *had* moved on since she left.

The shock stopped her dead in her tracks. Her hands fell open with surprise and dropped all her luggage on the tarmac with a crash. Imsey's Plant Centre had a whole new entrance and car park where the old sheds had been. A bright yellow mechanical digger was working behind the greenhouses Meg had been so sad to leave. It was burrowing across a field that had once belonged to their neighbour—but no longer. With growing disbelief Meg took in the message printed on a smart board beside the nursery entrance. It apologised to customers for any inconvenience caused during phase one of the nursery's expansion scheme.

Gianni's words came back to haunt her when she reached the plant centre's entrance. Not only was there now a gate, it was locked.

She was shut out of her own home.

Pulling out her mobile, Meg rang her home number. To her horror, a complete stranger answered.

'What's happened? Where's Mrs Imsey?' Terrified, Meg was already hurling her cases over the gate and starting to scramble over.

The voice went stiff with authority.

'I'm afraid Mrs Imsey is unavailable at the moment. May I help you?'

To Meg's intense relief, her mother suddenly appeared in the bungalow doorway and waved. Dropping her phone, Meg ran up the drive, but it was a very different woman who rushed towards her in greeting.

For one thing, Mrs Imsey was wearing a dress. And she only threw a single arm around her daughter to begin with, as she was busy signing off a mobile call herself. It was on a PDA that looked almost as impressive as Gianni's.

'Megan! There's lovely!' Engulfing her daughter in a proper hug, she almost squeezed the life out of Meg—until the unmistakeable strains of Percy Grainger danced from Mrs Imsey's mobile.

'Sorry, lovey, it's the design studio. Can you fend for yourself for a bit? There are some ready meals and chips in the freezer—' Mrs Imsey said, before starting to speak into her phone again.

Meg had no option but to stand and wait until her mother's call was over. She might be in the middle of her parents' drive, but she was all at sea. Except during family celebrations she had never seen her mother wear anything but overalls and wellington boots. Not only was Mrs Imsey now dressed in wool jersey and court shoes, she was using a mobile phone. And one that chirruped 'Country Gardens', too...

Meg knew she should have been glad, but the mention of junk food made her suspicious. Her mother would have considered it unthinkable a few months ago. She was torn between delight and unease. There was no need to wonder what had happened since she had been away. Gianni's words echoed through her mind like a passing bell. Her parents really had moved on. It was Meg who was living in the past now.

'I'll go down to the greenhouses and find Dad,' she mouthed to her mother. Initially, he had been more reluctant than his wife to take Meg's improvements on board. Now Meg couldn't wait to see him again. He would be her anchor in the middle of all these changes.

Her mother waved a frantic finger then covered the mouthpiece on her phone before pointing at the house.

'Your dad's in the office, installing some new software on his laptop. If you want anything special from the supermarket, he's going to be updating the grocery order later, but you'd better be quick!'

Meg gaped. When she'd lived at home, her father had only emerged from his beloved greenhouses at mealtimes and dusk—sometimes not even then. She had tried to get him to use the elderly office computer a hundred times.

Meg suddenly felt an awfully long way behind the

times. Looking at all the hustle and bustle going on around her once sleepy little home, she wondered if her parents had missed her.

Meg moved her things back into her old bedroom, but Gianni was right. It was no longer home to her. Life with him had made her a nomad, unable to retrace her steps. Although the clothes she had left behind in her wardrobe hung loosely on her now, she had grown. Her return felt like trying to fit a Boston Ivy into a three-inch pot. She wanted to escape, but didn't know how. Her parents no longer needed her. She was free to go, but now she was the one holding back. She had a Gianni-shaped hole in her life. Nothing, not even her family and friends, could fill that.

In desperation, she threw herself back into work at the nursery. Learning all the new systems and meeting all the extra members of staff was a refuge. It wasn't enough. She needed Gianni to keep her centred. Without him, her life had no balance. Despite her desperation, she was proud. Scouring the trade press to see if he would advertise the position of International Co-ordinator of Horticulture felt too desperate. So she resorted to inventing a new job for herself. Capitalising on her success at Chelsea earlier in the year, she designed and fitted out a trailer, specifically for transporting their plants to national flower shows. It was nothing more than frantic displacement activity. Concentrating on Imsey's Plant Centre stopped her agonising over the future she had lost…until something began working its way into her consciousness. She had started to feel decidedly strange. Her breasts became tender, and she couldn't remember the last time she had seen a period. That was hardly surprising, when her mind was so full of Gianni—but it was worrying.

She no longer lived each day to the full. All she did was exist. Getting up before dawn and working all day, she did nothing more than go through the motions. She opened up the business each morning, and closed it down last thing at night. When her parents persuaded her that she must have some time off, she spent it in her room. There she wrote up the notes she had made while working on the Castelfino estate. At least, that was what she intended to do. Instead, she sat at the writing desk her parents had bought her for her sixteenth birthday and stared out of the window. She had looked out over these fields and hedgerows all her life. Until today she had always been able to find something new and interesting about the view. The sight of redwings arriving to feast on hawthorn berries usually worked as a reminder to start making her Christmas lists. Today she stared at the cackling flock without seeing anything. Her mind was far away, on the other side of the Alps. Snow would be falling on those mountains, but they could look forward to spring. Meg couldn't. From now on she would be in suspended animation. It was for ever winter in her heart. She had sacrificed everything, and for what?

Stop it, she told herself viciously. *My heart is too full to bear, but it's nobody's fault but my own. I made the decision to cut my losses and run away from Gianni. If it wasn't for my stupid pride I could have stayed, at least for a little while longer. Now I have to live with the consequences of leaving. That means me—not the people I live and work with. They deserve better than the sight of me moping around the place!*

With a huge sigh and an even bigger effort, Meg put her hands flat on the desk to lever herself upright. Outside, life was going on without her. She might be dead to the world, but that didn't mean everyone else had to suffer. Beyond her bubble of grief, the sun was a ball of fire, touching the fields with gold. She stood up, but felt suddenly dizzy. She had to clutch at the desk for a second to steady herself. That was a shock. It was then she remembered she hadn't been able to eat anything more than a few crackers all day, because she had been feeling queasy.

An awful suspicion began to form in her mind. It might be nothing more than a vicious circle of grief killing her appetite, which made her permanently tired and sick at the very thought of food, but on the other hand…

It was ridiculous, of course. She couldn't possibly be pregnant. Gianni had been meticulous about taking precautions.

She couldn't be pregnant.

She couldn't be! She stared at the sunset, trying to think. It was hopeless. There was only one way to ease her mind. Picking up her purse, she headed for town. The pharmacists stayed open later there.

The next few days passed in a blur. If it wasn't for the huge wall planner blocked out in vivid inks and the reminders popping up on the business computer system, Meg would have been incapable of achieving anything. As it was she went through her routine on autopilot, selecting plants, packing the trailer and heading up to London to stage an exhibit of the Imsey Plant Centre's finest flowers. It was a nightmare. The streets were full of pregnant women. Buggies jostled for space on every pavement. Babies were everywhere. Meg had never noticed them before. Now they were all she saw, but only one mattered to her:

Gianni's child, growing inside her. She could think of nothing else. Normally the prospect of building a stand at one of the Royal Horticultural Society's monthly shows would have terrified her. Now it was one more thing to distract her when she had something far more important to worry about. Everyone she saw, wherever she looked, was part of a family. It should have made her glad. Instead her heart became heavier and heavier. The perfect picture of Mum, Dad and children would never be part of her life. She had no room for any man other than Gianni. A single parent could never afford to let their guard drop for an instant. All the responsibility would be hers—caring for her baby, earning the money to keep it fed, clothed and housed…and all the time that little face would remind her of the man she had left behind.

She arrived early at the hall where the winter flower show was to take place. Her mind could never leave Gianni alone, but the work had to be done. Her orchids were in perfect condition, and she wasn't about to sacrifice them. She had been up for most of the night, cushioning each bloom with cotton wool and securing every flower stem. Now all the tape and packing had to be removed. It was a fiddly job, but Meg knew exactly what she was doing. Her fingers flew over the work and soon she was settling each flower pot into the Imsey Plant Centre display. Before long her table had been transformed into a miniature rain-forest. As she was congratulating herself that there was still plenty of time before the show opened a shadow fell over her.

Meg's sixth sense instantly told her it was Gianni.

She was right. Whirling around, she looked up into the face she had longed to see, and touch, and kiss for so long.

A million thoughts tangled through her mind, but she was saved from making a fool of herself. Gianni was not alone. He was flanked by a man in a dark coat, and a teenager holding a very expensive looking digital camera.

'*Buon giorno*, Megan. These gentlemen are journalists. They produced a feature for a Sunday supplement on the work we have done together on the Castelfino project—'

'The work *you* did,' she interjected. The men smirked at Gianni. He ignored them, and speared Meg with a glare. He cleared his throat meaningfully.

'I happened to be attending a conference in England, and took care to check their copy while I was here. It was a good thing I did. I don't want a feature aimed at the lucrative Christmas market telling only half the story. They are missing your contribution and some photographs, and they needed *my* influence to get them in here before this place opened,' he said before she could ask why he had bothered to come with them. His words were fired like bullets from a gun. Meg saw straight away that Gianni didn't intend the journalists to get any sort of human interest angle.

'I don't know…' she began faintly. From his stance and the gaze he was directing carefully over the top of her head, this was not the way Gianni wanted to spend his time in London. It looked as though the pain wasn't all on her side. Fighting the urge to throw herself into his arms and beg forgiveness, Meg tried to put herself in his place. He was doing the right thing, despite the way she had treated him. She owed it to him to put on a brave face and toe the company line. So she smiled, and answered all the journalist's questions. After carefully leaving out all references to her stellar qualifications, she was horrified when her interviewer brought the matter up. With a quick side-long glance at Gianni, she glossed over the matter. After what he had said in the past, he wouldn't want reminding about them. The photographer worked as she talked, so the whole horrible process didn't take long.

As her visitors left all Meg's pent up emotion escaped in a low moan of anguish. Despite all the noise and bustle of exhibitors setting up around her display, Gianni heard. He stopped, dismissed the journalists and walked quickly back to the Imsey stand.

'What's the matter, Megan?'

With his companions heading out of the main doors, she expected him to smile. He always smiled when he asked how she was feeling.

But not today.

She swallowed nervously. 'Nothing—I'm fine. That interview was just a bit of a shock, that's all. I'm not used to things like that being sprung on me at a moment's notice. It made me nervous.'

'That was why I stayed with them. In case you needed some moral support,' he said tersely.

She thought of his morals, and her baby. Given the circumstances, Gianni couldn't possibly want this child as much as she did. He wouldn't want it at all. She came to a split-second decision. The less he knew, the less power he could have over her.

'I assumed you were making sure I didn't bad-mouth you to the gentlemen of the press,' she said casually.

His grim mask slipped a little, and he looked shocked. 'No. I know you're far too much of a professional to do that. I also knew you'd be too self-effacing when interviewed. I came along to ensure you got your fair share of the credit.'

'That's all?'

He didn't answer.

'Then thank you, Gianni,' she said quietly. 'When will the article appear?'

'In time for a big promotion I've been arranging in England. That's why I'm over here,' he said, quashing any idea that he had travelled from one side of Europe to the other to win her back. Meg knew then she had made the right decision. She could not possibly let him know about the baby. She would dissolve like meringue at the slightest hint of either his hatred or his pity. She needed him to carry on being the rigid, emotionless aristocrat standing before her.

'Well, as you're here, shall I supply you with another raft of plants for your latest harem?'

The joke almost lodged in her throat, but she got the words out somehow. Managing to smile was quite a different prospect. It was hopeless. Quickly, she busied herself gathering up a few last tufts of cotton wool and compressing them into a tiny ball, the size of her atrophied heart.

'Not quite. I only need one.'

Meg's blood curdled in her veins. There could be only one possible interpretation she could put on his words.

'Only one? Then it didn't take you long to find a replacement mistress.' Her movements were light and careless. They fluttered over the soft moss of the display, refining the tilt of each orchid bloom or broad, smooth leaf.

He shook his head. 'From the way you kept reminding me of all your qualities, I'm surprised you hadn't realised you were irreplaceable, Megan. For your information, I'm no longer in the market for a mistress. Not now, and not ever. That part of my life has come to an end.'

'Then…' She looked at all the plants she had so artfully arranged in her display. They were all in groups. She was the only singleton, now and for ever. 'That must mean you've found yourself a wife.'

'Possibly. The final details still have to be decided.'

Meg looked away so he would not be able to see the pain in her eyes. 'You make it sound like a business proposition.'

'That rather depends on the arrangements reached. This is my last night in London. I'd like you to bring the plant around this evening.' He pulled out his PDA, tapped a few buttons and cross-referenced its display with his wristwatch. 'I shall be free from seven p.m.'

It sounded chilling. Meg stared at him, knowing this should be the last time they met.

'Will your fiancée be there?' she asked gingerly.

His mouth became a tense line of disapproval at the word.

'I have a window of opportunity at seven. That's all,' he announced. Then he was gone.

CHAPTER TEN

Meg could not bring herself to be petty or mean-minded about the plant she chose to fill Gianni's order. She took her own favourite plant from the display. It had the most beautiful flowers, white petals overlaid with a pink flush and set off with a delicate yellow lip. She took great care in wrapping it. Crackling cellophane would protect it from the December chill, while the yards of pink ribbon she curled to decorate her offering made the finished plant a present she would like to receive herself.

The address of Gianni's Mayfair apartment was engraved on her heart from their first meeting. That didn't prepare her for the reality of it. A uniformed doorman showed her in. A phone call had to be made by Reception to check that she was a legitimate visitor. She was whisked up to a penthouse suite by a lift that was whisper quiet. Stepping out into a world of thick, plush carpet and gently hissing air-conditioning, she was faced with a sleek featureless door. There was no handle, knocker or any suggestion who might be behind it. Meg raised her hand, but she didn't have time to knock. A maid in a smart black uniform and white apron opened the door. She lifted the gift-wrapped orchid from Meg's hands, but was distracted by a movement from inside the flat.

'*Grazie*, Consuelo. You can go home when you've dealt with that,' Gianni's voice murmured out to greet her. Despite everything, Meg's heart leapt. When he moved into her field of vision, it stopped altogether. Instinctively, her hand moved to her waist. Then she let it fall away. Gianni mustn't suspect anything. Tonight, he looked every inch the career bachelor. Moving easily around his spacious apartment, he was in his element. He hadn't changed out of the suit he had worn for his meeting with the journalists, although he had lost his tie and jacket and his feet were bare. He had removed his gold cufflinks too, and his shirt sleeves fell back to expose his beautiful tan.

'There wasn't a chance to thank you for everything you've been to me. I wanted to spend some time catching up with each other,' he said to Meg as the maid pulled on her coat and wished them both a good night.

It sounded a hideous idea to Meg. The last thing she wanted was to be force-fed details of the woman who had overcome Gianni's lifelong aversion to marriage.

'How long do we have?' Meg asked as he led her further into his flat. She looked around with small, nervous movements. Desperate to find any trace of the Other Woman, she was sick with fear she might actually see something. There was nothing obviously feminine on display. Gianni's apartment was a masculine blend of clean lines and expensive furnishings. Silver curtains held back by golden ropes brushed a luxurious white carpet. Beyond the windows that ran the whole length of one wall, London by night was spread out in a kaleidoscope of flickering lights.

'We have as long as *I* like,' Gianni announced. 'I need

to explain something to you, and must be absolutely certain you have it straight in your mind.'

She nodded dumbly. Moving over to a low coffee table made of a single piece of solid beech, he picked up a crystal decanter of cognac. Two glasses stood on a silver tray. Splashing a finger of spirit into each, he offered one to her. Still lost for words, this time Meg shook her head. He shrugged.

'Suit yourself—I'll leave it on the table. You may feel like it later.' Holding his glass up in the soft glow of wall lights scattered around the room, he admired the clear golden liquid before taking a mouthful. It met with his approval, and he smiled. Seeing his face touched by a trace of the pleasure she had seen there so often, Meg smiled, too.

'I was wrong, Meg,' he said unexpectedly, diving in under her guard. 'I thought that to make you anything more than my mistress would turn you into a woman like my mother. She was a wife, and the ruin of my father. I thought committing to you would submerge everything special, unique and priceless about you beneath a tide of greed. Can't you see? I couldn't take the risk of getting emotionally entangled. As my mistress, I could preserve you as my ideal woman, for ever. Marriage would turn you into a wife, and the Meg I knew deserved better than that. You were soft, sweet and sensuous—the ideal mistress, perfect to visit after a hard day at the office. I wanted to keep *you*, not some shrew obsessed with gym membership and spa treatments. Seeing you turned into all the worst memories I had of my mother was the very *last* thing I wanted.'

It was a long speech, delivered as Gianni stared down

into his glass. Meg stirred, wondering what she could say. He hadn't finished. 'My earliest memories are all of conflict. My mother screamed the whole time, my father shouted, and it was all carried on in a windmill of gestures. My childhood was punctuated by the sound of crockery shattering against every surface. I didn't want to live like that. And then you arrived, wanting more than my body, or my money.'

Confused though she was, Meg couldn't let that go.

'I thought you said your mother died in childbirth?' she probed. In the past few moments her face had worked through every emotion. Fear and confusion had passed. She was now tense with suspicion. Her fingers running back and forth softly across her waistband, she waited for his reply.

'A child did cause the death of my mother, but it wasn't me. My half-brother was stillborn.'

Meg couldn't speak. Nothing she could say seemed appropriate. Finally, when Gianni's shoulders moved in a silent sigh, she reached out and placed her hand on his sleeve.

'Your father must have been devastated,' she said softly.

This time there were no explanatory smiles. He shook his head in despair.

'You have no idea.'

He swore, a bitter Italian explosion that he could not stifle. Meg looked away.

'As a child I assumed he was heartbroken. He was—but loss of trust damaged him far more than my mother's death. She'd conducted affair after affair, eventually falling pregnant to one of her many lovers. My father never spoke of it to me at the time, but shut himself away in the Villa Castelfino. I was sent off to school in England. Someone must have thought I'd be protected from the gossip and stories. They didn't count on the cruelty of children. In our isolation, both Papa and I grew shells of steel. The moment I left school I came home, hoping we could be a support to each other. I tried to help, but it was no good. He would never mention it. He encouraged me to go out and enjoy myself, on the absolute understanding that the woman I eventually chose to marry was perfect Bellini family material. Papa spent every moment of his life regretting his choice of wife, and didn't want the same thing to happen to me.'

'What a terrible example of married life.' Meg said slowly, thinking of her own parents' idyllic partnership. 'No wonder you never wanted to be tied down.'

'I wasn't going to let my heart lead me into disaster. My father married for love and was cheated. If my own mother couldn't be faithful, how could I possibly trust any other woman?'

'We aren't all alike.' Meg got her point across firmly. 'It's a good job my mum is nothing like yours. At least she wasn't, before I left for Italy…'

'Things have changed?' He gave her a knowing look. She nodded.

'I told you so,' he said, but with such regret Meg knew he was sympathising, not trying to score points.

'It's nobody's fault, Gianni. I left you because my feelings were hurt. When I got home, I realised you were right. Times change, people move on. I should have been confident enough in my own abilities to shrug off whatever you and your friends thought about my work. I know I would have proved you all wrong in the end. And I should have been big enough to part with you on better terms.' She stopped. There was a lump in her throat that threatened to betray her real feelings. 'We have to end this properly, right now,' she said in a rush.

'Of course.' Gianni's practised ease broke her heart into still smaller fragments. This must be a regular occurrence for him. A tearful girl, the fond farewell, the pretence of regret…

A mobile phone buzzed angrily from somewhere. Putting down his glass, he strode over to where his jacket lay on a chair. Retrieving the handset from an inside pocket of his suit, he muttered a curse and killed the call without answering it.

'That reminds me—you'll have to take my details off your BlackBerry,' Meg said, hoping he would ignore the quaver in her voice.

'I can't,' he said frankly, 'because they were never on there.'

The pain that had tortured Meg for so long swam into her eyes. Working hard to master her features, she managed to look up at him in undiluted defiance.

'But all your vital numbers are stored on there!'

Shocked by her tearful response, Gianni's retort was rapier swift.

'Not yours. Oh, don't look at me like that—what else did you expect? Would you rather I lied to you, and said it was on there? No, thanks. I leave deception to people like my mother.'

'Gianni! How could you be so heartless?' she said bitterly. 'If you ask me, I think you just use your father's experience as an excuse not to marry because you're too selfish! I'll bet in reality he couldn't wait to see you safely married!'

'What?'

Her jibe threw him completely off balance. For long seconds he stared at her, totally unable to summon up enough English to reply.

'While you were stuck in a time warp of commitment-dodging, your father was always more interested in the future. I spoke to him often enough to know the Bellini traditions wore him down. He was ready for change. I think he would have loved to see you married, Gianni. He'd probably got to the stage where he didn't care who she was, as long as she loved you for all the right reasons, and that you'd chosen her for all the wrong ones—such as your raging testosterone.'

'What do you mean by that?' Gianni retorted, but his surge of anger brought more turbulent emotions to the surface. He frowned. 'I was his heir. He *had* to care. When I think of the times he raised his eyebrows over breakfast when I was headline news again...when he asked me why I never brought any of the girls home to meet him, I thought he was being sarcastic. And the celebrity dinner parties he held in New York or Athens where all the guests had daughters...' Gradually his voice faltered. When it disappeared altogether he gazed into the middle distance as though in search of it.

'So that's your defence against marriage blown right out of the water. He wanted you to get moving. Now you've got no excuses left, Gianni. Say goodbye to me now, so you can go and present the orchid I brought you to the poor long-suffering woman who is going to become your wife.'

The mention of excuses brought him straight back to the present. Grabbing her hand, he began to pull her through the lounge. Meg thought he was about to throw her out of his suite altogether, but she was in for a shock. Instead of heading for the main door, he took her into an adjacent dining room. An intimate dinner for two was planned. The central table was set with a battery of silver cutlery and bone-china plates decorated with a discreet pattern in gold leaf. In the centre stood the orchid she had brought, still decked in its cellophane and ribbons. The lights were low, and the room warm and welcoming.

'An aristocratic Italian girl is the last thing *I* want,' he muttered, guiding her around the table. The far wall was almost completely filled by an enormous mirror in a heavy gilded frame. Below it stood a highly polished walnut sideboard. As they got closer Meg saw a young lemon tree in a terracotta pot standing in the centre of the sideboard. Everything glowed and shimmered in the light of dozens of candles.

Gianni looked as distracted as she felt. His tousled hair and open necked shirt gave him a reckless look, but his manner was anything but spontaneous.

'Your resignation was a real wake up call to me. I've spent every second since then examining my motives. I'm still convinced you did the wrong thing, Meg.'

'That doesn't surprise me.'

Before the accusation had fully left her lips Gianni grabbed her by the shoulders.

'Wait! Listen to me—you've driven a hole right through my reasoning, Meg. Do you hear that? All my life I've been working towards what I thought my future should be. I wanted a legitimate son to carry on my family name. That's still my objective, but you've made me realise I was going about it all the wrong way.'

Meg narrowed her eyes. 'How many ways are there to break a woman's heart, exactly?'

He flung his arms wide with exasperation.

'I thought I was being the ideal forward-thinking executive, but in reality I was always looking back over my shoulder. I was surrounded and haunted by the expectation of the past and the duty of being count.'

She watched him carefully, wishing she could read his expression. Gianni had hurt her more than she could bear, but she should have expected that. They weren't simply from different sides of the track, they were from opposite sides of Europe. Aristocrats were one thing. Foreign aristocrats were still more enigmatic. She loved Gianni so much it hurt, and would have done almost anything to take this look off his face. The only thing she could not bear to do was sacrifice her pride by asking how she could help. Meg might be meek, but acting as a doormat was not her style. She shook her head. With that, he indicated the potted lemon tree standing before them.

'And so I came to a decision. *Presto!* What do you think of this?'

From every branch hung a small package wrapped in red velvet. Each one was suspended from fine gold wire and the weight caused the little bush to bow and tremble in the warm air.

'It looks like a Christmas tree,' Meg said slowly.

'They're all for you.'

Hesitantly, she took a step forward. The little presents begged to be touched, taken and opened. Somehow, she couldn't do it. He must be trying to buy her off. In her fevered imagination they represented drops of her heart's blood, and they sprang from loving him. Slowly, she ran her hand over the back of his as he held her by the wrist. She knew every contour as well as her own. This would be the last chance she had to savour that smooth, taut skin. His fingers had to be peeled away from her. She had to release him so that both he and her baby could be free. It tore strips from her heart.

'Go on—they're yours,' he insisted. 'If you want them.'

'They're all for me? Why? I don't want anything more from you, Gianni. Not now.'

He started to say something but she held up her hand and stopped him. 'I never expected to see you again, but since I'm here there's something I really must tell you. I can't possibly keep it a secret. You won't like it, but I can't keep the truth from you—'

'Wait. I have a confession of my own,' he interrupted swiftly. 'It's one I should have made a long time ago, Meg. Let me say it while I can. If only I could have been honest with myself from the start, I could have saved us both so much pain.'

'Gianni…' Light-headed with lack of oxygen, Meg struggled for words but couldn't think straight, much less speak.

'When I first saw you, I was having the time of my life. All the women I wanted, more money than I could spend— I was the original man who had everything. But it was all a sham. All my life I've been fooling myself that happiness could be bought. I was wrong. It has to be earned. When I was a child, I watched my parents tear each other apart. The connection must have been made deep in my mind between marriage, anger and despair. My father tried to do the right thing by conforming to the model our ancestors carved out of ancient history. But after growing up to the sounds of screams and smashed crockery, I headed in exactly the opposite direction.'

'I suppose that's understandable,' Meg said faintly, her

stare unblinking. She couldn't take her eyes off the man who, always such an enigma, was struggling to open up in front of her.

'I used to hear my mother goading my father, right up to the end. She had so many lovers even she couldn't put an end to the press speculation about the identity of my half-brother's father.'

'Oh, Gianni…' Tentatively, Meg reached out towards him. He was staring at the ground as though his eyes could bore right through to the centre of the earth. It made her hesitate, her hand halfway to his shoulder.

'That's why I told myself I'd never get married. I'd seen what it was like, from the inside.' He recoiled with a grimace. 'But, *Dio*, in my book if a man makes love to a virgin, marriage is the only option. I should have made you my wife the very next day. The trouble was…I couldn't face the possibility that marriage would turn us into the sort of monsters I remembered from my own childhood. What if I failed in the one and only thing in life that truly matters—love? And to expose another innocent child to the hell I endured—I couldn't do it. Then again, I wasn't going to lose you. So I carried on with the fiction that you'd always be my mistress but never my wife. Every time I told you that, it was my guilty conscience talking.'

It went very quiet. For endless seconds, they neither moved nor spoke. Tears clawed at Meg's throat, eager for release, but she was determined never to weaken in front of him again. He'd admitted he'd wanted to marry her, but couldn't bring himself to do it. If she mentioned the baby now, he would think she was trying to force his hand. She stood in silent, bitter, lonely darkness until she could stand it no longer.

'Then I'll say goodbye,' she said in a small voice. 'You've unburdened that guilty conscience of yours, so there doesn't seem to be anything more to say.'

'Goodbye? Is that what you truly want, Meg?'

'What do you think?'

For once their roles were reversed. Meg's voice was low with determination. When at last Gianni spoke again he sounded unusually reluctant. 'You said you had something to tell me. I interrupted you, *tesoro*.'

The uncertainty in his voice was so unnatural Meg's eyes flew open.

'Don't call me that. You don't mean it.'

'Yes, I do. Of course I do. I've never meant anything more sincerely in my entire life.'

Meg stared at him. Now she really was confused. Perhaps she was hearing things. She certainly felt feverish enough to imagine his touch—

No, that at least was true. He had extended his hand until it was resting on her arm. His touch was as light as an orchid petal.

'Open your presents, Meg.'

Every ounce of his usual authority filled the order. Meg jumped towards the pretty little decorated tree before she could stop herself, but the second she could, she did.

'Go on. You know you want to.' His voice was slow and certain. Still she hesitated. 'Accept them, *tesoro*. If you don't, then no one else will ever get the chance. I shall take them back home unopened, and straight into the river Arno they go.'

His eyes were warm with all the feeling she had seen there in his unguarded moments. This must be another one. Hardly daring to hope, she lifted one hand a fraction.

Then she stopped. Gianni lowered his chin and slowly raised his eyebrows, encouraging her silently.

Her fingers automatically went towards the smallest present. Gianni moved as though to stop her, hesitated, but then decided that he couldn't leave well alone even now.

'No—don't take that one. Open this one first.'

She said nothing, but the look on her face as she accepted a different red velvet parcel told Gianni all he wanted to know.

'Believe me, it's not another example of me dictating to you. There is a reason why you should open these in a special order.'

He was moving uncomfortably under her scrutiny, and his voice was as close to apologetic as a man like Gianni was likely to get. Meg almost smiled, but couldn't bear to hurt his feelings.

Pulling open the fine gold ribbon, she unwrapped a battered leather case. It so obviously contained jewellery; she looked up at him in alarm.

'This must be one of the only occasions when a woman says "you shouldn't have" and means it from the bottom of her heart. Oh, Gianni, what have you done?'

'Open it, and see.'

His gaze was steady and level, but she could see a pulse in his neck. It was flickering almost as fast as her heart.

Obediently she dropped her gaze and concentrated on the small golden catch fastening the jewel case. The lid sprang open to reveal an extravagance of diamonds nestled in a bed of red velvet.

'It's a tiara.'

As quick as a flash Gianni lifted it out and set it on her hair.

'It feels funny…' she said with a puzzled smile.

'You'll get used to it.'

'No…no, I can't…I mustn't…'

Raising one hand to the gold and diamond crown, Meg tried to take it off. Gianni's hand met hers and held it there, in place on her head.

'Do you recognise it?'

'It looks like the coronet your mother was wearing in that portrait of your parents hanging in your suite.'

With his hand enfolding hers, Meg had no intention of struggling but she was worried. Her eyes flickered nervously over the little lemon tree. She was trying to remember exactly what else the *contessa* had been wearing in that frighteningly glamorous painting. As well as the coronet she had been draped in earrings, a necklace, a bracelet, rings…Meg racked her brains, wondering if there had been a wristwatch, too. That was the only thing she might have considered accepting, but nothing decorating the little tree looked remotely run-of-the-mill.

'I can't wear this,' she repeated.

'It's for you. It's *all* for you,' Gianni said quietly. Presenting her with a second, smaller package, he released her hand to let her unwrap it. Inside an antique case was a pair of stunning earrings to match the tiara. A waterfall of rose-cut diamonds fell from a fine filigree of eighteen-carat gold lace. Meg knew she couldn't possibly take them. These exquisite trinkets were exactly the sort of prizes awarded to women like Thomas Hardy's 'Ruined Maid'. Mistresses. If she fell under Gianni's spell again she would be lost for ever. He would trample over her heart, her life would never be her own and all the diamonds in the world could never restore her self-respect.

She could hardly find the words to speak. 'These are the

most beautiful earrings I have ever seen,' she breathed eventually. 'But I can't possibly accept them—or any of these lovely things!'

'I'll put them on for you,' he said, moving forward quickly. Before she could refuse, he silenced her with a look. Lifting the first earring out of its red velvet bed, he fastened it expertly into her lobe. Soon he had fixed the second network of precious stones to her other ear. 'If you can't wear them, Meg, then no other woman in the history of the world is going to have the benefit of them. I mean that. They're yours. You're entitled to them.'

She gazed up at him, her eyes troubled. 'Gianni, you owe me nothing. That's what I said, and I meant it.'

'Are you sure?' He looked at her uncertainly.

It was the first time Meg had seen him wear an expression other than supreme self-confidence. Suddenly she was scared. Her world had started spinning out of control when she'd discovered she was pregnant. The only dependable thing left in her universe was Gianni's certainty. To discover that was no longer set in stone terrified her. They couldn't both be adrift in wild, uncharted waters. Desperately, Meg tried to restore the natural order of things. When she delivered her bombshell, he would bounce back to furious normal.

'Look—Gianni—I thought nothing could ever tear this secret out of me, but you're forcing my hand…'

Instantly all the old Bellini pride returned. Gianni drew himself up and regarded her with hooded eyes. Meg took a deep, steadying breath. She had spent hours dreading his fury, planning her defence and going over and over what she would say. Now the moment was here, she felt strangely calm. Reliving every possible way he might explode had prepared her for the very worst. It had convinced her she could cope. After all, an angry Gianni was far less scary than the man who stood before her now, trying unsuccessfully to hide shadows of doubt.

'You need to know exactly how little all your wealth and possessions mean to me, Gianni? Well, I'll tell you.' Her palms were damp. She clenched her fists. Gianni's eyes darted to the movement, then up to her face. His suspicion stiffened her nerves. This was the man she knew—tough, uncompromising—a lone wolf if ever there was one. *With all the emphasis on the word lone*, she thought nervously.

'The truth is, Gianni…I loved working on the Castelfino Estate, and making the decision to leave was so hard…so very hard, I don't know how I survived.' She took a deep, noisy breath, bracing herself to put the awful truth into words. Her hand automatically went to her waist again, reminding herself of her new responsibility. 'I would soon have swallowed my pride and tried to get my job back. But now there's something stopping me, Gianni.'

He stared at her until the pulse throbbing in her veins rang through her head.

'Don't tell me—I know what you're going to say. You fell in love with me. When all I did was to tell you—and myself—over and over again that I didn't want any emotional ties?'

Unable to bear his scrutiny any longer, she closed her eyes and shook her head.

'No, it's not that.' Through all her pain she heard him take a sharp breath.

'I find it *very* hard to believe you didn't fall in love with me,' he said indignantly.

All Meg's tensions exploded in laughter.

'Oh, Gianni! Only you could say something like that at

a time like this! Of course I fell in love with you! That was the main reason I had to get away. I loved you, but you could never love me. When I found out you didn't even respect me, well, that was the end. And then when I discovered I was pregnant—'

She stopped with a squeak of horror. After all her careful build-up, the word escaped by accident. She was as shocked by her simple revelation as Gianni was. She had been mentally mapping out all sorts of complicated ways of breaking the news a little bit at a time. In the end, it popped out all by itself.

They stared at each other until finally Gianni broke the spell and looked away.

'I—I don't know what to say.'

He really didn't. Meg could see the truth of his words in the way his shoulders sagged momentarily as he absorbed the body blow she had delivered.

'Oh—no—this isn't how it's supposed to be!' she wailed. 'I've hurt you, and I never meant to! I didn't ever expect to see you again, so I thought I'd never need to tell you—that's why it happened like this! I should have taken more time to explain—oh, no, this is horrible—' Meg was gabbling, perspiring, gesticulating and crying but Gianni's response froze her instantly.

'No…no, it isn't,' he said slowly. 'Don't blame yourself, Meg. It takes two to make a baby. Although when it can have happened I have no idea…' He let her go and reached for one of the dining chairs. Pulling it away from the table, he lowered her gently into it.

'You shouldn't be standing—not in your condition,' he murmured. Planting his hands on either side of her, he looked deep into her eyes. She waited in awestruck silence.

'I've been fooling myself for too long. Deep down, all the parties, the girls, the excesses—it was all a hopeless search for love. When you walked into my life I started seeing things differently, Meg, but not clearly enough. On the night of the banquet my body spoke, not my mind. It cried out for you in the only way it knew you could never resist. A long-term commitment was something I didn't want to get mixed up with. At the time.' There was total certainty in his voice now. As he gazed into her eyes all Meg's doubts disappeared.

'Then…you don't mind about the baby?'

Leaning forward, he rested his brow against hers.

'My love, it is what I've always wanted—although it took you to make me realise it. I want to give my child all the love I never experienced when I was growing up. If you walk away from me now, we'll all lose out. All three of us.'

'I wouldn't…I couldn't…no, what I mean is—I want you, and this baby, more than anything I've ever wanted in my life, Gianni. But I can't be your mistress any more. I would have kept the baby a secret if we hadn't met up again today—and what will your fiancée say?' Meg flustered.

'I don't know. What *do* you say, Meg?' Gianni smiled, silencing her with a feather-light kiss. There was no resisting him, and Meg didn't want to. For a long time they were suspended in delicious silence. 'I want you now more than ever. I owe all the happiness that these past weeks have brought me to you. You warmed my heart as beautifully as you warmed my bed.' His voice became a low murmur as he buried his face in her hair, but Meg couldn't relinquish her last finger hold on respectability without a fight.

'I can't do this, Gianni. Really, I can't. My skin isn't thick enough. I can't go on being your mistress, and I can't bear to think of you marrying another woman. Imagine how much more painful it will be for me to become nothing more than a bystander in your life. I'll be sidelined in favour of your wife, and over the years as your legitimate children are born and grow, my baby and I will be pushed further and further away from you. We'll be abandoned and forgotten—'

'It isn't going to be like that.' His voice resonated through her entire body.

'But it will be! It *will*!' In a sudden panic Meg tried to pull away from him.

In the stillness of the dining room her priceless antique jewellery tinkled, the candlelight sending brightly coloured stars dancing in a halo around her head.

'No, it won't. I won't let it. Listen to me, Meg!'

'I've listened to you too often in the past, Gianni. This is hopeless! I can't be your mistress any longer!'

'I know!' he barked, silencing her instantly. Once her full attention was riveted on him he spoke with a quiet authority that almost stopped her heart.

'I want you to become my *wife*, Meg,' he explained slowly. 'I want you as my *contessa* as well as my lover. My partner. My companion. My *friend*,' he finished softly.

It took Meg several seconds to realise what she was hearing.

'But what about—' She looked across at the table set for two, crowned by the beautiful flower she had brought for presentation to Gianni's fiancée.

'Bellini men don't beg,' he said succinctly. 'The moment I saw you again today I knew I had to have you, and you alone, Meg. Now and for ever. I had the Bellini hoard wrapped and flown over especially, in time for your arrival tonight. I love you, Meg, and without you I'm only one half of the spectacular whole our family will be.'

There were no fanfares and no fireworks. Gianni simply spoke all the words she had longed to hear. It felt like coming home, without ever having been away. Slowly, delicately she leaned forward until her head was resting against his chest. She expected to feel the slow, steady beat of his heart. It would have been perfectly in accord with the indulgent way he silently stroked her hair and patted her shoulders. Instead, she got a surprise. A rapid pulse thrummed through his body in feverish excitement.

'Can I trust you, Gianni?' she whispered.

'With our baby's life,' he assured her, kissing the crown of her head with its sparkle of diamonds. Meg melted as he pressed the side of his face against hers. For a long time she sheltered in his arms, trying to catch her breath as she thought back over the pain of the last days. All she had ever wanted was to feel safe and secure in Gianni's love. Now she had a promise, and trinkets beyond her wildest dreams, but none of it meant anything at all without integrity. A single tear beaded her lashes and rolled down her cheek. His face pressed tightly against hers, Gianni felt it the moment it fell. Alarmed, he straightened up and held her at arm's length, studying her intently.

'You're crying!' He could hardly believe it. 'What's the matter? I only wanted to make you happy!'

'D-did you?' Blinded with tears, Meg gazed at him in hopeless doubt. 'If that's the case, w-why did you spend all that time keeping me at arm's length? Y-you never even put my details on your phone!' she sobbed, almost inaudibly. Chuckling, Gianni drew her towards him again.

'That's because I never needed to. They're here,' he

said softly, lifting her hand and pressing her palm against his chest. 'Every word you have ever spoken to me is carved in my heart, Meg.'

She felt it beating more slowly and steadily beneath her fingers. Gianni closed his fingers around hers and took them to his lips for a gentle kiss.

'Really?' she whispered.

'Really.' He nodded. 'Meg, my love, you are the only woman for me, now and for ever. I'm going to take you as my wife, my mistress and my soulmate. From the moment we met no woman has matched up to you in any way. I spent my whole life looking for love, but in all the wrong places. And when we found each other, I almost let you slip through my fingers. That's never going to happen again. I can promise you that.'

She leaned against him. He gathered her in to his body. Once upon a time Meg would have been terrified to admit she wanted someone she could depend on. Now she was safe in Gianni's arms, she could see things so much more clearly. He needed her every bit as much as she needed him. They were a team now. It didn't matter which one of them dealt with the little niggles and worries of day-to-day life, as long as they were solved.

As though reading her mind he held her close and whispered: 'I never thought I would find a woman I could rely on. You are all I need, my love. You—and our family,' he said simply, before his kisses swept her away to a place where nothing else mattered any more.

SECRETARY BY DAY, MISTRESS BY NIGHT

BY
MAGGIE COX

The day **Maggie Cox** saw the film version of *Wuthering Heights*, with a beautiful Merle Oberon and a very handsome Laurence Olivier, was the day she became hooked on romance. From that day onwards she spent a lot of time dreaming up her own romances, secretly hoping that one day she might become published and get paid for doing what she loved most! Now that her dream is being realised, she wakes up every morning and counts her blessings. She is married to a gorgeous man, and is the mother of two wonderful sons. Her two other great passions in life—besides her family and reading/writing—are music and films.

To dear Danika—
my delightful companion on a wonderful creative
break in Northumberland—with love and thanks

CHAPTER ONE

Now she knew what E.T. must have felt like—alone and abandoned, light years away from what was loved and familiar, on a planet that seemed totally alien and unwelcoming. No wonder he'd sought refuge in Elliott's garage. Right now, Maya wished she could find a handy empty or darkened room to hide away in. One glance along the burnished candle-lit table at the high-octane guests, the reek of class and money, merely confirmed what she already knew to be true—she didn't fit in. A 'fish out of water,' that was what she was. But the truth was she didn't *want* to fit in.

Up until now her temporary jobs as an admin assistant had been pretty problem-free. But for the past few weeks her agency had asked her to work for a PR agency—Maya's *worst* nightmare as far as employment went. As the cut-glass accents rose and fell all around her, the scent of social snobbery in the air as distinct as Chanel No. 5, she knew *why* she resisted being part of such a phoney world.

She'd been raised by a father who'd all but sold his soul to perpetuate a similar lavish lifestyle and glean the dubious respect of such people, and in pursuit of it he had sacrificed everything that had once meant something to him. His talent, money, self-respect and once good reputation had been squandered and degraded as he lost his grip on reality and the values he'd once so fiercely upheld. And as he'd sunk lower and lower into a pit of self-loathing and regret for what he'd done, it had only been a matter of time before he took the ultimate terrible step.

Maya shuddered.

The devastating memory killed her appetite. Now the food on her plate held little temptation for her, and even knowing it had been specially created in a Michelin-starred restaurant for the purpose of the occasion was no incentive. Along with the dinner had come the services of one of the restaurant's top chefs, supported by a small team of staff to supervise its plating and serving. As was his usual style, her flamboyant boss, Jonathan Faraday, had spared no expense in displaying the growing success of his well-known PR company.

Clamping down on the persistent little flutter in her belly that urged her to get the hell out of there while she still had her pride and dignity intact, Maya lifted her gaze determinedly to the urbane silver-haired man sitting opposite and gave him the brightest smile she could muster.

Bad move, Maya. His startled hazel gaze flashed an invitation in return, and with a sinking feeling she knew he thought she'd given him the green light at last.

Hell's bells! What was she supposed to do now? Because it paid well, she didn't want to lose her job, but neither did she want to sleep with her boss to keep it. If only his super-efficient, elegant PA Caroline hadn't been called to the hospital bed of her dying mother-in-law at the last minute Maya would be safe at home now, dressed in comfy sweater and leggings; settling herself down on her sofa in readiness to view the film she'd hired for the weekend, with a bowl of tortilla chips, some salsa dip and a glass of wine on hand to heighten the experience.

Instead, she'd squeezed herself into a black velvet gown that was at least half a size too small, with her breasts crammed into a bodice so tight that it gave her the cleavage of a pneumatic glamour model, while her generously applied mascara made her eyes smart because it was new and she was obviously allergic to it. And all this discomfort because Jonathan had insisted she attend the function at his house in Caroline's place. It didn't matter that Maya was just a lowly temporary assistant from the less glamorous echelons of the company—Jonathan had had his eye on her for some time. He could see she had talent, determination, he'd said, smiling—and he could see she was destined for better things... *He could see this was a good opportunity to get into her knickers...*

Sighing heavily, she absently pushed the artistically arranged concoction of cranberries and parma-ham round her plate with a fork. When the blatant caress of a shoeless foot stroked up and down her ankle Maya almost jumped out of her skin. Tucking her feet indignantly beneath her chair, feeling searing heat hotter than a blacksmith's smithy assail her cheeks, she stared across the table at her suave, supremely confident boss. Bad enough she'd had an inkling that she might have to fight him off if he had too much to drink. Jonathan could more or less be counted on to chase anything in a skirt when his rampaging testosterone had been even more boosted by alcohol, but Maya hadn't expected he would be quite so blatant about it from the off. And all he'd had so far was one glass of champagne as the guests had been welcomed into the drawing room. In the name of self-preservation she had deliberately kept an eye on his intake—so she was surprised and more than a little rattled that he seemed intent on staking a claim right away. *Damn it, she shouldn't even be here!*

'Excuse me.'

'Something wrong, Miss Hayward?' Jonathan swirled the ruby-red wine that a passing waiter had just poured into his glass, leaning nonchalantly back in his grand Regency-style chair to enjoy the view as his shapely young employee rose hastily to her feet.

'No. I'm fine.'

Why did he have to notice everything she did? Was she forced to announce to the entire table that she had a sudden pressing need to visit the Ladies' Room? Why couldn't he just talk to the stunning blonde sitting next to him? The woman had been batting her eyelashes at him practically since they'd sat down. But apparently in the bedroom department Jonathan Faraday didn't give women his own age the time of day—no matter how beautiful. He liked them young, so she'd heard on the grapevine. *Bad luck for Maya that she'd only just turned twenty-five...*

'I'll—I'll be back shortly.'

Escaping before he could delay her further—or, worse, find some nefarious reason to accompany her— Maya found herself hurrying down corridors, the echo of her heels hitting the parquet floor mocking her as she struggled to find her bearings. *Oh, why had she agreed to this farce?* Now she was stuck out here in the middle of nowhere, dependent on her lech of a boss for a lift home—and not until midday tomorrow, if what Caroline had said was true. Apparently Jonathan was in no hurry to get back to London until mid-afternoon at least. Maya's head swam a little. The glass of champagne she'd had had been a dangerous lapse in judgement. She should have insisted on orange juice or mineral water. If she was going to get out of this little escapade with her virtue intact it was essential she kept a clear head—so no more alcohol for her, even if Jonathan insisted.

Her green eyes flicked hopefully round. *She could have sworn there was a bathroom round here somewhere...* Pushing open twin cream doors with ornate gilded panels, she found herself in a long, high-ceilinged room, its panelling painted in tastefully calming hues of pink and cream. A welcoming fire blazed in the huge marble fireplace, tempting her to stay and re-establish some of her lost composure.

Gazing round, Maya was momentarily distracted by the elaborate array of expensive-looking art that adorned the walls, and the seductive glow of antique lamps turned down low that cleverly created the illusion that the large, elegant room was actually more intimately proportioned than it really was. Succumbing to necessity, she gave in to the luxury of breathing out completely. Her tight bodice almost cracked a rib, while her lush breasts appeared in dire peril of escaping their velvet confines any time soon.

What had possessed her to wear such an outrageous dress? Okay, Caroline had told her the dress code was black tie and evening wear, but surely she knew that, when she'd borrowed the garment from her smaller-built friend Sadie, she was courting trouble by wearing it? *Especially* when Jonathan Faraday was around!

* * *

'If Jonathan's the confectioner, then clearly you've got to be the candy.'

At the sound of an amused yet obviously mocking male voice, Maya spun round in shock, mortified that she'd been observed when she had stupidly imagined herself to be alone. Her hand flew self-consciously to her cleavage, her teeth worrying at her plump lower lip as she stared at the man who suddenly rose from the high-winged chair turned towards the fireplace. Why hadn't she noticed he was there straight away? A shiver of embarrassment and frustration sprinted up her spine. Staring transfixed at the imposing stranger, she felt his electrifying gaze welding her to a hypnotised standstill.

'And you are…?' *Not that she really wanted to know, when inside she was silently fuming at his impertinent assumption that she had somehow been invited purely for decoration.*

'I see you haven't done your homework, Miss…?'

Of all the arrogant…!

'I work for Mr Faraday.'

'Of course you do. You *work* for me too in that dress, if I may say so?'

Scorching embarrassment immobilised her. *Blast that stupid dress!* And blast her eye-catching curves, when life would have been so much easier if she'd simply been straight up and down and flat-chested.

'If that was meant as a compliment, then forgive me if I don't take it as one. It's not at all flattering to be viewed as some kind of decorative object…as if I don't possess even a modicum of intelligence! I've met people like you before, and I'm…' Maya paused to take a breath, before biting her tongue. 'Yes, well… I'd better not say any more. Time to go, I think.'

'What do you mean, you've met people like me before?'

'Never mind.'

'Oh, but I *do* mind. Explain yourself.'

It was too late to rescind her comment, and Maya sensed her shoulders drop with resignation and not a little annoyance. 'Enough to say I'm not part of the floor show or entertainment for the guests, however it might look. I didn't even want to be here in the first place!'

The stranger's well-cut lips parted in a puzzled smile. 'This is getting more and more interesting. Why didn't you want to be here, Miss…?'

'Hayward.'

It was difficult to say with any sense of accuracy what colour his eyes were in the muted glow of the lamps—it sufficed to register that they burned with a fierce, concentrated gleam across the distance between them, keeping Maya prisoner even though she desperately wanted to flee. Beneath the bold regard of that disturbing glance she shifted uncomfortably. *Was it her, or had the room suddenly acquired the temperature of some tropical oasis?*

'I'm only here because of work. All I meant was this

isn't my kind of scene and neither are the people. I apologise if I've offended you in any way with my frankness.'

'Apology accepted. I'm not offended at all. Just intrigued.'

'I'd still better go.'

'I wish you wouldn't.' The man walked towards her and a sharp spasm of recognition jolted through Maya's insides. *Blaise Walker*—movie actor turned lauded and brilliant playwright. No wonder he had made that dig about her not doing her homework. He was the guest of honour, no less! The guest that Jonathan had announced to the table a mere ten minutes ago as being unavoidably detained.

Now her face burned for another reason. She had just been bordering on rude to the man, and no doubt Jonathan would hear all about it. But what was Blaise doing, hiding out in here? Her growing unease deepened. One, because the man was even more devastatingly attractive in the flesh than in his photographs, and two, because she didn't really think her boss would like the idea of a mere admin assistant like her fraternising with such an important client—let alone verbally putting him in his place! She should make herself scarce...*now*.

'Well, I have to go. I'm expected back any time now.'

'Of course...it's no surprise that a woman like you would be missed if you were away too long.'

'Look...I didn't mean to disturb you in any way. I

was just trying to find the Ladies' Room, but I'm afraid I—I got lost.'

'This is a big house.'

Did he think she hadn't noticed? It was an extremely impressive one too—a real showpiece. The kind to which her father would have relished inviting his illustrious clientele—which had included rock stars, film actors and art sycophants, who had bought his paintings during his short but infamous career—for drinks and other 'recreational' refreshments. The minuscule square footage of her studio apartment would fit into it at least a hundred times over, she was sure.

Renewing her intention to make herself scarce, Maya moved back towards the still ajar twin doors.

'Anyway, like I said…I'm sorry for the intrusion.'

'An apology is hardly necessary when the pleasure was all mine. Perhaps when you've visited the Ladies' Room you might consider coming back for a while, to give us a chance to get properly acquainted?'

'No!'

She hadn't meant to sound quite so adamant, but any further explanation somehow got stuck in her throat. The way Blaise Walker was surveying her—disturbing eyes mocking in that haunting angular face of his, tarnished gold hair darkly glinting against the startling white of his shirt collar—Maya was finding it seriously difficult to think straight. She just prayed he wouldn't reveal her inadvertent intrusion and blunt opinions to Jonathan when they met up. Her boss might want to bed her, but he wouldn't take it lightly if his client intimated that she'd bothered him in any way. Her hand curved anxiously around the brass door handle.

'Sorry…' she muttered once more as she exited hurriedly into the hallway.

After she'd gone, Blaise sniffed the faint trail of stirringly sensual perfume that his entrancing temporary visitor had left in her wake and a charge of electricity zigzagged powerfully through his taut mid-section. It wasn't just the arresting notes of amber and warm tangerine that had stirred his previously slumbering libido. It was the intoxicating sight of almond-shaped green eyes fringed with sooty black lashes, long dark hair as glossy as a glittering moonlit sea, and audacious curves poured into the most seductive black velvet dress he'd ever seen.

With a brief shake of his head and a rueful smile, he went back to the comfortable winged armchair and the decanter of port his host had so thoughtfully provided, wondering when the last time was that a woman had so easily and carelessly refused him anything. His mind instantly provided him with the disturbing answer…*never*.

Blaise drank down the remainder of his drink with far less enjoyment than he'd anticipated and frowned. There was a certain lack of respect that manifested itself in him around anything that came to him too easily. That went for success *and* women. It was only natural that a beautiful, feisty female like his alluring visitor—a woman who was clearly not going to tumble into his bed at the click of his fingers—would inevitably arouse his interest. But, that said, despite Miss Hayward's indignant assertion that she wasn't 'part of the floor show', it was fairly obvious that she must belong to Jonathan. *She had to.* She hadn't even bothered to deny it.

Dropping the crystal stopper a little impatiently into the decanter, he carefully returned it to the small rosewood table beside the chair. Raking his fingers through his sleek golden hair, he briefly closed his eyes, wishing he hadn't allowed Jane, his agent, to convince him that he should capitalise on the current avid interest in his work from the theatre-going public and take advantage of some first-rate PR to promote his image.

All Blaise wanted to do was retreat to his remote house in the wilds of Northumberland, with nothing but the mournful soughing of the wind and the untamed beauty of the countryside for company, write to his heart's content and let the world go its own tedious way without him.

He'd briefly become acquainted with fame during his three-year stint as a film actor, and the maelstrom of public interest at the time, as well as the intrusion into his private life, had been a right royal pain! If there were actors who craved fame, with all its dubious rewards and lack of privacy, then he wasn't one of them. All he had been interested in was conveying the character he played to the audience with the utmost conviction and one hundred percent commitment. If he could do that then he wouldn't have short-changed the people who had come to see him.

He applied the same passionate approach to his writing. Hopefully, when this current circus of media attention was over, he could return to Hawk's Lair and pull up the drawbridge—for a little while at least. But, that said, it didn't stop him continuing to speculate about the gorgeous brunette who'd inadvertently wandered in on him, with all that creamy cleavage so tantalisingly on display and a temper that—did she but know it—made her even *more* provocative than she was already.

His creative mind was already speculating on how that pent-up passion might be expressed in bed. Even more, it made him fantasise about helping her out of that sexy little dress later on tonight if even so much as *half* a chance came his way…

They stopped outside her bedroom door, with Maya twisting her arm behind her back to clutch anxiously at the doorknob as she desperately sought an escape route out of her predicament. Her boss swayed in front of her, alcoholic fumes making her grimace. Jonathan's drinking was legendary, but he had surpassed his own reputation tonight. In fact, Maya was amazed that he was still standing, never mind trying to coerce her into bed. His chameleon-like hazel eyes—a little cloudy now from the effects of alcohol—dropped lasciviously to her cleavage. He put a hand out to the side of her, to help balance himself against the wall.

Ignoring her seriously startled expression as he loomed over her, he capitalised on the opportunity to move his body even closer, so that along with the fumes of alcohol her senses were assaulted by the overpowering smell of his French cologne.

'I thought the dinner went really well tonight, didn't you? But I'm really tired now, and I—' Maya moved suddenly and darted to the side of him, just in time to deflect an oncoming caress, her heart racing so fast she was almost dizzy.

Frustrated and cross, Jonathan swore. 'Screw the dinner! All I want to do right now is take you to bed. Think about it, darling. A girl like you deserves so much more than an admin assistant's pay to get by on. Be nice to me and I'll make it more than worth your while… You get my drift, don't you, sweetie?'

He raised a perfectly groomed silver eyebrow to drive home his clumsily executed innuendo, reminding Maya so much of a dastardly rogue in one of those old silent movies that she almost laughed out loud. All that was missing was the famous handlebar moustache and the scene would be complete.

'Yes, Jonathan. I *do* get your drift. But at the end of the day you're my boss, and I make it a rule never to complicate professional relationships by allowing them to become personal.' She sucked in a deep breath, trying not to let her voice falter. 'I'm one of your employees…albeit a *temporary* one. That said, I'm going to decline your invitation and say goodnight. In the cold light of day I'm sure you'll be glad I did.'

'What if I offered you a permanent position? Would that help you see things differently?'

'No.' Maya had no hesitation in making that clear. 'I'm afraid it wouldn't.'

'What a shame,' Jonathan sneered. 'And I thought you were such a bright girl too. Still…you're not getting off that easily.'

'What do you mean?' Her green eyes flashed her alarm.

'You're just playing hard to get, aren't you?'

Suddenly there was an expression on his face that put every impulse in Maya's body on red alert. *This is going to be trickier than I thought…* She panicked. Letting go of the doorknob, she raked her long hair away from her face, letting her hand splay protectively across her chest.

'I don't know what you're talking about. I'm only here tonight because my job required it.'

'Don't tell me you're that naïve?' Jonathan breathed, yanking her towards him. 'Common or garden assistants don't get invited to my house just to take dictation! I've been flirting with you for weeks now—don't pretend you didn't know what it was leading to.'

'I'm here because Caroline was called away at the last

minute. She told me you needed someone to stand in for her,' Maya protested, even as Jonathan shook his head.

'Caroline stayed away because I *ordered* her to stay away!' he growled. 'Seeing as you turned me down every time I asked you out, it was the only way I could think of to get you alone. Has the penny finally dropped, *Miss* Hayward?'

She twisted her face away as his mouth descended, pushing hard against his chest with both hands, in a split second seeing all her effort and hard work wasted as she denied Jonathan Faraday the prize he craved, knowing she would get nothing for her pains but her marching orders.

Oh, well. She'd just have to tell the agency to find her something else. It would be a cold day in hell before she succumbed to sexual coercion from a man just to keep her job—that was for sure!

'Come on, Maya—giving me the runaround is one thing, but I've been working myself up to fever-pitch knowing you were coming to my house this weekend. Just one little kiss, eh?'

He might have been drunk, but Jonathan was physically no push-over. He easily hijacked her arms to pin her against the wall, breathing heavily as he pressed his body hard against hers, seeing the sudden fear darkening her lovely green eyes and no doubt getting off on the thought of having his way.

That was until an authoritative male voice a few feet

away said coolly, 'I must say I'm surprised, Jonathan. For all your reputation as a ladies' man I never thought you'd descend to physically forcing your attentions on a woman.'

'What?' More than a little discomfited, Jonathan abruptly released Maya to negotiate an unsteady step backwards. Wiping his hand across his mouth, he straightened, then looked Blaise Walker defiantly in the eye.

'Don't be daft, man! She's been making eyes at me all evening. She was practically—'

'Gagging for it?' Blaise finished smoothly.

Maya wished the ground would open up and swallow her. Humiliation made her burn with rage at the injustice of it all. Did Jonathan's famous client really believe that? She could hardly bring herself to look at Blaise Walker as she pushed back her hair, then twisted her hands anxiously together in the sensuous velvet folds of her frock.

'From where I was standing, it looked like the lady was very definitely protesting at your attentions. Why don't we just check with her to verify the matter?'

Maya found herself in the worst dilemma. If she made Jonathan look like a would-be rapist then what would that do for his client relationship with Blaise Walker? On the other hand, she had her own reputation to consider, and she was damned if she was going to trash it all in the name of public relations... She'd more or less just kissed goodbye to her job anyway.

'As I told you before, I work for Mr Faraday,' she said

evenly. 'If he mistakenly got the impression I was considering anything else by agreeing to come here this weekend then I'm sorry—but he's most definitely *wrong.*'

Colouring in spite of her determination to stay strong, Maya flicked a glance at the handsome playwright, then tore it away again before his darkly brooding stare could make her reveal even more than she'd intended. Like the fact that she'd been genuinely frightened by Jonathan's unwanted attentions. Blaise was a tall man, whose breadth of shoulder alone seemed to dominate the long, high-ceilinged corridor, and in his black tuxedo and crisp white shirt his impressive physique and confident stance instantly commanded the kind of jaw-dropping attention that was hardly commonplace in her day-to-day reality. *No wonder he'd been such a successful screen actor.* It wasn't just his looks that would hook the audience in either. The man had genuine presence.

'Well. You have your answer, my friend.'

At Blaise's mocking stare, Jonathan had the grace to look momentarily repentant. Maya saw the sudden flush of colour beneath his artificial tan.

'Too much to drink, I expect,' he mumbled, shrugging his shoulders. Then, recovering quickly, he issued Maya with a belligerent glance that spoke volumes. 'You know what it's like—women are notorious for saying one thing when they mean another. I'm sorry you didn't feel you could join us at dinner, Blaise, but perhaps we can talk about the campaign in the morning?'

'I'm an early riser,' the other man responded coolly, 'and I like to go for a run before breakfast. Seven-thirty okay with you?'

Jonathan swayed a little, as if the mere thought of getting up so early on a Sunday morning after wining and dining the night away was like asking him to swim the English Channel when he could barely swim a stroke. He touched a slightly unsteady hand to his immaculate silver hair.

'Seven-thirty's fine. I'll see you then.' Without so much as a backward glance at Maya, he made his way carefully along to the opposite end of the corridor, pushed open a door right at the end and slammed it shut behind him, the sound resonating off the walls with the same jolting impact as cannon-fire…

Allowing herself the momentary luxury of leaning against the wall in support of her quaking limbs, Maya knew her sigh was hugely relieved. She'd had a lucky escape for sure. There was only one flaw. She was dependent on Jonathan for giving her a lift home tomorrow, because he'd insisted she travel with him. She couldn't leave now even if she wanted to. Unless, of course, she was willing to blow the last of her precious month's salary on an expensive cab ride to the nearest train station—and it was so late that she doubted any trains would still be running.

'Are you all right?'

Her eyes widened a little at the unexpected concern in Blaise Walker's voice, and the warm, gravelly resonance caused an involuntarily tingle in her body that reached all the way down to her toes.

'I'm fine…thanks.'

'Tell me straight—did he completely misread the situation?'

'There wasn't a situation to begin with! Except in his own twisted little mind, that is… It certainly wasn't in mine'

Maya could have died, knowing Blaise Walker's disturbing concentrated gaze was noting everything from the plunging cleavage of her tight-fitting velvet dress to the giveaway quiver of her fulsome lower lip. Flushing angrily, she tucked a glossy strand of black hair behind her ear and jutted her chin, green eyes flashing indignant emerald fire.

'He admitted to me that he got me here under false pretences. Is it likely, under the circumstances, that I would encourage him? Look, Mr Walker…I'm just a temp who was hired to work for his PR company. I work hard to earn my pay, and at the end of the day I go home. I shouldn't have to submit to the unwanted attentions of my boss for the privilege, should I?'

Considering the question, Blaise let his avid gaze fall on the agitated rise and fall of her chest. Her lush creamy breasts looked fit to burst from her gown at any moment, and God help him but all the blood in his body marched unerringly south.

'Clearly you shouldn't have to submit to anything of the kind, Miss Hayward. By the way—you do have a first name, I presume?'

'Maya.'

She hesitated at the door of her bedroom, exhaling a long, resigned breath as she twisted the brass doorknob and pushed it open.

'I'm sorry you had to witness that distasteful little scene. I really hope you won't let it prejudice you against using Mr Faraday's company to promote you. He has some good people working for him—I shouldn't like what happened to backfire negatively on them.'

'Your concern is admirable in the light of his quite appalling behaviour. But I guess we'll just have to wait and see what the outcome will be, won't we?'

After assessing her with a maddeningly enigmatic glance, Blaise turned and started to walk back down the corridor. When he'd travelled just a couple of feet away he looked back, and with a confident little smile said, 'I don't think you'll have anything more to fear from your troublesome boss tonight. With the amount of alcohol he's consumed no doubt he'll enjoy the sleep of the dead. One word of caution, though—I'd really advise against wearing that dress at any future function, unless you're prepared to handle the very *particular* kind of attention it generates…'

Lacking the courage just then to even meet his eyes, Maya mumbled a barely audible goodnight, hurried inside her room and bolted the door firmly behind her— as hurriedly as if she'd just been chased up the corridor by a herd of wild buffalo...

CHAPTER TWO

AWAKE since dawn, Maya chose not to linger in bed. Instead she got up, took a brief hot shower, then quickly dressed. Leaving her bags momentarily in the silent corridor, where behind closed doors Jonathan and his guests were still sleeping off the excesses of the night before, she took the risk of slipping a note under her boss's door. A note that clearly outlined the reasons why she couldn't stay and act as his assistant for the rest of the weekend and concluded with telling him that as soon as they returned to the office he could expect her resignation. Then, with her heart nervously tripping, Maya carried her bags downstairs.

If truth be known she couldn't wait to get away from this house—away from her licentious boss and the cloud of deceit that had brought her there—away from his shallow moneyed friends who, when she'd been trying to make conversation, had looked right through her but had not really 'seen' her at all. It gave her an uncomfortable sense of *déjà vu*, being around people like that. It was too reminiscent of her childhood and those interminable painful gatherings of her father's, with his so-called 'friends'—acquaintances who had petted Maya like a puppy when it suited them and told her to get lost when it hadn't, because she was cramping their style when they were drinking, drug-taking or trying to seduce someone.

Right now all she wanted was to return to her own little place, to what was comforting and familiar. She would have said to what was safe too, but since Maya had almost never experienced such a condition she bit her lip on the thought and shelved it away in some clandestine corner of her mind, where she would endeavour to forget about it for a while.

'So…I'm not the only early riser around here, I see.'

Intent on leafing through the Yellow Pages she'd found in the hallway for a cab number, Maya glanced round, startled at the appearance of the owner of that low, provocative male voice. *Lord, have mercy!*

Dressed from head to toe in enigmatic black, Blaise Walker resembled a dangerous secret fantasy come to blood-pounding, heart-racing life, with his dark gold hair swept sleekly back from his strong sculpted face and his sizzling bold glance that now, in the light of day, she saw was a magnetic Mediterranean blue. She couldn't attest to breathing at all as she stared back at him, but for several dizzying seconds the same roaring exhilaration pounded through her bloodstream that she imagined a Formula One driver must experience when he'd successfully negotiated a treacherous bend at devastating speed…

'Good morning. I'm always up early, I'm afraid… I'm not one of those people who can lie in bed 'til late. Besides…' sensing heat suffuse her, Maya defied any woman with a libido to say the word 'bed' in front of a gorgeous male specimen like Blaise Walker and *not* be consumed with heat '…just as soon as I can get a cab I'm making my way home.'

'So you've decided not to stay?'

'To be honest, I don't think that would be a very good idea—and I think my boss would probably agree. I don't doubt he can't wait to be rid of me after last night.'

'You mean because you didn't play along with his drunken and rather crass attempt at seduction?'

Casually sliding a hand into one of his trouser pockets, Blaise moved with compelling masculine grace towards Maya. A tantalising smile played round his well-cut lips that might have been mockery, curiosity, or perhaps even sympathy—who knew? That aside, his blunt description brought back afresh the sickening fear that had shuddered through her when Jonathan had been leering down into her cleavage and pinning her up against the wall.

'You call that seduction? It was horrible! Just horrible! He had no right to—' Her face flaming with embarrassment and a silent deepening fury at her boss's totally reprehensible and rough treatment of her, Maya raked a shaky hand through her newly washed hair. 'He'll be doubly embarrassed that you saw it happen. I expect he'll also be furious that I rejected him. I'd rather not stay here and find out his reaction, to tell you the truth.'

Moving her still trembling fingers down the appropriate thin page of the phone book, she located a number, then glanced back at the six-feet-something of powerfully arresting, hard-muscled male standing less than a foot away from her. Every cell in her body seemed to be drowning in the most compelling, exquisitely *painful* awareness of him, and she didn't feel a bit prepared to deal with the fact.

Feeling as if his sharp gaze saw every self-conscious move she made, she turned to lay the book back down on the polished chiffonier.

'I'd better phone for a cab. Excuse me…'

'Where do you need a lift to?'

'The nearest station.'

'To catch a train to where? London?'

'Yes…Camden.'

'Don't bother phoning a cab. I'll take you.'

'But the nearest station is fifteen miles away! What about Jonathan?'

'What about him?'

'Don't you and he have a meeting this morning?'

The blue eyes that reminded Maya of perfectly still

twin oceans that could no doubt seethe and turn stormy along with the best of deceptively calm seas stared back at her, as if the agreed meeting was of very little account indeed. Knowing from Jonathan's assistant Caroline what mercenary methods her boss regularly employed in order for his agency to represent the 'hot' names of the moment when up against the competition, Maya couldn't help but wonder what her boss had done to pull off this particular coup. In the world of theatre Blaise Walker's name was definitely hotter than hot. She knew that was true because she regularly scanned the Entertainment and Arts pages of the papers, to see what was on in the West End, and she had read the fulsome and glowing accolades his work commanded as well as seeing the 'Sold Out' notices on the billboards.

But now she worried that if Blaise Walker didn't make his meeting with Jonathan because he had given her a lift to the station then Jonathan would no doubt hold her completely responsible. Retribution in some form or other would quickly follow…maybe even manifesting itself in his refusal to give her a reference for her next job with her employment agency. It would be highly unfair and irregular, in light of Maya's un-blemished employment record, but Jonathan was more than capable of it—and *worse*.

'I'll *ring* him later. I'm pretty sure our Mr Faraday won't lift his head off the pillow until lunchtime at least…*if* even then,' Blaise remarked nonchalantly, dropping his hands to his hips. 'In any case, after what I witnessed last night, any inclination I may have had to let your boss do my PR has definitely disappeared. One hears things about people. As a rule I don't believe in listening to gossip, but having seen for myself the way the man conducts himself I've come to realise that much of the talk about him is probably quite close to the truth. The meeting I do eventually have with him won't be the one he was hoping for, I'm afraid. Now… are these all your bags?'

Staring uncomfortably down at her soft canvas hold-all, and the small leather tote bag that housed amongst other things her make-up, book and reading glasses, Maya was genuinely taken aback at the idea that Blaise had deplored Jonathan's treatment of her and was showing his displeasure by withdrawing his agreement to let his agency do his publicity. She realised she'd been nursing a real fear that he would side with her boss when it came to believing any attractive woman that worked for him was fair game. But now she also wrestled with the idea of allowing a man she barely knew, and who could potentially turn out to be just like some of those mercenary acquaintances of her father's—self-obsessed and making no bones about going after what they wanted no matter *who* they might hurt in the process—to drive her home.

Lifting her concerned emerald gaze to his, she frowned.

'You really don't have to bother, Mr Walker—'

'Blaise,' he insisted.

'It's easy enough for me to get a cab. At least then I won't disturb the rest of your weekend.'

'Oh, but you *have* disturbed me, Maya,' he answered enigmatically, a glint in his eyes that made her insides clench, 'but that's hardly your fault. Come on—let's get you to the station. I'll carry your bags.'

'Really…' Still unsure, she grimaced. 'It might be better in the long run if I just phoned for a cab.'

'If you're worried that I might have a tendency to behave in any way, shape or form like your disreputable boss then please let me assure you right now your concerns are groundless. I personally like my women willing, and I've never had to force one into my bed yet!'

Reddening at his frank confession, Maya shrugged and attempted a smile. 'Okay…'

Outside, a watery sun had broken through the early-morning clouds, and on the gravel drive where Jonathan's esteemed guests had parked a selection of gleaming and expensive vehicles Blaise Walker headed for a dazzling fire-engine-red classic open-topped MG sports car. Go-to-hell red, as her father had used to call that particular shade. Maya fielded the unexpected memory, but wasn't quick enough to suppress the little knot of tension that squeezed inside her.

Instantly Blaise picked up on her disquiet. 'Is anything the matter? Perhaps you were expecting something a little more sedate for your ride to the station?'

'I had no expectations at all,' Maya replied evenly. 'I'm just grateful for the lift.'

He replaced his concern with a captivating grin, and the sight brought the same sense of wonder with it to Maya as reaching the end of a frightening rollercoaster ride and realising that you'd survived. A feeling of totally giddy exhilaration flooded her body. In all her twenty-five years on the planet she'd *never* witnessed a smile as dazzling or as wildly, extraordinarily beautiful as that.

'You might want to find something to tie your hair back with,' Blaise suggested now. 'Could get a little windswept otherwise.'

Checking through her tote as he opened the rather compact boot in order to deposit her luggage, and seeing his own expensive bag ensconced there—*was he leaving this morning too*?—Maya produced a slender multi-coloured chiffon scarf and proceeded to tie her flowing dark hair up into a loosely fashioned ponytail.

'That okay?'

'You look adorable.' Her companion grinned. 'Get in and make yourself comfortable. The door's unlocked.'

Folding her long-legged, slender, jean-clad frame into the passenger seat, Maya relaxed as far as she was able in the small space provided. Easing back into the softly luxurious leather seat, she silently admired the immaculate burr walnut veneer that covered the dash and centre console, and the amazing craftsmanship that had produced what her father had once informed her was one of the country's bestselling sports cars *ever*.

He should have known, because when she was little he had owned two of them—one in red, like this, and another in black. *Of course they were long gone now.* Sold to help pay off some of the horrendous debts his wildly reckless lifestyle had accrued...

Hearing the lid of the boot slam, she turned to see Blaise lower his own tall, athletic, black-clad frame into the driver's seat. Even though his legs were long, like hers, Maya was quietly amazed at how effortless he made every movement look...like a sublime symphony...every note in perfect accord and nothing remotely out of sync. A waft of quietly stirring aftershave imbued with sultry notes of sandalwood and musk assailed senses already tested to their limit by his charismatic presence. She tried to steel herself against it.

'This is a concourse model, isn't it?' she commented, her fingertips lightly touching the walnut veneer on the dash.

'Yes, it is. It's an original model, but I paid a small fortune to get everything restored down to the last nut and bolt back to the way it was. You know about classic cars?' her companion asked in surprise.

'Not really. I just knew someone once who had a model like this.' Maya stared out through the windscreen instead of into the disturbing blue eyes that seemed to be playing such havoc with her insides. The huskily soft chuckle beside her was equally disconcerting.

'You probably know a lot more than you're admitting, right? That's okay… I don't mind you being a woman of mystery. It simply makes me want to get to know you even more.'

He shouldn't have been surprised, but she was even more alluring and beautiful dressed in jeans and a simple white cotton shirt than she'd been in that eye-popping black dress that had paid such mouthwatering homage to her curves last night. And that dress had caused him one *hell* of a sleepless night, he recalled now, his hands tightening on the MG's steering wheel. Seeing Jonathan Faraday's drunken paws all over her had also been a factor in ensuring Blaise's sleep was fitful. *He had been a breath away from laying the man out flat.* Maya had clearly been frightened by Faraday's clumsy inebriated attentions, and all his latent protective instincts towards women had rushed to the fore. She would have had only to indicate to him by a mere glance that she wanted him to step in and her licentious boss would have been nursing much more than a hangover this morning.

When he was about ten years old, Blaise's actor father had struck his mother savagely across the face during one of their many bitter rows—an event that, after that shocking first time, had become a more or less regular feature of his childhood, he was sorry to say. *Blaise had leapt on him, kicking and screaming.* He had truly wanted to kill him at that moment. The same strong feelings of fury and resentment had roared through his bloodstream last night in the corridor, when he'd seen Jonathan behave like some despicable Neanderthal.

Now Blaise realised just how much the bewitching Maya Hayward had been on his mind since she'd inadvertently burst in on him in the drawing room last evening, leaving a trail of sexy perfume in her wake and stirring the kind of fantasies that would be strictly rated 'adults only'. He definitely wanted to get to know her better. It had been quite some time since he'd enjoyed an exciting affair, and this could potentially be his most exciting liaison yet.

When he'd found her in the hall searching through the phonebook the pure raw desire that had coursed through him had been fierce enough to almost make him stumble. Now he realised Jonathan Faraday's loss was definitely his *gain*, and he made no apology for the mercenary-sounding realisation whatsoever...

At some point during the journey it started to rain, and Blaise had no choice but to put the MG's top up. His bewitching passenger didn't even notice, however. To his surprise and amusement she'd fallen asleep—head on one side and her soft breathing making him feel strangely calm and peaceful—as he smoothly steered the vehicle onto the motorway heading towards London. *Almost straight away he had decided he would forgo the ride to the station and take her all the way home instead.* The faintest suggestion of a smile touched his lips. It had been worth staying at Faraday's house last night to now have the opportunity that had opened up to him. The only possible impediment to him getting to know Maya more intimately, he mused, was if there was a man in her life already. The idea caused a totally disproportionate stab of jealousy to slice through his middle.

Glancing sidelong at her now, he let his gaze skim the arresting, fulsome curve of her breast nestling beneath crisp white cotton, and the long, slender length of her denim-clad thigh. The hot, sweet need that immediately surged through Blaise's bloodstream made him clench his jaw to contain it, and it was only out of pure necessity and commonsense that he returned his full attention back to the road…

She felt warm and safe, and the sound of the rain pattering on the roof somehow gave her a wonderful sense of inviolability and protection. The experience was so delicious that Maya just wanted to stay there, eyes shut tight against the world, for a little while longer, reluctant to surface from sleep and even face the day at all…

But suddenly a strongly disturbing instinct made her peer out from beneath her drowsy lids—only to find that she wasn't in her bed at home, but in a car, being driven on the motorway at quite a lick in the outside lane. Beside her was a man with the chiselled profile of a model. Her heart pounded in shock.

'How long have I been asleep?' Her voice was husky and she sounded like someone else. Sitting up straight, she adjusted her previously cramped position with a relieved groan.

'Practically since we started out.' A fleeting grin appeared on her companion's carved, compelling features.

Maya stared. 'Was the station closed or something?'

'No. It wasn't closed. I just decided to take you to London myself. It's no big deal. I came to the conclusion that I should head home to Primrose Hill anyway, so it's not too far out of my way.'

'You have a place in London too? I thought Jonathan told me you lived in Northumberland?'

'I do. But when I'm working at the theatre it makes sense to stay in town. A play of mine has just completed a six-month run and will soon be on its way to Broadway, so I'll be going back to Northumberland in the meantime to rest and continue working on my latest project. Whereabouts in Camden are you situated?'

Maya told him, with not a little sense of unreality in her voice. Her softly shaped dark brows drew together in genuine puzzlement.

'I can't believe I fell asleep like that. It must have been all that upset last night. I don't think I slept a wink afterwards, to tell you the truth. But to fall asleep with someone I hardly even know driving me...that's a first!'

Briefly Blaise turned his head to survey her. 'I hope we can very soon rectify the fact that you hardly know me, Maya. It should be fairly obvious to you by now that I'd very much like to see you again?'

She fell silent for a moment. 'You mean like on a date?'

Digesting this bombshell, twin feelings of surprise and apprehension flooded her.

'Is that so shocking?' Directing the MG into a long line of traffic heading towards Greenwich, Blaise smiled.

'Not shocking, exactly...but I am surprised, yes.'

'And are you pleased or *not* pleased about it? Maybe you're seeing someone already?' he fished.

It had been two years since Maya had been in a relationship. A relationship in which her trust in someone had been utterly violated. The memory was still liable to churn her guts from time to time whenever she thought about it.

'I'm not seeing anyone else. But then I'm not really interested in dating at the moment. Particularly as I've probably just talked myself out of a job! There's no guarantee that my agency will have another position for me straight away, and I might have to look round other places as well.'

'Do you enjoy working for Faraday?' Blaise's voice was definitely disgruntled.

'Not for him personally...but I have enjoyed working with my fellow colleagues and the job itself.'

'Well, then, let's not jump the gun here, shall we?'

'What do you mean?'

'There hasn't been any mention of you being let go yet, has there?'

'No, but—'

'Then why don't you cross that bridge when you come to it? Right now it's all hypothetical. If you really want to keep your job then I'll have a word with Faraday myself and tell him it was *me* that made you leave early. There shouldn't be a problem. Although why you would want to work anywhere *near* the man is beyond me!'

'It's kind of you, but you don't need to talk to him on my behalf. Besides…' Maya shrugged awkwardly. 'I left him a note telling him that I couldn't work for him any longer after what happened, and if I take back what I said to try and ameliorate the situation then no doubt he'll endeavour to make my life as miserable as possible as a punishment. No…it's probably for the best that I leave. I wasn't exactly ecstatic at being asked to work for a PR agency anyway.'

'Why was that?'

'I'm just not mad about celebrity culture, I suppose.'

'Can't say I blame you.' Blaise grimaced a little. 'But if you're going to be free for a while then you'll have time to make a date with me to go out to dinner…right?'

CHAPTER THREE

MAYA had directed Blaise to pull up in front of a slim four-storeyed house in a narrow side-street not far from Camden Lock. The area was a Mecca for locals and tourists, flocking to the outdoor and indoor markets selling an eclectic mix of crafts, jewellery, music, clothing and artefacts from all round the world. The soft late summer rain had long since ceased, and the sun had made a welcome reappearance. With the sports car's top rolled down again it was easy to detect the exotic aromas of food, incense and the other myriad scents that permeated the air.

The surrounding pavements and roads were heaving with cars and people, and it had taken quite some time to negotiate the busy, packed streets to reach Maya's address. But now they were there, and Blaise realised his stomach was clenched tight as a drum as he lifted her bags from the boot of the car, waiting expectantly— not to mention a little *impatiently*—for her to finally address the question of a dinner date. He could already tell by the vibes he was getting that she had no intention of inviting him in for a coffee or anything like that and, resigning himself to the fact, he had to irritably bite back his frustration.

'Well…thanks so much for driving me all the way home. It was above and beyond the call of duty and very sweet of you.'

Sweet? Blaise almost choked on the ironic laughter that bubbled up inside him. *Should he regard such a comment as a compliment, or as a sign that he'd definitely lost his touch?* Smiling ruefully at the lovely brunette in front of him, he couldn't help noticing the anxiety reflected in her mesmerising green gaze, and he was intensely curious as to the cause of it. *Had some other jerk like Faraday messed around with her? Hurt her, perhaps?* The knot in his stomach gripped even tighter.

'It was my pleasure. Perhaps you'll think about meeting up again some time soon?' He was fishing in his wallet for a business card. 'I'll be in London at least until the end of next week. After that I'm returning to Hexham.'

'Hexham?'

'It's a market town near where I live in Northumberland.'

She took the card he proffered and folded it in her hand without so much as a glance. 'I will. I'll definitely think about it.'

Would she? Contemplating that she might *not* was

definitely a massive blow to Blaise's pride. To practically be given the brush-off by a woman he'd made it more than clear that he liked was something that had never happened before, and was *not* an experience he was in a hurry to replicate.

'Well…' he shrugged his powerful shoulders with pretended good humour '…that's all I can ask. Take care of yourself, and don't worry about Faraday. You'll have no problem finding another position—I'm sure of it. And if you do—give me a call and I'll see what I can do.' Lightly he clasped her arms, sensing her bewitching perfume sensually invading him. Then he kissed her continental style, on both cheeks, and moved away. 'Goodbye, Maya.'

'Goodbye. Drive safely.'

As he gunned the engine and roared away from the kerb, Blaise saw in his rearview mirror that she stood on the pavement, watching him. Grimly he clenched his jaw, ruthlessly brushing aside any doubt or imagined obstacles that might arise to prevent him seeing her. Of *course* he would see her again! Now that he knew where she lived, why the hell should he *not*?

For the first time since setting eyes on Blaise Walker that morning Maya finally felt as if she could breathe freely again. Never before had a man unsettled her and yet perversely commanded her attention quite as much. It seriously troubled her. No doubt if her friends found

out he'd given her a lift home they'd think she was *mad*
for not agreeing to a date! But then none of them had
experienced what Maya had experienced in associating
with people from similar privileged circumstances. People who were part of an elite, almost *oppressive* circle
of wealth, fame and privilege that was a million light
years from the kind of ordinary lives Maya and her
friends lived... *Wolves in sheep's clothing*, as her young
teenage self had thought of them. All glitz on the outside
but frighteningly shallow and cruel within.

She realised she was definitely apprehensive that
Blaise could potentially turn out to be like that. No
doubt her friends would be *more* than impressed with
his dazzling good-looks, achievements and wealth if
they were in her shoes—but then they still thought that
money and fame were some kind of Holy Grail to
instant happiness while Maya sadly knew different.

With a sigh that was part relief at getting away from
that horrible weekend party and—*shockingly* disturbingly—part lingering regret that she'd more or less indicated to Blaise that she wasn't at all interested in
going out on a date with him, she let herself into the tiny
studio flat, dropped her bags onto the rush-matted floor
and moved across the room to open the window and let
in some fresh air.

As she turned back to survey the small domain that
was both her living room and her sleeping quarters,
when she turned down the functional bed-settee each

night, Maya's gaze alighted on the medium-sized portrait hanging on the opposite wall. *It was a painting of herself at fourteen...* Her dark hair was in thick plaited ropes, and there was an expression in her eyes that easily reflected the painful shadows in her teenage heart. It had been painted at her father's insistence, during one of his more mellow periods. A rare time when he hadn't been drinking and partying into the early hours and had perhaps had an inkling of his daughter's deep unhappiness at his neglect of her.

'Smile, darling!' he had coaxed from behind the easel that had been permanently set up in what had once been the dining room of the grand Georgian residence they'd lived in. The space had been commandeered as her father's studio due to the exceptional quality of the light that had flooded in through the huge windows.

'I don't feel like smiling,' Maya had answered, in typical sulky teenage fashion but with an ache in her heart big enough to fill an ocean.

The portrait had turned out to be the last picture her father had ever painted.

After that, more late-night drug- and drink-fuelled parties had beckoned, with his so-called 'friends', and there had been no more mellow periods ever again. Three years after that he'd taken his own life, and at seventeen Maya had lost her home as well as her father.

Impatient at the deeply disturbing memories that made her feel heavy as lead, she glanced at the time on her watch, making a decision. She would forgo unpacking her stuff and instead go into Camden Market and have a coffee at her friend Diego's coffee bar. She'd sit and scan the Sunday newspapers, deliberately bypassing the doom-laden stories for the lighter ones, and instead of letting her mind be racked with regret and pain she'd watch the endlessly interesting characters that came and went in the market, imagining what *their* lives were like instead of dwelling on her own, and the day could just unfold however it willed…

'What do you mean, give her a job?'

Jane Eddington—Blaise's quick-minded, sharp-suited American agent—threw Blaise one of her most piercing and suspicious glances over the top of her high-fashion reading glasses.

'Someone really *has* stirred your sugar, honey, haven't they? You've never gone this far before in order to get a woman into bed! Don't tell me there exists in the world a female who *can* actually resist your charms, Blaise—myriad and devastating though they are?'

'Your encroaching years are making you cynical, Jane…and it doesn't suit you,' Blaise countered with a scowl.

'I'll ignore that distinctly ungentlemanly remark and simply say this: you've just spent the past twenty minutes verbally blasting Jonathan Faraday *again* for being an out-and-out sleaze and a snake for trying to coerce this girl into bed against her will, and now you're doing the same…albeit more covertly…by asking me to give her a job just so you can conveniently call on her whenever the mood takes you!'

'Please don't insult me by suggesting I'm remotely like that poor excuse for a human being! He's put Maya in an untenable position and practically forced her to resign. She really does need a job and I want you to hire her. You're always saying you need extra help around here.'

'Maya? Is that her name?'

With a mocking little smile, Jane adjusted her glasses and met the piercing azure glance of the answer to every woman's prayer currently perching his Savile Row-suited, perfectly taut male bottom on the edge of her desk.

'You know that name means illusion, don't you? Perhaps you've dreamt the lady up out of pure sexual frustration and the fact that it's been…what? At least six months since your last affair?'

With an impatient sigh Blaise shook his head and pushed to his feet. 'You know far too much about me, and it's not healthy.'

'Look, darling… I really would like to help you out, but I hired a girl only just last week. She starts on Monday.' With a glance that was perfectly guileless, Jane removed her glasses, laid them down amongst the detritus of paperwork on her desk and with the air of an old-fashioned headmistress folded her arms.

'What's her name?' asked Blaise.

'I forget. I know I've written it down somewhere…'
She waved her hand vaguely towards the pile of paperwork in front of her.

'Hmm… Well, if you won't do me this one small
favour and employ Maya at the agency then I'll simply
have to suggest that she comes and works for me personally. No doubt there are at least a dozen jobs she can
do to help me out. As you know, I've started the new
play, and so as long as she has an inkling of how to do
research, type and make the odd cup of coffee she'll
probably work out just fine.'

'And that's *really* all that you want her to do for you,
is it, Blaise?'

Despite the impatience that had been building inside
him like a pressure-cooker for the last few days—
because it had been *that* long since he'd last set eyes on
Maya and no phone call from her had been forthcoming—he sensed a devilish smile hitch the corners of his
lips upwards. '*Darling,*' he drawled sarcastically, 'I
really don't think it's any of your damn business!'

Glasses perched firmly back on her nose again, Jane
shot to her feet with a deep frown between her perfectly
arched slim brows.

'You mean you'd really take her to the wilds of
Northumberland with you? In the five years I've been
your agent I've never known you to take a woman up
there—especially when you're working!'

For answer, Blaise tunnelled his fingers through the

sleek strands of his dark gold hair and strode casually across to the door.

'They say there's a first time for everything. I'll be in touch. Hope your new girl works out okay. I'll look forward to meeting her when I get back to London.'

With a knowing little smile and a mocking salute, he abruptly turned and went out through the door…

'Oh…it's you!'

Staring back into the deep blue eyes of one of the country's finest playwrights as he stood casually on her doorstep, looking for all the world as if he made a habit of calling on her at odd hours of the day or night, was like being hypnotised. Maya sensed her heart clang loudly in alarm. Clutching the sides of her short towelling robe tightly together, and with her long hair still dripping from her shower, she hardly knew what to say or think. She couldn't deny that the man had been on her mind pretty much constantly since he'd given her a lift home that disastrous weekend, but quite frankly finding him on her doorstep was as startling as if Prince William or Harry had unexpectedly made her a visit!

'Yes, it's me.' He grinned, unabashed. 'How are you?'

'I'm—I'm fine…surprised to see you, that's all.'

He considered this for a long moment, before flashing Maya another disturbing smile. 'And you don't like being taken by surprise, I take it?'

'I don't know. I mean—'

'I'd like a word with you, if I may? Can I come in?'

'Well, I—'

'You're not about to leave for work, are you? I thought as it was after ten you would have left by now if you were going.'

'I wasn't planning on going anywhere today other than the supermarket, for some groceries. And as for going to work… Jonathan Faraday decided not to wait for Monday to accept my resignation, but rang me on Sunday night instead, to suggest that I didn't bother to go back at all.'

Shrugging off the wave of anger that arose inside her at the crude, almost aggressive way Jonathan had spoken to her, as if this whole sorry mess was *her* fault, Maya stood up a little straighter as she sensed her shoulders start to slump.

'Anyway, I decided to give myself the week off to take stock of things. I've told the agency I'll start back at work next Monday.'

'You know you could doubtless sue him for unfair dismissal, citing sexual harassment?'

'And give myself even more grief?' Maya shook her head with a bitter little laugh. 'He's probably done me a favour. At least I won't have to put up with his sleazy behaviour any more!'

The implacable look on her visitor's mesmerising face gave her no clue as to his thoughts right then, and Maya sensed her stomach sink. *Did he think she was a fool for not putting up more of a fight for her rights than she had?* Right then she could have *wept* at the injustice of it all. No matter how hard women had fought for equality it was still a man's world when all was said and done—and didn't birds of a feather flock together?

'I'd still like to come in, if that's okay? I promise this won't take long. I can see that my timing could have been a bit better.'

'I was in the shower when you rang the bell.'

'So it appears.'

His definitely interested gaze made a casually bold appraisal of Maya's partially clothed state. *It was as though the beam of a red-hot laser touched her everywhere at once.* In contrast, an icy drip of water slid down the back of her neck from her wet hair and caused a convulsive shiver.

'You'd better come up, then. You'll have to let me finish dressing and drying my hair before we talk.'

'Don't feel you have to do that on my account.'

His huskily voiced drawl made another wave of heat submerge Maya, and she quickly turned back inside the house, before he could witness the fierce, revealing blush that scorched her cheeks, and headed up the stairs. Her teeth nibbling worriedly on her lower lip, she wished she could relax about Blaise being right behind her, but it was seriously challenging knowing his gaze was doubtless lingering on the natural sway of her shapely hips, and he would be fully aware that beneath her robe she was as bare as the day she was born…

* * *

Having reluctantly watched his very diverting hostess disappear into a bathroom on the landing, and having been directed by her to enter the room next to it, Blaise breathed out to try and ease some of the inevitable tension that had gathered inside his chest. He knew he was taking a risk, forcing the issue rather than waiting for Maya to ring him, but damn it he was going back up north the day after tomorrow, and he simply couldn't wait any longer for a phone call that—going by the deafening silence of the week—was probably not even forthcoming. It wasn't his style to chase a woman, but it was as if something stronger than his own will— *some force of nature he could not ignore*—was now in charge where this girl was concerned. It compelled him all the more to find out why.

Noticing a little pottery vase of yellow and white freesias on the mantelpiece above a small fireplace swept meticulously clean, Blaise briefly bent his head to sniff their distinctive piquant scent. Glancing round, he interestedly examined the rest of the room. *Not that there was a lot to see.* A simple light brown couch, submerged beneath a veritable bazaar of silky cushions in varying shades of purple and red, faced an armchair that looked like a refugee from a charity shop. With its frayed arms and flattened seat, it had definitely seen better days. Apart from a small pine wardrobe tucked away in a corner, and a stout oak bookcase with its shelves literally crammed with paperbacks and hard-backs, Maya's furniture was very slim pickings indeed.

He sensed a frown forming. He knew stagehands at the theatre who lived more luxuriously than this! As he released a sigh, his gaze inadvertently collided with the most stunning portrait of a young girl. Apart from a couple of film posters it was the only picture in the room. Even at a distance he could see it was a sublime work. Moving closer, Blaise realised two things that made his heart almost jump out of his chest. Firstly, the portrait was of a teenaged Maya—a very vulnerable-looking and beautiful Maya, on the cusp of young wom-anhood—and secondly, the artist who had painted it, confirmed by the scrawled name at the very bottom right-hand corner, was only one of a handful of British artists whose work could literally command *millions*.

Blaise should know, because he was the envied owner of one of his paintings himself. A searing, frank depiction of a well-known actor his father had mentored, it had captured him on stage during dress re-hearsals for the play that had made his name. It had been left to Blaise by his parents after they'd passed away, and it hung in pride of place at his house in the North. He could have sold it a thousand times over, such was the worldwide demand for this particular artist's work. and he'd long craved to own another one.

Rubbing a troubled and curious hand round the back of his shirt-collar, he felt the skin between his brows pucker again. *How had Maya come to know such an acclaimed artist and sit for him?* More than that, why was she living in a one-roomed studio flat in a hardly prosperous area of Camden when she had in her possession a portrait that was without a doubt...*priceless*?

The noisy whirr of a hairdryer briefly distracted him. Casting a quick glance over his shoulder, Blaise returned his stunned attention back to the portrait. Captivating didn't come close to describing it. Even if you didn't know the girl whose cat-like almond-shaped green eyes gazed back at you with the kind of wounded glance that made a man feel personally responsible for whatever had hurt her, and broke something open inside him that he'd probably prefer *not* to have disturbed, you'd know you were witnessing something quite *extraordinary*.

The door opened and the sitter for the portrait—now clothed in light blue denims and an ethnic patterned silk top, with her pretty feet disturbingly bare—ventured an uncertain smile in his direction. The second her shy glance met his, a deep, magnetic tug of pure, undiluted sexual awareness made everything inside Blaise clench hard.

'This is you...right?' Fielding the sensual heat that now gripped him with a vengeance, he indicated the painting he'd been studying. Her tentative smile vanished.

'Yes.'

'The artist is world renowned...how did you come to sit for him? Was he a friend of your family's, perhaps?'

Maya's ensuing heavy sigh was laced with irritation.

'People are always so impressed by fame and celebrity, aren't they? It doesn't always follow that the person concerned is the best example of a decent person you could know or even *like*. Why don't people ever think about that? Because in my book that's the thing that really counts.'

CHAPTER FOUR

'I HEARD that Alistair Devereaux had his challenges. He must have had to take his own life.'

Maya winced. 'So you know about that?'

'He was probably one of the most inspirational and influential artists of his generation. How could I *not* have known that he'd killed himself?' Blaise's brow creased. 'But you still haven't told me how you came to sit for him.'

Eight years he had been gone, but the pain never seemed to lessen… Maya experienced the familiar tumult of despair and shuddering shock that she always felt when the subject of her father's death came up, and she restlessly linked and unlinked her hands as she mentally stumbled to stay upright against the great swell of hurt that surfaced in her heart. She could see that Blaise was clearly puzzling over how on earth someone like her could have sat for one of the country's most illustrious artists, and she couldn't help resenting the unspoken judgement that out of habit she naturally assumed.

'He was my father.' An edge of defiance under-
lined her tone.

'Your *father*?' Genuinely taken aback, Blaise stared.

'That's right.'

'I wasn't aware that he'd left children behind.'

'Well, he did…*me*.'

'But your name's Hayward, isn't it?'

'After he died I started using my mother's maiden
name.' Maya lowered herself into the armchair because
her legs suddenly felt disconcertingly wobbly. Visitors to
her humble little home inevitably remarked on the
portrait—why should Blaise Walker be any different? *The
picture was the only beautifully crafted thing in the room,
and therefore it was bound to draw attention.* But most of
her friends didn't even know who the artist was, and Maya
had not been in a particular hurry to enlighten them.

Now, linking hands that were suddenly icy, she
watched silently as her enigmatic visitor lowered his
tall, fit frame onto the couch, moved cushions out of the
way to get comfortable, then briefly speared his fingers
through his hair.

'Why? Because it was difficult to live with the attention from the press and the public?' Blaise speculated.

'Something like that.'

'What about your mother? Presumably she must
have outlived him?'

'No. She died when I was four. I hardly remember her.'

'That's tough.'

Silence, then… 'So you were left on your own?'

'I managed.' Embarrassment was crawling over her skin with debilitating heat, and Maya shrugged. Then, riding the crest of her unease, she observed her handsome visitor with a steely look. She'd had enough of this awkward exchange, and the truth was after the week she'd just had she was in no mood for playing games with anyone—*least* of all with another man who was possibly only after one thing.

'I don't mean to be rude, but what do you want with me, Mr Walker? You must be a very busy man, and it's really not clear to me why you're here.'

Meeting her gaze equally frankly, Blaise leant forward to rest his elbows on his knees. 'I was hoping you'd call,' he said.

A flame of hope flickered and blazed with the strongest compulsion in Maya's heart. *Then cynicism and hurt moved swiftly in to douse it.*

'I didn't call because I'm not interested in seeing anyone at the moment… To be absolutely blunt with you it's the very last thing I need! The only thing I really need right now is—'

Her guest cut across what she'd been going to say with that devastating smile of his—the one that seemed to have the disturbing ability to suspend her thoughts and dive deep down into her most secret core, awakening every fragile dream and hope that slumbered there, making them flare into vibrant and dangerous life again.

'How do you know that I'm not the perfect answer to what you need if you don't even give me a chance?'

Oh, he was good. For a fleeting, vulnerable moment Maya almost wanted to give him that chance—but then she quickly remembered who he was. *Hadn't she had enough examples of men in the arts like him, who completely disregarded women's feelings and lied to them as easily as breathing?* Artists were a selfish, self-obsessed breed. She'd learned that to her cost...her father being a case in point. His constant lies and unfulfilled promises about taking care of her had demolished every bit of trust she'd had, and it had been obvious that he preferred to put his work and so-called friends first. She was under no illusions about what men like him could or couldn't deliver when it came to close personal relationships.

Now, as she levelled her glance at Blaise, every single one of her defences slammed and then double-locked into place.

'You have no idea what I need...none! But I'll tell you this much—it isn't another man who'll lie to me and make promises he has no intention of keeping! And it isn't a man who hasn't the slightest inkling of who I really am and...worse than that...can't see past what I look like to even trouble to find out!'

'Maybe you've just been seeing the wrong kind of men, Maya.'

'And maybe we should just change the subject.'

Pushing to her feet, she crossed the room to a curtained-off area that secluded the small confined space that was the kitchen.

'Do you want some tea or coffee? I have fruit tea if you don't want caffeine.'

Her heart still thudding with emotion, she splashed water into the kettle and then inserted the plug into the wall socket. She sensed a tangible, perturbing shift in the air with the realisation that Blaise had stepped up behind her.

'I didn't come here to distress you,' he said, quiet-voiced, and it was as though sensuous strokes from the softest sable brush had skimmed across Maya's skin. A deeply sensual pull in the pit of her stomach made her long to close her eyes, so that she could revel in the pleasure of it for a little while longer.

'You told me you were intending to quit Faraday's agency and, apart from wanting to see you again, I came here to offer you a job.'

She turned at that and blinked at him, disconcerted to find him suddenly so close. In those electrifying few moments as she gazed at him every thought in her head was emphatically silenced—even the one that insisted she wasn't interested in dating anyone...*especially* someone like Blaise Walker, whose looks and credentials were too reminiscent of her father's phoney celebrity friends all those years ago and threatened to awaken ghosts she'd prefer to let lie dormant.

'A…a job?' she echoed, unable to stem the sudden quaver in her voice.

'I need a personal assistant for a few weeks to help me gather information for my new play. I'll be working from my house in Northumberland, so if you don't mind being away from London for a while, the job's yours.'

'And why would you offer *me* such a job? You must know people who are far more qualified and capable, I'm sure.'

'If you must know, I spoke to someone at the temp agency you work for and they told me you're hard-working, quick to learn and extremely reliable.'

Maya knew she was well liked at the agency, and that she did indeed do her job well, but it was still a bit of a shock to learn that Blaise had personally spoken to someone to discover that for himself.

'And this job you're offering…it's on the level, as they say? I mean…' she flinched a little '…you're not just stringing me along?'

'It's a real bona fide job, Maya.' He dropped his hands to his hips and one corner of his mouth nudged fleetingly towards a smile. 'And I swear I'm not stringing you along. In fact, if you want, I'll give you my agent's number and you can verify it with her. Her name's Jane Eddington and her office is in Shaftesbury Avenue. She's been a theatrical agent for years and is well known in the business.'

'I believe you… If you went to so much trouble to find out if I could do the job then I don't think I need to check.'

There was a brief look of surprise on his face, then his features seemed to relax.

'To put you in the picture, the play I'm writing has a strong historical context and needs quite a bit of research. I normally get secretarial help via Jane, but I've decided to try a different approach this time. To have someone I can directly call upon for help who's staying in the house with me while I'm writing makes much more sense.'

'I see.' Maya swept some long strands of silky, still slightly damp hair behind her ear. *To get away from London for a while, away from the noise and constant restless movement of people and traffic, definitely had its allure.* But she didn't doubt it wouldn't be easy taking on this particular assignment. She already sensed a powerful magnetic pull between herself and Blaise, and that revelation alone potentially signalled the sort of emotional turmoil she should definitely be running a mile from, given her history.

But on the other hand she really *did* need a job, and it had been a long time since any kind of lucky break at all had knocked on her door.

'It sounds like the work might be very interesting,' she admitted cautiously, 'and frankly it's a much more appealing prospect than sitting by the phone waiting for the agency to ring.' She forced herself to gaze steadily back into the long-lashed blue eyes that confronted her...at all that sculpted, breathless masculine beauty

and burning intelligence...and knew with sudden
stunning clarity that she would have to doubly strengthen
her emotional armour against falling for such an incredible man. Even now Maya's heart throbbed with
anxiety.

'Does that signify a yes or a no?' Blaise enquired, a
definite hint of impatience in his tone. 'I have to have
your answer today, I'm afraid. I'm going back the day
after tomorrow.'

'What kind of remuneration are you offering?' she
asked, dry-mouthed, uneasy at discussing money—but
she had living costs and bills to pay, just like everyone else.

He told her, and her jaw almost hit the floor at what
he was willing to pay for her services.

'Okay,' she heard herself reply, managing to keep her
voice surprisingly steady given the circumstances. 'I'll do
it. I'll need to make some arrangements with my neighbour about keeping an eye on the flat for me while I'm
gone, but...well, when would you want me ready by?'

'We leave the day after tomorrow. I'll pick you up
around six-thirty or seven in the morning, to beat the
traffic. Pack enough for a few weeks, and don't forget
to bring something waterproof. There might still be
sunny skies around at the moment, but it's almost
September and the region is notorious for sudden heavy
showers of rain.'

Linking her hands in front of her, and feeling suddenly awkward now that the business part of their dis-

cussion was ended, Maya nodded towards the just boiled kettle.

'Right, I'll remember that. Would you like that drink I offered you now?'

Blaise glanced at his watch and she caught a tantalising glimpse of a strong-boned wrist scattered with fine dark blond hairs. Something inside her—some long-suppressed need to know the sheer physical touch of a man again *without* the attendant complications and potential deceit—was shaken dangerously awake.

'I don't think so.' The summer blue eyes locked onto hers for an instant. 'I've got various appointments I need to keep this morning, so I'd better get going. I'll see you the day after tomorrow, as arranged.'

Relief and regret pulsed through Maya at the same time. Right then she was finding it hard to stem the sense of vulnerability and need that Blaise's presence so disturbingly seemed to arouse, and because of that she definitely wanted him to leave. Yet deep in her heart some perversely opposite feeling silently protested because he wasn't going to stay longer.

'Six-thirty or seven, you said? I'll be waiting.'

She followed him to the door and down the stairs, and now it was *her* turn to study him more closely... Her skin prickled with warmth as her gaze swept the back of his tarnished gold head, the strong, masculine shoulders lovingly encased beneath the fine wool of his suit jacket, the long and no doubt hard-muscled legs negotiating the worn carpeted staircase with languorous yet athletic ease. Maya's too acute awareness was all but deluged by all she saw.

Just before opening the front door, Blaise turned back for a moment. 'I'm glad you've agreed to take the job. Where I live there's a wild beauty that if I'm away too long inevitably lures me back. Perhaps you might find it has the same effect on you, Maya?'

A flash of a strangely enigmatic smile, a turn of the head, a final glimpse of that perfect knife-edged jaw and he was gone...

There was taking risks in life and then there was knowingly setting out on a course that was hell-bent on delivering nothing but trouble... Blaise couldn't help reflecting on the latter as he expertly directed the silver Jaguar onto the long fir-tree-lined drive that led to the place he called home—a stately Jacobean dwelling nestling within towering conifers, with wisteria tumbling down its aged stone walls.

Maya had been the ideal travelling companion. She'd been perfectly amenable to conversation—*if* a little guarded—but had largely left him alone with his thoughts as he drove. Thoughts that had been inevitably consumed with *her*, did she but know it, along with constant musings on how he was going to survive the next few weeks working on his most challenging play with her distracting presence around... The woman had the *saddest* eyes Blaise had ever encountered. With the knowledge that her illustrious father had taken his own life, and having been on the receiving end of that defensive diatribe she'd launched into about men not being able to see past what she looked like, he could understand why she had such a fierce need to self-protect.

One glance into those melancholy green eyes of hers and he should have been instantly warned to steer well clear, instead of offering her a job and inviting her to stay with him in the one place where he could work in peace without intrusion. Yes, right now Blaise seemed determined to court the *worst* kind of potentially disruptive trouble as far as he was concerned…*woman* trouble. But here was the thing…regarding the gorgeous but clearly wounded Maya Hayward, he just couldn't seem to help himself…

'We're here. Welcome to Hawk's Lair.' He rolled his shoulders to ease out the stiffness accumulated there from miles of concentrated driving, then turned to smile at the slim, dark-haired woman beside him. It had been a long journey, and to be frank he was extremely relieved to have reached their destination. But instead of having his gesture reciprocated, he saw his passenger's lush pink mouth tighten worriedly, and the tension she exuded was tangible. Blaise sensed a muscle flex in his cheek.

'Struck silent, huh?' he teased, but felt an odd kind of tension of his own seizing his muscles.

'I didn't realise—' She swallowed, tucked some strands of that waterfall of black flowing hair behind her ears, and looked as though she were trying hard to compose herself.

'What?' he demanded.

'I didn't realise the house would be quite as…as grand as this,' she answered, her glance wary.

'It's a Grade One listed building, but it's still my home,' Blaise remarked matter-of-factly. 'I inherited it from my parents. You might be surprised to know that sometimes it didn't seem large *enough* when we lived there together.'

'Any particular reason why?'

'My father was apt to outbursts of quite violent temper. It just wasn't easy being around him for my mother and me.'

'I'm sorry.'

'No need to be. It's all in the past.'

Sensing the muscles in his taut stomach bunch tight at the way he'd so easily glossed over what he had been through, Blaise shrugged, silently cursing himself for being so frank…*too* frank. In future he would have to more closely guard against such off-the-cuff personal revelations.

Feeling a sudden urgent need for some fresh air, he stepped out of the car onto the gravel drive into the rapidly cooling afternoon. 'I'll get our bags out of the back,' he threw over his shoulder.

* * *

Up ahead, the front door of the house opened and a huge Irish Wolfhound bounded towards the car. It was a faintly surreal sight. In the process of making her way round to the front of the car, Maya felt her heartbeat drum painfully at the realisation that the hound was making a beeline for *her*. Remembering a childhood incident when she had been winded by the powerful bulk of an Alsatian running at her at full pelt, she froze in horror, her whole body tensing in expectation of being similarly winded again as the large dog drew nearer.

'No, Sheba! Stay!'

The forceful tone of Blaise's commanding voice cut through the mild breeze that was blowing round them and the dog came to a sudden obedient standstill, pink tongue lolling, massive head slightly bowed as it looked sheepishly towards him.

'You okay?'

It took a couple of seconds before Maya found the breath to reply. Her heart was still pounding like a hammer inside her chest. 'I'm fine... I think...'

'She was just excited to see you...weren't you, girl?'

He stooped to ruffle the hound behind the ears, and she responded by rolling on the ground in apparent ecstasy.

Maya sensed her heartbeat slowly return to normal, but she was still disturbingly emotional at the raw childhood memory that had suddenly flooded back to her. The incident had occurred at one of her father's infamous parties. The Alsatian had belonged to a world-famous rock star that Alistair Devereaux hadn't wanted to offend because he'd just spent a 'shed-load' of money buying one of his paintings, and he'd made no effort whatsoever to comfort his shocked and sobbing daughter other than to tell her to 'stop making a fuss about nothing and go to bed'.

'All animals are basically wild and unpredictable.' Standing tall again, Blaise was studying Maya with a direct look that left her with nowhere to hide. 'But I'm fairly certain Sheba wouldn't have hurt you. She was just excited to meet someone new.'

'Why do owners of dogs always assume that those without dogs always assume that those without dogs don't mind if they jump up at them or practically knock them down?' Maya snapped, shocked at her own lack of control over her temper, and her failure to keep her voice at all steady.

'There's been an incident in the past when that happened to you? I mean when somebody's dog knocked you down and hurt you, perhaps?'

CHAPTER FIVE

How did he guess? Was it so obvious she was scared
out of her wits because a similar thing had happened before? 'Yes, a large dog did knock me down. It happened
when I was about ten years old, and when it slammed
into me I couldn't get my breath. I really thought I was
going to die.'

'Come over here.'

'What?'

A genuine expression of concern was written on the
handsome face that gazed back at her over the car bonnet,
and Maya felt as though she were still that frightened ten-
year-old girl, badly shaken and in need of reassurance.
There was a movement to the side of her and she noticed
a much older man with neatly combed silver hair dressed
in navy overalls standing watching them.

'I said come over here.'

Still nervous of the Wolfhound that now lolled at
Blaise's feet as though she was some playful kitten, rather

than the huge, potentially *threatening* beast she actually was, Maya sucked in a shaky breath and walked forward.

'Give me your hand,' Blaise directed.

For reasons unknown to her right at that moment, she obeyed. The most delicious warmth spread through her entire being as he guided her palm gently to Sheba's head and helped her stroke it over the trimmed thick slate-grey fur that covered the dog's skull. The animal turned trusting brown eyes towards her, letting Maya know she was enjoying her touch and was not remotely hostile. Breathing was suddenly easier and she relaxed.

'See?' Blaise grinned, eyes sparkling like dazzling twin lakes shot through with sunlight as he observed her, causing a miniature firework display to be ignited in the pit of her stomach. 'She likes you. Given time, she'll become your friend and want to protect you.'

'Will I need protecting?' she quipped, her own gaze falling into his as if she was falling into the sky. He disconcerted her by saying nothing and intensifying his glance. Then, still holding onto her hand, he straightened to his full height and turned towards the elderly man in overalls.

'Come and meet Tom. He and his wife Lottie used to look after the house for my parents, and now they do the same for me.'

'Sorry about Sheba running at your lady-friend, Mr Walker,' Tom apologised, inclining his head deferentially towards Maya. 'She always knows when it's your car coming up the drive, no matter what vehicle you're driving, and I couldn't hold onto her.'

'That's okay. No harm done, I think?'

'No,' Maya agreed, smiling tentatively. To her secret disappointment, Blaise let go of her hand to clap Tom on the shoulder.

'I know she misses me when I'm away…as I miss *her*. Well, Tom, this is Maya Hayward and, as I explained to Lottie on the phone yesterday, she'll be staying at the house and working with me over the next few weeks. Is her room ready?'

'Lottie's got it all in hand, Mr Walker. But first I think she's getting a cup of tea ready for you both in the kitchen.'

'Then we'll go and find her. Will you bring our bags in? Thanks, Tom.'

The interior of the house was full of original features and beautiful artefacts, but instead of the slightly dissipated, neglected air that the various homes of her childhood had held there was a sense of grace, order and calm that had the unexpected effect of issuing a sense of calm inside Maya too.

The kitchen was large and high-ceilinged, and just as ordered as the rest of the house with its oak furniture, neat rows of blue and white porcelain on the imposing dresser and every surface gleaming with obvious care and attention. The elderly woman wearing a cheerful floral apron, who was clearly responsible for its upkeep, made no bones about displaying her pleasure at welcoming her handsome employer home again.

'There you are—and about time an' all, if you don't mind me saying so! You've been away so long I thought that all that fame and adulation in London must have gone to your head…made you forget where you really belong!' she exclaimed, and without further ado opened her arms to embrace Blaise.

'Never!' He grinned, hugging her ample frame hard. And if Maya was slightly shocked at the familiar, clearly fond way the housekeeper addressed him, she was also a little envious. To have someone waiting for you at the end of your travels to welcome you home— as if they'd been counting the days until your return— was something she had never experienced.

As Blaise stepped away from the older woman, she sensed the backs of her eyelids prickle with threatened tears. *Get a grip, Maya! What do you think you're doing? He's hired you to come and do a job for him, and he'll start to think you're some kind of emotional wreck if you carry on like this!* The familiar critic in her head that was always there to bring her back down to earth mercilessly laid into her.

'And you must be Miss Hayward?' Lottie turned her attention to Maya, warmly gripped her hand and patted it.

'Please,' the younger woman replied a little self-consciously, 'call me Maya.'

'What a beautiful name! An extremely apt one too, if you don't mind my saying so, my dear.'

'Before I show Maya to her room, we're in need of one of your excellent cups of tea, Lottie,' Blaise teased, pulling out a couple of carved oak chairs from the kitchen table and indicating with a look that Maya should sit.

'It's all ready and waiting for you, my dears. The teapot's been keeping warm for the past five minutes, and I've made some of your favourite ginger biscuits to go with it.' She bustled around, arranging plates, cups, spoons and a dainty jug of milk, and finally brought the pretty china teapot to the table, removing its clearly home-made knitted cosy to pour the tea. Then she fetched a scalloped cream plate full of the most mouth-watering and delicious-looking home-made ginger biscuits that Maya had ever seen.

'Help yourselves. I'll leave you now and go and see if Tom has brought your bags in. If you want to top up the pot, there's fresh hot water in the kettle.'

Carefully sipping her scalding hot tea, Maya relished the silence that suddenly descended. It gave her a chance to get her bearings and compose herself, even though her heart felt as if it missed a precarious beat every time she glanced across the table at Blaise.

'Your housekeeper…Lottie…she seems like a lovely lady.'

'She is. She's been mothering me since I was little. In fact, sometimes I think she forgets that I'm a grown man!'

As if *any* woman couldn't see that Blaise Walker was a man, Maya reflected, her avid glance privately examining the strongly delineated beauty in that indisputably masculine face, the stop-you-in-your-tracks blue eyes, the broad, hard-muscled shoulders beneath his casual but exquisitely tailored sports jacket.

'When did you lose your parents?' she asked, half expecting him to ignore the question. Or at the very least divert it.

'About ten years ago. Funny…it doesn't seem that long.' The azure gaze was far away for a moment. 'They were touring in Vienna with a company of local actors they'd been mentoring and the train they were travelling in derailed. They and the guard were the only fatalities.'

'I'm so sorry. So they were actors too?' Maya hadn't realised that. Was that why Blaise had initially gone into acting and not play-writing?

'Wait a minute…' The search engine inside her head whirred to a surprised stop. 'I vaguely remember hearing the news about that accident on the news… Henry and Letitia Walker were your *parents*?'

'Yes, they were.' Blaise's wary glance levelled with hers for a moment, then moved uncomfortably away again. 'Would you like some more tea?'

Again, after his surprising revelation about his father's temper, the firm reminder of his fierce need for privacy reared its head, and Maya was forced to digest the astonishing information she'd just learned in silence.

But discovering who Blaise's famous parents had been was like just learning he was the offspring of one of the high-profile glamorous couples that dominated celebrity culture today. In their time, the Walkers had commanded just as much interest and notoriety. Silently, Maya digested the fact that Blaise was also the child of famous parents.

'No. I'm fine, thanks.'

'Then have a couple of Lottie's delicious ginger biscuits. If you don't, I may just be forced to eat the whole lot myself!'

'You've got a sweet tooth, then?'

''Fraid so.'

'Blaise?'

'Yes?' Wariness made the arresting summer eyes darken—just as though a storm was coming—and Maya knew he thought she was going to question him further about his parents. He'd already indicated that his family life had had its problems, and he was probably fairly prickly about having the fact speculated on by a comparative stranger. But, knowing how she guarded her own privacy where her father was concerned, she could at least accord him the same respect.

'I won't pry into your private life, I promise. I'm here to work, and I'll try my best to do a good job for you helping with your research. You won't regret hiring me.'

'I'm sure I won't.'

His tone was brisk and all business, and Maya's throat ached with sudden unexpected hurt.

'Now, finish your tea and I'll show you where your room is. You'd probably appreciate a chance to relax then freshen up before dinner and to be frank…so would I.'

The almost companionable silence of their drive down had been replaced by a much more strained one at dinner. Stealing glances across the table at a subdued Maya, dressed in very becoming forest-green amid the flickering candlelight, somehow Blaise sensed himself become uncommunicative, on edge, and even inhabiting a state of *regret* about inviting her to come and help do the research needed for his play. Her incandescent beauty, so beguilingly captured in that incredible coveted portrait by her father when she was just fourteen, shone out no matter what she was feeling, and his painfully growing attraction for her was making a mockery of any more noble intentions he might harbour. Candidly, all Blaise could really dwell upon was his almost primal need to lose himself inside her, to feel her without censure, to experience the heat and passion he sensed lay simmering just beneath the surface of all that transparent sadness and have her incredible body join with his all night long.

With any other woman he desired the idea of becoming sexually intimate would not be nearly so complicated. But after that incident with Sheba upon their arrival at the house Blaise had again glimpsed the vulnerability and fear of being hurt in Maya's painfully truthful gaze, and setting out to deliberately seduce her would make him feel like an unscrupulous carbon copy of her detestable ex-boss. *He simply couldn't live with himself if he behaved like that.* Maya was a woman to be gently wooed and made to feel safe in a man's arms, he realised…not thoughtlessly and lustfully tangled in his sheets for a few hot nights then kissed goodbye!

Already he sensed she was the kind of girl most men probably dreamed of marrying. She had it all…beauty, intelligence, sensitivity and kindness. But, given the fine example of marital bliss he had witnessed growing up, and having seen how his father's once vigorous passion for his mother had frighteningly deteriorated into resentment, jealousy and even *violence* down the years, marriage and even a long-term relationship with a woman raised the terrifying possibility that he would turn out just like his father. *He had his genes, didn't he?* And his temper too, if he was truthful.

No…his *grande passion* was his work, and he was more than content to let that be his focus for the foreseeable future…

'Your glass is empty,' intoned the soft voice from across the table. 'Shall I pour you some more wine?'

'No, thanks.' Having been lost in the disturbing maze of his thoughts, Blaise came firmly back to the present. Unable to help himself, he let his glance sweep lazily and

contemplatively across the lovely features before him,
then drift down to the demure V of Maya's dress. It was
a neckline that might conceal her curves far more successfully than that black velvet bombshell number he'd
first seen her in, but it still paid delectable homage to
enough smooth satin skin to make him want to see more.

'I've had enough. Besides…alcohol's not the answer.'

'Not the answer to what?'

'To what's bothering me right now.'

'What *is* bothering you, Blaise? I don't want to pry,
but if I could help in some way…?'

Along with that soft-voiced suggestion, Maya's
wide-eyed, innocent gaze sent a provocative charge of
undiluted *lust* straight to Blaise's loins, leaving him
aching, aroused, and frustrated as hell that he could do
damn all about it right then. *Especially* when the lady
who had provoked his uncomfortable condition seemed
completely oblivious to his dilemma!

'Blaise?' she prompted, sounding concerned.

'It's nothing to worry about. I was only thinking
about the play and how much there is to do. Tomorrow
I need to crack on with it, and in order to do that my
mind needs to be clear and sharp. What I'm saying is
that I think I'll call it a day. Hope you don't mind? I'll
see you in the morning, Maya. Sleep well.'

And with this sudden declaration he pushed to his
feet, dropped his napkin on the table next to the polished
candelabra with its soft flickering candlelight, then

swiftly exited the room. No doubt leaving his beautiful new assistant to perplexedly ponder at her leisure on his sudden and rather abrupt need to leave…

The next morning, as he walked into the kitchen craving his usual cup of strong black coffee, the frustration of the previous night had scarcely improved. Even a hot, invigorating shower had failed to banish either the sensuous aching that had seized his body *or* the thoughts in his head that seemed obsessed with just one thing and one thing alone…*making love to Maya*.

A relentless tide of lust and desire for her had mercilessly tormented Blaise all night, keeping him awake practically from midnight to dawn. Only when the softly smudged pinkish-grey light of morning had streamed through the bedroom windows—windows that he invariably left uncovered and opened in the summer—had he perversely managed to close his eyes and fall into a deep sleep.

'Good morning.'

The reason for his disturbed night stood in front of him, stirring a mug of coffee at the kitchen counter. She was dressed in fitted black jeans that hugged hips and thighs goddess-like enough to send every male from here to Alaska howling in delight at the sight of her and thanking the universe that he'd been born a man. On her top half she wore another fitted white cotton shirt that couldn't help but make much of the fact that her waist was *tiny* and her bust was… Well, he couldn't think of a single epithet just then that would do it justice. All Blaise could do instead was recall the sight of it contained in that knock-out black dress he'd first seen her in, and he was turned on all over again…*instantly*. To complete the highly arresting package she made, a small carved butterfly on a fine gold chain nestled at the base of her smooth skinned throat, and her emerald eyes gazed back at him like those of one who had slept the sleep of the innocent and woken as refreshed and rested as it was possible to be.

Because Blaise felt so grouchy, it was a double kick in the guts to encounter her fresh-faced loveliness and know that in comparison he must look like a man who had just crept out of some God-forsaken cave in the desert, where he'd slept on rocks all night!

'Good morning.' His voice sounded as if he'd been gargling with rusty nails too. 'Sleep well?'

'It's the best night's sleep I've had in years! Honestly, I'm not joking. The sofa-bed I use at home is hardly the most comfortable thing in the world, and I usually wake up in the morning aching all over and feeling like I've been kicked by a donkey!'

'Doesn't sound very appealing, I have to say.'

'Trust me…it's not. Would you like some coffee? Lottie had the percolator going when I came in and told me to help myself.'

'Please.'

'And how about some breakfast? I told Lottie I could see to it, as she'd got a pile of ironing to be getting on with.'

'Not for me, thanks, but you go ahead if you want something.'

'I'm fine. I never eat much in the mornings...so just some coffee for you, then?'

'That's all, thanks.'

He sat down at the table, scraped both hands backwards and forwards through his already tousled hair, and tried to force his distracted mind to focus on the play. In the entire history of his writing career never had anything been more seriously difficult...if not downright *impossible*...as he watched Maya cheerfully pour his coffee and bring it across to him, his gaze fixated on the gentle sway of those womanly hips in her spectacularly well-fitting jeans.

'I'm really looking forward to starting work today,' she enthused, gracefully dropping down into the oak chair opposite.

'Are you?' Sarcasm scarcely cloaked the frustration in Blaise's tone 'Well, if you're feeling so full of get up and go perhaps you'd care to write the play *for* me?'

'Is something wrong?'

A fleeting shadow of hurt passed across the vividly crystal irises and Blaise silently cursed himself. 'I had a rough night, that's all. And before you say it...I'm *begging* you...please don't ask if there's anything you can do to help!'

CHAPTER SIX

HIS gaze was hot, focused, and *definitely* aroused. Suddenly Maya knew very well why he had warned her not to offer to help. He had worn that same drowsy lustful 'I could eat you up' glance when he'd looked at her last night at dinner…just before he had declared that alcohol wasn't the answer to whatever was bothering him.

But last night she had somehow fooled herself about what should have been as plain as the nose on her face. Before Blaise had offered her this job he had made it more than clear that he wanted to see her again, that he was attracted to her. Now Maya could no longer hide from the fact that he *wanted* her. The idea caused a lava flow of heat to erupt inside, making her squeeze her thighs together and squirm in her seat. Her body *definitely* responded to the libidinous signals Blaise was giving her, and indeed *echoed* them—yet because of her devastating past *acting* on her feelings was a frightening leap she just wasn't ready to contemplate. Especially when she already knew that it had no future in it.

'Is this going to get in the way of us working together?' she asked quietly, staring down at the table. She continued, 'Because I really want the chance to show you…to prove that I'm a fast learner where learning new skills is concerned and that I can be a genuine asset to you.'

'*Nothing* gets in the way of my writing… Just because I'm attracted to you it doesn't mean I'm going to throw the baby out with the bathwater! I still have a play to write.' The broad shoulders lifted in a tense little shrug that couldn't help but reveal his frustration. 'And I still need someone to do my research. As far as I'm concerned, you've got every chance of proving you can do a good job, Maya.'

'Good.' She relaxed.

'But sex *can* be recreational too, you know.'

His words swept through her like a violent tornado.

'For you maybe…but not for me'

'Is that because you got hurt by someone, or just because you're holding out for something more serious?'

'Won't you talk to me about the play?' Taking a swift sip of her rapidly cooling coffee, Maya prayed her question was diverting enough to steer Blaise away from the far more *dangerous* ground he was currently intent on travelling…

Drumming his fingers on the table, he let a knowing little smile touch his lips 'Because it's safer?'

'Probably… But I do really want to know what you're writing about and hear your suggestions on what I need to research first.'

Sheba chose that very moment to pad into the kitchen and glance hopefully at them both. Studying the Wolfhound with far less wariness than she had yesterday, Maya smiled.

'It must be just like having a small horse in the house, having Sheba about the place!'

'Something like that,' Blaise agreed, beckoning the animal to him and ruffling her fondly behind the ears. The dog sat, happily allowing him to make the fuss she'd obviously been seeking and clearly adoring him.

'I suppose we ought to take her for a walk before starting work.' He glanced across at Maya, his gaze friendly and with no hint of tension in those superlative blue eyes at all.

'You want me to come too?'

'Good opportunity to show you some of the countryside and talk about the play at the same time,' he answered, rising to his feet with Sheba swiftly following suit…

Hadrian's Wall was between seventy-six and eighty miles long, she'd learned. For the past two hours Maya and Blaise had negotiated merely four miles of it, with Sheba bounding along in front of them. Built on high ground, it had been a fairly steep climb. But Maya loved walking over the uneven crags alongside the wall, seeing the lichen scattered between the rocks, and clumps of gorse and purple-flowered comfrey wherever they glanced, climbing uphill one minute and then downhill the next, with the wind in her hair and the heady fragrance of genuinely unpolluted, clean fresh air in her lungs.

Blaise threw her an enquiring look as they moved steadily uphill again, clearly noticing that her breath came a little quicker at the exertion. Below them was a glorious panorama of the most wonderful countryside Maya had ever seen, consisting of clumps of ancient trees, verdant fields and tarns, sparkling rivers glinting in the midday sunlight, and every so often she simply had to stop and take stock of what she was seeing. To drink it in and count her blessings that she was privileged enough to be there, enjoying it.

'How are you holding up? It can be quite a climb in places.'

'I'm doing fine. It's challenging, because I'm a little bit out of shape at the moment, but I honestly love it,' Maya replied, emerald eyes shining.

'I would never have called you out of shape, Maya.' His tone huskily wry, Blaise let his glance deliberately track up and down her body for a moment. Heat invaded her.

'I mean I'm probably quite unfit. Living in London, I just don't get the exercise that I'd probably be motivated to get out here, where I can breathe in all this wonderful fresh air instead of traffic fumes. You're so lucky living in such an amazing place.'

She could hear her heart pounding in her ears, and frantically hunted for a way to keep the conversation neutral.

'You said that the main character in your play is a young Roman soldier responsible for helping guard and patrol some of the sentry posts along the wall?'

'That's right.'

'Where did he come from? Rome?'

'No. The soldiers came mainly from a place in Belgium—known in ancient times as Tungria.'

'Oh? Can you tell me a bit more about what happens to him?'

He had told her a little of the story, and what he needed her to research, and right from the start Maya had been intrigued by it. It was the heartbreaking tale of a young boy in Roman times—a boy with a head full of dreams of glory, running away from home and his family's farm to join the Roman army—who, when he got to Britannia, met a local girl from one of the settlements and fell in love. The soldiers then had been forbidden to marry, and their liaison had to be conducted in secret.

'Well…' Blaise gazed out into the middle distance for a couple of moments, considering Maya's question. 'Eventually the soldier is killed, during a night attack on the wall, but before he dies he finds out that his sweetheart is pregnant with his child, and he vows to find a way for them to return to his village so that they can marry. Frankly, he is tired of being a soldier—killing men in skirmishes and attacks to preserve land for a conquering army—and has become increasingly disenchanted with his role. He soberly reflects on the benefits of a simple rural life, raising a family and earning a living from what he can grow on his land.'

He continued thoughtfully, 'Yes, we can travel all round the world in pursuit of our dreams, only to realise the treasure we were so avidly in search of is already right here in front of us.' He jerked his head towards the stunning vista surrounding them. 'The taking of a life is a dreadful thing, and violence can never be the answer,' he added, sighing, 'however much we seek to justify it. First we need to examine the violence in ourselves, I think. Ultimately, that's what the play is about.'

As he'd been speaking, a gust of strong wind had torn through the tousled dark gold lock of hair that flopped onto his brow, and Maya stared transfixed at the chiselled beauty of features that were suddenly thrown into stark and breathtaking relief. She was utterly fascinated that to highlight the theme he'd chosen—and he was writing a play about youthful dreams turning into a nightmare—he had used *a story about love…*

Before she realised it, she heard herself ask, 'What were your own dreams as a boy?'

On the brow of that windblown hill, Blaise studied Maya for what felt like an eternity before replying. When he did eventually answer her question, his voice sounded calm and steady. 'To express myself creatively in the way that I chose and be good at it…and funnily enough to be happy.'

'And *are* you happy?'

'Are you?'

'That's not fair!' Maya protested, taken aback at how easily he'd turned the tables on her.

'Then answer me this instead… What were *your* dreams as a young girl?'

Knowing that he was definitely issuing her with a challenge, Maya dug her hands into the pockets of her denim jacket and wondered what to tell him. In the end, because the penetrating beam of his gaze left her with no hiding place, she elected to be honest.

'To grow up, find someone I wanted to be with for ever—someone who really loved me—and have a family. I was never ambitious for a big career or wealth or anything like that. But…' she dipped her head and stared at the ground '…it was a childish dream. Now that I'm grown up I'm fully aware just how difficult such a deceptively simple dream is to achieve, and I just take one day at a time and try to enjoy what I *have* got.'

'What about artistic talent? You didn't inherit any desire to maybe do what your father did?'

'No…I didn't. I can't draw or paint to save my life. Are you disappointed?'

Feeling a sickening sensation of genuine hurt well up inside her in case he was, Maya turned away from the lancing gaze that so easily took her apart and started walking down the hill again, her heart still hammering as her booted feet carefully negotiated the uneven crags that covered the ground.

Sensing a flash of something beside her, she glanced down at a panting Sheba, the large noble head held ever so slightly at an angle as she came to a halt, just as if she was asking her what was the matter and could she help? The thought was so preposterous that she found herself smiling. Reaching out, Maya gently stroked her hand over the slate-grey fur that covered the dog's extensive back without any fear whatsoever.

'It's all right, Sheba. I'm fine…honest.'

Asking her if she'd had any desire to follow in her father's footsteps had obviously been too close to the bone and Blaise should have known better. Especially when he had fielded many similar questions himself over the years, because of his own famous parentage. Yet somehow an increasing desire to get Maya to open up to him, to make a real connection with her, had unexpectedly manifested itself inside him. He'd never experienced such a powerful need around a woman before and, startled, he let the idea wash over him, feeling what it was like. Her confession that her one-time dream had been to be with someone who really loved her and to have a family had also perversely made him want to instantly back away…to maintain the emotional distance that he realised both of them subconsciously fought hard for.

Contemplating her now as she stroked Sheba, the gusting wind turning her long flowing hair into a riotous cloud of ebony silk, Blaise remembered the upsetting memory she'd revealed about being winded by a similarly powerful dog when she was small, and the fact that she'd taken the courageous step of petting the animal in front of him with such apparent ease filled him with honest admiration for her sheer gutsiness.

'Let's press on, shall we?' he called out, lest any more warm feelings of admiration take precedence over the play he was meant to be thinking about. 'We've got a lot to do today.'

Deftly negotiating the jagged crags that separated them down the hill, Blaise arrived beside the stunning brunette and the Wolfhound in next to no time, and with not even the merest hint of being out of breath added, 'Lottie will have lunch prepared in another hour. And she's a stickler for timekeeping when it comes to meals at Hawk's Lair.'

'That's such an evocative name. Where did it come from?' Maya asked, and he saw the telltale smudges of what he suspected was the residue of tears beneath her emerald eyes.

For a moment his heart squeezed with regret, and he had to fight the strongest urge to wipe them away.

'My father started out in a local repertory company

in the small Scottish town where he came from and once performed in a play that had the title.' Blaise shrugged. 'My mother had seen him in it and thought the name so romantic that when they bought the house here, she insisted on calling it Hawk's Lair.'

'And was it a romantic play?'

'No…it most definitely wasn't! It was a stinging satire about a corrupt politician.'

'Still,' Maya said quickly, but not quickly enough to hide her apparent disappointment, 'it's a great name.'

'Maya?'

'Yes?'

'It was crass of me to ask if you had any ambition to be like your father.' He lifted her chin and cupped her small perfect jaw in the cradle of his hand. 'Do you forgive me?'

'Of course.' But she moved quickly away as she said it, turning only briefly back to enquire, 'That sycamore tree you mentioned earlier that's supposed to be a famous landmark… How far did you say it was from here?'

Fuelled by her challenging walk to see the famous Roman wall, along with Lottie's excellent lunch of grilled fresh salmon, new potatoes and a warm salad, Maya was just as eager as Blaise to start work.

During lunch he had expanded a little bit more on the play, and just what he was looking for research-wise, and as they'd talked she'd become more and more transfixed by the animation she heard in his mellifluous voice. Animation that she also witnessed etched in the sublime contours of his handsome face. It was a master-class in inspiration, and by the end of it Maya fervently wished that she had some up until now undiscovered talent so that she could help him move forward with what she'd learned.

After lunch they made a brief detour to the extensive library on the floor upstairs, where Blaise informed her she could find just about every history book she'd need, then came back downstairs to his huge study. He showed Maya into the smaller connecting office, where she was set up with a computer, use of the internet, printer, scanner, and a small but extensive bookshelf crammed with books in which to search for information.

'I've asked Lottie to make dinner for eight tonight instead of seven…do you mind? I'd like to work on as long as possible before we break again.' Standing by the door leading back into his study, Blaise briefly checked his watch before settling his arresting gaze once again on Maya.

She almost had to shake herself out of the trance she'd fallen into. That voice of his was a seductive weapon, bent on the complete capitulation of the listener, she was certain. Along with the sheer sensual heat that radiated from his hard, leanly muscular body, it made her knees almost buckle and every muscle she possessed contract with an answering devastating warmth.

'I—I hope you don't think this sounds too weird…' to cover her confusion she started to babble '…but when we were out there walking alongside the wall, I could almost hear the marching feet of the Roman soldiers— as though…as though the sound was contained and preserved in the very earth… Do you know what I mean?'

What she told him was absolutely true, but the way Blaise was studying her made Maya feel as if he'd just moved his body right up next to hers and demanded she kiss him. His pupils had contracted with genuine surprise at what she'd said.

'I do know what you mean. I've had the same thought myself many times when I was up there. The place is full of ghosts from the past. You're obviously very sensitive and receptive to that sort of thing.'

Ghosts from the past… Maya shuddered softly. She certainly knew about those. 'Well, I'll let you get on. I'm fine with dinner at eight.'

'Good.' Delaying his departure by another couple of disconcerting seconds as his glance lazily drifted across her face, Blaise finally moved away back into his own office and closed the door behind him.

Maya had returned to her room to change for dinner. Having showered and got ready in double-quick time himself, Blaise sat on the edge of the huge king-sized bed he occupied alone and tried to think over the progress he'd made on the play.

*Trouble was…every time he tried to focus on the
day's work the TV screen of his mind kept switching
to the channel where Maya had the starring role.* Too
restless to patiently sit and wait for her, he got up and
went out into a corridor lined with much of the highly
covetable art both he and his parents had collected
over the years. Maya's room was about halfway down
the corridor from his and, scrubbing his hand round
his newly shaven jaw, Blaise rapped smartly on the
oak panelling. Half hoping she'd answer the door
wrapped in just a towel, or that short little robe she'd
had on that morning he'd called on her unexpectedly
in Camden, he felt his lips twitch with a wry grin. He
was behaving like a schoolboy who had just hit
puberty with a vengeance! But then this was one
bewitchingly beautiful woman, and when he was
around her it just didn't seem possible for him to
behave like anything else.

She wasn't just beautiful either…she was intelligent
and sensitive too. Not to mention *damaged* by whatever
had gone on in her past. The grin on his lips vanished
as he soberly considered if he wouldn't live to regret
inviting her to work for him after all.

'Hi. Am I taking too long? Just let me put my shoes
on.'

Fragrant and bare-footed, Maya greeted him at the
door, her long dark hair flowing down over the black
silk sleeveless top she wore with matching palazzo-

style trousers, dazzling green eyes bright as newly polished crystal. Blaise took one look at her and knew he had never wanted anything in his life *more*...

CHAPTER SEVEN

'THERE'S no hurry. I just thought we'd go down to dinner together. Go put your shoes on…take your time. I'll wait.'

'Why don't you come in, then?' Her skin flushed a little as she said this, and Blaise saw with satisfaction that she was equally as affected by seeing him as he was her.

Accepting her invitation, he entered the room and shut the door behind him. Hurrying across to the wardrobe to retrieve a pair of flat gold sandals, Maya sat back on the bed to put them on, inadvertently giving him a highly arousing glimpse of her scarlet-painted toenails. But then out of the corner of his eye he saw the portrait of her as a child propped up against a striped slipper chair, and a jolt of surprise shot through him.

'You brought the picture.' Drawn by its beauty, as he had been before, he found himself standing in front of it, all the better to study it more closely.

'I always take it with me on longer trips.' A rustle of

silk, the scent of some sweetly floral perfume, and its owner suddenly stood there beside him.

'Presumably you have it well insured?'

As soon as the words were out of his mouth Blaise sensed the abrupt shift in Maya's mood. Crossing her arms over her chest, she turned her head to glare at him.

'I don't care about its monetary value!' she exclaimed passionately. 'Do you think that means anything to me?'

'Then what *does* it mean to you, Maya?' he asked gently.

Moving back towards the bed, she collected the cream pashmina she'd left lying there. 'It's a piece of my father. The piece he couldn't give to me when he was alive.'

Seeing her wrestle with whatever powerful emotion was flowing through her, Blaise judged it best not to speak right then. Instead he moved across the room to join her…*waiting*.

'You see…he was always busy working, or—or partying with his celebrity friends, and he didn't always have much time for me. That day—the day he started work on the portrait—he was more like the father I'd dreamed of him being. And although I was grumpy, because he rarely ever gave me much attention and I barely knew how to handle it when he did, I secretly loved him doing that portrait of me. That's why I wouldn't sell it…no matter how much it's worth.'

'And that's all he left you after he died? His career was amazing. He must have had other assets, surely?'

'What assets? Everything he had was either sold to help pay off his debts or given away to some—some sycophant whilst he was intoxicated! We even lost our house… But he'd died before that happened, and it couldn't have mattered less to me that everything material had gone.'

Suddenly understanding why she lived in a poky studio flat, with not much evidence of anything of material value, Blaise took the soft pashmina out of Maya's hands, threw it back on the bed, then placed his hands either side of her waist. It was slender as a reed—no more than a man's hand span—and he easily sensed the heat from her body through the silky material of her blouse.

'What was he like as a man…your father? Will you tell me about him?'

Clearly startled by the question, Maya momentarily withdrew her gaze, as if to regroup her thoughts, but to his satisfaction did not move out of the circle of intimacy he'd instigated.

'Like many artistic people he was very complex…brilliant and *driven*, but easily led too. His weakness was anything addictive—anything that was ultimately bad for him. When he lost my mother he lost a little of his grip on reality, I think. He tried to take care of me in his own muddled fashion, but he really wasn't the type of man who could cope with children. He just didn't have a clue what I needed. Often he left me on my own for long periods. At one time we lived in a house a bit similar to this, and I can remember at nights huddling in a corner of my bedroom terrified of every sound, every creak of a floorboard or tree branch moving in the wind, convinced someone was going to break in and either kill me or…or take me away.'

The long, tremulous sigh she released feathered over him, and Blaise realised that his heart was pounding like a sledgehammer in his chest at what she'd told him. Now a couple of the disparaging references she'd made to fame started to make sense. *What had Devereaux been thinking of, leaving his young daughter to fend for herself?* Surely the neglect of a child was one of the most despicable cruelties of all? The man had obviously been too wrapped up in chasing his desires and addictions to tend to his daughter's welfare, and in Blaise's book that was pretty damn unforgivable.

'No wonder you were frightened.' There was a slight break in his voice as his hand lifted to brush away some soft dark hair that had drifted across her cheekbone. 'You had a right to be. You were just a child, Maya.'

Her lip visibly trembled. Then her stunning eyes filled with tears. 'Don't do that!'

'Do what?'

'Be so understanding and…and say nice things to me. Kindness is the hardest thing to cope with of all. Better that you just tell me to forget about the past and concentrate on the present. Isn't that what people say?' Anguished, her beautiful emerald gaze latched a little desperately onto his. 'Trouble is…sometimes I *can't* forget about the past. I feel like I'm still waiting for him to come back, you know? Still waiting for him to walk through that door and say all the things I longed for him to say to me when I was a little girl…most of all to tell me that everything would be all right…even if it was a lie. But of course he won't come back, will he? He even took his own life to get away from me!'

'Is that what you believe? My God, Maya, that's got to be a million miles from the truth!'

'Is it? How do you know?'

'Because people aren't in their right minds when they take their own life. They're so locked in their pain that they can't see any other way of escaping it. That's the only reason they would make such a dreadful decision. It's nobody's *fault*, and you definitely shouldn't be blaming yourself for what happened. I also know that you absolutely deserve people to be kind to you…to treat you well. Your father was ill and needed help. Maybe right now what *you* need is a little help and kindness too?'

'That's where you're wrong. People's help or kindness usually comes with a price attached, I've found. Frankly I'd rather fend for myself.' She tried to twist away from him, but Blaise held her fast, forcing her to look at him.

'I don't believe you.'

In a heartbeat, his lips were on hers. No thinking, no planning, no intent to seduce… He merely acted on pure primal *instinct* and a genuine need to provide solace to the woman in his arms in whatever way he could. But once he'd laid his lips against hers, and her mouth had opened to him as easily and effortlessly as a flower opening its petals to the sun, a fire caught hold of him—a rampaging torrent of want, need and desire that was like a forceful, unstoppable river...

His arms wound tightly about her, Blaise was kissing her as if he was drunk on the taste of her and it was utterly *blissful*. Just as Maya had always guessed it would be. She had no reservations about kissing him back either. In a state of heightened emotion already, she knew her blood was pounding with the kind of carnal heat that she'd read about in books and passionate poetry but had no personal experience of. Her hands moved urgently down over his hard, fit body, pushing at the black fine wool sweater he wore, touching the warm, taut flesh of his ribcage and stomach underneath, aching to explore even more of him.

He too was impatient with her clothing, and he lifted the silky top that clung to her body, moving the sensuous material urgently up over her lacy black bra, kneading her breasts through the flimsy cups, teasing her burgeoning nipples with rough, warm fingers and making her want to plead with him for more of the same exquisite treatment with no end in sight.

When his hands travelled down to her hips, to impel

her hard against him, she came into contact with the full dizzying strength of his desire. It strained hard against the fly of his jeans and left Maya in no doubt that he was as turned on as she was. With a hungry little groan she moulded his taut firm behind through the black denim he had on, a sudden wild need driving her to have him possess her...*now*. She didn't want to wait. The desperate demand of her body to have him void the ache inside her in the most primeval way was too great for either conscience or patience to play any part in at all, yet somewhere in her mind she knew it was dangerously crazy as well.

But gradually, bit by devastating bit, Blaise made the decision to call a halt to the madness and broke off their passionate kiss. He lifted his head to study her. His blue eyes reflected back a hot, restless sea of need and desire that easily matched her own as they ruefully met hers.

'Lottie is expecting us down for dinner, and I can't do anything to delay that right now, but I don't want to leave you in a state of wanting either. Why don't you lie on the bed for me?'

Dazed by his mellifluous voice and that tantalising instruction, Maya tugged her top back down over her bra. 'What—what for?'

'Maya...do you really need to ask?'

Eyeing him nervously, Maya found herself doing as he'd asked her—just as if her body made its own decisions without even consulting her mind. Turning her head, she watched him move across to the lamp beside her bed like a fluid ebony shadow—the only relief his dark gold hair—and switch it on. Then he flicked another switch and the main light went off. Her very ribs aching with the tension that was building inside her, she forced herself to try and relax even as the room was bathed in a soft, intimate glow.

Returning, Blaise slipped off her shoes—and even the touch of his hands at her bare ankles sent hot darts of torrid pleasure bolting almost violently through her. Then, crouching down by the bed in front of her, he eased her long legs towards him. In another fluid, commanding motion he moved upwards to undo her zip, tugging her black silk trousers down over her hips and legs in a rustle of sensuous silk before discarding them onto the bed.

Her breath catching in her throat, Maya leaned forward to see what he would do next. Never had her heart beat with such clamouring, urgent need—and it had to be said *fear* too. This was simply out of her remit. To be so vulnerable with a man again was like cracking open a fissure in her heart that had not yet healed. It would all end in tears…she knew that. But it was with devastating intent that Blaise met and held her enraptured gaze. In response, her skin prickled hotly, as though a thousand tropical winds were blowing over her and through her. She was hardly conscious of breathing as he hooked his thumbs beneath the black lace sides of her panties and then, with a firm downward tug, deftly removed them too.

Biting her lip, she lay back on the bed, her body trembling so hard that she physically hurt. With the tight, coiled feeling inside her hitting an impossible ceiling, she knew she was on the brink of climaxing already because of Blaise's sensual attentions.

It wouldn't take much to tip her over the edge, she realised.

'Try to relax…trust me. I'm going to give you just what you need…I promise…' His voice flowed over her like warm, luscious honey in the most seductively hypnotic tone she'd ever heard.

Telling herself she was only fulfilling a very basic need—a need she'd long denied herself with a man— Maya shut her eyes. Almost instantly she opened them again. Shock and dizzying hot pleasure poured through her in a volcanic rush as his velvet tongue laved at the soft exquisitely sensitive folds at her centre, across the aching bud there, and then thrust commandingly inside her.

Maya hardly knew how she stayed on the bed the pleasure was so intense. All she could do was gasp and moan out loud, her fingers clutching desperately for purchase into the luxurious silk counterpane, her body helplessly writhing as Blaise's thrusts became more and more purposeful. And then she couldn't hold back any longer. An ecstatic cry left her throat as she convulsed with the power of her climax, and still he tormented and thrilled her with that erotic tongue of his—holding her slender thighs firmly apart until she writhed and convulsed no more.

All but exhausted by the ecstatic release he had helped her attain, Maya slowly returned to the world and dazedly sat up. Quite aware of how wild and wanton she must appear, with her long hair falling in a tousled silken mass round her shoulders and the lower half of her body bare and exposed, she self-consciously drew her knees together, feeling her sense of vulnerability magnify. It was the most vulnerable and exposed she had ever felt with a man, and her anxiety at what she'd dared let him do flowed over her, almost stealing every bit of the wild, unfettered pleasure she'd just enjoyed.

If she knew herself to appear wanton, then Blaise looked downright *lascivious* as he got to his feet. Leaning over her, he tilted her face towards him and delivered a most *knowing* masculine grin.

'That was just for starters,' he teased, then gently moved the pads of his fingers downwards over her cheeks, where the damp trails of her tears still glistened. 'I wanted to help you forget the past and come back to the present.'

'You—you certainly did that.' One corner of her mouth somehow quirked upwards in a smile that, given what she'd just allowed him to do, was ridiculously shy.

'We'll continue where we left off later. I want you

in my bed tonight, Maya… In fact the truth is I want you anywhere I can have you.'

Without hesitation she touched his smoothly shaven jaw, forcing her anxiety away and for once bravely meeting the burning gaze that surveyed her without withdrawing, 'I want that too,' she answered softly, and this time it was Blaise's audible intake of breath that feathered over her…

Neither of them was able to do full justice to the beautiful dinner Lottie had prepared. *Not when a different sort of hunger was gnawing at them instead.* With the candlelight glowing between them on the polished dining table, even conversation seemed extraneous. When Blaise asked her to pass him one of the condiments in its antique silver container Maya reacted just as if he'd just asked her to peel off her clothes and lie naked on the table. Her skin *burned* where his fingers inadvertently brushed against hers, and when she glanced up into his eyes he was studying her so fervently that her breath was suspended for a couple of moments.

'What is it?' she whispered.

'I want to know how long it's been since you've been with someone,' he replied.

'I haven't been with anybody for at least two years.' Troubled, she blushed hard at the idea that he might believe her to be promiscuous in any way. After all, she'd just allowed him the most intimate access to her body—*more* intimate than she'd ever let any other man come *close* to getting.

'Was it a long relationship?'

Thinking about Sean Rivers was not something Maya liked to do very often. Even now she shuddered at how bitterly their liaison had ended. 'It lasted about six months, so…not very long at all.'

'Why did it end?'

'Because I trusted him a bit too much and he threw my trust right back in my face.'

'Oh?'

'Something happened.' She took a small sip of wine, the alcohol bolstering her courage. 'His name was Sean, and for a while I thought I was in love with him…thought that he loved me too. He was the first man I'd ever met who made me think our relationship could go somewhere. When we were together he—he was tender, kind, caring. We'd talk and talk for hours, on every subject under the sun…even about becoming engaged.'

Maya's glance was far away for a moment as memories of that liaison came flooding back. 'He was all the things I thought I'd ever wanted in a man. Then one day I received a text from him…an intimate, private message—the sort of thing that a man sends to the woman he loves. Only it wasn't for me…he'd sent it to me accidentally. That was the day I discovered he was having an affair with somebody else.'

Swallowing hard at the aching memory of yet again

being betrayed by someone she'd trusted, Maya reached up to curl a few silken black strands of hair behind her ear. 'My friends said I should have seen the signs. But people also say that love makes you blind, don't they? Anyway, I didn't see them—the signs, I mean. I stupidly believed everything he said and I paid for it. I rang him straight away and told him I never wanted to see him again. I *didn't*. Clearly the other woman meant much more to him than I did.'

'That's tough. I'm sorry you had to find out the truth in such a crass way,' Blaise commented thoughtfully, slowly twisting the stem of his crystal wine glass between long fingers as he regarded her. 'But better that you found out his true character sooner rather than later.'

'And what about you as far as relationships are concerned?' Maya dared, watching how the candlelight cast some of his amazing sculpted features into shadow and the others into mesmerising relief—including the sexy little dimple that cleaved into his chin. Sensing that guard of his descend almost immediately, she half expected him not to tell her, and she couldn't help but feel a little crushed that he would withhold such information after what she'd just revealed about her ex.

A sickening fear arose inside that he would turn out to be some kind of international playboy, with a woman in every port, and that he would break her heart. *But what if she could steel her heart against full-blooded involvement with Blaise?* What if she could accept a short-term affair instead? An affair with no expectations on her part other than more of the scalding passion she had enjoyed earlier? What then?

'My most enduring relationship has always been with my work,' he answered, with not a small touch of his trademark irony in his tone. Before continuing he drained the rest of the shimmering ruby wine in his glass. 'I've always adored women…but as yet I've never found one I wanted to spend the rest of my life with.'

'Did you even *want* to?' Maya questioned unhappily, suddenly knowing that, for Blaise, the notion of happy ever after with a woman he adored was probably not even on the agenda, if the truth be known. Now she considered again the possibility that he was one of those men who liked to play the field, to have his cake and eat it, as the old saying went.

And why wouldn't he when he moved in the kind of circles where beautiful available women must be ten a penny? The small corner of Maya's heart that had started to blossom beneath his kind words and sexy attention started to close up again—like a flower denied sunlight—and the sensation of an icy breeze rippled through her instead…even though she'd already tried to resign herself to a brief affair with him.

Sensing the downturn in her mood, Blaise smiled coaxingly at her. 'Come on, Maya. Let's not spoil this thing we have between us already.' Frustration edged his tone.

'Oh?' she pushed to her feet, too upset to stay sitting. 'And what is this "thing" we have between us, exactly… *recreational sex*? Of course…how could I forget?'

CHAPTER EIGHT

SHE'D left the table before Blaise could fully register the fact.

'Damn!' What had he said to make her act so unreasonably? He didn't like the way he was suddenly feeling: as if *he* were one of those despicable men that had jerked her around—and he included her tragic father in that list. He'd been perfectly up-front from the start, hadn't he? Even though he'd offered her the job as his temporary research assistant he'd made it crystal-clear that he desired her too, so what was she getting upset about? Covering his face with his hands, Blaise swore softly.

Minutes later, he found himself standing outside Maya's bedroom for the second time that evening. As he rapped on the door, he was genuinely shocked at what a heightened state of emotion he was in. Not since he was a child, witnessing that first terrible row where his father had hit his mother across the face, had he felt so affected. God! What was the matter with him? He'd become expert over the years at disguising his feelings, and sometimes wondered if he hadn't done *too* good a job. Most of the women he'd had relationships with had all but *despaired* that he was even capable of experiencing emotion, yet here he was, turned every which way imaginable because of the woman whose room he now waited outside.

'I'm sorry I stormed off like that.' The door opened and there she stood.

'I somehow think maybe I owe you an apology too.' But even as the words left Blaise's lips confusion bolted through him…confusion *and* arousal. Dressed only in a short striped nightshirt, her feet and long legs bare and the neckline of the shirt opened provocatively low enough for him to easily glimpse the sexy, tantalising curve of those voluptuous breasts, Maya stared steadily back at him. His reaction was inevitable. He hardened instantly, as though a searing torch of flaming heat had glanced against his loins.

'What's all this about?' he asked huskily, marvelling that he was able to speak at all when he was confronted by what was probably the most alluring sight even *his* fertile imagination could devise.

'I thought you were meant to be clever? You write all these amazing plays about the human condition, and you can't work out why I'm standing here dressed like this? I've been waiting for you, Blaise. If you want to have an affair with me then I've decided that's exactly what I want too. I promise you I'll have no expectations other than that.'

'Is that right?'

'Yes. It's what you wanted, isn't it? After all…we're both grown-ups here, aren't we?'

Her cheeks turned visibly pink as she made this declaration but, gazing into her hypnotic dark-lashed emerald eyes, Blaise could see that though a part of her might be mad at him for clearly not wanting anything more than an affair with her she was still equally as aroused as he was. Stepping over the threshold into the room, the intimate space lit only by that same diaphanous glow that had lit it earlier, he knew his hungry glance devoured her. Devoured her like no tempting dessert he'd ever sampled.

Taking a long, slow breath, he remarked carefully, 'Never mind what *I* want. I'm moving no further from this spot unless I know for sure that this is absolutely what you want too, Maya.'

'It is. It *is* what I want. I've told you already, haven't I?'

'You're sure?' He raised her chin to bring her revealing ardent glance level with his,

'Yes…yes!' she cried. 'Of *course* this is what I want! What do I have to do to prove it to you? I've tried going for love and it turned out to be far too painful for me to ever want it again. An affair is all I'm looking for, Blaise.'

'Okay. You've convinced me.' Now Blaise's hand moved to the open V of her nightshirt, and in a heartbeat he tore it down the centre, causing the tiny white buttons to fly in all directions. Pushing the gaping material aside, he let his gaze feast on Maya's beautiful breasts, with their perfectly *edible* café mocha tips, before ravenous need drove him to sample each one in turn, suckling, tasting and wetting them with the heat and moisture from his swirling, greedy tongue.

Her fingers were in his hair, urging him on, and Blaise slid his hands between her legs and pushed into her with his fingers. Her damp heat engulfed him, and her slender body quivered and sagged against him as a long, low moan left her throat.

Tugging his sweater over his head and unfastening his jeans, he yanked Maya roughly against him, branding her mouth with a hot, sexy kiss that was *beyond* hungry, beyond any carnal craving he'd ever experienced before, as basic and animal as a kiss could be and with no pretence of gentleness whatsoever. *Not even a drop.* At one point Blaise even tasted blood on his lips, and couldn't be sure whether it was his or Maya's. All he knew was that a storm was building between them—a storm whose only way of stopping was to burn itself out. *Well, he was burning.* So burning hot and turned on that he thought he might lose his mind if he didn't take her soon.

Even as the erotic realisation filled him, electrifying

his body to the exclusion of everything else, he was dragging Maya down to the luxuriously carpeted floor, the body he took pride in keeping so fit jammed skin to skin against hers. Inserting his hands between her thighs, he pressed them apart and then, opening his fly with a rough groan, he placed the tip of his heavily aroused sex at her most feminine core. Earlier…she'd *tasted* like heaven. Now he would find out if she *felt* like it too.

Arching up off of the floor, Maya let her slumberous, inviting glance fall hungrily into his. 'What are you waiting for?' she gasped. 'I want you so much… If you care about my sanity take me now…*please*…'

'Maya, you hardly have to ask… I'm all yours… *All* yours for however long you want me… I promise you.'

With one scalding hot thrust he filled her, and for the most dizzying unforgettable moment Blaise *did* lose his mind. She was exquisite…tight and silky as a hot satin glove. As he began to move deeper and harder inside her she whimpered, and again he kissed her, drowning out her erotic little cries with his demanding, voracious mouth, driving into her body as if it was the only destination he'd been seeking all his life and he would not soon relinquish it…

Maya had quickly come to terms with the realisation that all Blaise wanted was her body. *After all…why should he be different from any other man who had been interested in her?* Feeling upset by Blaise's remarks earlier, about adoring women but not finding one he wanted to commit to, Maya had stemmed the flood of emotion that threatened to unbalance her and given herself a firm reprimand. Facing the facts, she'd decided, was more empowering than succumbing yet again to grief and hurt because life had once more confirmed her worst fears—that she must indeed be unlovable. If this wild, tempestuous coupling was all she would ever have with Blaise then she would honestly accept it, and not wound herself further by wanting more.

In fact…tonight she'd decided she could be whoever she liked—for instance a passionate, daring woman who could truly be mature about what might turn out to be a hot one-night stand, or even several hot nights of passion, but who wouldn't rack herself with recriminations when the affair came to its inevitable end.

Now, as Blaise voraciously claimed her body, Maya's hands locked tight onto the impressive iron muscle in his shoulders—the touch of his skin warm and silky, his muscled forearms and lean torso dusted with a smattering of darkly golden hair through which she glimpsed his darker, flat male nipples. He was raining kisses on her mouth, her throat, her breasts, his seductive masculine scent and strong, hard body saturating her senses—making her forget that a world even existed outside this room. Wriggling beneath him on the carpet, Maya adjusted her slender body to accept his possession even deeper inside her, wrapping her long legs round his waist, one hand moving to the back of his neck to guide his lips voraciously back to hers whenever he removed them.

Somehow she'd become *addicted* to the taste of him. It seemed impossible that she would ever get enough of those scalding, inflammatory kisses... But suddenly Blaise tore his mouth from hers, to stare back into her eyes for a stunning moment that would be forever etched in her memory with the most exquisite clarity. Maya stared back, hardly knowing what to say or think. Then he delivered another one of those sexy, knowing little smiles of his, the azure blue eyes twinkling in the lamplight, making him look as if he'd invented the very word *temptation*...in fact was the *personification* of it. Then, slowly and deeply, he started to rock her hips towards his.

A stunned gasp was torn from her throat as her release came, quick and fast, stealing her breath as it convulsed her, even as Blaise's own movements started to match it. Her heart thumping hard enough to jump right out of her chest, Maya stared up at her lover, knowing the *exact* moment when his own powerful climax held him in thrall and sensing the scalding force of his seed spurt deep inside her.

They'd been so swept away by the power of the wild, raging river of need that engulfed them that neither of them had thought about protection.

Now, as she carefully lowered her legs to the floor again, her feet touching the soft carpet once more, she rested her hands on the smooth flesh of Blaise's back, sensing the slick rippling muscle beneath his skin contract and then still beneath her fingers. Her sigh of longing and resignation at what they'd done hovered softly on the air between them. She would never regret it, but would Blaise?

Scraping his fingers through his mane of gold hair, he ruefully moved his head from side to side, his gaze boring deeply down into hers. 'I'm so sorry, Maya… there's no excuse. I should have protected you, but you're so beautiful and incredible that the possibility of thinking straight around you went right out the window! I guess I just got rather carried away. If anything happens I—'

'Shh.' Maya put her fingers against his lips. 'I got carried away too, Blaise,' she confessed shyly, 'but don't worry…it's the wrong time of the month for anything to happen.'

'Next time I promise I'll take more care.' Smoothing her hair gently back from her forehead, Blaise was regarding her almost tenderly, making no sudden move to separate his body from hers despite his rueful confession that he should have used protection. In fact, to her great surprise, Maya already sensed him becoming aroused again inside her.

'Do you mean…like *now*?' she asked, wide-eyed.

'See what you do to me?'

His lips met hers in a long, lingering kiss that ignited the fireworks inside her all over again, but just as Maya started to surrender to more of the same drugging, irresistible lovemaking Blaise regretfully withdrew from her body.

'But I'm not doing this again without protecting you. I'm also concerned that you're going to get carpet burns if we stay on the floor like this! I think the bed might be more comfortable, don't you? You get in. Give me a couple of minutes and I'll be right back with what we need.' On his feet again, Blaise yanked up his trousers and did up his fly. Then he reached for Maya's hand to assist her. His wonderful chest was left provocatively bare.

Self-consciously, Maya drew the torn sides of her nightshirt together over her own naked breasts. 'Blaise?'

'What is it?' Immediately he moved in closer, sweeping the sides of her nightshirt aside and possessively cupping her hips with his warm, slightly callused hands as he concernedly examined her face.

'If you're coming back to bed…does that mean you'll be spending the night with me?'

His ensuing laugh was low and sensual, and almost rough with undisguised need. 'Try ejecting me, darling, and you'll have a genuine fight on your hands!'

'Good morning, my love!' The housekeeper paused in the kitchen doorway, clearly startled by the sight of Maya sitting with her chair pulled out from the pine table and the huge Irish Wolfhound lying at her feet, as though keeping guard over the lovely young brunette.

'You're up and about early. Give me a few minutes and I'll get you a nice cup of tea.'

'Don't bother about tea, Lottie, thanks all the same.' Getting to her feet, Maya dusted down her jeans. As if on cue, Sheba also rose, gazing up at her with an expression that looked like longing in her eyes. 'I thought I'd take Sheba for a bit of a walk before breakfast…is that all right?'

'Of course it's all right. My Tom usually takes her, but he'll be glad of a break this morning before he tackles the day's work, I'm sure. There's always plenty to do round a big place like this, and today he's mowing that huge front lawn. You don't need to bother with a lead, lass—just don't let madam here dictate the pace, or you'll come back fit for nothing!'

Out in the grounds, breathing in air that was akin to having pure oxygen injected into her lungs, Maya tramped grass still damp with morning dew. The Irish Wolfhound loped along beside her quite agreeably. Strangely, she found unexpected comfort and companionship in the animal's presence. She had never had a pet when she was a child— her father hadn't allowed it—but being around Sheba made her realise that she actually liked the idea. However, her thoughts did not dwell on the subject for long. Not when every cell in her body was still vibrating with the memory of Blaise's passionate loving last night, and her skin carried the tender spots to prove it.

Extricating herself from that warm, cosy bed this morning, she'd been so careful not to disturb him, but thankfully the calm, rhythmic rise and fall of his heavenly chest had indicated that he was enjoying the deepest of deep sleeps—one he wouldn't wake from in a hurry. The fact hardly surprised Maya when they'd spent most of the night lost in each other's arms, driven to greater and greater heights of ardent fervour by this— this *maelstrom* of need and desire that they seemed to generate so electrifyingly between them.

She'd risen early because she'd needed some time on her own to absorb what had occurred. Her only other lover had been Sean, and although she had lost her virginity to him he had hardly set her on fire with his quickly over with attentions. Even at the time Maya had known in her heart that her relationship with him had been nothing but a Band-Aid for what really ailed her…a deep, gnawing loneliness coupled with a sometimes desperate need for love that wouldn't go away.

But nothing could have prepared her for the passionate revelation that was Blaise Walker… Tugging open the neckline of her waterproof jacket, she sniffed. Even though she'd showered thoroughly, and washed her hair twice, it was as though he'd left his provocative masculine scent all over her… Or was she just imagining that was so because she'd simply not been able to get enough of him? Would a woman *ever* be able to get enough of such an incredible man? Now Maya knew that he'd ruined her for anyone else. Any other man she might be with in the future would only ever get barely a *quarter* of what she felt for Blaise. But even considering that there might be another man in her future was akin to feeling as if she was already betraying herself. She simply couldn't do it…not after what she'd just experienced. If this so-called affair of theirs *did* develop into something deeper on her part could she honestly handle it as easily as she seemed to be trying to convince herself that she could?

Sheba chose that moment to nudge her with that huge head of hers. It took Maya a couple of seconds to realise what she wanted. 'I'm sorry, poppet… I didn't think to bring a ball to throw for you.' She fondly ruffled the thick grey fur. 'Maybe I can find a stick for you instead? Come on, girl…let's go see what we can find, eh?'

Blaise drank his coffee, checked the time on his watch and gazed out of the window for the umpteenth time. He'd woken in a state of almost instant arousal at the thought of engaging Maya in some sexy, languorous early-morning lovemaking, and instead had been confused and disgruntled to find that she had already risen without him. As he'd swung his legs out of bed, then scraped his fingers through his hair, he'd quickly added frustration to the list of woes he was mentally compiling because of her desertion.

Walking into the kitchen, he had felt his jaw all but hit

the floor at Lottie's cheery announcement. 'Miss Hayward has taken Sheba for a walk…wasn't that kind of her?'

Kind? Blaise had echoed ironically. Abandoning him in preference to taking his dog for a walk wasn't kind…it was pure sadistic torment! Yet part of him knew an honest admiration for Maya too, at the realisation she was obviously trying to overcome a childhood fear by taking Sheba out.

He found himself reflecting on what a tough road she'd been travelling. Just the thought of that idiot that she'd gone out with who'd so clumsily revealed what he was up to, with an accidental text to Maya's mobile phone, made Blaise want to find him and teach him a lesson he wouldn't soon forget!

Then, realising that the idea had been generated by a too-easy familiar fury sweeping through him, he experienced genuine revulsion that he was perhaps becoming more like his father every day. Clenching his jaw, he shook his head, as if to rid himself of such a demoralising, painful thought. Now, hearing Maya's velvet-soft voice in the hallway in brief conversation with Tom, another far more agreeable sensation gripped him instead. With almost bated breath he waited for her to come through the kitchen doorway.

'Hi there.' Her smile was a little lopsided—almost *shy*—but to Blaise's eyes she looked simply wonderful, with her pink cheeks, her dark hair mussed by the wind, dressed in well-worn jeans and a red waterproof jacket.

'Good morning.' He sauntered across to her, not hesitating to tug her gently but firmly into his arms. 'You deserted me. I woke up and there you were... gone.'

'I just—I just needed some fresh air, so I took Sheba with me for a walk. The grounds here are really beautiful—just like a stately home.'

'With the aid of a couple of part-time gardeners Tom does a sterling job taking care of it all. But let's not talk about the grounds or the gardens, hmm?'

'I think we should talk about the play. I can't wait to get started on the research today.'

To Blaise's chagrin, Maya ducked out of the way of his intended kiss, and stepped out of his embrace too.

'So it's to be all business, is it?' He knew he sounded unreasonably annoyed—almost *petulant*—but right then he didn't care. 'Just as if last night never happened?'

Maya frowned. 'I want to do a good job for you, Blaise—remember I told you that? And I don't want you to think that I'm somehow expecting special privileges because we slept together either. I'm here to work, and that's how I intend to proceed from now on.'

'Really?' Irritation made Blaise feel like breaking something. He could hardly believe she was acting so cool with him...as if she'd just had a one-night stand she was quickly regretting, instead of being consumed by the thought of how soon they could get together again, as *he* was.

Maya didn't answer him…just stood there calmly unzipping her jacket.

'Well, if that's the way you want it, then so be it. Get yourself some breakfast, then come and find me in my study. I'll expect to see you there in exactly twenty minutes…no later!'

As he headed out of the room, he was so mad that he could hardly bring himself to look at her…

CHAPTER NINE

WHEN Maya turned up in Blaise's study, just under twenty minutes later, it was to find him writing furiously away in long-hand at his desk. She knew he must have heard her enter, but he didn't glance up to acknowledge her presence for at least two or three minutes. Already aware he was not very happy with her, but also aware that an artist at work should never be disturbed unless it was an emergency—a rule that had been drummed into her by her father—she deliberately kept quiet.

To be honest, it was no hardship for Maya just to watch him. Although she kept experiencing an almost irresistible urge to touch him…to slide her hand round that exquisite sculpted jaw and bring his mouth close to hers, so that she could tease and taste and remind herself of what she'd so freely enjoyed doing last night. But because he looked so serious she also wanted to brush back that rogue lock of dark gold hair from his forehead as he bent over his large spiral notebook and make him look at her instead.

Eventually, he did glance up. There followed an un-comfortable moment when Maya felt like a blundering insensitive stranger who had walked in on him.

'You took your time,' he commented grumpily. 'Pull out that chair and sit down. Got something to write in?'

'No—yes… I mean give me a second.' She dashed into the adjoining office to sweep a notebook and pen off the top of the desk. A little red-faced, she returned and drew out a chair, her notepad and pen at the ready.

'Before we start,' he began, his intense, all but scorching blue gaze closely examining her, 'do up the top buttons on your shirt.'

'What?' Embarrassed, in case her blouse had unwit-tingly come undone and she was revealing more flesh than was seemly, Maya saw that the buttons were fastened almost right up to her neck. Only the very top one was left free, and all that revealed was the slender column of her throat.

'There's just one button not secured, and I'm not fas-tening that because it makes me feel too claustrophobic'

'Well, then, go and put something on that's a little less provocative.'

'What? It's a perfectly respectable blouse and not the least bit provocative!' Defensively, Maya touched her hand to her chest. Instantly she saw Blaise's gaze go straight there and his jaw tightened.

'Well, *I* find it provocative!'

'That's hardly my fault.'

'It is your fault,' he insisted belligerently, 'because you chose to wear the damn thing!'

'This is ridiculous. You're only behaving like this because—'

'Because what, Maya? I'd really like to hear your thoughts on the matter.'

She squirmed uncomfortably as a wave of scorching heat all but glued her to the chair. 'It's because—oh, I don't know!'

'Liar.'

'All right, then. You find what I'm wearing provocative because clearly you're frustrated,' she exclaimed in exasperation, wishing that just looking at him didn't drive every other thought from her head other than the one that said she wanted him so badly it hurt.

'Damn right I'm frustrated,' he replied, and there was a lascivious gleam in his eye that made Maya squirm even more. 'How in hell am I supposed to work when just the sight of you is driving me crazy?'

Not knowing how to answer that question, Maya examined her linked hands in her lap and felt everything—including the tips of her ears—burn.

'Perhaps...'

Getting up, Blaise walked slowly round the desk to join her—reached out and started gently massaging her shoulder. Feeling her body *and* her resolve melt at his touch, Maya was momentarily dazzled by the glint of a gold signet ring set with a diamond that he wore on his little finger.

'Perhaps what?' she asked, turning to regard him.

'Perhaps between the two of us we can find a way to alleviate some of my frustration…before we start work, I mean…' His voice was huskily sinful. It rolled over her like tropical waves of heat lapping at the shore of her already highly sensitised body.

'Blaise, please don't—'

'Please don't what?'

He was smoothing his hands down the sides of her arms, his palms glancing deliberately against her breasts. Hot needles of pleasure and desire caused Maya's nipples to surge and prickle to the point of pain inside her bra.

'This is madness, Blaise. I can't—I can't think straight when you do things like that to me.'

'I'm not asking you to think.'

'But I'm here to work, not to—not to succumb to your highly provocative ways of distracting me!'

'No?'

He bent to kiss her, but Maya stoically turned her face away at the last moment, and his intended kiss glanced off the side of her mouth instead.

'We—you really need to work, and I'm meant to be helping you.'

There was a well-timed—or perhaps *not* so well-timed—knock at the door. Stepping instantly away from her side, Blaise cursed softly under his breath.

'Come in!' he called out, his tone definitely disgruntled.

Lottie walked in, carrying a tray with a full cafetière alongside a plate of biscuits. 'Thought you might like some coffee to keep you both going while you work,' she said brightly, carefully depositing the tray on the desk.

'Thanks, that's great.'

Her employer's smile was tense. Maya knew he was definitely put out by the intrusion. The housekeeper glanced sideways at her. 'That's a very pretty blouse you're wearing, my dear.'

'Thank you.' Maya didn't dare look at Blaise after this comment. However, Lottie's interruption did give her some valuable time to restore common sense to the situation, and she seized the opportunity to effect some much needed distance between them, even knowing he would probably taunt her about it later.

'Excuse me, but I need to go and sort out which books I'll need for our research.'

'For God's sake, Maya, I—'

But she'd already left the room before Blaise had even finished the sentence.

Maya had absolutely done the right thing, disappearing for a while. Blaise had had no choice but to get down to some work. It wasn't easy when his mind was taunted by too erotic images of her, but once he started to write the story totally absorbed him, drawing him into the drama that was unfolding on the cinema screen of his mind and making him forget everything—even *her*.

Yet that wasn't completely true. In the play, the female lead of the piece had helplessly turned into Maya, and Blaise found to his surprise that he was becoming more and more emotionally involved in the character than with any other female part he had ever written. *It was a strange process, what he did for a living.* He believed he was far more capable of expressing emotion in his writing than he was in day-to-day life. Subconsciously he supposed he blamed his parents for that. God knew they'd expressed enough stormy emotion throughout their married life to make any child of theirs either abhor it or shun replicating it as far as possible.

Disturbingly uncomfortable echoes from the past gripped him for a few frozen moments…so much so that he swore he could hear his mother's anguished cries coming back down the years to haunt him. Such an incident had not occurred for ages. He couldn't help wondering why memories of his not so happy family should surface now. Determinedly, Blaise refocused on his work. After writing a particularly stirring scene between his female lead and her soldier suitor, he reached for the half-full cafetière and poured himself another cup of coffee. At least two hours had passed since Lottie had made it, and the dark bitter brew was barely warm, but he drank it all the same, mulling deeply over the words he had put onto the page in front of him.

The door to the connecting office opened and Maya reappeared.

'I don't want to disturb you, but I've been looking through some of the books on my shelf and making notes about what you might need—it's just an educated guess, I'm afraid, since we haven't discussed it in any length, but I thought I'd go upstairs to the library and see what I could find there.'

'Maya?'

'Yes?'

Blaise found himself hypnotised by her wide innocent gaze. 'I've scribbled down a short list of some things that might be useful.' Tearing out a page from his own book, he held it out to her. Glancing down at the contents, she couldn't hide the unfeigned excitement in her eyes, causing him to muse silently that she was the first woman he'd been intimately involved with who had expressed a genuine interest in his work. A frisson of unashamed pride and pleasure rippled through him.

'I'll crack on, then.'

'Take your time. We'll catch up later and talk over what you've got. I'll also need you to type out what I've done today.'

'That won't be a hardship. I'd love to see how the story's progressing.' Reaching the door that led into the hallway, Maya paused to venture a friendly smile. 'I hope the writing is going well for you,' she said encouragingly.

'I'm not doing badly so far.' He grinned back. 'By

the way, I didn't congratulate you on conquering your fear around dogs and taking Sheba for a walk earlier.'

'I loved being with her. And I think it's just like you said it would be…somehow I got the sense that she's looking after me and wants to protect me.'

Did she but know it, the expression on her face just then was like a lost little girl who'd just been found, and all Blaise's suppressed longing for her of that morning came hurtling back to the fore again…

When Maya arrived upstairs, a cloak of silence descended like muffled snow all around her. As she walked down the long, stately corridor towards the library, a shiver chased down her spine. *There were ghosts here…just like she'd sensed when they'd been walking by the wall outside…* Only these weren't ghosts of marching Roman soldiers—these were ghosts of family now gone.

She wondered why Blaise barely talked about his parents. After all, he had inherited the family home, and had already told her he'd lived here with them when he was young. Had something unpleasant happened between them? He'd already indicated that his father had had an explosive temper. Was that why he seemed so reticent about discussing his childhood?

Frowning, Maya reached the library and pushed open the door. It was cool inside and, tucking her pad against her chest, she folded her arms to get warm. The room was stunning, decorated in the style of its

Jacobean ancestry, but with some smart contemporary pieces of furniture dotted around too. Best of all, it was lined with bookshelves from floor to ceiling that were jam-packed with books, and in the middle of the far wall was the most beautiful inlaid marble fireplace. Above it hung a striking portrait of a handsome young dark-haired man. Moving closer to examine the picture, Maya felt a jolt a bit like a small lightning strike, jagged through her insides. The name of the artist was scrawled at the bottom right-hand corner, plain for all to see...*Alistair Devereaux*.

How did Blaise come to own one of her father's paintings? Why had he never told her about it? Studying the painting, with its exquisite confident brushstrokes and bold use of colour, Maya was catapulted back in time. Suddenly memories of all her father had meant to her—his love for her, his neglect of her and finally his complete and utter desertion of her—crashed down over her head. Furiously wiping her tears away, she was poignantly struck right then by how dangerously strong her feelings were becoming towards Blaise.

She should look out. If she got too close to him would *he* ultimately neglect her, reject her and desert her? Why shouldn't he do all those things? she asked herself. He was in the arts, as her father had once been, was well known by the media and fêted by an adoring public. What she knew of him so far seemed to suggest that he was fairly wary of commitment too... She'd be an utter idiot to let her heart be ensnared by such a man—no matter how charming, handsome, talented or good in bed. She'd best just stick to her resolve of having an affair and expect nothing else…*because she knew without a doubt that her self-preservation depended on it…*

At dinner that night, after what had turned out to be a very satisfying day's work, Blaise returned his half-drunk glass of Chardonnay to the table, avidly studying Maya's softly shadowed features in the flickering candlelight.

'By the way, tomorrow I'm giving you a car for your use while you're here. I thought you might like another MG, since you seem to know so much about them. What do you think?' he asked.

Carefully Maya touched her white linen napkin to her lips. She was wearing a very becoming multi-coloured maxi-dress, its swirls of soft verdant green in the pattern of the satiny material complementing the vivid emerald of her eyes, and Blaise found himself admiringly musing if there was a colour in existence that didn't complement her? He very much doubted it.

'Are you sure? If it's anything like the one we drove to Camden in it must be your pride and joy.'

'I trust that you're not going to be reckless and drive it into a brick wall. And if you do…' He lifted his broad shoulders in a careless shrug. 'I think I'll get over it. At the end of the day it's only a car.'

'My father was extremely possessive and protective

about his cars. If any one of them had been damaged in any way, I don't think he would have got over it so easily.'

'Was he as possessive and protective about you?'

'I think you already know the answer to that question.' She gazed at him steadily, and there was an air of defiance about her unwavering stare. When Blaise didn't probe further, she sighed, saying, 'I have a question for *you*. Why didn't you tell me you owned one of my father's paintings? The one in the library—though for all I know you may have others you haven't told me about.'

'I only have the one. The portrait of a young actor my father was mentoring. It was left to me when my parents died. To tell you the truth, I did plan on telling you about it, but I guess I just got wrapped up in work and forgot.'

'You didn't think I'd be interested in such a pertinent piece of information, seeing as the painter *was* my father?'

'Seems to me you have a lot of unresolved business concerning your father, Maya, and I get the feeling it really haunts you.'

'And it seems to me that you have a lot of unresolved business concerning your past too, Blaise! Or else why are you so reluctant to even talk about it? It's like you've built some kind of—of fortress around the subject, with a sign saying "Keep out".'

Inside his chest, Blaise's heartbeat accelerated. He'd been anticipating some pleasant and relaxed small talk over dinner, before finally doing the thing he craved the most…taking Maya to bed and enjoying a long, uninterrupted breathless night's lovemaking. What he *hadn't* been anticipating was that she would be challenging him on the one part of his life that he kept strictly private. The one topic that *wasn't* open to casual after-dinner conversation. He twisted his lips into a grimace.

'We all have skeletons in the closet, Maya. Why don't we just leave mine where they are?'

'What are you so afraid of? Aren't playwrights supposed to be bold and daring? Aren't they interested in exploring the mistakes of the past? Isn't that what you're doing in the play you're writing now?'

'What about your father's mistakes?' Blaise demanded, sensing his temper rise. 'It's clear you've been pretty damaged by them. What the hell good does it do to keep on revisiting the past? Answer me that!'

Across the table, Maya's shoulders drooped a little in an expression of defeat. 'You're right. I probably *am* damaged by what my father did—the way he lived and the way he died. I suppose I'm just trying to understand it all, really…that's all. I'm trying to understand it so that if I have children of my own I won't ever do what he did—put myself and my career and my so-called friends first, so much so that the children are neglected and left to fend for themselves. I'll show them every day that they mean the world to me, and love them so much that they'll never have a moment's doubt that they're not my top priority—no matter what else is going on in my life!'

Seeing the determination *and* distress mirrored in her lovely features, Blaise felt his heart helplessly contract. Recalling his own father's vile temper, and what the consequences of that had been like for him and his mother, he realised his home life had been a *fairytale* compared to what Maya had been through. There were no doubts in his mind that she would make a terrific mother one day…not to mention a wonderful wife to some very, very fortunate man.

'I found his body after he'd hung himself,' she told him softly.

CHAPTER TEN

SHAKING his head in disbelief, Blaise sensed his stomach violently turn over. 'What?'

Maya stared down at the table. Her long dark hair fell gently forward, partially shielding her.

'He was in his studio… I'd just returned from buying some groceries—he never thought about food when he was working and the cupboard was bare.' She glanced up and grimaced. 'I called out to him but he didn't answer. I knew he was working, trying his best to get something new going after a long period of not being able to work at all, so I put the food away and made us both a cup of tea.'

'You don't have to go on if this is too painful.'

'I want to. I haven't spoken to anyone about it for a long time, and I—and I need to.'

'Then I want to listen.'

'Anyway…I knocked on the door and called out again—not so loud as to disturb him from his train of thought, just clear enough that he could hear me. Still he didn't answer. I carefully opened the door and glanced in.'

Her chin wobbled a little, and Blaise's breath was suddenly trapped inside his chest.

'He was hanging by a rope he'd tied onto the chandelier—it was a fairly hefty, lavish affair—and little shards of glass lay shattered and broken beneath his feet on the table that he'd dragged over so that he could—so that he could—' Covering her face with her hand, she began to cry softly.

For a frozen second Blaise couldn't make himself move. Then he was on his feet, moving swiftly round to her side, pulling her gently upright and guiding her head down onto his chest. Almost immediately her hot tears dampened his shirt, and he rained tender little kisses over her silken hair, breathing in her sweetly perfumed shampoo and feeling her slender body shudder against him.

'Cry as much as you want to, sweetheart,' he crooned. 'I won't let you go. I'll just keep on holding you.'

'This isn't what you hired me for…to behave like some emotional wreck and have you take care of me.'

'Are you crazy? Do you honestly think it's a hardship for me to hold you like this after what we've shared?'

'All these years,' she whispered against his shirt, 'I've kept on thinking that if I'd only got back sooner… or if I hadn't gone to the shops at all…he might—he might still be here…'

'No, Maya…sweetheart, I think you're wrong.'

'How do you know?' Trustingly, hopefully, she raised her face to his.

Folding his palms round her slim upper arms, Blaise breathed in deeply. 'It sounds like he'd let himself descend too low into the pit of despair to be rescued by anyone…' Unable to resist, he traced the tracks of her tears with the pad of his thumb. 'Least of all you. He was meant to take care of you, Maya…not the other way round.'

'What if he tried his best to take care of me but he just couldn't? I can't keep on blaming him for that.'

Even now she was still protecting him, Blaise realised with incredulity. After all the man had put her through!

'You don't have to keep on blaming him, but he absolutely did not try his best to take care of you, Maya. Whatever you say, however much you may want to jump to his defence, he didn't try his best at all. He may have been an incredible artist, but it was his only daughter he should have lavished his love and devotion on first…even before his art.'

'To be honest, I think that sometimes he used his painting to escape the world—but don't we all do that in one form or another at times of stress or worry? Try to escape? Can I tell you something else? I don't always feel so forgiving towards him. Sometimes I *hate* him for what he did…how he behaved, how he put people who didn't even care about him before me. But the truth is I also loved him very much.'

'Most relationships are that complicated.'

'You know the strangest thing? After his funeral I had the strongest sense that he was looking after me at last. Instead of going to pieces, which is how I feared I might react, I felt this really warm sensation of peace and love wrap itself round me. It stayed with me for months…even when everything had to be sold to pay off his debts and I was forced to leave our home.'

'Where did you go?'

'A friend of mine was sharing a house with two other girls and they offered me a room. A couple of months before that—knowing that my father was in financial difficulty—I'd left school and got myself a job in an office, so that I could help support us. Anyway…'

She shrugged matter-of-factly, and her lips formed a tentative smile. As subtle as the gesture was, the sweet curve of her lips acted like a ray of pure sunlight, dazzling him.

'You're perfectly right. It doesn't do any good to keep revisiting the past—it can be an exercise doomed to make you miserable. It's what's happening now that we need to concentrate on, isn't it? I've told myself not to keep dwelling on things, and I *do* want to try and put everything that happened behind me, but still…it was a terrible thing, you know? To witness, I mean…'

'To even *imagine* it is terrible enough, Maya. And you had to cope with that devastating event all on your own. That takes tremendous courage.'

'I suppose I've never thought about it like that before. That I had courage… But I must have had it even to want to continue. And I have continued…I haven't given up. *I'm* still here and I have to count my blessings. I've got the rest of my life to live, right? I'm determined to put my whole self into whatever I do next—not have only half of me show up, which I think is what I've been doing all these years. It's time to move away from all the sadness—to go forward with a bit more optimism.'

'If anyone can do that, *you* can, Maya.'

'Blaise?'

'Hmm?'

'Thank you.'

'For what?'

'Listening.'

Her gratitude almost undid him—particularly when he thought it was singularly undeserved. 'Any time.'

'If *you* ever need someone to just listen…I'll be there for you too.'

Steadily he rested his gaze on her lovely face, but said nothing.

'I don't know why, but sometimes I get the feeling there's something from the past that really bothers you, Blaise. You don't show it outwardly—I mean you're very confident and successful at what you do—but it's just a sense I get. Is it—is it to do with your family?'

Stultifying mental shadows pressed close, and his

usual battle with the tide of hurtful memory gripped Blaise in a vice. 'Another time,' he replied gruffly. 'Another time perhaps I'll talk to you about it.'

Lowering his glance, he saw the doubt in her eyes and knew she had every right to doubt him. Resistance to discussing both his family and his fears about repeating his father's reprehensible behaviour was so strong in him that he took the path of avoidance every time...*every time*. Inside, he bitterly despaired that he would ever be any different.

The truth was that Maya was far more courageous than he could ever hope to be. She was willing to deal with the dark cloud of memory that sometimes enveloped her, had made a pact to try and move away from it, to be more optimistic about life. Perhaps all Blaise could do was keep on pouring his stifled emotion into his work instead? And maybe he should properly confront the fact that in all likelihood he would spend the rest of his life alone because of his inability to face up to things. One thing he was certain of: he would not venture into a long-term commitment with a woman with such a high risk of failure hanging over his head. *For who would stay with a man that might potentially harm them?* He especially wouldn't do that to a woman like Maya—someone who had already been hurt almost beyond imagining.

Maybe he had been selfish to embark on this passionate odyssey with her? She surely deserved better than just enjoying some explosive sex with a man who—despite his genuine concern for her—fully intended to kiss her goodbye some time soon? When she'd talked about her ex he had heard disappointment and hurt in her voice that her imagined happy future with him had come to naught, and in such a cruelly painful way too. Surely a short affair with Blaise would only confirm her opinion that all men were louses? *Users…who didn't give a damn about her as long as they got what they wanted?*

Dropping his hands to rest them lightly either side of her hips in her long satin dress, Blaise couldn't resist impelling her body closer to his, even though he was in turmoil about his right to intimacy with Maya at all.

Her scent made him feel hypnotised…drugged. And he wanted her again, with no lessening of the fierce need and burning desire that had seized him from almost the first moment he saw her. Reverently he touched his lips to her infinitely soft cheek.

'Let me take you to bed, Maya. It won't make the hurt go away, but it might help you forget for a while… And the truth is I need to make love to you… need it more than anything else in the world right now…'

When he reached out his hand for hers, Maya hesitated only a moment before silently slipping her palm into his…

Her fingers splayed lightly across Blaise's hipbone, Maya snuggled closer to his wonderful naked masculine form in the bed. 'Your skin feels like rough warm silk,' she told him, smiling up into his handsome face in the lamplight.

'And yours…there are no words to do such delicious softness justice. Except perhaps to say that I think heaven must feel like this. You're a revelation to me, you know? Yes, a revelation—as well as one very irresistible and tempting woman, Maya Hayward.'

'How tempting?' She touched him in the place where he was most sensitive and *most* aroused. Beneath her gently exploring fingers she sensed the warm silken length of his manhood pulse even harder into life. They had already shared some of the most combustible languorous kisses Maya could imagine—her lips still bore the exquisite aftermath of his alternately demanding then gentle mouth. Now she watched him rip open a slim foil packet to release the protective sheath inside, his brief examination of her teasing expression hot, libidinous and hungry.

'Climb on top and I'll show you, sweetheart.'

'You mean sometimes actions speak louder than words…even for a playwright?' She grinned.

Along with her seemingly insatiable desire for this man, there was a new lightness and playfulness skipping through her bloodstream that she hadn't known was even possible. Loving the sensation of her inner thighs gripping Blaise's lean, arrow-straight hips, she didn't take her gaze off his as he thrust upwards inside her with devastating intent. His blue eyes were like living, dangerous electricity, and she immediately felt him fill her to the hilt. He stayed there, rocking her gently, so that she was intimately acquainted with every wonderful inch of him, his hands clasping her hips.

Her head momentarily falling back, Maya shut her eyes. That sense of lightness pulsing through her body wasn't just because she'd finally decided to leave the past behind and move on...*it was because she was in love, she realised*. Her eyes shot open again. Blaise might not yet trust her enough to share whatever it was that troubled him, and he might have clearly hinted that he wasn't a man who welcomed long-term commitment either, but there it was. *She loved him*. Hugging the knowledge to her, she gazed down at him with a new sense of wonder and appreciation.

'Hey,' he said, his seductively low-pitched voice breaking a little, 'keep on looking at me like that and you may just have to stay right where you are for the rest of the night. Think you could handle that?'

Leaning towards Maya, he cupped her face, drawing her mouth urgently down to his before she could reply. As the heat and hardness of his demanding kiss avidly claimed her, she willingly returned his passionate fervour with all her heart, suddenly finding herself praying hard that one day, despite her intention to only enjoy a brief affair, he might love her back...that his love might lead to the dream of a happy, fulfilling union with a man that constantly eluded her.

'I think I could handle anything you wanted to give me, Mr Walker,' she murmured, nuzzling her face deep into the beguiling warmth of his neck…

He was outside walking by the wall again, with the wind in his hair and—it had to be said—a spring in his step. He didn't waste time speculating *why*. The reason was back at the house, eagerly continuing research for the play on Blaise's behalf and by all accounts loving every minute of it. It had taken a monumental effort on his part not to say to hell with it and keep Maya in bed for the rest of the day. But the plain fact of the matter was that he had a play to write, and it wouldn't progress any further if he lost himself in any more distractions…*delightful and engaging as they might be*.

No, he needed to delve deeper into his protagonist's character, needed to see what else it was besides a dream of a more exciting future that drove him to leave his family and join up with the Roman army, to travel to a foreign land and guard a border he had never even seen before.

After an hour and a bit of walking across the uneven crags, he felt the wind pick up and become ever more gusting as he passed the odd intrepid fellow walker on the way. Then finally, his head down and his mind intent on developing the storyline, Blaise had his answer. When it came he sucked in a breath and sensed his insides roll over.

It had been there all the time, hovering on the edge of his consciousness from the moment he'd come up with the play's concept, but unbelievably he had been playing the avoidance game again. Now it seemed there was no longer any place left to hide…

'How's the play going?'

'Hello, Jane.' Blaise rocked back in his chair with the phone receiver next to his ear and grinned. 'How's life in the great metropolis?'

'Answer my question first, and then I'll tell you.'

'The play's going fine. For the past two weeks I've hit a real blue streak.'

'Inspired, no doubt, by your visiting muse? How is she, by the way? The fact that she's still with you after two weeks and hasn't high-tailed it back to London tells me a lot.'

'Does it, indeed?'

'Yes—it tells me about her tenacity, for one thing…as well as about her resilience in continuing to work in the face of how temperamental and demanding you artistic types can be.'

Blaise frowned. 'Her father was an artist,' he said thoughtfully.

'That explains it, then. You're utterly charming and beguiling, darling, but we both know that when you're working sparks of artistic temperament are apt to fly!'

'I've changed!' he said jokingly. Then a second later

realised he meant it. He *had* changed since he'd been around Maya. She'd definitely been responsible for bringing out a much more mellow side in him—a side where he was a little less angry when things didn't immediately go his way, where he could actually relax in a woman's company and not feel the need to escape and be on his own at some point.

'She's great, by the way,' he remarked, finally answering Jane's question. Even just thinking about Maya made him grow warm. Right now she was in the adjoining office, typing up yesterday's work, and later that afternoon he was taking her into town so that they could enjoy tea at a five-star hotel.

'My, my...' Jane's voice lowered meaningfully. 'How the mighty are fallen.'

'What do you mean?'

'Are you falling for this girl, Blaise? I mean... *really* falling?'

He rocked forward again, feeling the skin between his brows pucker. 'You know I don't do happy-ever-after, Jane, so don't go getting your hopes up and looking at hats to wear to my wedding, will you?'

'You sound happier than usual—that's all I meant. When you talk about this woman your voice lights up.'

'Happiness doesn't last...*especially* where romantic relationships are concerned. Living with someone day after day is apt to take the rose-tinted edge off the illusion...or so I've heard. Why can't I simply enjoy what I have right now with Maya without it necessarily having to lead somewhere?'

'That's your prerogative, of course. Speaking as a friend, I just don't want to see you grow old and lonely on your own, I guess.'

'Well, I appreciate your concern, but do you honestly believe there *won't* be pretty and obliging women around to keep me company—*even* into my dotage?' Blaise chuckled, but the sound had a definitely *hollow* ring to it, even to his own ears…

CHAPTER ELEVEN

MAYA stared at the pretty watercolour of violets on the wall by the door to Blaise's office, feeling stunned and faint. She wished she could erase from her mind the words she'd just heard Blaise speak but knew that it was impossible. It was obvious now that she'd merely been deluding herself that he was beginning to feel something deeper for her because they'd been spending more and more time together. The bond she'd imagined they shared was nothing but a foolish and ridiculous pipe-dream on her part!

All their liaison had probably been about for a dedicated commitment-phobe like Blaise was great sex.

Shockwaves of distress and pain rolled sickeningly through her. With her hands shaking, she put down the sheaf of paper she had just printed out to add to the small growing pile on the desk that was the play, then opened the door to step out into the adjoining office.

Having finished his phone conversation, Blaise

glanced up and saw her. He was dressed in his trade-mark black again, the sombre colour somehow rendering him impossibly charismatic, adding a hint of seductive danger to good-looks that were already off-the-scale compelling. It also highlighted the dazzling glints of gold in his hair and the intense Mediterranean blue of his eyes. *The quick, easy smile on his handsome face all but broke Maya's heart.*

'I'm—I'm up to date with the typing and printing out,' she told him, desperately trying to control the quaver in her voice. 'I'd like to get a breath of fresh air now, if you don't mind?'

Eyes narrowing, Blaise got up and walked round the desk to join her. 'Is everything all right?'

'Of course.'

'Maya?' he pressed, clearly not believing her.

Twisting her hands in front of her, she suddenly couldn't contain the pain that was tearing her up inside and sensed it helplessly spill over.

'I was just wondering if I'd outstayed my welcome... if it wasn't time for some other "pretty and obliging" woman to replace me?'

The colour drained from his face. 'I was talking to my agent...you were listening to that?'

'Not intentionally.' She lifted her chin. 'I was about to come and tell you that I needed to get out for a while and inadvertently I heard you talking. It wasn't easy to hear...what you said, I mean...but I'm glad I heard you say it all the same. It was the wake-up call I needed. I'd rather dangerously started to fool myself about us, you see.'

'What about *us*?'

Did she imagine it, or was there suddenly a steely undertone to his voice? A firming of the fortress he had already built around his heart to keep out would-be threats to his emotions? Her spirits sank even lower.

'We're more than just two people working together—we've become lovers. I know I said I only wanted an affair, but naively I started to think that after enjoying intimacy together night after night it might make you want something a bit more. I thought that things had been progressing a little deeper between us than my just being your temporary assistant and bedmate.'

'You *do* mean more to me than that, Maya…much more. You're an exceptional and beautiful woman, and I find myself in awe of what you've had to overcome in life to even get this far. I couldn't have accomplished what I've done so far on the play without you, and—'

'Let me finish.' She folded her arms across her chest, and her hurt glance was withering. 'And my contribution has been invaluable? Was that what you were going to say next? For God's sake, you make me sound like some naïve little schoolgirl who should be grateful for every crumb of praise and attention you deign to throw my way!'

'As wonderful as it's been, I thought you knew—

thought you realised that even though we're sleeping together this isn't going to be a permanent situation.'

Blaise's words fell on the air like daggers, slicing Maya in two. Lifting the heavy weight of her dark hair off the back of her neck, she pursed her lips, fielding the waves of pain that made her whole body tremble with distress.

'Sometimes a situation can change from—from what you expected into something else…something even *better*…if you let it…' she offered quietly.

When Blaise's intense examination of her turned into the deepest frown, making her sense both his regret *and* frustration that she was instigating a situation he was clearly uncomfortable with and probably deplored, a shattering moment of shocking self-discovery assailed her. *She was no different from her father…for she too had become an addict.* Yes, she'd become addicted to a man who clearly only wanted her for the pleasure her body could give him—and even that for just a brief time. For, after she'd gone, Maya was certain it wouldn't be long before Blaise found himself another 'adoring and willing' woman to warm his bed.

Because she had this terrible aching need to experience real love from a man she'd allowed herself to be seduced by him—even when in her heart she'd always known their liaison was doomed not to last. And when he had shown such depth of understanding and compassion towards her after hearing about her difficult and painful past, she'd fooled herself into believing that he must really care for her. That was why his announcement that he'd thought she *knew* their relationship was not destined to last had struck her like a hammer-blow. What a blind fool she'd been! How could she once more have made the same destroying mistake in a relationship? Would she ever be able to trust her instincts again? Swallowing hard, Maya knew all she could do right then was think about leaving and chalk up her experience as another painful dalliance with the universally recognised school of hard knocks.

'Maya, listen…' Blaise was saying. 'You deserve the best man that's out there. Someone who can be the real hero I sense you need. But that man isn't me.' Regretfully he shook his head, dropping his hands in a futile gesture to his arrow-straight hips. 'I don't want you to go, and I'm not looking to replace you with anyone else—I swear it. But neither do I want to lead you on and make you hope for something that I'm just not in a position to deliver.'

'Because you refuse to let a woman get close enough to even try? What you're telling me is that you'd rather just "adore" as many women as possible and let the chance or possibility of something more enduring…something more *meaningful*…pass you by? That sounds like a pretty lonely, not to mention *empty* existence to me, if you don't mind my saying so. Not that you give a damn *what* I think! And by the way…you've got me all wrong.'

With her heart pounding loud enough in her chest for

her to hear every unhappy beat, Maya squared up to Blaise without flinching.

'I'm not looking for a hero. All I want is a man who's willing to spend the rest of his life with me because he loves me. I'm not looking for perfection. Just someone a little flawed, like myself, who'll be as accepting of my less than perfect qualities as I would be of his. We'd work together to try and overcome them. And finally I want someone who doesn't believe the grass is greener somewhere else—who is happy with what he already has. I want a man with the innate capacity to be loyal, as *I* would be loyal to him. I'm going out for that walk in the fresh air now, and when I get back I'll be packing my bags.'

She turned at the door, jerking her head towards the office she'd been occupying. 'By the way, you'll find the work I did this morning on my desk. You'll have to hire somebody else to type out the rest, but I'm sure as long as she does what you want, is easy on the eye and obliging, you'll hardly even notice that it's not me!'

New York, six weeks later

'Want to go for a beer or a cocktail somewhere?' Shrugging into his cashmere coat in the theatre foyer, amid the crush of well-wishers and the congratulatory smiles of satisfied patrons, critics and colleagues, Blaise felt distinctly uneasy as his diminutive agent gave him one of her slow 'I've got you taped' assessing glances.

'That lonely apartment you've been living in for the past month getting to you already?' she probed, her small, cropped blonde head erect, hazel eyes narrowed like a cat about to pounce on some poor unsuspecting mouse.

'I can get as much company as I need whenever I choose,' he snapped back, glancing round as a pretty redhead squeezed deliberately by him—one of the ensemble actresses in the production—giving him both a coy and invitational smile before reluctantly disappearing through the rotating theatre doors when he didn't respond.

'That's hardly in dispute, darling,' Jane replied, eyes rolling. The edges of her scarlet painted mouth softened somewhat. 'But when your mind is fixed on one particular person's company alone not even Angelina Jolie herself could fill the gap. Heard from her at all since you came to New York…? Your sad-eyed raven-haired little temporary assistant, I mean?'

'No.' Appalled at how bleak he sounded, Blaise shifted from one lean hip to the other. 'She has no idea that I left the UK a month ago. But then why should she? After she left I didn't keep in contact. It was only after spending two impossible weeks in Northumberland trying to work on that damn play alone that I decided I finally couldn't stand it and came here.'

Reaching for his usual acerbic humour to deflect any further near-the-knuckle questions from Jane, he defensively squared his jaw.

'Are you thirsty or aren't you? Even the most faded

blooms appreciate the odd drink of water to stop them from shrivelling up and dying, so I'm told!'

She whacked him with her shiny patent leather designer handbag—*hard*.

The foyer had emptied quickly, and outside on the sidewalk umbrellas were hurriedly opening to face the downpour that was spilling from the skies onto the somewhat chilly New York night.

'Faded bloom, my backside! At least I'm going back to my hotel to the man I've been married to for twenty years and who still thinks I hung the moon! Whereas *you*…'

Rubbing his arm where she'd hit him, Blaise scowled. 'Whereas *I* am apparently destined to walk into the sunset alone…*boo-hoo*. No doubt you think I deserve it.' He shook his head as if to shake off the deepening sense of gloom that made him feel heavy as concrete.

For six long weeks he hadn't even had the guts to pick up the phone and speak to Maya, let alone beg her for-giveness…which was exactly what he should have done. Instead he'd let her leave, as if she was as dispensable and replaceable as one of the stack of inexpensive pens he kept in his desk drawer. He either had to face the fact that he was too scared to overcome the childhood fears his family life had left him with, give them up and move on—or realise that he was a genuine twenty-four-carat *bastard* who seriously needed the help of a good psychologist. All he knew was that nothing meant anything to him any more since he'd let Maya go…not even his work. *Including* the play that was currently setting Broadway alight after just two nights.

'Seriously, I could do with a couple of drinks, and I don't want to drink alone tonight. You're about the only one I know who'll talk straight to me and isn't after something… I make no apology for my cynicism, but I do ask your forgiveness for any unkind remarks I may have made earlier. I was actually quite pleased when you rang me to say you were coming over here for a short visit to see how the play was doing. Can you forgive me for my previous bad manners?'

'Sure I can. Lucky for you I was born with such a sweet nature.' Latching onto his arm, Jane reached up on her four-inch stiletto heels and planted a noisy smacker on his cheek. 'Plus I never could resist a handsome well-spoken man when he grovels so nicely!'

'I'm not grovelling, so don't get too carried away. I still only tolerate you because you're my agent.'

'Yeah, and next week they're crowning me the Queen of England!'

'No, no, no, Maya, *querida*! Let me get that. You mustn't lift heavy things now, remember?'

Straightening up from the box of crockery she'd just been about to lift onto the granite worktop of her new flat's kitchen, Maya glanced at her helpful friend Diego with a mixture of exasperation and gratitude. Sturdily built, with the shoulders of a flanker in a rugby team, the Spaniard had practically single-handedly packed and moved the contents of her old studio flat to her new two-bedroom abode down the road in Kensal Rise.

Never mind his usually macho sensibilities—he'd been like the proverbial mother hen round Maya ever since she'd confided to him that she was pregnant. Although not before he'd furiously vowed to 'rough up' the ne'er do well who had thoughtlessly got her in the family way, leaving her to face the prospect of motherhood on her own. When he'd told her that his aunt had a house in Kensal Rise that she rented out, and that the ground-floor flat had recently become vacant, Maya had increased her working hours for the temp agency to meet the new rent, and had even been putting a little by towards the day when she would have to give up her job completely to take care of her baby.

'I'm not going to harm myself if I lift a few light boxes, Diego!' she chided her friend, wincing as he deposited the full-to-the-brim cardboard box onto the counter with a little too much gusto and she heard something inside rattle alarmingly. 'I'm only eight weeks pregnant, and I don't even show yet.'

The Spaniard's dark brown eyes visibly softened as they moved down to Maya's still flat belly beneath her loose white shirt and faded jeans.

'Yet the fact is that you are growing a little one inside you who needs you to be careful and not take unnecessary risks that could harm him or his mother.'

'You know what, Diego?' Her lips tugging upwards in an affectionate smile, exasperation forgotten, Maya touched her palm gently to his roughened cheek. 'One of these days, when you meet the right woman, you're going to be the best father in the whole wide world.'

'And if my wife is as good and beautiful as you, Maya, I will be the happiest man in the whole wide world too!' His pleased grin was quickly followed by a concerned frown. 'Does that crazy, irresponsible man of yours even know what he has done? What he has so foolishly given up?'

Maya flinched, her heart and stomach turning over at the thought of Blaise—at her profound longing to see him again, and at the dreadful hurt and sense of rejection she'd experienced when she'd had to walk away from him in Northumberland and go home. Acute apprehension also deluged her at the prospect of telling him she was pregnant with his child. She'd read in the papers that for the past few weeks he'd been in New York, overseeing the London play that had transferred there. But sooner or later he would be home again, and Maya would have to tell him her news.

After the initial great shock of discovering her condition, she'd been consumed with instant love and strong feelings of protection towards her unborn infant. In her eyes it was an utter miracle, and she felt truly blessed. Even though it wasn't the future she'd dreamed of…to raise a child alone. But how would

Blaise react to the news? *Would he be angry or deadly calm?* Would he reject the reality of her pregnancy completely and deny all responsibility? Or would he want to take charge and calmly make arrangements for the baby's future like some distant, remote stranger, displaying no love or concern for the child's welfare whatsoever?

'He—he's not a man that finds commitment easy, Diego. I think something must have happened when he was young to make him fear it somehow, but he won't discuss it. I told you that. And, to be fair, I guessed that even before I—before we—' She blushed hotly. 'It's unfortunate, but I'm sure when he hears the news he'll want to do the right thing all the same.'

'And if he does not,' Diego growled crossly, folding his arms across his ample chest in his treasured FC Barcelona T-shirt, 'as God is my witness he will have to answer to me!'

Hawk's Lair, Northumberland

His eyes glued to the details of the art auction, and the brief words about it at the beginning of the newspaper article, Blaise sucked in a deep breath, heavily blowing it out again as he tried to get his head round what he'd just read.

'Would you like some more coffee, my dear?' Lottie was hovering beside him, keeping one eye on the sizzling pan of bacon and eggs she was cooking for his breakfast on the stove as well as stealing a curious glance over his shoulder at what he was reading.

'Yes… I mean no, thanks. I've got to go and make a phone call. Excuse me.'

'What about your breakfast?' the housekeeper exclaimed, her voice dismayed as Blaise shot out of his chair and strode to the door.

'Sorry, Lottie… I've got far more important things to think about this morning. Give it to Tom. I'm sure he'd welcome a second breakfast!'

CHAPTER TWELVE

WHEN the phone call came to an end Maya had to sit down, because her legs were shaking so much. She'd scribbled something down on the notepad she now gripped between her hands like a life-raft, and, staring down at what she'd written, she felt a hundred differing emotions storm through her like a cyclone. There was a burning sensation behind the backs of her eyelids, and suddenly tears were sliding and slipping down her cheeks in a hot stream. Not troubling to wipe them away, she slowly moved her head from side to side, as regret and a sadness almost too hard to bear welled up inside her.

'It's time to say goodbye,' she whispered brokenly, 'but I promise I'll never forget you.'

A minute later she got up, put on her trench-coat because outside it had started to rain, locked the door, and then walked rapidly down the street towards the bus stop to catch a bus that would drop her off near Diego's place.

Today was the beginning of a whole new life for her after what she'd just heard, and she needed to share her hopes and fears for the future with a friend...a *good* friend.

It was late in the afternoon by the time Maya got to Camden. The sky had darkened early because of the storm clouds that had gathered overhead, and most of the shoppers were heading homewards. Diego's distinct, brightly painted coffee bar, with its blue-and-white neon sign flickering in the window, was almost empty. The man himself was behind the counter, avidly scanning the sports page in a newspaper, while his young assistant Maria was busy wiping down tables. He glanced up in delight when he heard the bell over the door jangle and saw who it was.

'Maya, *querida*! How are you today?' Moving round the counter with all the grace of a much slimmer man, he enveloped her in a fierce hug. 'Is everything all right? I am surprised to see you when I know the smell of coffee makes you queasy in your condition.'

'I couldn't let a small thing like that stop me visiting you.' Maya smiled, then realised Diego was examining her a little too closely, concernedly shaking his head. 'You have been crying, *querida*...what has happened? Sit down and tell me everything.'

Her friend ordered Maria to bring her a banana milkshake—for the baby!—and they sat opposite each other at a newly cleaned table, under the eye-catching poster of a flamenco dancer dressed in sultry red and black decorating the wall behind them.

Having only just begun her story, Maya glanced round at the sound of the bell jangling above the door and sucked in a shocked breath. *It was Blaise.* She blinked hard to make sure she wasn't dreaming, but she'd know that flawless azure gaze, the carved jaw and the chin with the sexy little crease down the centre anywhere. Her insides mimicked the same intense flamenco as the dancer in the poster.

'What are you doing here?' she asked, and her mouth felt dry as a sun-baked beach at the height of summer. 'I thought you were in New York?'

'I came to find you,' he replied hoarsely, for long moments just standing still and surveying her. Maya knew her gaze must match his for sheer hunger as she stared back at him. He looked every inch the successful Broadway playwright, dressed in a stylish mackintosh, the gold in his hair glistening with damp from the rain.

'I went to your old place and a neighbour told me you'd moved. She wouldn't give me your new address, but she told me that a friend of yours owned this coffee bar and would probably give you a message for me.'

'This is Diego,' Maya murmured, her glance shifting away from his for the briefest second towards the older man sitting opposite her. 'This is his place.'

'Pleased to meet you.' Moving towards their table, Blaise stuck out his hand.

The Spaniard made no move to take it. Instead he abruptly pushed himself to his feet, his expression definitely suspicious. 'And you are…?'

'Blaise Walker.'

'So you are the man that—'

'It's all right, Diego.' With a pleading look Maya managed to still what he had been going to say next. 'I'm sure Blaise isn't staying long…are you?'

'I wouldn't be too sure about that. I need to talk to you, Maya…however long it takes.'

'I need to talk to you too. So maybe—maybe we should go back to my place? We can get a bus just down the road…'

'My car's parked round the corner.'

Feeling queasy, as well as apprehensive, Maya got slowly to her feet. With trembling fingers she attempted to refasten the buttons on her coat, but quickly gave up and left it open. Whatever she and Blaise had to say to each other, it wasn't a conversation to be aired in public. Yet her stomach was fluttering wildly with nerves at the mere thought of being alone with him again. Not only that but probably having to say goodbye to him a second painful time after he'd said what he had to say and then left.

'Diego, I'll give you a call later on tonight, okay?'

'Make sure you do,' the Spaniard replied gruffly, now regarding Blaise with not just suspicion but also antagonism in his eyes. 'I am not happy about how you looked when you came in, and I want to hear what you were going to tell me and make sure everything is okay.'

'It will keep...and I'll be fine. I promise.'

Saying nothing, his expression implacable, Blaise held the door open for her to precede him out into the rain.

She'd lost a little weight, he saw with a flicker of alarm. Her cheekbones were more pronounced, the smooth, perfect skin stretched over them like pale satin, making her spellbinding emerald eyes seem huge and her luminous beauty even more incandescent. But so many feelings, sensations and fears kept hitting him that it was difficult for Blaise to stay with one train of thought for long. Ever since he'd let her go the only thought that had been and still *was* constant was that he missed her. He missed her so much that it was as if he'd been inflicted with some agonising chest wound that wouldn't heal. He'd called himself all kinds of imbecile for doing what he'd done, but insults and fury hadn't helped. Not when there was still the same underlying fear that daily ate away at his soul—a corrosive terror that almost paralysed him and stopped him from doing what his heart all but begged and pleaded with him to do.

When he'd seen that article about the art auction in the newspaper it had finally galvanised him into action...finally told him it was time to conquer his fears and make the one decision he needed to make above all others.

His gaze flicked interestedly round the recently painted living room of Maya's new flat, noting the more comfortable furnishings and furniture and the sense of space that had been so severely lacking in her previous tiny abode.

During the car journey to get here she had haltingly told him about the opportunity that had come up to move to a bigger place—how she had eagerly grasped it with both hands and how Diego had helped her move. Having met the surly Spaniard who owned the coffee bar Maya liked to frequent, Blaise silently owned to feeling quite put out that she was friends with such a man…*a man who had looked at him as if he'd like to punch a fist right in the centre of his gut.* He smirked grimly.

A couple of pretty cards wishing her happiness in her new home graced the magnolia-painted mantelpiece, he noticed, fighting to gain control over the growing feelings of jealousy and possessiveness that poured through him. *Who had sent her the cards? Was she seeing someone?* Sitting quietly on the sofa across the floor from where he stood, her long legs encased in sheer black hosiery and her hands calmly folded in the lap of her deep burgundy skirt, Maya met his glance steadily, with no hint of the strong emotion that currently tormented Blaise.

'What made you sell the portrait?' he heard himself demand, his heart thudding because it wasn't the first thing he wanted to do. Even now he had to wrestle with the almost overwhelming urge to just haul her up from where she sat and kiss her senseless.

Her emerald gaze remained steady. 'You heard about the sale?'

'How could I not? It made the news in most of the papers, I should think.'

'I needed the money.' Her slender shoulders lifted in what looked like a resigned shrug. 'It was as simple as that.'

'You needed the money before, if the place you lived in was any indication!' Blaise couldn't contain the impatience in his voice. 'Why decide to sell it now?'

'Because there's not just myself to think about any more.'

'You're seeing someone else?'

Everything inside him constricted with despair, fury and tension. *Why had he left it so long to contact her after she left? Why? Why? Why?*

'I'm not seeing anyone else.' Sighing, she rose slowly to her feet, her hands linking restlessly together. 'I'm pregnant, Blaise. I'm afraid I made a mistake about it being a safe time.'

'Pregnant?' The word filled his mind like a snowstorm, blotting out all other thoughts.

'That's why I needed to sell the portrait. I'm keeping the baby, whatever you decide to do, and I didn't want him or her brought up in an atmosphere of tension and uncertainty like I was. I wanted to give my baby a better start and a more secure future.'

'You're going to have a baby? *My* baby?' Again the knowledge deluged him, making it almost impossible to think with any clarity. Then came the terrible fear that he couldn't possibly be a proper father to the child—not if there was the remotest chance that he would turn out like his own father. But in the next instant that unhappy thought died away, and Blaise started to feel genuine excitement and joy pulse through his bloodstream. It took two to make a baby, and ideally two to be his parents and take care of him. Whatever happened, he and Maya were in this together.

'There's no doubt that the baby is yours, Blaise.' Her teeth nibbled a little anxiously at her soft lower lip. 'I've been with no one else.'

'I'm not suggesting anything like that.' He frowned. 'Are you okay? Have you seen a doctor?'

'Both me and the baby are doing just fine.'

'But the portrait…it meant everything to you. I can't believe you sold it. It was a little piece of your father, you said.'

'At the end of the day it's just a painting…if a valuable one. I was shocked to learn just how valuable. But I'll use the money wisely… I'm sure—I'm sure if my dad were alive he'd want me to use it to help take care of his grandchild.'

'Were you going to let me know about the baby?'

A shadow of hurt flickered in her eyes. 'Of course… But I knew you were in New York with the play, and that I'd have to wait until you came back to tell you face to face.'

'How far along are you?'

'Nine weeks.'

Blaise rubbed his hand round the back of his neck, thinking hard. Impatiently he pulled his tie loose from his shirt collar so that he could breathe easier. *It wasn't every day that a man who had been contemplating a decidedly lonely future learned that he was to become a father, and it took some sinking in to get used to the idea.* But the more he contemplated it, the more he sensed a wild exhilaration and sense of purpose gathering momentum inside him, instead of fear and apprehension consuming him.

'So…I'm to become a father?'

'Are you angry?'

'Are you serious? How can I be angry when this must be the most incredible piece of news I've ever heard?' In front of Maya now, Blaise caught hold of her worryingly chilled hands and held them, infusing them with the heat from his own.

'You mean it?'

'Yes, I mean it! Though I understand why you have your doubts. I'm not proud of the way I behaved, Maya. The way I so easily let you leave and made no attempt to stop you or contact you afterwards.'

Saying nothing, she simply listened.

'I would never have expected you to raise the baby on your own,' he continued, his voice hoarse with regret that she might have believed that. 'I would always have supported him—and you.' Lifting those cold, slender hands to his lips, he tenderly kissed each one in turn.

'So what exactly are you telling me, Blaise? That you want joint custody when the time comes?'

'No, that's not what I'm saying at all.'

'Then—'

Letting go of her hands, Blaise urgently encircled Maya's slender waist to impel her hard against him. For a moment his senses were saturated by her warmth and those delicious feminine curves, and the unmatched feeling of holding her in his arms again almost over-whelmed him.

'I was such a fool to let you go…' He dragged the pad of his thumb over her plump lower lip, sensing heat inflame him as he saw it quiver. 'I had my reasons…but in the cold light of day they seemed preposterous when I started to examine them. But before I tell you about that, I need to ask you something.'

'What is it?'

'Will you marry me?'

Her expression was genuinely shocked, as if that was the very *last* thing she'd expected Blaise to ask her. He could only blame himself for that, he mused bitterly.

'But you're not a man who wants commitment.' She was looking distinctly puzzled. 'You adore women but haven't found one yet that you want to spend the rest of your life with. You made it clear that the possibility of us staying together long-term wasn't even on the cards…that we could enjoy a brief affair but nothing more—least of all marriage.'

'I was wrong. I was wrong because I *did* meet someone I wanted to spend the rest of my life with…*you*, Maya. I used to trot out that rubbish because I couldn't get past the fear that if I committed to a woman I would turn out like my father…become bitter and resentful and harm her in some way.'

'Harm her? Why would you believe that?'

'Because that's what my father did to my mother, and I seem to have inherited his propensity to lose my temper.' He dropped his head for a moment, acutely uncomfortable at finally admitting what he'd been most afraid of.

'Everyone has a temper, Blaise. Even the most seemingly docile people… It's normal…human.' Gently, Maya touched her hand to his cheek and made him look at her. 'It doesn't mean that they're going to be violent.'

'My mother said to me once that she prayed I wouldn't turn out like my father. She loved him passionately, but she was afraid of him too. He'd always been hell to live with. Growing up with such a volatile man was a nightmare sometimes. I never forgot what she said to me. Every time I sensed rage in me I'd wonder—was that a sign? Was I going the same way as him? I even started to jeopardise the new play I've been writing because I wasn't fully exploring the lead character's motivation for leaving home. It wasn't just about him trying to make a dream of happiness come true—*his* father was violent too. That's what ultimately drove him away.'

'It must have been very painful for you all these years—not being able to tell anyone how you felt. I've learned that keeping our fears to ourselves is never the answer, Blaise. They just get bigger and bigger if we don't bring them out into the open and see them for what they really are. They're just ideas we get about ourselves because of something that happens. They're not the truth. I thought similarly to you. I thought because my father behaved like he did, and put all his friends before me, that must mean I was unlovable. When Sean deceived me with another woman it confirmed that view. I felt totally rejected and worthless. I thought our whole relationship had been a lie, based on my fantasies about a happy future together. But then I met you, Blaise, and for the first time I *really* and truly fell for someone.'

'Well, let me tell you now, the notion that you must be unlovable is totally ludicrous!'

Fastening his hands either side of her curvaceous hips, Blaise gave her a brief, hungry, hard kiss on the mouth. When he lifted his head again he was beaming.

'You are the most lovable woman I've ever known… that's ultimately why I couldn't resist you. And I'm going to spend the rest of my life showing you that it's true… It was my own stupid fault, but you broke my heart when you left, Maya.' Lightly he swept back a stray ebony strand of hair where it glanced against her cheek. 'I haven't been able to work, eat or sleep since you went. I'm sure everyone in New York thought I was a miserable git!'

'No...' Softly but emphatically the word left Maya's lips. Incredibly, she was regarding him just as Jane had described the way her husband looked at *her*—as if he'd hung the moon.

'You're not morose or violent or any of those dark things, Blaise... You're just a man who's been hurt. That's hardly a crime.'

'Well, I'm certainly no hero—not the one you deserve. But I am a man who loves you very much and can't live without you.'

'I didn't mean to break your heart.' Maya sighed. 'I only wanted to try and help mend it.'

'Marry me,' he said again, dropping a tender kiss at the side of her mouth. 'Marry me and put me out of my misery once and for all.'

She could hardly believe the urgency in his loving demand. It seemed like a dream when Maya had more than half expected him to reject her all over again after he heard about the baby. She was gratified that he had at last told her why he had let her walk away. Not because he didn't want her...but because he was afraid if he properly committed to a relationship he might end up hurting her physically, just like his father had done to his mother. She could understand how having a fear like that must have haunted him.

The weeks without him had been some of the most despairing Maya had ever spent. All she'd been able to do was think about him, remembering with longing how passionately they had made love and aching down to the very marrow in her bones to see him again. *Her yearning had been multiplied when she'd found out she was carrying his child.* Now he had asked her to marry him, and there really *was* only one answer she could give him.

'I love you, Blaise… I'm not a bit afraid that you would ever hurt me *or* our child, and of course I'll marry you.'

'Wait here.'

'Why?'

She watched in vague alarm as he swiftly left the room. Seconds later she heard the front door open. With her heart helplessly knocking against her ribs, Maya waited anxiously for his return. When he came, he was carrying something square, carefully wrapped in brown paper. He placed it into her hands. The rain had dampened his hair again, and she longed to thread her fingers through the thick gold strands and bring his face down to hers for a long, lingering kiss. Stifling the urge, she stared at the package he'd given her.

'Open it. It's for you,' he urged softly. 'Think of it as an early wedding present.'

Carefully tearing some of the paper packaging away,

Maya gasped when she saw what it was…*her portrait.* Confused as well as elated, she caught her lip between her teeth to stop her emotion from overwhelming her. 'You bought the portrait…to give to me?'

'I knew something had happened when I saw it was up for sale. You would never have sold it unless there was some absolutely compelling reason.' Relieving her of the picture, Blaise laid it against the couch and came straight back to her. 'There's only one place where that portrait belongs, and that's with *you*, sweetheart.'

Reaching out, Maya put her hands against his chest, her expression wide-eyed and shocked.

'But you paid a fortune for it, Blaise! So much money that just the thought of it makes my head spin!'

'If I'd spent ten thousand times that amount it wouldn't be as valuable as you are to me, my darling.'

'I don't know what to say… I'm so overwhelmed that I think I'm going to—'

Blaise's lips covered hers, his tongue slipping hotly into her mouth. He pressed her body close into his even as the tears in her eyes spilled over onto her cheeks. Crying and kissing him at the same time, Maya knew her heart was so full she could hardly comprehend so much joy was possible. Her legs went weak as a newborn lamb's as his deepening kiss and hungrily searching hands on her body made her melt and yearn and ache to hold him closer, without the barrier of clothing.

As if reading her mind, he suddenly scooped an arm

behind her back and lifted her up into his arms, his extraordinary eyes hazy with longing, his well-cut lips quirking in a teasing, provocative grin that made Maya dissolve inside even more.

'As much as I love them, and earn my living by them, I think the time for words has definitely passed, don't you? Where's the bedroom, my darling wife-to-be?'

SWEET SURRENDER
WITH THE MILLIONAIRE

BY
HELEN BROOKS

Helen Brooks lives in Northamptonshire, and is married with three children and three beautiful grandchildren. As she is a committed Christian, busy housewife, mother and grandma, her spare time is at a premium, but her hobbies include reading, swimming and gardening, and walks with her husband and their two Irish terriers. Her long-cherished aspiration to write became a reality when she put pen to paper on reaching the age of forty and sent the result off to Mills & Boon.

CHAPTER ONE

SHE'D done it! It was finally hers. A place where after all the trauma and misery of the last few years she could pull up the drawbridge—metaphorically speaking—and be in her own world. Answerable to no one. No matter it was going to take her years to get the cottage sorted; she could do it at her own pace and it would fill her evenings and weekends, which was just what she wanted. Anyway, if it had been in pristine condition she wouldn't have been able to afford it.

Willow Landon heaved a satisfied sigh and then whirled round and round on the spot before coming dizzily to a halt as she laughed out loud. She was in control of her life again, that was what this cottage meant, and she was *never* going to relinquish that autonomy again.

She gazed round the small empty sitting room, and the peeling wallpaper and dusty floorboards could have been a palace, such was the expression on her rapt face. Walking across to the grimy French doors in which the glass was cracked and the paintwork flaking, she opened them onto the tangled jungle of a garden. Monstrous nettles and brambles confronted her, fighting for supremacy with waist-high weeds and aggressive ivy, which had wound itself over bushes and trees until the whole had become a wall of green. It was impossible to see any grass or paths, but she thought she could spy what looked like an old potting shed in front of the stone wall at the end of what the estate agent had assured her was a quarter of an acre of ground.

She shut her eyes for a moment, imagining it as it would be when she'd finished with it. Roses and honeysuckle climbing the drystone walls, benches and a swinging seat on the smooth green lawn and little arbours she'd create, a fountain running over a stone water feature. She'd cultivate lots of old-fashioned flowers: foxgloves, angelica, lupins, gillyflowers, larkspur, and pinks—*lots* of fragrant pinks and wallflowers and stock. And she'd have her own vegetable plot. But those plans were for the future. For now she'd simply clear the jungle and rake the ground free of the worst of weeds and debris for the winter. The most pressing thing was to get the house in shape, and that would take plenty of elbow grease, patience and money. The first two she had, the third would filter in month by month when she saw what she had left after paying the mortgage and bills.

Her mobile phone rang, and as she fished it out of her jeans pocket and saw the number she sighed inwardly even as she said, 'Hi, Beth,' her tone deliberately bright.

'Willow.' Her name was a reproach. 'I've just phoned the flat and one of the girls told me you moved out today. I can't believe you didn't tell us it was this weekend you're moving. You know Peter and I wanted to help.'

'And I told you that with you being seven months pregnant there was no way. Besides which you're still trying to get straight yourself.' Beth and her husband had only moved from their tiny starter home into a larger three-bedroomed semi two weeks before. 'Anyway, I've had loads of offers of help but it's not necessary. I shall enjoy cleaning and sorting out at my own pace. I've got a bed and a few bits of furniture being delivered this afternoon, but there's so much to do here I don't want to buy much as each room will need completely gutting and the less I have to lug about, the better.'

'But to attempt to move on your *own*.' Beth made it sound as though Willow had gone off to Borneo or outer Mongolia on some hazardous expedition. 'Have you got food in for the weekend?'

Before Willow could reply there was the sound of someone speaking in the background. Then Beth's voice came high and indignant. 'Peter says I'm acting as though you're eight years old instead of twenty-eight. I'm not, am I?'

Willow smiled ruefully. She loved her sister very much and since their parents had been killed in a car crash five years ago they'd become even closer, but she had to admit she was relieved Beth would soon have her baby to fuss over. At thirty, Beth was definitely ready to be a mum. Soothingly—but not absolutely truthfully—she murmured, 'Course not. Look, I've taken some holiday I had owing to get straight. I'll pop in for a chat soon.'

'Great. Come on Monday and stay for dinner,' Beth shot back with alacrity.

Again Willow sighed silently. The planning office in Redditch where she'd worked since leaving university was a stone's throw from Beth's new place, and not far from the house she'd shared with three friends for the last twelve months. The cottage, on the other hand, was an hour's drive away, the last fifteen minutes of which on twisting country lanes. Until she'd got familiar with the journey she would have preferred to drive home while it was still light. Now, in late September, the nights were dropping in. But if she suggested going to see Beth for lunch instead it would mean virtually a whole day's work at the cottage was lost. 'Lovely,' she said dutifully. 'I'll bring dessert but it'll be shop-bought, I'm afraid.'

They talked a little more before Willow excused herself by saying she had a hundred and one things to do, but she didn't immediately get to work. Instead she sank down on the curved stone steps that led from the French doors into the garden. She breathed in the warm morning air, her face uplifted to the sun. Birds twittered in the trees and the sky was a deep cornflower blue. Silly, but she felt nature had conspired with her to give her a break and make moving day as easy as it could be. It was a good start to the rest of her life anyway.

A robin flew down to land on the bottom of the three steps, staring at her for a moment with bright black eyes before darting off. She continued to gaze at the spot where the bird had been, but now her eyes were inward-looking.

This was what the cottage signified: the start of the rest of her life. The past was gone and she couldn't change it or undo the huge mistake she'd made in getting involved with Piers in the first place, but the present and the future were hers now she was free of him. It was up to her to make of them what she would. Just a few months ago she had wanted the world to end; life had lost all colour and each day had been nothing more than a battle to get through before she could take one of the pills the doctor had prescribed and shut off her mind for a little while. But slowly she'd stopped taking the pills to help her sleep, had begun to eat again, been able to concentrate on a TV programme or read a book without her mind returning to Piers and that last terrible night.

She lifted up her slender arms, purposely channelling her mind in a different direction as she stretched and stood up. It had taken time, but she was able to do this now and she was grateful for it. In fact it had probably saved her reason. Whatever, she was herself again—albeit an older, wiser self.

Turning, she went back inside and through the house to the front door. Her trusty little Ford Fiesta was parked on the grass verge at the end of the small front garden, which, like the back, was a tangle of weeds, nettles and briars. The car was packed to the roof with her clothes and personal belongings, along with a box containing cleaning equipment and the new vacuum cleaner she'd bought the day before. She had roughly four hours before her bed and few items of furniture were due to be delivered, and she'd need every minute. The old lady who had lived here before she'd finally been persuaded to move to a nursing home had clearly been struggling for years to cope. The nephew who had overseen her departure from the cottage had apparently cleared it; removing the carpets and curtains—which the estate agent had assured Willow had been falling to pieces—along with everything else. What was left was mountains of dust, dirt and cobwebs, but from what she could see of the grimy floorboards they would be great when stained. And at least she could really put her stamp on things.

Four hours later she'd emptied the vacuum bag umpteen times, but at least the dust from the carpet underlay, which had disintegrated into fine powder, was gone, and most surfaces were relatively clean. The cottage wasn't large, comprising a sitting room, kitchen and bathroom downstairs, and two bedrooms upstairs. There was a kind of scullery attached to the kitchen by means of a door that you opened and stepped down into a six-foot by six-foot bare brick room with a tiny slot of a window, and it was evident the old lady had been in the habit of storing her coal and logs for the fire here. There was no central heating and in the kitchen an ancient range was the only means of cooking. The cottage had been rewired fairly recently though, which was a bonus in view of all the other work she'd need to do, and it had a mains supply of water.

The furniture van arrived and the cheery driver helped Willow manoeuvre her bed and chest of drawers upstairs. There was a built-in wardrobe in the bedroom she'd chosen to sleep in. A two-seater sofa and plumpy armchair and coffee table for the sitting room completed her purchases; her portable TV was in the car, along with her microwave.

That night she fell into bed and was asleep as soon as her head touched the pillow, and for the first time since she had left Piers there were no bad dreams. When Willow awoke in the morning to sunlight streaming in the uncurtained window, she lay for a long time just listening to the birds singing outside and drinking in the peace and solitude. The house she'd shared with her friends for the last months had been on a main road and the traffic noise had filtered in despite the double glazing, but that had been nothing to the noise within most of the time! And before that—

She sat up in bed. She wasn't going to think about the years with Piers in any way, shape or form. New resolution. New start. Off with the old and on with the new. She could *so* do this. She'd always had her fair share of willpower.

The next couple of days were spent cleaning and scrubbing every room, but by the time Willow had dinner with Beth she was satisfied the years of dirt were dealt with. OK, the place needed serious attention, but the roof was sound and she'd keep to her original plan and do a job at a time as the money dictated. Buying furniture had taken every spare penny but she could work on the garden for the rest of her holiday.

She drove home without mishap after an enjoyable evening with Beth and Peter, and the next day began the assault on the garden. By the weekend she was scratched and sore and aching in muscles she hadn't known she had, but she'd cleared a good-sized section of land. Sunday afternoon the sun was still shining and she decided to have a bonfire. That was what people did in the country, after all.

At some time there must have been a small picket fence separating part of the garden. This had long since rotted, but the remains were useful as a base for the bonfire, along with armfuls of other pieces of wood she had found and old newspapers. When she'd opened the door of the dilapidated pottingshed a couple of days earlier, she had found it stacked from floor to ceiling with old newspapers, magazines, cardboard egg boxes and food wrappers. The old lady must have deposited her paper and cardboard there for years before the garden became too overgrown for her to reach it.

Willow piled the brambles and nettles and other vegetation she'd cleared as high as she could. It would take ages to burn the contents of the potting shed alone, but she had until it got dark. She had positioned the bonfire at the end of the garden some feet from the high stone wall. Beyond this, she understood from the estate agent, was the garden of a larger manor house. The house in question was set in extensive grounds and obscured from view by massive old trees, but the landscaped gardens visible from the lane spoke of considerable wealth. It had been the country residence of the local squire who had owned most of the village set in a dip below Willow's cottage in the old days, apparently, and her cottage had been the gatekeeper's property before the cottage and garden had been sold off. These days the manor house was the weekend home of a successful businessman, according to the estate agent.

Once the bonfire was well and truly alight, Willow began to enjoy herself. There was something immensely satisfying in burning all the rubbish and she fetched more piles of newspapers from the potting shed, throwing them into the crackling flames with gay abandon. This would save a good few trips to the local refuse site if nothing else.

Quite when a sense of slowly mounting unease turned into panic, Willow wasn't sure. Her gung-ho approach with the newspapers had resulted in a large quantity of pieces being picked up by the breeze—still merrily burning—and sailing over the wall in ever-increasing numbers. She tried to knock a pile that was smouldering off the fire with a big stick, but only succeeded in fanning the flames.

She had followed a tip of Peter's and drenched the wood at the bottom of the bonfire in petrol before she'd piled the rubbish on it; now there was no stopping the blaze. Increasingly alarmed by the power of the monster she'd created, she retreated to the cottage to fetch a bucket of water to throw on the flames now leaping into the sky with ever-increasing ferocity and strength.

She was still filling the bucket in the kitchen when she heard shouting. Turning off the tap, she picked up the half-full pail and hurried into the garden in time to see the figure of a man hoisting himself astride the stone wall, his curses mingling with the roaring fire and the wild frenzied barking of what sounded like a pack of rabid dogs.

'What the hell are you playing at?' he snarled at her as she approached. 'Have you lost your reason, woman?'

How rude. The abject apology she'd been about to make died on her lips. She stared into a pair of eyes so blue they were dazzling—which wasn't helpful in the circumstances—and stopped dead in her tracks, which caused a good portion of the water in the bucket to slop over onto her grubby work trainers. 'This is my property,' she said coldly. 'And this isn't a smoke-free zone.'

'I've got nothing against the smoke,' he bit back, his tone acid. 'It's your determination to start fires all over the neighborhood I'm objecting to, and the danger to life and limb. One of my dogs has had its fur singed as it is.'

'I'm sorry,' she said, equally acidly.

'You sound it.' He ducked as a particularly large piece of burning paper wafted past his left ear. 'There's bits of this stuff floating in my swimming pool and all over the grounds, and my dogs are playing a game of Russian roulette as we speak. Damp it down, for crying out loud.'

'I was about to when you materialised.'

'With that?' He eyed her bucket with scathing disgust.

'You might as well use an eggcup. Where's your garden hose?'

'I don't have one.' She glared at him, her eyes narrowed.

'Give me strength…'

As he disappeared back into his own garden Willow stared at the spot where he'd been, her cheeks burning, and not wholly because of the heat from the fire, which was intense. What a horrible individual and how dared he growl at her like that? Anyone would think she'd done this on purpose. Couldn't he see it was an accident? She'd hardly meant to send stuff into his stupid garden.

As the breeze mocked her by gathering a handful of paper and causing it to pirouette over the wall she groaned softly. He had a point, of course he had a point, and she would have apologised if he hadn't rushed in all guns blazing. She slung the remaining contents of the bucket on the fire. It treated the paltry amount of water with the contempt it deserved and blazed fiercely as if to confirm she was fighting a losing battle.

She was just about to run back to the house for more water when there was a scrambling noise and the man re-appeared. 'Stand back,' he said tersely.

'What?' She stared at him, taken by surprise.

'I said, stand back.' He bent down to someone on his side of the wall as he spoke, adding, 'OK, Jim, I've got it.'

Willow saw the garden hose in his hand a moment before the jet of water hit the flames. For a minute or two all was hissing and spitting and belching smoke, ash from the fire covering her and the surrounding area along with droplets of water. She had instinctively moved when he'd shouted at her, but she was still near enough to the bonfire for the spray to reach her. She stood, utterly taken aback as she watched him douse the flames as though he was enjoying himself. He probably was.

'That's done it.' He passed the hose back to the unseen assistant and turned to look at her. 'Never start a bonfire without having the means at hand to put it out should something like today happen,' he said with what Willow considered sickening righteousness, and then he grinned at her.

She stared at him. The piercing blue eyes were set in a tanned face that was more rugged than handsome and topped by black hair that reached the top of the collar of his open-necked shirt. His smile showed dazzling white teeth and he seemed totally at ease on his perch on the wall now the imminent danger was over. 'Morgan Wright,' he said calmly when she continued to gaze dumbly at him. 'As you may have gathered I'm your next-door neighbour.'

'Willow Landon,' she managed at last, suddenly aware of how she must look as the blue eyes washed over her. 'I— I moved in last week. I've been doing some gardening,' she finished lamely.

He nodded. He was dressed in a blue shirt with the sleeves rolled up and black denim jeans, and his whole appearance was one of strength and virile masculinity. Willow knew she was filthy, her hair bundled up into a ponytail and no make-up on her face. She had never felt at such a disadvantage in the whole of her life. 'I'm sorry about the fire,' she said stiffly after a moment had ticked by, 'but I was about to see to it, like I said.' She took a deep breath and forced herself to add, 'But thank you for your help. I'm sorry to have bothered you.'

His eyes had narrowed slightly at her tone. 'Self-preservation,' he drawled after a moment's silence. 'There's a wooden summer house on my side of the wall and I'd prefer not to see it go up in smoke just yet.'

'I hardly think that would have happened.' She eyed him coolly.

Dark eyebrows rose in a wry quirk. 'Your mother ought to have warned you about being so friendly,' he said, his blue eyes laughing at her. 'Folk could get the wrong impression.'

She knew she was being unreasonable in the circumstances. Unforgivably unreasonable. And she wasn't usually this way. Somehow, though, everything about this man caught her on the raw. She swallowed hard, willing her voice not to falter when she said, 'Thank you again. I'd better start clearing up,' as she turned away, wishing he would disappear as quickly as he'd arrived.

'Want some help?' The deep voice was unforgivably amused.

'No, I can manage.' She didn't look at him as she spoke.

'I've no doubt about that but the offer still stands. Two pair of hands make light work and all that.'

'No, really.' She met the blue gaze again and the impact was like a small electric shock. She felt muscles clench in her stomach as everything in her recoiled from the attraction, but her voice was steady when she said, 'I think I'll go and have a wash and leave the clearing up until tomorrow, actually. Give it a chance to die down completely.'

'Good idea—you don't want to burn yourself.'

Again his eyes were laughing; the covert mockery was galling. Warning herself not to rise to it, Willow pretended to take his words at face value. 'Exactly. Goodbye, Mr Wright.'

'Morgan. We're neighbours, after all.'

She nodded but said nothing, walking back to the cottage and aware all the time of his eyes burning into her back. She didn't look round when she reached the door but she knew he was still sitting on the wall watching her; she could feel it.

Once inside the cottage she leant against the door with her eyes shut for a long moment. Great, just great. What an introduction to her nearest neighbour. Now he would think she was a dizzy female without a brain in her body, which wasn't exactly the sort of impression she wanted to impart to folk hereabouts.

He had been laughing at her the whole time. Well, not the whole time; he had been too angry at first, she amended, opening her eyes with a soft groan. And she hadn't made things any better, going for him like that. But he had been so totally supercilious and aggravating. And that little lecture about having a hose handy when she had a bonfire; how old did he think she was? Still in nursery school?

She levered herself off the door. She was wet and cold and dirty and it was going to take ages to clear up outside tomorrow. She just hoped Mr Know-It-All stayed well clear. If she saw him again for the rest of her life it would be too soon…

CHAPTER TWO

MORGAN waited until the door had closed behind Willow before he jumped down into his garden. He landed beside his gardener-cum-handyman, who eyed him wryly. 'I could be wrong but I got the impression she didn't appreciate your help overmuch.'

'Don't you believe it—she was bowled over by my charm.'

'Oh, aye, you could have fooled me. Pretty, was she?'

Morgan smiled. Jim and his wife, Kitty, had been with him for ten years since he'd moved into the manor house after making his first million or two as a young man of twenty-five. They lived in a large and very comfortable flat above the garage block, and ran his home like clockwork. Kitty was a motherly soul and a wonderful cook and house-keeper. Now in their early sixties, the couple had been unable to have children of their own. Morgan knew they looked on him as the son they'd never had and he, in his turn, was immensely fond of the tall, distinguished-looking man and his small, bustling wife.

'Hard to tell exactly what she did look like under all that dirt,' he said offhandedly, turning and surveying the littered grounds as he added, 'I'll help you start clearing up this lot.'

He thought about what Jim had said, though, as he began to fish pieces of blackened paper out of the swimming pool with the large pool net. Green eyes and red hair, nice combination, and a good figure, but definitely a prickly customer. The way she'd glared at him... He stood for a moment, smiling slightly to himself. It had been a long time since a woman had scowled at him like that; since he'd discovered he had the Midas touch where property was concerned and risen to dizzying heights in the business world they normally fell over backwards to be seen on his arm. There was no vanity in this thought, merely a cynical acknowledgement of the power of money.

Beginning work again, he pictured her in his mind's eye. There had been a nicely rounded, firm little *derrière* in those jeans as she'd marched away down the garden, her silky red ponytail swinging in indignation.

To Morgan's surprise, he felt a certain part of his anatomy respond to the memory, becoming as hard as a rock. In answer to his body's reaction, he said out loud, 'She's too young.' She didn't look a day over twenty, all bright-eyed and bushy-tailed. He preferred his women to be sophisticated and worldly-wise, happy to be shown a good time but without any delusions of till-death-us-do-part and *definitely* charming, easy company. He worked hard and played hard and he was sufficiently wealthy to do both on his terms.

His mouth hardened, although he was unaware of it. When he had first entered the business world he'd been taken for a ride once or twice, but it had been valuable experience and he'd learnt from it. Very quickly he'd understood he couldn't afford to take anyone or anything at face value. The same applied to his love life. At twenty-four, just before he'd hit the big time, he'd met Stephanie. Stephanie Collins. Blonde, bright, beautiful. When they began dating he thought he was the luckiest man in the world but after six months she'd sent him a typical 'Dear John' letter and disappeared into the blue yonder with a balding, wrinkled millionaire. Ironic, really, because if she'd waited a year or so he could have given her everything she'd ever wanted and without being pawed over by a man old enough to be her grandfather. But, again, the episode had taught him plenty for which he was grateful.

He nodded mentally to the thought. In fact the Stephanie thing had woken him up to the fact that the whole for-ever scenario wasn't for him. His parents having been killed in a car crash when he was just a baby, he'd been shunted round various relatives until he'd gone away to university at the age of eighteen. From that point he'd made his own way in the world, but until Stephanie he hadn't faced the need he had of belonging to someone, of putting down roots and having a home that was his. The need had made him realise he was vulnerable and he hadn't liked that.

Morgan straightened and threw the net to one side. No, he hadn't liked that at all. But then the money had started to roll in. He had been able to buy this place and also a chrome and glass one-bedroomed apartment in London where he stayed weekdays. And nowadays all he required of his women was honesty, which was why he made a point of only dating successful career women who were as autonomous as he was. And he was satisfied with that. His square chin came up, thrusting slightly forward as though someone had challenged him on the statement.

One of the dogs pushed its nose into his hand and he didn't have to look down to see who it was. Bella had been the first of the German Shepherds he'd bought a couple of years after acquiring the manor house and she was still his favourite. As a puppy she'd had a weak stomach and been prone to vomiting attacks that could swiftly put her life at risk; many a time he'd sat up all night giving her sips of a rehydrating formula prescribed by the local vet. Maybe it was that that had created the special bond between them. She had grown into a strong, beautiful animal who was as intelligent as she was gentle, but in spite of her sweet temper she was the undisputed leader of his five dogs. And she always knew when he was disturbed about something or other.

'I'm all right, girl.' He looked down into the trusting brown eyes. 'Thinking a bit too much, maybe, that's all.' He glanced over to where Jim was still picking up fragments of charred paper, his progress hampered by the other four dogs who were chasing bits here and there. Then his gaze moved over the beautifully tended grounds until it rested on the fine old house in the distance, the mellow stone and mullioned windows set off perfectly by the exquisitely thatched roof.

He was a lucky man. He nodded mentally to the thought. Answerable to no one and in complete control of every aspect of his life. And that was the way things would stay. Snapping his fingers at Bella, he made his way to the house, the dog following at his heels as she always did, given half a chance.

Kitty looked up from rolling pastry as he walked into the kitchen, her round, homely face enquiring. 'Put the fire out, did you?' she said, asking the obvious. 'What was the lass thinking of to do that? I hope you read her the Riot Act—she could have had the roof on fire. Bit simple, is she?'

Ridiculously he didn't like that. Remembering the spark in the green eyes, he said quietly, 'Far from it. She struck me as impetuous, that's all.'

'Oh, aye?' Kitty was a northerner and always spoke her mind. 'Plain daft, I'd call it. Still, let's hope she's learnt her lesson.'

Morgan wondered why he was feeling defensive on the girl's behalf when she'd behaved so foolishly. With Bella following he walked through to the drawing room at the front of the house, the windows of which overlooked wide sweeping lawns and manicured flowerbeds. Pouring himself a whisky from the cocktail cabinet in a corner of the room, he flung himself into a chair and switched on the massive TV with the remote. An inane quiz show came on the screen and after channel-hopping for a while he turned the TV off, drained his glass and made his way to his study.

The room was masculine and without frills, a floor-to-ceiling bookcase occupying one wall and his massive Edwardian twin-pedestal desk dominating the space. The study could appear cosy in the winter when Kitty saw to it a good fire was kept burning in the large ornate grate, but now the room merely had the air of being functional. He sat down at the desk.

Morgan gazed musingly at the tooled-leather writing surface without reaching for the stack of files he'd brought back to work on. When he'd got home at the weekend Kitty had been full of the news the village grapevine had passed on. A woman had bought Keeper's Cottage and was living in it alone, and to date she'd had no visitors. He hadn't been particularly interested; if he'd thought about it at all he'd probably jumped to the conclusion the woman in question was a middle-aged or retired individual who wanted a bit of peace and quiet from the hurly-burly of modern-day living.

He raised his head, his eyes taking in the tiny dancing particles of dust the slanting sunshine through the window had caught in its beam.

But the occupant of Keeper's Cottage was far from being old. The woman who had glared at him with such hostility was very young and attractive and clearly had a mind of her own, which begged the question—why had she chosen to live in such seclusion? Did she work? And if so, where? Who was Willow Landon and why didn't she like men? Or perhaps it was *him*, rather than the whole male gender, she didn't like?

This thought caused his firm, sensual mouth to tighten and he leaned back in the big leather chair for a moment, drumming his fingers on the padded arms.

This was crazy. Annoyance with himself brought him reaching abruptly for a file. It didn't matter who Willow Landon was or what had brought her to this neck of the woods. He'd probably never talk to the woman again; in all the time he'd lived here he had made a point of not becoming friendly with the neighbours. This was his bolt hole, the place where he could be himself and to hell with the rest of the world. His London apartment was where he socialised and conducted out-of-hours business affairs—other affairs too, come to it.

Morgan opened the file, scanning the papers inside but without really taking them in. He had ended his latest liaison the week before. Charmaine had been a delightful companion and—being a high-grade lawyer with nerves of steel and keenly intelligent—she was at the top of her profession and much sought after. Only he hadn't realised she thought it perfectly acceptable to endow her favours to other men on the occasions she wasn't seeing him. Unfashionable, perhaps, but he had always had an aversion to polygamy and he had told her so, as he'd thought quite reasonably.

Charmaine had called him pharisaical after throwing her cocktail in his face. What was the difference, she'd hissed, in sleeping with other men before and after an affair, and not during? They both knew they didn't want a for-ever scenario, and they had fun together and the sex was great; why couldn't he just go with the flow and enjoy it? Other men did.

He had looked into her beautiful, angry face and known any desire he'd had for the perfectly honed female body in front of him had gone. He didn't want to go where someone else had been the night before; it was as simple as that. He gave and expected fidelity for as long as a relationship lasted, and he couldn't operate any other way. The scene that had followed had been ugly.

Smiling grimly to himself, Morgan cleared his mind of anything but the Thorpe account in front of him. He needed to check the figures very carefully because something hadn't sat right with him when he'd glanced at them at the office. He had found his gut instinct rarely failed him.

Sure enough, a few minutes later he found a couple of discrepancies that were enough to raise question marks in his mind about the takeover that was being proposed. He'd have to go into things more thoroughly once he was back in the office, he decided, slinging the file aside and raking his hand through his hair.

The movement brought the faint smell of woodsmoke into his nostrils and he frowned, his earlier thoughts taking hold. Women were a necessary indulgence but they were a breed apart, and Charmaine had reminded him of the fact. Not that he'd needed much reminding. And that applied to all women—angry, green-eyed redheads included. She certainly had a temper to go with the hair, that was for sure. His mouth twisted in a smile. Not that he minded spirit in a woman. It often made life interesting. He'd never understood men who liked their women to be subservient shadows, scared to say boo to a goose.

He stretched his long legs, reaching for another file and feeling faintly annoyed at how he'd allowed himself to become distracted. Within moments he was engrossed in the papers in front of him and everything else had vanished from his mind, but the faint scent of woodsmoke still hung in the air.

CHAPTER THREE

'How *embarrassing*. Poor you.' In spite of her words Beth's tone was more eager than sympathetic and her face was alight with interest. 'And this guy who owns the place, he must be worth a bit if the manor house is just his weekend home?'

'I've got no idea how wealthy he is or isn't.'

'Is he young or old? I mean, grey-haired or what?'

'What's his age got to do with anything?' Willow found she was regretting mentioning the episode at the weekend to her sister now. She had called in for a coffee and quick chat after work mainly, she had to admit, because she was still smarting from Morgan Wright's condemnation and wanted someone to commiserate with her. She might have known Beth wouldn't play ball.

Beth shrugged. 'I just wondered if he was tasty, that's all.'

Willow had to smile. 'He's a man, Beth. Not a toasted sandwich.'

'Is he, though?' Beth had got the bit between her teeth.

'Is he what?' said Willow, deliberately prevaricating.

'Fanciable.' Beth grinned at her. 'Hunky, you know.'

She was *so* not going to do this. 'I didn't notice, added to which he's more likely than not married. Attractive, wealthy men of a certain age tend to be snapped up pretty fast.'

'So he *is* tasty?' Beth sat forward interestedly.

Willow changed the subject in the one way that couldn't fail. 'So you've finished the nursery now, then? Can I take a look?'

She oohed and ahhed at the pretty lemon and white room, which already had more fluffy toys than any one child could ever want, along with a wardrobe full of tiny little vests and socks and Babygros, and then made her escape before Beth returned to their previous conversation. Her sister rarely let anything drop before she was completely satisfied.

The weather had broken at the beginning of the week and it had got progressively colder day by day. Today, Friday, was the first of October and the month had announced its intentions with a biting wind and rain showers. It started to rain again when she was halfway home, but this was no shower, just a steady downpour that had her scurrying out of the car and into the house in record speed once she was home.

After several days of battling with the Aga cooker she'd finally got the knack of persuading it into action just before she'd resumed work, but she hadn't lit it all week, making do with microwave meals. She could imagine the kitchen was a warm, cosy place with the range in action, but each evening she'd lit a fire in the sitting-room grate and sat hunched over it for the first hour until the chill had been taken off the room.

Putting a match to the fire she had laid that morning before she'd left for work, she walked through into the kitchen to switch the electric kettle on, shivering as she went. The last few days had pointed out her main priority was to get oil-fired central heating installed in the cottage as quickly as she could; the sitting-room fire would be a nice feature to keep but was woefully inadequate as the sole means of warmth.

Once she was nursing a hot mug of coffee she returned to the sitting room and threw a couple more logs and a few extra pieces of coal on the fledgling flames, fixing the guard round the fire before she went upstairs to change into jeans and a warm jumper. That done, and in spite of the fact the room was freezing, she sat for some time on the bed sipping the coffee as she stared at her reflection in the long thin mirror on the opposite wall, her mind a million miles away.

It had been a tiring week at work with several minor panics and she was still getting used to the long drive home, but it wasn't that that occupied her thoughts, but how her life had changed in the last twelve months and especially in the two weeks since she had moved into the cottage. OK, it might be pretty basic right now but it was *hers*. She had done this on her own. Why hadn't she had the courage to leave Piers long before she had done and make a new life without him? Why had she tried and tried and tried to make the marriage work long after she had known she'd married a monster? A handsome, charming, honey-tongued monster who had fooled her as completely as he did everyone else. At first. Until she'd tied the knot.

Why? a separate part of her mind answered. You know why.

Yes, she did. She nodded her acquiescence. Piers had been the master of mind games and he had moulded and manipulated her to his will so subtly she hadn't been aware of his power over her until it was too late. He had convinced her she was worthless, useless, that she couldn't manage without him, and she had believed him utterly. Because she'd trusted him, fool that she was.

Rising abruptly, she walked closer to the mirror and stared into the slanted green eyes looking back at her. What had attracted Piers to her that night nearly six years ago? There'd been other, prettier girls in the nightclub. But he'd chosen her and she'd been thrilled, falling head over heels in love with him from the first date. Seven months later her parents had been killed and when he'd asked her to marry him just after the funeral she'd accepted at once, needing his love and comfort to combat the pain and grief. A month later they were Mr and Mrs Piers Gregory. And she had been caught in a trap.

Marry in haste, repent at leisure. An older, wiser friend had murmured that to her when she had announced her wedding date but at the time she'd been too much in love and too heartbroken about her parents to take heed to the warning.

Shaking her head at the naive girl she had been then, Willow made her way downstairs. On entering the sitting room she was slightly alarmed by the roaring fire, although it had warmed the room up nicely. Hastily banking down the flames with some damp slack, she walked through to the kitchen and made herself another coffee. Give it a few minutes and she'd toast the crumpets she'd bought for her tea in front of the fire once it was glowing red; there was nothing nicer than toasted crumpets with lashings of butter. And this was definitely a comfort night.

She had just picked up the mug of coffee when a sharp pounding on her front door almost made her drop it. Her nerves jangling, she hurried into the tiny hall and opened the door, her eyes widening as she took in the tall dark man in front of her. And he looked just as angry as when she'd first seen him.

'Are you aware your chimney's on fire?' Morgan said grimly.

'What?' She stared at him. 'What are you talking about?'

'Look.' To her amazement she found herself hauled forward by a hard hand on her arm as he pointed to the roof of the cottage. Massive flames were lighting the night sky.

Wrenching herself free, Willow stared aghast at the chimney. Never having lived in a house that accommodated coal fires, she'd had no idea a chimney could catch fire.

'I've called the fire brigade and they should be here shortly.' Even as he spoke the sound of a siren in the distance could be heard coming rapidly nearer.

'You called the fire brigade?' Willow echoed in horror. 'Can't it just go out? I won't put any more coal on.'

'Are you serious?' Morgan stared at her through the rain, which had settled down to a fine drizzle. 'You could lose the whole cottage. The chimney is on *fire*, for pity's sake.'

'But a chimney is supposed to have smoke and flames go up it,' she answered sharply. 'That's what they do.'

'Up it, yes. If it catches fire that's a whole different ball game. Did you have it swept before you lit the first fire?'

'Swept?' He could have been talking double Dutch.

'Give me strength.'

He shut his eyes for a moment in a manner that made Willow want to kick him, but then the fire engine had screeched to a halt and in the ensuing pandemonium she forgot about Morgan.

Half an hour later the fire engine and the very nice firemen left and Willow stood staring at the devastation in her sitting room. She was barely aware of Morgan at the side of her until he murmured, 'What is it with you and fire anyway?'

She wanted to come back at him with a cutting retort, but she knew if she tried to speak she would cry. Swallowing hard, she picked her way across the wet, sooty floor and reached for the photograph of her parents on the mantelpiece. Wiping the black spots off the glass, she held the photograph to her when she turned to face him. 'Thank—thank you for calling the fire brigade.' The fireman had said she'd been minutes away from having a major catastrophe on her hands. 'I want to start cleaning up now, so if you don't mind…'

He didn't take the hint. 'I'll help you mop up the worst and then I suggest you leave the main clearing up till tomorrow. Nothing will seem so bad after a good night's sleep and a hearty breakfast.'

Willow stared round the room and her expression must have spoken volumes because Morgan smiled the lopsided grin that she'd registered the first time she had met him before saying wryly, 'OK, it might, but this'll take hours and it'll be better in daylight.' He shivered, adding, 'Haven't you any heating in this place? It's as cold in here as it is outside.'

Willow's eyes went involuntarily to the blackened fireplace.

'No central heating? No storage heaters or fan heaters?'

She shook her head. 'Not yet, but I will do something soon.'

'OK, this is what we do,' he said after a moment's

silence. 'We mop up like I said and then you're coming home with me for a hot meal and a bath before you spend the night at my place. I'll bring you back in the morning and we'll tackle the cleaning then. At least you'll be in a better frame of mind to cope.'

Was he mad? Adrenalin surged in a welcome flood, enabling her to straighten and say steadily, 'Thank you, Mr Wright, but that's really not necessary. I can manage perfectly well.'

'I've seen the results of you managing…twice.'

Willow's chin raised a notch. 'Thank you,' she said for the third time, her voice thin, 'but I'd like to be on my own now. I'm not a child so please don't treat me like one.'

She saw the amazingly blue eyes narrow in irritation. 'Are you always this stubborn?'

The smell of soot was thick in her nostrils and she was so cold her fingers were numb. All she wanted was for him to leave so she could sit down and howl. 'Please go,' she said weakly.

It was like talking to a brick wall. Somehow in the next few minutes she found herself covering the floorboards with a thick layer of newspapers—Morgan had fetched these from the potting shed and to his credit he didn't make any comment whatsoever—before fetching her handbag and coat and locking the front door of the cottage. She felt shivery and shaky and it was just easier to comply rather than argue, besides which she was cold and hungry and the thought of tackling the cleaning-up process tonight was unbearable.

It wasn't until Willow reached the rickety garden gate that she noticed the Harley-Davidson parked down the lane on the grass verge. As Morgan walked over to the powerful machine she stopped dead. 'That's yours? You came on that?'

'Yep.' She could see his blue eyes glittering in the deep shadows as he turned and smiled. 'When I saw the flames I figured I'd better get round here as fast as I could.'

She waved her hand helplessly. 'But you live next door.'

'A minute or two can make all the difference with fire. I didn't know whether I was going to have to pull you out of a burning house at that stage.' He shrugged. 'It can happen.'

He started the engine and the quiet of the night was rudely shattered as he drove to her gate. 'Get on.'

She had already noticed that he was even taller than she had thought him to be when he was perched on the wall. Morgan Wright was big, very big, and it was muscled strength that padded his shoulders and chest. In fact he gave off an aura of strength from his face—which was rugged with sharply defined planes and angles and no softness— to his feet, which were encased in black leather boots. The thought of clambering up on the bike and holding onto the hard male body was blushingly intimate, but she could hardly walk beside him. She had no choice but to agree.

Blessing the fact she had changed from her pencil-thin office skirt to jeans, Willow slid onto the bike, her handbag over one shoulder. Morgan wasn't wearing a coat, just jeans and a shirt, and as she put her arms round his waist the warmth of his body flowed through her fingers. She felt him jerk.

'Hell, you're like a block of ice,' he muttered.

Funnily enough, she was aware of that herself. 'Sorry.'

There was no chance to say anything more before they roared off. After some two hundred yards Morgan turned into his own grounds through open six-foot wrought-iron gates. The drive wound through mature trees and bushes, which hid the house from the road, but then a bowling-green-smooth lawn came into view and the manor house was in front of them. It was quite stunning.

The motorbike drew to a halt at the bottom of wide semi-circular stone steps, which led to a massive studded front door that could have graced a castle. Willow could hear dogs barking from within the house and they sounded ferocious.

'Are you OK with dogs?' Morgan asked as he helped her off the Harley. 'There's a few of them so be prepared.'

'If they're OK with me,' she said more weakly than she would have liked. 'And I prefer they don't look on me as food.'

He grinned. 'They've already been fed for the night.'

'That's comforting.'

He took her arm, leading her up the steps. 'My house-keeper and her husband will be back shortly—they're visiting a friend in hospital—and dinner'll be about eight, but that'll give you time for a long hot soak. You're shaking with cold.'

Willow was glad he was already opening the door and she didn't have to reply. For the life of her she couldn't have said if it was the icy night air making her tremble or the enforced intimacy with the very male man at her side. And he smelt delicious, the sort of delicious that would cost a small fortune for a few mls and definitely came courtesy of a designer label.

Contrary to what she had expected the dogs didn't come at them pell-mell but in an orderly group that sat at their feet without any jostling. 'I'll introduce you and you can give the obligatory pat—that way they'll know you're a friend and off the menu. They never eat my friends.'

Morgan's lazy tone and the laughter in his eyes informed her he was well aware of her unease and enjoying it. Willow looked at him coldly. She didn't know why but everything about Morgan Wright irritated her, ungrateful though that was in the circumstances. Criminally ungrateful, to be truthful.

Introductions finished, the pack padded off led by the large female called Bella, much to Willow's relief. It wasn't that she disliked dogs but she'd never had anything to do with them, either as a child or an adult. Her mother had been allergic to most types of pet hair and although she and Beth had had a hamster each, which they had kept in their bedrooms, it wasn't the same as an animal free to roam like these dogs. And they were so big, especially their jaws. In fact they resembled wolves more than pet dogs, in her opinion. She gazed after them, her eyes taking in the luxury of her surroundings from the pale wood floor to the beautiful paintings adorning the cream walls in the massive hall. Everything was perfect.

She suddenly became aware that Morgan was looking at her with unconcealed appraisal. 'Freckles,' he said, as though that made up the sum total of her appearance. 'Lots of them.'

She inwardly winced. The hundreds of freckles that covered most of her creamy skin had been the bane of her life from when she was first teased about them at nursery school. Reminding herself that he was going the extra mile in being neighbourly and that he had probably saved her cottage—if not her life—this night, she forced herself to smile and say, 'Goes with the hair, I'm afraid. But you learn to live with what you can't change.'

'You don't like them? I do.' He continued to study her.

If he were covered in an infinity of them he might think differently. Willow shrugged. 'There's worse things to contend with than freckles.' Much worse.

His gaze hadn't left her face. 'And your eyes are truly green without a fleck of brown. Unusual.'

She wasn't about to stand there like a lemon submitting to his scrutiny. Moving past him, she looked to where a magnificent winding staircase led to a galleried first floor. 'This is a beautiful house. How long have you lived here?'

'Just over ten years.' It was as if she had reminded him to play the host as he added, 'Can I get you a drink or would you like that bath first? Or both, come to it.'

'The bath, please.' The bright lighting in the hall had brought an awareness that her jeans and jumper were covered in soot and she must look like something the cat had dragged in. Morgan's jeans and shirt were bearing evidence of the events of the evening too. Somehow, though, he still looked good.

'I think I'll join you.' As her eyes shot to meet his a dawning mockery in the blue gaze made it clear that he knew the conclusion she'd jumped to. 'Not literally, of course,' he added smoothly. 'You in your bath and me in mine.'

The second bane of her life, which again went with the red hair, rushed in on a tide of crimson. She didn't blush quite so readily these days but this one was a corker and she knew it. 'Of course,' she managed with a coolness that was rendered null and void by her beetroot face. 'What else?'

'What else indeed.' He smiled gently.

Hateful man. OK, he might have the good Samaritan thing down to a fine art, but he hadn't stopped laughing at her since the first moment they'd met, except when he was yelling insults, that was. He'd already made it quite clear he thought she was the original hare-brained female, and she wasn't. She *wasn't*. She had survived a destructive marriage and built a new life for herself, and that alone merited enough Brownie points to fill the ocean. Several oceans on several planets.

'I'll show you your room.' Morgan's voice was pleasant and Willow nodded her head with what she hoped was dignified hauteur. She thought she saw his lips twist, but maybe not.

He stood aside for her to precede him when they reached the staircase, and she found she had almost forgotten how to walk as she climbed the stairs. Her jeans were old and had shrunk to fit her body like a comfortable second skin, but it didn't feel so comfortable with the laser-like blue eyes behind her. The old adage of 'does my bum look big in this?' was at the forefront of her mind with each step. It didn't make for easy walking.

When they reached the wide gracious landing Morgan led her to the first door on their left, pausing and opening it before he said, 'You should find everything you need in the en-suite and there's a robe and slippers in the wardrobe.'

'Thank you.' She smiled politely. 'You're very kind.'

'See you downstairs later for that drink.'

She nodded, fairly scuttling into the bedroom and shutting the door behind her. Only then did she let out her breath in a long sigh. She'd been mad to come here; whatever had possessed her? She didn't do things like this. She had always envied people who acted impulsively and took risks, knowing she was the exact opposite herself. Not that spending the night at a neighbour's house in such circumstances was exactly a risk…

A mental image of Morgan Wright came to mind and she groaned softly. Or it wouldn't be if the neighbour in question were any other than Morgan. But no, she was being silly. What did she think he was going to do, for goodness' sake? Steal into her bedroom and have his wicked way with her like the villain in an old black and white movie? He'd offered her a bed and a hot meal for the night, that was all, and she ought to be grateful. She *was* grateful, but she wished he weren't so…

Her mind couldn't quite categorise what Morgan Wright was, and after a couple of moments she gave up the attempt and walked further into the room. It was gorgeous—large and airy and decorated in soft shades of silver and cream, with touches of dark chocolate in the bed-coverings and curtains. The en-suite was equally impressive, the chocolate marble bath sunk into the floor with elegant silver fittings and the massive shower at the other end of the bathroom large enough for a rugby team. A profusion of soft fluffy towels were stored on glass shelves, along with toiletries of every description. Willow even noticed two new toothbrushes and a tube of toothpaste. The two basins, toilet and bidet were all in chocolate marble but the tiled floor, walls and ceiling, along with the bath-linen, were the same light cream as the bedroom. And this was just a guest room!

Willow stared at her reflection in the mirror that took up half of one wall opposite the bath. And groaned again.

Five minutes later she lay luxuriating in expensive foamy bubbles, tense muscles slowly beginning to relax as the hot water did its job. Her toes didn't reach the end of the bath and the marble had been formed to provide a natural pillow for the occupant's head; she felt she could stay in it all night.

She roused herself at one point to wash her hair, but then slid under the water to her neck again for a last indulgent soak, and she was like that when a knock came at the bathroom door. Shooting to her feet so quickly she sent a wave of water washing onto the floor, she grabbed a bath towel and wrapped it round her as she said, 'Yes? What is it?'

'It's Kitty, dear. Morgan's housekeeper. Just to say I've done my best with your clothes for now, but if you want to leave them outside your door when you go to bed tonight I'll have them laundered for you in the morning so they're nice and fresh.'

'Oh, no, no, that's all right.' Willow stepped out of the bath and made her way to the door, opening it as she said, 'Please, they'll be fine till I get home tomorrow morning,' to the small, smiling woman waiting outside. 'I feel bad enough arriving unannounced for dinner as it is. I'm so sorry.'

'Go on with you.' Kitty flapped her hand. 'I'm just glad Morgan had the sense to invite you after what happened. Men don't always think on their feet, do they?' She winked conspiratorially.

'I guess not.' Actually she suspected Morgan would.

'Still, all's well that ends well. I can give you the name of the chimney sweep we use if that's any help? Nice lad, he is, and he makes a good clean job of it. Doesn't charge the earth either.'

Willow smiled ruefully into the round little face. 'If you could see the state of my cottage right now a bit of dust and soot from a chimney sweep would be nothing. I...I feel so stupid. You must all think I haven't got the sense I was born with.'

Kitty, who had been airing her views on the ineptitude of 'city' dwellers to her husband for the last twenty minutes, clicked her tongue. 'Not a bit of it, lass. How were you to know the chimney needed sweeping? I blame the estate agent—they should point out these things as part of their job. Quick enough to take their cut, aren't they? But that's typical of today's generation. There's no pride in a job well done any more, more's the pity. People do as much as they can get away with.'

'I hope you're not including me in that statement.'

As the dark smoky voice preceded Morgan strolling into the bedroom through the door Kitty had left open Willow's hands tightened instinctively round the bath sheet. For a moment she had the mad impulse to step back and shut the bathroom door but she controlled it—just. Her eyes wide, she stared at him.

Morgan had changed into a fresh shirt and jeans and his damp hair was slicked back from his face. The five o'clock shadow she had noticed earlier was gone too. Ridiculously the thought of him shaving to have dinner with her caused her stomach to tighten, even as she told herself he probably always shaved twice a day. His open-necked grey shirt showed the springy black hair of his chest and his black jeans were tight across the hips. Every nerve in her body was sensitised, much to her aggravation.

He seemed faintly surprised to see her still wrapped in a bath towel, his voice soft as he drawled, 'Not ready yet, then.'

'No, I— No. No, not yet.' Oh, for goodness' sake, pull yourself together, girl, she told herself angrily, annoyed at her stammering. You're perfectly decent. Only the look in his eyes hadn't made her feel that way. Even more alarming, she had liked the warm approval turning the blue of his eyes to deep indigo. For the first time in a long while she'd felt…womanly.

'We'd better leave you to get ready.' Kitty took charge, her voice suddenly brisk. 'Dinner's at eight, dear. All right? And there's a hairdryer in the top drawer of the dressing table.'

As the little woman bustled off Morgan smiled a lazy smile. 'Red or white?' he asked softly, the words almost a caress.

'Sorry?' She hoped she didn't look as vacant as she sounded.

'The wine with our meal. Red or white?'

Her hair was dripping over her face and all she wanted was to end this conversation and put a door between them. 'Red, please.' Actually she didn't mind but she wasn't going to say that.

One eyebrow lifted. 'Funny. I'd got you down as a white-wine girl,' he said easily.

In spite of herself she couldn't resist asking, 'Oh, yes? Why?' even as she mentally kicked herself for giving him the opportunity for more mockery. As if he needed an opportunity!

He shrugged. 'Girls of a certain age seem to go for white wine.' He smiled charmingly. 'Or that's what I've found.'

Did they indeed? And of course a man like Morgan Wright would know. The green eyes he'd spoke about narrowed. 'What age is that?' she asked evenly, determined to show no reaction.

'Twenty, twenty-one.'

Willow didn't know whether to feel pleased or insulted. If he was judging her age purely on her appearance, then that was fine, but if this was another way of saying she was silly and immature... Warily, she said, 'It's my twenty-ninth birthday in a few weeks.' And make of that what you will.

'You're joking.' He let his gaze travel over her body, top to toes. 'It's obviously a gene thing.'

It was actually. Beth looked years younger than she was and their mother had often been taken as their older sister. She nodded. 'Advantage as one gets older but definitely irritating when you're asked for ID at a nightclub,' she said as coolly as she could considering her face had decided to explode with colour again.

He didn't seem to notice her discomfiture. 'Never had that problem myself,' he said with a crooked smile. 'I think I was born looking twenty-one.'

Willow could believe it. Morgan Wright was one of those men who made it impossible to imagine him as a child. The flagrant masculinity was so raw, so tough and virile she couldn't envisage him as a vulnerable little boy. She shivered although she wasn't cold.

'Sorry, this is undoing all the good work the hot bath's done. You get dressed and I'll see you downstairs. The sitting room is to your right once you're in the hall, incidentally.' He had turned as he spoke, and, having reached the bedroom door, shut it quietly behind him.

Willow stared after him for a few moments before she pulled herself together. She found the hairdryer Kitty had spoken of and dried her hair so it fell in a sleek curtain framing her face. She was lucky with her hair. Thick and silky, it was no trouble as long as she had a good cut.

Grimacing, she dressed in her grubby jeans and jumper, although thanks to Kitty's ministrations they were more presentable than when she'd arrived. Fishing out the odd bits of make-up she always kept in her handbag for an emergency, she applied eyeshadow and mascara before finishing with lip gloss. The result wasn't spectacular but better, and better was good considering this man always seemed to see her when she looked as if she'd been pulled through a hedge backwards.

She stopped titivating and stared into the green eyes in the mirror. He must think she was some kind of nutcase and she hadn't done much to convince him otherwise. Perhaps she *was* a nutcase, at that. At uni she'd always been one of the more restrained ones, looking on with a mixture of embarrassment and envy when some of her more wild friends had gone skinny-dipping on a day out by the river or related their antics at the latest wild party they'd attended. But now they were all lawyers or doctors or 'something' in the fashion industry, and a few had successful marriages to boot. Whereas she…

This train of thought was too depressing to follow, besides which it was two minutes to eight. Taking a deep breath, Willow smoothed her jeans over her hips, trying to ignore the sooty smell, and smiled at the face in the mirror. 'You're going to be fine. He's a man, just a man, and this is one night out of the rest of your life. It isn't a big deal so don't make it one.'

And talking to yourself was the first sign of madness.

CHAPTER FOUR

MORGAN WRIGHT wasn't a man given to second-guessing himself. In fact he'd built his small empire by going for the jugular and to hell with it if he'd got it wrong—which, it must be said, he rarely did. He was at the top of his game professionally and comfortably satisfied with life in general. So why, he asked himself as he sat absently ruffling the fur on Bella's head, the rest of the dogs piled round his feet, was he regretting inviting Willow to stay the night? It didn't make sense.

A muscle knotted in his cheek and he swallowed the last of the Negroni he'd made for himself after coming downstairs. The bittersweet cocktail was one of his favourites and he usually took his time and enjoyed it in a leisurely way, but tonight the mix of Campari, sweet vermouth and gin barely registered on his taste buds. He was all at odds with himself and he didn't like it.

He set the squat, straight-sided glass he always used for his pre-dinner cocktails on the small table beside him, frowning. He would have bet his bottom dollar she was no older than twenty, but if she was to be believed you could add practically another decade to that. And he didn't doubt her. What woman would add years to her age, after all? No, she was nearly twenty-nine.

He raked back a quiff of hair that persisted in falling over his forehead, and the restrained irritation in the action brought Bella's eyes to his face as she whined softly.

'It's all right, girl.' He patted the noble head reassuringly even as a separate part of his mind asked the question, but was it? He didn't like the way his new neighbour made him feel, that was it in a nutshell. He was way past the sweaty palms and uncontrollable urges stage, damn it. That had died a death after Stephanie and since then he'd made sure his head was in full control of his heart and the rest of him. He had a couple of friends who'd let their hearts rule their heads and both of them were paying for it in hefty alimony payments and only seeing their kids every other week-end—if they were lucky. Women were another species, that was the truth of it. Love, if it even existed, was too fragile a thing to trust in, too weighted with possible pitfalls. Like another wealthier, more successful patsy coming along.

Knowing his thinking was flawed, he rose abruptly from his seat and walked across the room to stand looking out over his grounds. OK, there were men and women who loved each other for a lifetime—maybe. But how many of these 'perfect' relationships were for real? How many merely papered over the cracks for reasons of their own? Thousands, millions.

'Ten minutes to dinner.'

Kitty interrupted his thoughts and as he swung round and nodded it was as though the small, plump woman standing in the doorway was a challenge to his thoughts. He couldn't doubt the strength and authenticity of what Jim and Kitty had, but they were the exception that proved the rule. There were hundreds of millions of men and women in the world; you had more chances of winning the lottery than finding what the women's magazines called a soulmate.

'The lass not down yet?' Kitty asked cheerily.

'No, not yet.' He hoped she'd take the hint and disappear.

Kitty came further into the room, her voice dropping as she murmured, 'I wonder what's made a young lass like that buy Keeper's Cottage? Someone of her age should be sharing a flat with friends and having fun. Tisn't right to bury yourself away like she's done.'

His voice dry, Morgan said, 'She's older than she looks.'

'Oh, aye?' Kitty nodded. 'That makes more sense. How old is she, then?'

'Nearly twenty-nine,' Morgan said expressionlessly.

'Is that so?' Kitty nodded again. 'Fancy that.'

Morgan grinned. Kitty was trying very hard to appear nonchalant but he could see the matchmaking gleam in her eye. The little woman had been on a mission to find a 'nice' wife for him for years; it was an irresistible challenge to her despite knowing his views on the subject. Walking across to her, he gently tucked a strand of grey hair behind her ear as he murmured softly, 'Forget it, Kitty. Between you and me Miss Willow Landon doesn't like me very much so there's no hope in that direction, OK?'

It clearly wasn't. Visibly bristling, Kitty stared at him. 'I don't see why after the way you've helped her.'

'Personality clash,' he said briefly. 'That's all.'

'Personality clash? And what's that when it's at home?'

Wishing he'd kept his mouth shut, Morgan took a deep

breath, then let it out. 'She's been polite and grateful so don't get on your high horse, woman. I just meant I'm clearly not her type any more than she's mine.'

A slight noise in the doorway brought their heads turning. Willow was standing there and he suspected she'd heard his last remark from the colour in her cheeks. As if that weren't enough the sight of her—hair falling to her shoulders in silken strands, eyes as green as emeralds and her soft, half-open mouth—sent a jolt of desire sizzling through his veins. Mentally cursing Kitty and her match-making and not least the primal urges this young red-haired woman seemed able to inspire so easily, Morgan decided prevarication wasn't an option. As Kitty beat a hasty retreat he said quietly, 'Sorry, you obviously weren't supposed to hear that.'

'Obviously.' The green eyes were as cold as glass.

Damn it. Following the line that honesty was the best policy, Morgan shrugged. 'The thing is, Kitty tries to pair me off with any and every woman who strays across her path. It must be her age. Menopausal hormones out of control or something.'

The attempt at humour was met with a steely face. 'Let me endeavour to make one thing perfectly clear, Mr Wright. I wouldn't have you if you were the last man in the world and came wrapped in gold encrusted with diamonds.'

Certainly clear enough. 'The very point I was attempt-ing to make to Kitty.' His mouth took on a rueful quirk. 'I was trying to save you any embarrassment because Kitty can be a little…persistent when she gets a bee in her bonnet. In the event I seem to have made a pig's ear of things.'

The green gaze continued to study him for a moment.

Morgan felt he understood how an insect felt when impaled on a pin. Then he saw her head go back as she strolled further into the room. 'No problem,' she said coolly. 'Just so we are absolutely clear.'

Morgan was well versed with women and he knew he was still in deep water. 'Cocktail?' he offered as Willow held out her hands to the blazing fire in the deep, ornate fireplace, her back to him. 'I always indulge when I'm at home at the weekends.'

She didn't look at him when she said, 'Thank you, a margarita would be nice.' Her voice verged on icy.

Morgan prided himself on his margaritas. After filling a mixing glass with ice and stirring with a spoon, he tipped the ice away before topping up the glass with fresh. A dash of dry vermouth and he continued stirring, aware the figure by the fire had turned to watch him. After straining the liquid he again added more ice, along with a large measure of vodka.

It was when he strained the cocktail into a frosted martini glass rimmed with salt that Willow said, 'Don't tell me. You used to be a cocktail waiter in your youth.'

His youth? He wasn't exactly at the age to push up daisies yet. Smiling, he handed her the cocktail. Her fingers touched his for a moment and a light electric current shot up his arm. 'I worked in a cocktail bar for extra money during my uni days,' he admitted easily. 'It was a good job. I enjoyed it.'

'One of those where you throw the bottles over your head and at each other?' she asked with sweet venom.

His laugh was hearty and he saw her lips twitch in response. 'The very same. At the weekends we put on quite a show.'

'Dream job for a student, I should imagine?'

'You better believe it. On lean days we'd fill up on the snacks and stuff the owner put out for the clients; he knew but he didn't mind, not while we were pulling the punters in. The tips were great too; lots of rich Americans looking for some fun and entertainment with their drinks.'

'*Lady* Americans?' she enquired too casually.

His smile deepened. 'Is that disapproval in your voice?'

'Of course not.' She tossed her head. 'Why would it be?'

He watched with interest as her blush became brilliant. Putting her out of her misery, he busied himself fixing his second Negroni as he said casually, 'Myself and the other guy in the bar were propositioned now and again as it happens. Ladies looking for a holiday fling with no strings attached, mainly.'

He turned and saw the look on her face before she could hide it. His voice amused, he drawled, 'You're shocked.'

This time she didn't deny it. After taking a sip of her drink, she said, 'It's your life.'

He decided not to tell her he'd got a steady girlfriend at the time and had left the women to his friend who'd worked with him. This idea she'd got of him being an English gigolo was too entertaining. 'And it's been a rich one to date,' he said, deadpan.

This time she almost gulped at her cocktail.

It was mean perhaps, but he found he got a buzz from teasing her, probably because he'd felt off kilter since the first time he'd set eyes on his red-haired neighbour. Ridiculous, but Willow Landon bothered him deep inside, in a small private place no one ever reached. It was irritating and inconvenient, he told himself, but it would pass. Everything did.

'So you've been here ten years?' Her voice sounded a little desperate as she made an obvious attempt to change the subject. 'You're not bored yet? No plans to leave?'

'None.' He gestured for her to be seated as he added, 'Disappointed?' just to rile her a little more.

'Why would I be concerned whether you live here or not?' she said stiffly, sitting primly on the edge of a chair.

Her skin was the colour of honey peppered with spice and the red hair was a combination of endless shades. Fighting the urge to touch her, Morgan walked to the chair furthest from Willow's and sat down, stretching out his legs and taking a swig of his Negroni. There was a short silence and as he looked at her he found he'd tired of the game. Leaning forward suddenly, he said quietly, 'We got off to a bad start, didn't we? And it hasn't improved since. Can we come to a truce? I promise I'll try not to annoy you if you try and relax a little. If nothing else it will make life easier the next time I rescue you from a burning building or whatever.'

For a moment he thought she was going to freeze him out. Then a shy smile warmed her face, her eyes. 'Do you think there's going to be a next time?' she murmured ruefully. And before he could answer, went on, 'In spite of my track record so far I promise I'm not an arsonist in the making.'

He grinned. 'I never thought you were. Unlucky maybe…'

She inclined her head. 'Thank you for that—you could in all honesty have said stupid. It must appear that way.'

His smile died, a slight frown taking its place. 'Why would I be so crass? We all make mistakes. Life is a series of learning curves. It's when we *don't* learn from them the problems start.'

She nodded, but as Morgan stared at her there was something deep and dark in the clear green eyes that disturbed him. 'You don't believe that?' he asked gently.

She finished her cocktail before she spoke and a slow heat had crept into her cheeks. '*I* believe it. It's just that…'

'Yes?' he prompted quietly, wanting to know more.

'I suppose I've found others aren't so generous. Some people expect other people to be perfect all the time.'

Some people? It had to be a man who had hurt her enough to cause that depth of pain. Telling himself to go lightly, he said softly, 'I guess you get flawed individuals in every society who are either selfish enough or damaged enough to expect perfection. Personally I'd find being with a "perfect" person hell on earth, having enough faults myself to fill a book.'

'That sort of person doesn't see their own faults though.'

Her voice had been curiously toneless. Morgan kept all emotion out of his voice when he said, 'Are you speaking from experience? And you don't have to answer that if you don't want to.'

Her eyes flickered and fell from his, but her voice was steady: 'Yes, I am.' She glanced at the clock on the mantelpiece. 'That's a beautiful clock. Unusual.'

Morgan accepted the change of conversation with good grace although he found he was aching to know more. 'It's a French timepiece I picked up at an auction in France some years ago. The clock itself is mounted in a stirrup and horseshoe. I like unusual things. Things that don't follow a pattern. Unique things.'

Her gaze moved to the two bronze figures either side of the clock, each in the form of dancing fauns. 'I can see that. Are the fauns French too? They're very beautiful.'

'Italian, eighteenth century.'

They continued discussing the various objects of art in the room in the couple of minutes before Kitty put her head round the door to say dinner was ready, but Morgan found it difficult to concentrate. Who was this man who'd hurt her so badly? If it was a man. But it had to be; he felt it in his bones. What had he been to her and how had she got mixed up with him in the first place? Not that it was any of his business, of course.

He took Willow's arm as they walked through to the dining room where Kitty had set two places. She had lit candles in the middle of the table and the lights were dimmed; clearly their discussion about her matchmaking had had no effect at all.

Willow's hair smelt of peach shampoo, which was fairly innocuous as perfume went; why it should prompt urges of such an erotic nature the walk to the dining room was a sweet agony in his loins, he didn't know. He glanced down at the sheen of her hair as he pulled out her chair for her and resisted the impulse to put his lips to it.

Pull yourself together. The warning was grim. He was acting like a young boy wet behind the ears and on his first date with a member of the opposite sex, not a thirty-five-year-old man who had shared his bed and his life with several women in his time; some for a few months, some longer. Experience told him Willow Landon was not the sort of woman who would enter into a light relationship for the hell of it, she was too...

What was she? the other section of his mind, which was working dispassionately, asked. Clingy? Trusting? Stifling?

No. None of those. The opposite in fact. She didn't

strike him as a woman who had marriage and roses-round-the-door in mind. From what he could ascertain so far the male of the species didn't feature highly in her estimation. But neither was she the kind of woman who would enjoy an affair for however long it lasted and then walk away with no tears or regrets. He didn't know how he'd come by the knowledge but he was sure of it.

'This is lovely.' Willow glanced round the dining room appreciatively. 'Do you always eat in such style?'

Morgan glanced round the room as though he were seeing it for the first time, his gaze moving over the table set with fine linen, silver and crystal. 'Always. Kitty takes her duties very seriously,' he added dryly, reaching for the bottle of red wine. He poured two glasses and handed Willow hers, raising his as he murmured, 'To chimney sweeps and the good work they do.'

She giggled.

It was the first really natural response he'd had and he had to swallow hard as his heart began to hammer in his ribcage. He drank deeply of the wine, needing its boost to his system. It was a fine red; enough complexity showing from the skilful blending to bring out the cherry and berry flavours without spoiling the soft oaky flavours of the French and American wood. He'd drunk enough cheap plonk throughout his university days to always buy the best once he could afford to do so.

Kitty bustled in with the first course, cajun-spiced salmon with honey crème fraîche. It was one of her specialities and always cooked to perfection so the flakes of flesh fell apart when pressed with a fork.

He watched Willow take her first bite and saw the green

eyes widen in appreciation. She ate delicately, like an elegant, well-mannered cat, her soft, full lips closing over the food and tasting it carefully. With a swiftness that surprised him he found himself wondering what it would be like to feel her mouth open beneath his, to bury his hands in the silken sheen of her hair and thrust his tongue into the secret recesses behind her small white teeth. To nibble and suck and tease her lips…

'This is delicious.' She glanced up and saw him looking at her and immediately her face became wary even though her smile was polite. The withdrawal was subtle but there nonetheless.

What the hell had gone on in her life? Morgan nodded, his voice easy when he said, 'She's a strange mixture, is Kitty. She and Jim only like the plainest of food, no frills or fancies, as she puts it, but her main interest in life is cooking fantastic dishes that are out of this world. Her tofu miso soup has to be tasted to be believed and likewise her baked Indian rice pudding with nuts, fruit and saffron. I do believe she and Jim are probably sitting down to steamed white fish and three veg as we speak, though. Good solid northern food that sticks to the ribs.'

'Don't they ever eat with you?' she asked in surprise.

'Not when I have guests. Another of Kitty's set-in-concrete ideas.' Deliberately keeping his voice casual, he said, 'Do you like cooking?'

Her small nose wrinkled. 'I suppose I don't mind it but I'm not the best in the world by any means. I do experiment at weekends now and again, but I rely on my trusty microwave during the week when I'm working. Ready meals mostly, I'm afraid.'

Aware he was itching to know more about her—a lot more—Morgan warned himself to go steady. 'Tell me about your job,' he drawled as though he were merely making polite conversation. 'What do you do and where do you work?'

He ate slowly as she spoke, pretending he wasn't hanging on every word. When she came to a natural pause he asked the question he'd been working round to all evening. 'So what made you buy Keeper's Cottage? It's a bit remote, isn't it?'

The barrier that went up was almost visible. 'I liked it.'

'There must have been other places you liked closer to your work, surely? Places you could have shared with friends, perhaps?'

For a moment he thought she was going to tell him to mind his own business. He couldn't have blamed her. Instead, after a long pause, she said coolly, 'I've done the sharing-with-friends thing for a while and I decided I wanted my own house now. I...I like my own company. Being independent is important to me.'

Neat hint for the future. Morgan smiled. 'There's a hell of a lot wants doing to the cottage as far as I understand.'

Willow shrugged. 'I'm in no rush. Things will happen in time.'

'And it's tiny. Charming,' he added hastily. 'But tiny.'

'It's more than big enough for one.'

He'd finished his salmon and took a long swallow of wine, blue eyes holding green when he murmured, 'What if you meet someone?'

'I meet people all the time, Morgan, and it doesn't affect my living accommodation.'

Her voice had been light, even suggesting amusement, but her fingers were gripping the stem of the wineglass so tightly her knuckles showed white. Vitally aware of her body language, he gave the required response of a lazy smile but found he wasn't ready to do the socially acceptable thing and leave well alone. 'I mean someone special,' he said softly. 'You're a very attractive young woman and most women in your position want a partner eventually, maybe even children one day. It would be a shame to work at getting the cottage exactly how you want it only to have to move to a bigger place.'

Her pupils had dilated, black showing stark against the clear green. Slowly she took a sip of wine, then said, 'For the record I've done the partner thing, OK? Husband, everything. I didn't like it and I have no intention of repeating what was a mistake now I have my freedom again.' Rising to her feet, she added, 'I just need to pay a visit to the cloakroom. I won't be long.'

He rose with her but didn't say a word because he couldn't. He felt as though someone had just punched him hard in the stomach. And the ironic thing, he acknowledged soberly, was that he had probably asked for it.

CHAPTER FIVE

WILLOW fled to the downstairs cloakroom, berating herself with each step. Stupid. She'd been absolutely stupid to reveal what she had. And to add that bit about her freedom...

She closed the door of the cloakroom behind her and stood with her hands pressed to her hot cheeks in the cool white and grey room. Staring at her face in the large oval mirror above the washbasin, she saw her cheeks were fiery.

He'd think she'd been insinuating she was on the market again but this time for a no-strings-attached affair or something similar. Any man would. She should just have stated she had no intention of concentrating on anything other than her career for a long, long time. That would have been enough. Impersonal and to the point. Instead she'd launched into an explanation that had embarrassed them both. And Morgan *had* been embarrassed, she could tell from the look on his face. He hadn't known what to say. In fact he'd done a goldfish impression as she'd left.

Which was probably a first.

The thought came from nowhere but in spite of her agitation it made her smile for a moment. She dared bet

Morgan Wright was never taken by surprise and usually had an answer to everything.

Shutting her eyes tightly, she groaned under her breath. He really must think she was a nutcase now. First she nearly set his summerhouse on fire and covered his garden in ash, then she nearly set her own house on fire and now she was bending his ear about her disastrous marriage. What on earth was the matter with her? But he *had* asked.

Her eyes snapping open, she shook her head at herself. No excuses. He'd been making friendly dinner conversation, that was all. He hadn't asked for a precise of her lovelife to date, for goodness' sake. She hadn't been thinking clearly enough, that was the trouble. When he'd mentioned children he'd touched a nerve. She had always thought she'd be a mother one day; she'd never really imagined anything else. Perhaps she'd hung in there with Piers long after she'd known she should have left because of the dream of babies and a family? By the time she'd petitioned for divorce she'd known she'd rather be barren for the rest of her days than have Pier's child though.

Of course you didn't have to be married or with someone to have a baby these days—the world was full of single mothers who'd got pregnant knowing they had no intention of staying with the father of their child for ever. One of her city friends had been quite open about the fact she'd purposely conceived knowing she didn't even want to see the man again once she was pregnant. A high-powered businesswoman who was as ruthless in her lovelife as her worklife, Jill had already hired a full-time nanny before her baby was born and, now little Lynsey was six months old, appeared as happy as a bug in a rug with life.

But she wasn't like Jill. Sighing, she brushed her hair back from her face. And what was right for one person wasn't necessarily right for another. She wouldn't want Jill's life, which consisted of seeing Lynsey for an hour or two in the morning and even shorter time in the evening, and weekends. She knew herself well enough to realise she was an all-or-nothing kind of girl, and if she couldn't have it all—a permanent relationship, babies, roses round the door—she'd rather have nothing. Not that her life was empty; it wasn't. She had loads of good friends, a job she enjoyed and a home she'd fallen in love with the minute she'd seen it. Beth being pregnant had unsettled her, that was all. But it would be fun being an aunty and she could slake some of her maternal longing on the poor little thing in due time.

Willow continued to give herself a stern talking-to until she left the cloakroom a few minutes later, by which time she was in control of herself once more. Feeling slightly silly at the way she'd panicked and left the table, admittedly—but reason had reasserted itself and she was confident Morgan hadn't assumed she was inviting herself into his bed. She was out of practice at conversing over dinner with a member of the opposite sex, that was the trouble, she told herself ruefully as she retraced her steps. Despite offers, since Piers she hadn't dated.

When she entered the dining room Morgan was sitting where she'd left him, staring broodingly into his wineglass. For a second she studied his face, noticing the strength in the square-boned jaw, the cleanly sculpted mouth and straight nose.

His attractiveness went far beyond looks, she thought

with a sudden jolt to her equilibrium. In spite of being a very masculine male, there was nothing bullish or brutal about him. It would be easier to dismiss him from her mind if there were.

Morgan looked up, the brilliant blue eyes unreadable. 'Did I offend you just now? And please be honest, Willow.'

'What?' Completely taken aback, she stopped in her tracks before recovering and taking her seat at the table as she said, 'No, of course not. You didn't, really.'

'Upset you, then? And again, be honest.'

She stared at him. He clearly didn't believe in pushing awkward issues under the carpet. She was about to make a dismissive reply and change the subject when she saw there was real concern in the hard face. She hesitated, colour creeping up her cheeks, and then said in a rush, 'You didn't offend *or* upset me, Morgan, I promise you. It's just that—' she took a deep breath '—I don't normally wear my heart on my sleeve.'

He nodded slowly, his voice soft when he said, 'Is it still painful to talk about?'

He had refilled her wineglass while she'd been in the cloakroom and she took a long sip to gain some time. She wanted to say she didn't wish to discuss this any further so it was with something akin to surprise she heard herself say, 'I don't love him any more if that's what you mean.'

He took the wind out of her sails for the second time in as many minutes when he said quietly, 'I don't know what I mean, to be truthful. I hadn't imagined...' He shook his head at himself. 'I guess because you *look* so young I hadn't considered something like marriage. Nothing so serious or...permanent.'

Tonelessly, she said, 'I met Piers six years ago and we married eight months later. I—I was very unhappy.' She stared into the wineglass, swirling the ruby-red liquid as she spoke. 'He wasn't who I thought he was before we married. I knew I'd made a terrible mistake within the first few months but—' she shrugged '—I thought I could make it work if I tried. I was wrong. Something happened—' a few drops of wine escaped the glass, staining the linen tablecloth like blood '—and I left. We're now legally divorced. End of story.' She raised her eyes, her smile brittle. 'Just one of many said little tales happening up and down the country.'

'Perhaps. But this is *your* tale and marriage.'

'Was.' As she spoke Kitty bustled in with the main course, and Willow had never been so glad of an interruption in all her life. 'Something smells wonderful,' she said brightly.

'Steak with red-wine butter,' said Kitty cheerfully. 'You don't go in for all that slimming carry-on, do you?'

'Not me.' She had lost so much weight in the aftermath of the break-up with Piers she'd fought for months to gain weight, not lose it, having gone down to skin and bone— as Beth had put it. She'd never been voluptuous but she liked her curves.

'Good. Can't abide lettuce eaters. There's toffee-ripple cheesecake with fudge sauce for dessert. It's quite rich so you won't manage much but it's one of Morgan's favourites.'

'All your desserts are my favourites, Kitty.'

Kitty gave a rich chuckle. 'Go on with you.' But she was red with pleasure as she left them.

Willow looked at him. She was beginning to realise Morgan was more complex than she'd initially thought.

She'd felt comfortable putting him down as a wealthy bachelor with a different girlfriend for each day of the week and a jumbo ego the size of a small mountain. The first part was probably still true, but he didn't act like a man who had an inflated opinion of himself. He was obviously intelligent and determined—no one got to where he had without possessing such qualities along with a healthy dose of tenacity and intuitiveness—but he wasn't brash or conceited. And the way he was with Kitty was lovely.

She frowned to herself. She would have preferred he stayed in the box she'd put him in; it was far more comfortable. Determined to deflect more searching questions, as the door closed behind Kitty she said, 'Well, now you know all about me, how about you? Ever been tempted to walk up the aisle or are you much too sensible for that? You strike me as the confirmed-bachelor sort.'

Morgan smiled as she'd meant him to. 'I got my fingers burnt a long time ago when I was knee-high to a grasshopper,' he said lightly. 'I decided then I wasn't a for-ever-after type.'

'Then we're two of a kind.' That sounded too cosy and, feeling flustered, she took a big bite of her steak. It was wonderful. 'I'm surprised you aren't as big as a house if you eat like this all the time,' she said, raising her head.

The piercing blue eyes were waiting for her. 'Ah, but I'm only here weekends,' he pointed out softly. 'Weekdays I live in London in a very modern, functional apartment, the kitchen of which, I must confess, is rarely used.'

'You eat out all the time?'

'I work out at the gym most nights and they have a good

restaurant, which prides itself on the healthy options. I feel I can indulge at weekends. That's my excuse, anyway.'

'That doesn't sound as though you leave much time for a social life.' The words had popped out before she realised how nosy she sounded. She just hoped he didn't think she was prying.

There was a sexy quirk to Morgan's mouth when he murmured, 'Oh, I manage fairly well. On the whole.'

She just bet he did. Her gaze fell to his hand as he drank from his wineglass. His hands were like the rest of him, powerfully masculine, and his forearms were muscular and dusted with dark hair. The room was large and impressive and yet he dominated it with his presence. She could imagine he would be devastating to come up against in the business world. Devastating altogether. Not a man you could easily forget.

Even more flustered, she concentrated on her meal for the next little while, which wasn't hard because every mouthful was heavenly. Morgan did the same, eating with obvious enjoyment and making amusing small talk, which needed very little response on her part. Nevertheless she was aware she was as taut as piano wire and conscious of every little movement from the hard male body opposite her, even when she wasn't looking at him. He was an…unsettling man, she decided as Kitty cleared away their empty plates and brought two helpings of toffee-ripple cheesecake, Morgan's being large enough for half a dozen people.

He saw her glance at his plate and smiled the crooked grin that was becoming familiar to her. 'Kitty thinks I'm a growing boy. And I don't want to disillusion her, now, do I?'

It was somehow disturbingly endearing, and to combat

the quiver of something she didn't want to put a name to Willow's voice was deliberately dry when she said, 'Be careful you don't grow too much. Those extra pounds creep up on you, you know.'

'Not me. Fast metabolism.'

'All in the genes?' she asked, just to make conversation and echoing what he'd said to her earlier.

'Probably.' His voice was pleasant but dismissive.

'Your father's or your mother's?'

He stared at her for a moment and Willow saw what she could only describe as a shutter come down over the brilliant blue of his eyes in the second before he shrugged. 'Your guess is as good as mine. They died when I was too young to remember them.'

Quickly, she said, 'I'm sorry. Mine died a few months before I got married but I still miss them dreadfully. So does my sister. She's expecting a baby soon and it would have been nice for Mum to be around to see her first grandchild.' She was gabbling but the look in his eyes had thrown her. 'Do you have any brothers or sisters?' she added weakly.

He shook his head. 'No, there's just me. The one and only original. Like that clock you liked so much.'

Willow smiled because she knew he wanted her to and for the same reason didn't pursue what was clearly a no-go area. Her tenseness had given her the beginning of a headache, but she felt every moment in Morgan's company was electric so perhaps it wasn't surprising. She didn't think she had ever met anyone who was such an enigma.

They took coffee in the drawing room where Kitty had placed the tray on a low coffee table pulled close to the fire, a box of chocolates and another of after-dinner mints next to the white porcelain cups. When Morgan sat down on a two-seater sofa in front of the table Willow felt she had no option but to join him, anything else would have appeared churlish, but she took care no part of her body touched his.

She declined cream or sugar in her coffee; the cocktails had been potent and so had the wine and suddenly she felt she needed all her wits about her. The coffee was strong but not bitter and the chocolate she chose was sweet and nutty. The red glow from the fire, the mellow light in the room, the different tastes on her tongue and not least the dark man sitting quietly beside her created a whole host of emotions she could have done without. She felt tinglingly, excitingly alive and had to force her hand not to shake when she replaced her cup on the saucer and turned to Morgan. 'Thank you for dinner and everything you've done,' she said steadily. 'I'll try and be out of your hair as soon as possible tomorrow.'

'No need.' His voice was deep, smoky. She had to clench her stomach muscles against what it did to her. 'Stay as long as you like. I wasn't doing anything special this weekend.'

'Nevertheless I'd like to make a start on clearing up as soon as I can,' she prevaricated quickly. 'Get it over with.'

'I'll help you,' he offered softly.

'No, that's all right, you've done enough already.'

'Two pairs of hands will make lighter work.'

'No, really.' She could hear the tightness in her voice herself. Swallowing hard, she forced a smile. 'But thank you.'

'Is it me or are you like this with all men?'

His voice had been calm, unemotional, but the effect of his words brought her pent-up breath escaping in a tiny swoosh. Feigning a hauteur she didn't feel, she said, 'I'm sorry?'

He had settled himself in a corner of the sofa half-turned towards her and with one arm stretched along the top of the seat. The casual pose emphasised her own tenseness, which was unfortunate. 'You're as jumpy as a kitten around me,' he murmured. 'A little Titian-haired kitten with enormous green eyes that doesn't know whether to bite or purr.'

Willow bristled immediately, the welcome flood of adrenalin sharpening her voice as she said, 'I can assure you I have no intention of doing either and I am most certainly not "jumpy", as you put it. I'd just prefer to tackle my house myself, that's all.'

'So you're not frightened of me or nervous in any way?'

'Of course I'm not. Don't be so ridiculous,' she said firmly.

'That's good.'

He shifted position slightly and her bravado faltered before she steeled herself to remain perfectly still. He was only reaching for his coffee, for goodness' sake! What was the matter with her? She had to pull herself together and fast.

Morgan drank deeply from his cup, took a couple of chocolates and then settled back into the contours of the sofa, his eyes on her wary face. 'So,' he drawled lazily, 'Keeper's Cottage is the place where you hide away from the big, bad world?'

He had hit the nail square on the head but Willow would rather have walked stark naked through the village than admit it. 'Not at all.' She found she was glaring at him and quickly moderated her expression. 'I simply liked the area, the cottage, and it was the right price. It all came together at the right time.'

'I see.' His tone reeked of disbelief.

'I'm not hiding away like a hermit after my divorce, if

that's what you're suggesting,' she said hotly. 'Not for a minute.'

'That's good,' he said again.

'But even if I was—which I'm not—it would be my own business and no one else's. *No one else's.*'

'Of course it would,' he said soothingly.

Willow drew in a deep breath. 'Has anyone ever told you you're the most aggravating man in the world?' she said stonily.

Amused blue eyes considered her discomfiture. 'Not that I can remember. There have been other accolades, though.'

Willow took refuge in dignified silence—only because she silently acknowledged she wouldn't win in a war of words with Morgan. After another two chocolates she ran out of something for her hands and mouth to do. His eyes were waiting for her when she nerved herself to glance his way.

'This might not be the best time to confess, but I've arranged for a team of professional cleaners to go into the cottage first thing tomorrow,' he said coolly. 'I hope that's OK?'

'*What?*' She literally couldn't believe her ears.

Her voice had been so shrill he winced when he said, 'Come on, they'll do in a few hours what would take you a few days.'

'You've hired *strangers* to go into my home? How *dare* you?'

'They're not strangers, they're a small family firm I've used professionally several times and they're totally trustworthy.'

'They're strangers to *me*,' she ground out furiously.

He gave her a hard look. 'So you'd rather struggle for days and still not do such a good job as they'll accomplish.'

'Absolutely.' She glared at him.

He folded his arms over his chest, stretching his long legs as he studied her with an air of exasperation. 'You like to make it almost impossible for anyone to help you, obviously.'

'I don't want strangers in my home,' she repeated stubbornly. 'I'm sorry but you'll have to cancel them.'

'You mean it, don't you?' His voice carried a faint air of bewilderment, which would have made her smile in different circumstances. 'You'd really rather do it yourself.'

Willow tilted her chin. 'I know you were trying to be kind,' she said steadily. 'I appreciate that, really. But I am more than capable of looking after myself and I like to do things my way. I do not want a cleaning team in my cottage.'

Morgan said nothing for a few moments. Then he nodded slowly. 'Fair enough. I'll ring them and tell them they're not needed. OK?'

'Thank you.' She relaxed a little. Bad mistake.

'And in the morning I'll help you make a start and you can tell me exactly how you want things done.' He reached for another chocolate as he spoke, popping it into his mouth before offering her the box. 'OK?' he said mildly. And he smiled.

She stared at him. After rejecting his proposal about the cleaners she didn't feel she could refuse his help again. Besides, he was talking about it as though it were already a fait accompli. Her brow slightly furrowed, she said hesitantly, 'I don't want to put you about any further.'

'You're not.' He grinned a slightly wolfish grin. 'Have one of the dark ones with the cherry on top. They're delicious.'

CHAPTER SIX

OK, so he'd lied about the cleaners but it was only a small white lie. And perfectly acceptable in the circumstances.

After an hour or two of tossing and turning Morgan had given up all hope of sleep and decided to take a shower. Now, as he stood under the cool water with his face up-turned to the flow, he found his mind was still centred on the flame-haired, green-eyed girl sleeping under his roof.

She would never have agreed to let him accompany her to the cottage tomorrow without a spot of subterfuge, and the job of cleaning up was too much for one, he told himself self-righteously. Hell, he was doing her a favour after all. He'd brought home a briefcase full of papers needing his attention this weekend; it wasn't as if he didn't have anything better to do.

Turning off the water, he raked back his hair and stepped out of the shower. The bathroom was black and white, the white bath, basin, toilet and bidet offset by gleaming black wall and floor tiles and a large strip of mirror that coiled round the room at chest height and reached the ceiling. The room had a voyeuristic quality, which Morgan didn't apologise for in the least, having designed it himself, along with the equally luxurious and dramatic bedroom, again in black and white.

After drying himself roughly with a towel he walked through to the bedroom stark naked, flinging himself on the ruffled black sheets and switching on the massive high-definition LCD TV. He flicked through umpteen channels before throwing down the remote with a grunt of irritation, his mind replaying the last few minutes before he'd left Willow at her bedroom door.

He'd wanted to kiss her so why the devil hadn't he? he asked himself testily. Just a light, friendly kiss, nothing heavy. A social exchange that would have emphasised he was merely being neighbourly in having her stay. But he hadn't wanted her to get the wrong idea, to imagine he was coming on to her. She was already like a cat on a hot tin roof most of the time—he hadn't liked the idea of unsettling her further.

Nice rationalisations, another section of his mind stated dryly, but that was all they were. The truth was he hadn't dared trust himself to kiss her. He had the feeling once his mouth connected with hers it might mean a whole lot of trouble.

Groaning softly, he rolled over and stood up, pulling on his black towelling robe. If he wasn't going to be able to sleep he might as well make himself a pot of coffee and do some work in the study. He'd brought home the details of a merger he was contemplating and he wanted to get the facts and figures securely under his belt for a meeting on Monday morning. His main business interests revolved around the buying and selling of companies—always at a profit—and he had a team of people working for him at the premises he owned in the city. This project was a little different, however. A friend he'd been at uni with had approached him asking for his help. His friend owned a glassmaking business, which had been handed down through his family for generations, but it was in severe financial trouble. The proposal was that for a share of the business he plough in the necessary funds to keep it floating but, friend or not, he didn't intend to try to patch up a ship that was too full of leaks. He needed to go through the papers very carefully so he knew exactly what was entailed.

The dogs were sprawled in the hall when he padded downstairs, his bare feet making no sound. Bella raised her head, wagged her tail and settled down to sleep again and the rest of the pack—as always—followed her lead. As he approached the kitchen he saw a dim light shining from under the door and, forewarned, opened the door quietly. She was sitting on one of the stools at the island in the center of the room sipping at a mug of something or other. The sight of her—her slim figure wrapped in a white towelling robe and her shining mass of hair loose about her shoulders—took his breath away for a moment. 'Willow?' he murmured softly. 'Is everything all right?'

The jump she gave almost sent her off the stool and onto the floor as she swung round to face him. 'Morgan, I didn't hear you.'

'Sorry.' He raised his hand placatingly. 'I didn't mean to startle you. I was just going to get myself some coffee.'

'No, no, that's OK, you didn't startle me.'

He clearly had. She still looked scared to death.

'I—I couldn't sleep,' she stammered. 'Strange bed. I thought I'd make myself some hot milk.'

Hot milk. He could give her something much more satisfying than hot milk to help her sleep. There was nothing like a long bout of lovemaking to relax tense muscles. 'I couldn't sleep either but in my case it's not the bed,' he said blandly. 'My solution was going to be coffee and work.' He waved his hand vaguely in the direction of his study.

She was as flushed as if she'd read his illicit thoughts, her eyes dropping to the mug in her hand. She had small hands, he thought, although her fingers were long and slender. Nice nails. Long but not too long. How would it feel to have them rake his back gently in the moment he brought her to a climax? To have her moan and pulse beneath him? To cry out as he tasted and pleased her until her thighs shook and she sobbed his name in utter abandonment? They would be good together; he knew it.

His erection pulsed, almost painfully so, and conscious the towelling robe did little to hide his arousal he kept his back to her while he fixed himself a pot of coffee, making small talk as he did so. Hell, what a situation to be in. In spite of himself he wanted to smile. If anyone had told him a few weeks ago he'd be lusting after a woman to the point of making a damn fool of himself—a woman who wasn't remotely interested in him, incidentally—he'd have told them they were crazy.

Once his body was under his control again, he reached for a cake tin and opened it to reveal one of Kitty's unsurpassable moist fruit cakes. 'Fancy a slice?' he asked as he turned and showed Willow the cake. 'It's second to none. I can guarantee you won't taste fruit cake like this again.'

'You've convinced me.'

She smiled such a friendly smile it made him feel a swine for his lecherous thoughts.

He cut them both a generous portion and joined her on the other stool. After her first bite, she said, 'It *is* fabulous. I thought my mother had the record for fruit cake but Kitty would have given her a run for her money.'

'What happened with your parents?' he asked softly. 'Was it an accident?'

She nodded, her silky hair fanning her cheeks. Quietly and softly she told him the details and, although her voice was matter-of-fact, the pain in her eyes told its own story. He didn't like how it affected him. He didn't like how *she* affected him, but he reminded himself it didn't really matter in the scheme of things. The circumstances that had thrown them together this weekend were unlikely to be repeated, and as long as he kept his lurid thoughts—and his hands—to himself, there was no harm done. Apart from a few sleepless nights perhaps.

Aiming to bring the conversation and her thoughts to happier things, he said quietly, 'You said your sister is expecting a baby soon. How does it feel knowing you'll be an aunty? Are you looking forward to it?'

She smiled, wiping a crumb from the fruit cake from the corner of her lips, and as his gaze followed the action his traitorous body responded sharply, causing his breath to catch in his throat.

'I can't wait,' she said with genuine warmth, 'but at the same time it doesn't feel quite real. I mean, Beth's my sister, the person I argued and fought and shared secrets with over the years. Her stomach's getting bigger and she's developed an obsession for chocolate and cherry muffins, but it's hard to believe there's a little person in there. Does that sound silly?'

Secretly enchanted she had let her guard down for once, Morgan shook his head. 'Not at all. I'm a mere man, don't forget. I find the whole process baffling. Well, apart from the beginning, of course. I worked out the birds and the bees some time ago.'

She giggled, blushing slightly, and as he looked at her parted lips he wanted to kiss her so hard it hurt. As he raised his eyes to hers they were smiling into his and for several seconds, seconds that quivered with intimacy, their gaze held. When her eyes dropped to her plate and she ate a morsel of cake with uncharacteristic clumsiness, dropping half of it onto the worktop, he knew he had been right.

Willow Landon was no more indifferent to him than he was to her. Which presented a whole load of new problems. Big ones.

By the time Willow returned to her room all the good work the soothing hot milk had wrought was completely undone. Morgan had escorted her to the door, said goodnight very politely and disappeared along the landing to his own room without a backward glance, thereby rendering all her fears null and void.

Fears? a little voice in the back of her mind queried nastily. Don't you mean hopes? Desires? Longings?

Her jaw tightened and she leaned back against the bedroom door, her legs trembling as she fought for control.

She was *not* attracted to Morgan Wright. 'I'm not,' she reiterated weakly, as though someone had argued the point. 'No way, no how.' She had no intention of getting involved with a man for a long, long time—if ever—and certainly not one like Morgan. If and when someone came along she could see herself dating now and again, he'd have to be a mild, retiring type who was easy-going and happy to meet her halfway on any issues that might crop up. Morgan didn't meet the criteria in any direction.

Not that he'd asked her for a date, of course. And wouldn't. It didn't need the brain of Britain to work out the sort of female Morgan would take to bed when the need arose. Without a doubt they'd be stunningly beautiful and sexy and probably highly intelligent as well; he didn't strike her as a man who would be satisfied with merely an accommodating body. He'd expect mental as well as physical stimulation from his partners.

Levering herself away from the door, she walked across to the bed and sank down. She had known all along it was madness to come into his home. One of the reasons she had bought the cottage was because of its secluded location. It was far enough away from the nearby village to ensure there'd be no pressure from neighbours intent on including her in this, that and the other, or—which was even more pertinent—if any tried, she could cold-shoulder them without having to bump into them each day.

She raised her head and glanced around the luxurious room, her conscience kicking in as it usually did.

She was grateful to Morgan for his help, she really was, and she didn't want to hurt his feelings or anyone else's for that matter, but it was somehow essential that her life was her own again down to the smallest decision. She had done the whole trying-to-please-everyone thing to death. She was never going to relinquish the tiniest fragment of her autonomy again.

Wasn't that verging on callous? questioned Soft-hearted Willow reprovingly. Wasn't that selfish and mean?

No. It was sheer self-survival, answered Unmovable, Resolute Willow grimly. Pure and simple.

Easing out a breath, she stood up. She was going to brush her teeth and go to sleep, and if Morgan insisted on helping her clean the cottage in the morning she'd thank him sincerely when they'd finished and then that would be the end of this... She sought for a word to describe what she was feeling and then gave up. 'Whatever,' she muttered grumpily to herself as she marched into the en-suite to brush her teeth.

Willow awoke to bright autumn sunshine streaming in the window the next morning. Sleepily she told herself she should have closed the curtains the night before, but then she checked the time by her wristwatch and shot into a sitting position. *Ten o'clock?* It couldn't be that late, surely? Pushing her hair out of her eyes, she refocused her gaze. Ten o'clock it was.

Springing out of bed, she galloped into the bathroom for a quick wash and brush-up and was dressed and ready to venture downstairs within five minutes, her hair pulled back in a high ponytail and her face clean and scrubbed. She couldn't believe she'd slept so late. When he had left her the night before Morgan had mentioned he normally breakfasted about eight in the morning at the weekends. What must he be thinking? And Kitty—the housekeeper would obviously have expected her employer's guest to eat with him. Yet again she had done the wrong thing.

The big house was quiet and still when Willow opened

her bedroom door and stepped onto a galleried landing flooded with light. Old houses were sometimes dark and somewhat forbidding, but due to the number of large windows on every floor of this one it breathed airiness and space. She stood for a moment breathing in the slightly perfumed air, the source of the delicate scent becoming apparent when she descended the stairs and saw a huge bowl of white and yellow roses on a table at the foot of the staircase. They had obviously been arranged by Kitty earlier.

She didn't have time to think about the flowers, though. As Willow reached the bottom step Morgan uncurled himself from one of the easy chairs dotted about the vast hall, throwing down the magazine he'd been reading before her arrival.

'I'm so sorry,' she said before he could speak. 'I never sleep late, never, and you told me what time breakfast was. I hope I haven't put Kitty out and—'

'Easy, easy.' He smiled with warm amusement in his eyes. 'In this house the weekends fit in with the occupants, not the other way round. You clearly found the bed comfortable at least.'

In truth she had tossed and turned until dawn, but her inability to sleep had had nothing to do with the bed and all to do with the tall dark man in front of her. 'It was lovely, thank you.' She could hear the breathlessness in her voice and was annoyed by it. The night before she had decided she was going to be very calm, cool and collected in her future dealings with Morgan Wright and here she was acting like a gauche fourteen-year-old.

'Jim's taken Kitty shopping once I persuaded her we were quite capable of sorting ourselves out for breakfast,' he said lazily. 'I suggest we eat in the kitchen if that's OK? It's easier and Kitty's not here to object.'

'That's fine by me but you should have eaten earlier.' She felt awful having clearly put a spanner in the house's normal weekend routine. It was so rude.

'Why would I do that?' he said quietly, walking her through to the kitchen at the end of the hall.

Morgan opened the door and stood aside for Willow to precede him into the room. The kitchen was fabulous. She'd seen it in dim light, last night, but she'd been too fraught to take in how stunning it was. The flowing lines of the spectacularly beautiful black granite worktops, which glittered like a starry night's sky, the wide expanse of light wood cupboards and array of every modern appliance known to man were impressive. 'Wow,' she breathed. 'Now this *is* a kitchen.'

'Like it?' He smiled, obviously pleased. 'This is Kitty's domain but I designed it myself and know my way around.' He walked to a refrigerator that could have accommodated several families, opening it as he said, 'There's orange, grapefruit, apple and mango, black grape and cranberry juice. Which would you like? Oh, and a couple of smoothies, banana and loganberry.'

'No pineapple?' she asked, tongue in cheek.

He looked at her and she looked at him. He stood enveloped in the golden sunlight streaming through the wide kitchen window, his black jeans and white shirt making him a living monochrome. Her heart stopped and then galloped as he smiled slowly, his blue eyes warm as he said, 'Touché.'

'I'll have black grape, please,' she said weakly after a long moment when she could find her breath to speak.

He wasn't supposed to be able to laugh at himself. Her heart was now thumping like a gong in her chest and she wasn't able to control her breathing. That wasn't who Morgan Wright was. *Was it?* But then she didn't have a clue who he was.

She sat down at the kitchen table, which had been set for two. Not by Kitty, she was sure. A basket of what looked like home-made soft rolls and a pat of butter were in the centre, and Willow suddenly felt ravenously hungry. As Morgan handed her a glass of juice she said, 'May I?' as she nodded at the rolls.

'Help yourself.' He grinned. 'Cooked this morning by Kitty's fair hand. No shop-bought bread in this establishment.'

'You're spoilt,' she said a moment later, her mouth full of the delicious bread. 'Absolutely spoilt rotten.'

'You're right.' He'd begun to cook bacon and eggs and the aroma was heavenly. 'And long may it continue.'

They ate sitting side by side in the sunlit kitchen, finishing off with some of the best coffee Willow had ever tasted. Replete, she stretched like a slender well-fed cat. 'I've never eaten three eggs at one sitting in my life.' She glanced at him and he was smiling. 'It's not good for you, you know,' she said reprovingly. 'Very bad for your health, in fact.'

'Eating?' he murmured mockingly.

'Eating too many eggs.'

'You've been listening to the experts, I take it?' he drawled lazily. 'Give it another decade and they'll be saying you should eat a dozen a day or something. Their advice changes with the wind. There's always someone saying something different.'

'So how do you know what's right?'

He gave her a long, steady look and suddenly they weren't talking about eggs. His eyes held hers locked. 'Go with your heart,' he said softly. 'Always with your heart.'

There was a silence that stretched and lengthened. 'And if your heart lets you down and leads you astray?' she said shakily. 'What happens then?'

'There's no guarantees in life,' Morgan acknowledged after a moment, 'but what's the alternative? To live in fear and never experience the freedom of casting all restraint aside?'

'Eggs aren't that important to me in the overall scheme of things,' she said with forced lightness. 'I could live without them.'

'Pity.' He studied her face. 'What if you wake up one day years from now when it's too late and you're old and set in your ways and regret all those breakfasts you never had? What then?'

'At least my cholesterol will be under control.'

'And control is important to you?' he asked smoothly.

Again he'd put his finger on the nub of the issue but this time she wasn't going to let him get away with it. Remembering their conversation of the day before, she said carefully, 'Probably as important as it is to you, yes.'

His mouth quirked to the side, a self-deprecating smile that intensified his attractiveness tenfold. 'Ouch,' he murmured lazily. 'I guess I set myself up for that one.'

Willow slid off her chair. 'I'll help you clear up so all's as it should be when Kitty comes back.'

'No need, it won't take a minute to load the dishwasher. Why don't you get your bag and meet me in the hall and we'll go to the cottage and start?' he said easily.

Willow hesitated. She knew she didn't want Morgan in her cottage. It was too—her mind balked at dangerous and substituted—irksome. But she also knew he'd made up his mind he was going to help.

Her expression must have spoken for itself because he said, very softly, 'Get your bag, Willow.'

They worked like Trojans the rest of the day until late in the evening. Kitty arrived with lunch about one o'clock but apart from that they didn't take a break. Willow had to admit Morgan did the work of ten men and by seven o'clock the cottage was cleaner than it had ever been. Morgan had thought to bring a large container of upholstery shampoo with him and her sofa and armchair were now damp but free of smuts. The new sitting-room curtains she'd bought the week before had been washed, dried in the sunshine and ironed and were now back in place at the squeaky-clean window. Ceiling, walls, floorboards and fireplace had been washed down and Morgan had even given the kitchen a once-over, although soot hadn't penetrated too far within its walls. The bathroom door had been shut so that room hadn't needed any attention.

Kitty had insisted she was cooking an evening meal for them when she'd brought lunch, and Willow had to admit she wasn't sorry as she took a quick shower and washed her hair, vitally conscious of Morgan sitting on the French window steps nursing a cup of coffee. She was exhausted, the result of working flat out all day and not having slept properly the night before. Not to mention the nervous tension with being around him.

She left the bathroom cocooned from head to foot in

towels and scurried up the stairs to her bedroom, even though there was no need to panic. Morgan wasn't the type of man to take advantage. He wouldn't have to, she thought wryly as she hastily got dressed in cream linen trousers and a jade-green cashmere top, which had cost an arm and a leg a few months ago. Morgan would have women falling over themselves to get noticed by him.

After drying her hair into a sleek curtain, she left it loose and applied the minimum of make-up, along with silver hoops in her ears. She wanted to look fresh and attractive but not as if she was trying too hard. After dabbing a few drops of her favourite perfume on her wrists she was ready. Taking a deep breath, she checked herself in the mirror. Wide green eyes stared anxiously back at her and she clicked her tongue irritably. For goodness' sake! She looked like a scared rabbit!

Smoothing her face of all expression, she tried a light smile. That was better. She was going to have dinner with him, that was all, and once tonight was over it was doubtful they'd run into each other again. In fact she'd make sure they didn't. Morgan was only in residence at weekends and she could avoid being home until late for the next little while. The planning office was crying out for a few folk to work Saturdays on a new project in Redditch, and on Sundays she could catch up with friends and visit Beth. It would all work out just fine.

Not that she expected Morgan to try and see her. Why would he? He was way out of her league in every way. But she didn't want him to think she was hanging around at weekends in the hope of bumping into him. That would be the ultimate humiliation.

Neurotic. The word vibrated in her head from some deep recess in her psyche and she pulled a face at the girl in the mirror before turning away defiantly. She wasn't neurotic, she argued silently, but even if she was she'd prefer that than Morgan Wright thinking she was interested in him.

Morgan was still sitting on the steps when she walked into the sitting room, his head resting on the side of one of the open French doors and his eyes shut. He hadn't had the advantage of a shower and the shirt that had been white that morning was white no longer. She had approached noiselessly and now she stood for a moment looking at him. The hair, which was longer than average for a man—or certainly a businessman—had flicked up slightly on his collar and he had smudges of dirt on his face. Beneath the shirt hard muscles showed across his chest and shoulders and his forearms were sinewy beneath their coating of soft black hair. He looked more like someone who spent his days working outside than anything else. Tough, strong, brawny. Even slightly rough and hard-bitten. Piers had been tall but slender and even beautiful in a classical Adonis sort of way.

Shocked by the knowledge that she was comparing the two of them, she must have made a noise because the next moment the brilliant blue eyes had opened. 'What's the matter?' He was instantly on the alert, rising to his feet with an animal grace that belied her earlier thoughts. 'What's happened?'

'Nothing.' She forced a smile. 'Nothing at all.'

'Nothing? Willow, you were staring at me as though I was the devil incarnate.'

'Of course I wasn't.' Somehow she managed to keep any shakiness out of her voice and smile. 'You imagined it.'

His expression hardened. 'Tell me,' he said flatly.

'There's nothing to tell. I...I was thinking your office staff might have a job to recognise their immaculately turned out boss tonight, that's all.' It was weak but all she could think of.

'I don't believe you.' His blue eyes searched her face, demanding the truth. 'What have I done to make you look like that? Forgive me, but I think I've a right to know.'

'Nothing. Really, you haven't, you know you haven't. You—you've been very kind.' He wasn't buying it. 'Very kind.'

'So tell me,' he said again. 'What were you thinking?'

Willow stared at him helplessly. 'I was thinking of my ex-husband,' she admitted flatly, knowing he wouldn't like it.

Morgan's eyes narrowed to blue slits. 'From the little you've said about him it's no compliment you look at me and see him. Are we similar to look at? Is that it?'

'No, that's not it. At least, what I mean is, you don't remind me of him. Just the opposite, in fact.'

She could tell he was unconvinced even before he folded his arms and said stiffly, 'So what brought him to mind?'

Inwardly groaning, she sought for the right words. 'Piers was very handsome,' she said slowly. 'And charming.'

He stared at her. 'Willow, this isn't getting any better.'

'What I mean is, it was all false. A front. The real Piers—' She shook her head, shuddering in spite of herself.

Willow wasn't aware of him moving and taking her into his arms, it happened so quickly, but amazingly she didn't fight the embrace but sank into it, closing her eyes as she rested against his chest. She felt his mouth on the top of her head in the lightest of kisses before he murmured, 'Don't look like that. He can't hurt you any more, it's over. He has no hold on you now, Willow.'

'I know.' She *did* know, but occasionally the memory of that last terrible night in their apartment would take over despite all her efforts to keep it at bay. Maybe Beth was right. Perhaps she should have seen a counsellor and talked things through with someone trained to help in such cases, but she had been determined to rise above the tag of victim. She still was. And as Morgan had just said, it was over now. He couldn't hurt her any more.

Making a desperate effort to pull herself together and both shocked and mortified at how the evening had degenerated into something much too raw, she moved out of Morgan's arms as she said, 'You're not like him in any way, that's what I was thinking. I promise. Not in looks or anything else.'

'Good.' Gently he pulled her close again. His kiss was thorough but gentle, the sort of kiss she had fantasised about as a young schoolgirl. She was overwhelmed with a drowning, floating sensation that was sweet and sensual at the same time and mind-blowingly addictive. She felt a soft warmth blooming deep within her body and parted her lips to strengthen the intimacy between them, not really aware of what she was doing and led purely by an instinct so strong it was overpowering.

She was pressed against the muscular wall of his chest and could feel his heart thudding his arousal. It was exhilarating, heady, to know he wanted her. In these moments of time it was all that mattered. And she wanted him too.

His fingers had tangled in her hair, tilting her head back as his lips moved over hers with more urgency, his mouth meltingly sexy. He'd moulded her into him as he'd deepened the kiss and she felt as though they were already making love standing up, every contour of his hard male body pressing against her softness. It should have shocked her but it didn't.

'Willow…' He groaned her name and something in his voice echoed in her. She wanted him. Right here and now, on the floor of her sitting room, she wanted him.

It was like a deluge of icy cold water as her mind registered how much she'd lost control. She jerked away, stumbling backwards as she gasped for air. 'No.' The word sounded plaintive, weak, and she took another breath before she said more strongly, 'I don't want this. I'm sorry but I don't want this. This is not who I am.'

Morgan was quite still. For a moment something continued to blaze in the blue eyes and then it was veiled. His control was almost insulting when he nodded, a faint smile touching his lips as he murmured, 'No problem, put it down to one of those crazy moments, OK?' As she continued to stare at him he added softly, 'I'm not a wolf, Willow. You're quite safe. No is no in my book.'

A single beat passed. She knew she had to say something. They both were aware she had been there with him every moment. Flicking her hair from her hot face, she found she couldn't look at him when she said, 'I—I didn't mean to make you think—'

'I didn't.' His voice was firm but not annoyed. 'It's fine.'

Willow swallowed hard. 'What I mean is—'

'Stop it, OK? Like I said, it was one of those crazy

moments that happen sometimes between members of the opposite sex. Now, I don't know about you but I could eat a horse so how about we see what Kitty's rustled up this evening?'

She met his eyes then. His features were expressionless and she couldn't tell what he was thinking. It was easier to take his words at face value, besides which she didn't know how to explain to him what she couldn't explain to herself. If someone had told her that morning she would want Morgan Wright to take her with every fibre of her being she would have laughed in their face, but she had. And in this moment of absolute honesty with herself she knew this had been brewing from the first time she'd laid eyes on him, but she hadn't wanted to acknowledge the fierce attraction this man held for her.

Feeling the ground beneath her feet had changed to shifting sand, she knew she couldn't dodge the truth. Gathering all her courage, she said woodenly, 'I don't make a practice of giving the wrong signals, I just want you to know that. I've never slept with anyone except my ex.'

'If you're trying to tell me you aren't the sort of woman to hop in and out of bed with any man who catches your fancy, I'd already worked that out for myself.' He raked back his hair and went on in a tone laced with unmistakable sincerity, 'You're still working things through after the breakup, I can see that, so don't beat yourself up about one kiss. That's all it was, a kiss. Forget it, Willow. I already have.'

But it hadn't been, at least not for her. It had been an introduction into a realm she'd never imagined even existed. She'd loved Piers—at first, that was—but his lovemaking had never done what one kiss from Morgan had accomplished.

Her green eyes darkened but, telling herself she had to follow his lead and lighten the mood, she nodded and smiled. 'You're right,' she said as casually as she could manage.

He returned the smile. 'Of course I'm right,' he said lazily. 'It goes with the name.' Shutting the French doors, he locked them and then turned to where she was standing, leaning forward and touching her lips lightly with his before she'd realised what he was going to do. 'We're friends,' he said easily, taking her arm and leading her out of the cottage into the warm October shadows, 'so relax. You've got nothing to fear from me.'

Willow took a breath and tried to ignore what the feel of his warm flesh on hers was doing to her equilibrium. She might not have anything to fear from Morgan—although that was a mute point—but she had plenty to fear from herself where this man was concerned. She had to remember that and be on her guard. Morgan had been kind to her and she was grateful, but there was much more to him than met the eye. Much more.

CHAPTER SEVEN

WILLOW awoke in her own bed the next morning and listened to the faint echo of the bells in the village church calling the faithful to the Sunday morning service. Sunlight spilled through the window but the air was cool as she slipped out of bed and made her way downstairs to the kitchen wrapped in her thick robe. It was sparkling clean after Morgan's spring clean.

After making herself a pot of coffee she poured a cup and wandered through to the sitting room. The sofa and chair were still a little damp from Morgan's ministrations the day before and so she opened the French doors and sat on the steps, much as he'd done. The air was actually warmer in the garden than it was in the house, she thought with a stab of surprise. The solid walls of the cottage had the effect of cooling the rooms somewhat. Morgan had given her the name and telephone number of a local plumber the night before so she could see about having central heating fitted before the worst of the winter.

Morgan… She bit down on her bottom lip pensively. He'd behaved like a perfect gentleman after that one scorching kiss. They'd eaten Kitty's wonderful dinner, talked, laughed a little and enjoyed coffee with a fine liqueur before he'd seen her home to her front door. He'd tucked her hand through his arm as they had walked the short distance down his drive and into the lane before reaching the cottage, and although she'd known it was merely a casual gesture it had seemed strangely intimate to feel the pressure of his body close to hers. Once at her door she had prepared herself for the goodnight kiss. Only it hadn't come. Not even a fleeting peck like the one he'd given her after the scorcher. She could have been his maiden aunt, she thought crossly.

Willow frowned to herself, inhaling the fragrant scent of coffee as she idly watched two blue tits hanging from a nut feeder she'd hung from one of the trees bordering the garden, their distinct blue crests on tiny black and white heads vivid in the sunshine.

Not that she had *wanted* him to kiss her, she assured herself firmly. The close embrace hours before had been enough to convince her that where Morgan was concerned she'd be playing with fire. No, far better to keep it light and easy. And that was exactly what he'd done. Her frown deepened. Which was fine.

She finished the coffee and fetched another cup, settling herself down again in the same spot and feeling intensely irritable.

She was being ridiculous. She nodded to the thought. *And* hypocritical, which was the one human failing she loathed above all others. A hot arrow of guilt pierced her. She couldn't insist Morgan kept his hands—and his mouth—to himself and then feel miffed when he did exactly that. She was being monumentally unfair and capricious and unreasonable, but *why* hadn't he mentioned seeing her again? Why had he just walked off without a word?

Because you're just the neighbour he helped out.

She lifted one shoulder in answer to the thought, the motion defensive, almost aggressive. In that case he'd had no right to kiss her as he had, had he? She took a long pull at the coffee, scalding hot though it was. He hadn't; it had been grossly unfair.

She *was* being ridiculous. He'd explained that kiss as one of those things that happened now and again between members of the opposite sex, and that was what it had been. It wasn't his fault that it had been the most devastatingly, incredible, *amazing* experience of her life and had left her wanting much, much more.

Her heart jolted violently and then jump-started itself into a machine-gun gallop. She put her hands to her chest as though to calm it down, her mind racing.

No, no, no. She shut her eyes tightly as she struggled for calm. He had said friends and that was exactly what their relationship—*relationship?*—was. Friends. Neighbours. Nothing more. Nothing less. Anything more would be disastrous.

She opened her eyes. The blue tits were back, having been disturbed temporarily when she'd gone to fetch her second cup of coffee. They twittered happily, positively frolicking on the nuts.

She had no right to feel let down. No right at all, and yet she did. More than she could have imagined. Which only proved she had been absolutely right when she had told herself that Morgan Wright was dangerous and to be avoided.

* * *

'So she didn't stay another night?' Kitty said disapprovingly.

Morgan clenched his teeth but when he spoke his voice was cool and controlled. 'No, Kitty, she didn't.'

'Pity.' Kitty sucked her breath through her teeth. 'Pity.'

'Pity?' Even as he told himself not to bite, he responded.

'I think so. She seems a nice young lady.'

'Ah, but I go for the bad ones, Kitty. You should know that by now.' He grinned at her with a lecherous wink.

Kitty treated his mockery with the contempt it deserved and ignored it as she plonked Morgan's breakfast in front of him. 'So when are you seeing her again?' she said stolidly.

Morgan deliberately finished the last of his coffee before he said, 'I've no idea. When she needs rescuing from a burning building or something similar? That seems to be the pattern.'

Kitty surveyed him, hands on hips. Even her apron seemed to rustle with indignation. 'You didn't arrange to see her again? A lovely young woman like that? Why ever not?'

He had asked himself the same question countless times and the answer didn't sit well with him. Willow had the potential to complicate his autonomous controlled life and he needed that sort of aggravation like a hole in the head. In fact it scared the hell out of him. Pouring himself more coffee, he said casually, 'Why would I arrange to see her, Kitty? She's a neighbour who needed a helping hand, that's the only reason she came here in the first place.' He took a sip and burnt his mouth.

'Maybe, but she did come and you seemed to get on well.'

Get on well? He was drawn to Willow with a strength that he hadn't felt before and that was the very reason he had to avoid contact. Shrugging, he murmured, 'She was polite and grateful, but I think getting on well might be pushing it a bit. Besides which—' He stopped abruptly. Was it wise to go on?

'What?' Kitty's ears pricked up immediately.

'Nothing.' And then he decided to tell her. If nothing else it might stop her infernal matchmaking. 'She's not in the market for any sort of relationship, as it happens. She was married and I gather the divorce wasn't an amicable one. Once burnt, twice shy. She doesn't date and she intends to keep it that way.'

Kitty snorted. 'Poppycock. The lass might be a bit wary, but that's better than some of these brazen types that are around these days. That's the one thing I can't abide in a woman, brazenness.'

What she meant was the brazen types *he* dated, Morgan thought wryly, being fully aware of Kitty's opinion of his lifestyle and in particular his women. He unfolded his Sunday paper, signifying the conversation was at an end, his voice dismissive when he said coolly, 'She's a neighbour, that's all, Kitty. And I'll have a round of toast to go with the bacon and eggs, please.'

For once Kitty wasn't playing ball. Folding her arms across her plump little stomach, she said grimly, 'You let this one go and you'll regret it, m'lad. That's all I'm saying.'

For crying out loud! His tone deliberately weary, he said, 'I can't let go of what I don't have. End of story.' And he raised the newspaper in front of his face.

He didn't enjoy his breakfast and the paper was full of

rubbish. Irritable and out of sorts, he decided to take the dogs for a long walk to blow away the cobwebs and get himself back on course so he could work that afternoon.

Pulling on a leather jacket, he whistled the dogs and left the house a few minutes later. There was a pleasing nip in the air, foretelling the frosts that were sure to come later in the month. The October day was fresh and bright, shallow sparkles of sunshine warming the fields that stretched either side of the lane beyond his house. He walked in the opposite direction to Willow's cottage and the village, a host of magpies in the trees bordering the lane chattering across the autumn sky.

Shortly after leaving his property, he turned off the lane onto a footpath that led between fields recently ploughed under the stubble of the old wheat crop, the dogs gambolling ahead but taking care to stay on the footpath like the well-trained animals they were. The landscape was already turning into a glorious world of golden tints from copper to orange and Morgan stood for a moment, breathing in the sharp air and looking up into a blue sky, which until recently had been full of swallows gathering together ready to migrate and screaming their goodbyes.

Everything was fine. He nodded to the thought. Nothing had changed. His world was ticking along nicely and under his control.

He continued to tell himself this throughout the rest of the walk and by the time he returned home he was ready for his Sunday lunch. He ate a hearty portion of Kitty's Yorkshire pudding and roast beef with roast potatoes that were crisp on the outside and feathery soft on the inside, and disappeared into his study for the rest of the afternoon. By the time he re-emerged as a golden autumn twilight was falling he had the facts and figures of the papers he'd been studying clear in his head.

He met Kitty in the hall and she was carrying a tray holding steaming coffee and a plate of her delicious home-made shortbread. 'Though you might want a break,' she said fussily. 'You work too hard.'

Morgan hid a smile. This was her way of saying he was now forgiven. 'Thanks, but I'm just on my way out,' he said, and it was only in that moment he realized he'd been intending to call round and see Willow from the moment he opened his eyes that morning. 'I'll be back as and when,' he added, 'so don't worry about dinner. I'll grab a sandwich or something when I come in. Your roast was enough to keep a man going for twenty-four hours.'

He left before she could ask any awkward questions and for the same reason took the Harley. It would have been a giveaway if he'd walked. Kitty had a nose like an elephant as it was.

When he knocked on the door of Willow's cottage his heart was slamming against his ribcage with the force of a sledgehammer and his mouth felt dry. In any other situation he could have laughed at himself. This evening, though, he didn't feel like laughing.

The door opened and he hoped his nervousness, his rush of wanting, wasn't obvious to her. She stared at him wide-eyed, her delectable mouth slightly open, and he had to swallow hard before he could say, 'Just wondering how the sofa and things are drying out.' Weak, but it was the best he could do.

'They—they're still a bit damp.' She smiled warily.

He nodded. 'Are you cold?' he asked, noticing she was wearing a big baggy furry kind of top over her jeans.

'I haven't been able to light a fire.'

No, of course she hadn't. He wasn't about to look a gift horse in the mouth. He nodded again, in a I-thought-as-much kind of way. 'I know a nice warm little pub not far from here that does wonderful meals and the Harley's waiting.'

She blinked a couple of times and then, as though regaining control over her composure, she smoothed her hair in a little-girl gesture that spoke of confusion. 'Is—is this you being friends?' she said with a monosyllabic breath of laughter.

'Absolutely.' If ever there was a situation where a lie was called for, this was it. 'Scout's honour and all that.'

Their gazes met and held for a moment before hers skittered away. He didn't know whether she liked him or not, Morgan thought triumphantly, but she damn well wasn't unaffected by him and he'd take any encouragement he could get right at this moment. 'And it's also being a good neighbour,' he added, deadpan. 'Such a quality is highly thought of in this part of the country, believe me. Part of the countryman's code and unbreakable.'

She smiled and lust, pure and hot, knifed through him. Well, hot at least. White-hot, in fact.

'OK.' She lowered her head, her hair falling in a sleek curtain either side of her face. 'Come in a minute while I change. I can't go anywhere in these old things.'

Once in the cottage the chill was obvious, even through his leather jacket. He stood, hands thrust in his jeans pockets and his gaze directed at the ceiling above which she was changing. The place was an ice-box. Concern for her brought his mouth into a straight line, moments before he told himself it was none of his business. She had made it clear the day before she was in charge of her life. Furthermore, that she wouldn't appreciate any efforts to alter the status quo. He had to respect that.

She reappeared, and his voice sounded husky even to his own ears when he said, 'Ready?' She looked like all his Christmases rolled into one: gorgeous, self-possessed and as sexy as hell. And yet the demure little top she was wearing covered her to the neck and halfway down her arms, even though it clung in all the right places. A hundred women could wear it and it wouldn't stir his pulse above normal, but on Willow...

'This is very kind of you, Morgan.'

She meant well, but he found he'd had enough of the label. 'I never do anything I don't want to do, Willow.' He smiled to soften the statement as he helped her on with her jacket. 'I'm your typical selfish male. We're born that way.'

'But honest.' She was smiling back at him as she reached for her handbag. 'Well, you are at least. Aren't you?'

'I try to be.' He nodded. 'Yes, I think I am.' Then he grinned. 'Most of the time anyway.'

'Well, I guess that's not bad for the male of the species.' Her voice was light but there was something in her tone that jarred on him. Whether she was aware of it or not, he didn't know, but immediately she followed with, 'Some females too, come to think of it. Women are more inclined to tell little white lies so as not to hurt someone's feelings, I've found.'

'You mean with answers to questions like, "Does my

bum look big in this?"' he replied lazily, to put her at ease, even as he thought, What the hell did her husband do to her to make her so sceptical? She wasn't like this before him, he'd bet money on it.

'Exactly.'

Once outside he nodded at the Harley parked across the other side of the lane. 'Hope you don't mind the mode of transport, but it won't be long and this beauty will be consigned to the garage if we get the sort of floods we got last year during the winter.'

She didn't answer this directly, saying instead as they walked over to the motorbike, 'What sort of car have you got?'

'Cars, plural. An Aston Martin and a Range-Rover.' But you won't have to hold onto me in those and I wouldn't feel your body pressed against mine. His eyes glittering, he gave her the spare helmet he'd brought with him and then helped her up behind him. She smelled gorgeous, some flowery thing with undertones he couldn't put a name to but which made his body harden. 'OK? Hold on tight.' Real tight, don't be shy.

He turned briefly to smile at her before he switched on the engine and her voice sounded breathless when she said, 'I'm not used to riding on a motorbike. How far away is the pub?'

'Not too far.' Unfortunately.

In fact it was ten minutes, being in the next village, the winding lanes that twisted and curved making it far longer than the crow flew and imposing their own speed limit. The pub was a pretty little thatched affair, complete with brasses and narrow mullioned windows and solid oak furniture. Having secured comfy seats by the big open fire-place in which a blazing fire roared, Morgan fetched two halves of beer and the menus.

'Warmer?' He took a long swallow of his beer, looking at her over the rim of his glass. She looked good enough to eat.

She nodded, her gaze not holding his but dropping to the menu in her hand as she said, 'Much. And starving too.'

They were seated at a table for two, so close he could reach out and touch her if he wanted to. And he wanted to, he acknowledged silently. But he didn't. 'The pan-fried crispy pork with red-onion gravy is seriously good here,' he said conversationally. 'But the steaks are great too. Local butcher. But perhaps you'd prefer fish or a risotto?'

'The pork sounds lovely.' She tucked her hair behind her ears as she spoke, the movement not so much wary as guarded. He wondered if she ever let that guard down. Whatever, Willow Landon was one hard female to get to know, but, remembering that burning kiss and the way it had shook him up, it would be worth the trouble. Nothing worth having came easy.

Madness. The word resonated as it bounced round his head. This was madness and he knew it, so why had he asked her out tonight when this had every chance of ending badly?

He knew why. He wanted to make love to her more than he'd wanted to make love to a woman for a long, long time. There was a gnawing hunger inside him for her body, which had been with him since he'd first met her, and it was damn uncomfortable. If he took her to bed then maybe it would assuage the primal need and she'd stop featuring in his dreams every night.

That being the case, why wasn't he going all out to

weaken her defences? another part of his mind asked caustically. He'd had enough experience with women to know the right buttons to press, for crying out loud. It was all part of the mating game.

Because Willow was different.

An alarm went off in his mind, causing him to raise his head with a jerk as a waitress appeared at their table for their order. He raised one eyebrow to Willow. 'The pork?' And at her nod, said to the waitress, 'Make that two.'

'This is nice.' She glanced round the pub as she spoke, her voice warm. 'Do you come here often?'

'Usually just the odd weekend when Kitty and Jim go to visit relatives in the north-east. Kitty always leaves meals she's prepared, but it's the putting it in the oven and getting it out at the right time I fall down on. I tend to work and invariably the meal's cremated by the time I remember.'

'She's very fond of you, isn't she?' She smiled warmly.

'As am I of her and Jim. We rub along together fairly well.'

She nodded. 'They're nice people, what my father would have called salt of the earth.'

The fact that it really mattered that she liked Kitty and Jim was another warning shot across his bows, but again he chose to ignore it. Lifting one ankle to rest it across the opposite knee, he settled back in his seat. 'Tell me about your father,' he said quietly. 'Were you close to him and your mother?'

She was silent for a moment. 'Very close. Beth was too.'

He found he wanted to know more. 'What were they like? As parents, I mean.' He wanted to picture her as a little girl.

She glanced at him, a small, uncertain look. 'They were great,' she said awkwardly.

Suddenly he understood. 'It doesn't hurt to hear about other people's parents,' he lied softly. 'Tell me, if it's not too painful to talk about them,' he added quickly.

'No, Beth and I talk about them often.' She bit her lower lip, her small white teeth worrying the flesh for a moment. 'Where do you want me to start?'

His eyes had flared at the action, but he didn't betray the desire it had induced in his voice when he said, 'The beginning. You as a little girl in pigtails and white lace.'

She smiled, as he'd wanted her to, and relaxed a little. 'I so wasn't a white lace sort of child.'

'But you had pigtails? Cute little red pigtails and freckles?'

She nodded. 'Plenty of freckles.'

'Pigtails and dungarees, then, and scabby knees and ink-stained fingers. And those sandal things, jelly beans, aren't they?'

'Now you're nearer the truth.' She took a sip of her beer and began, 'Well, Mum was a stay-at-home mother and Dad had a nine-to-five job, very traditional…' She talked about her home, their family holidays, how she and her sister had smuggled home a 'pet' crab because they'd been desperate for a pet, after which their parents had bought them a hamster each…

He listened, fascinated, but consciously untensing his jaw several times as the scenes her words invoked brought the old familiar longing tightening muscles.

The subject came to a natural conclusion when the waitress brought their meals, but for a few moments the feeling he'd grown up with—that of being on the outside looking in—was strong before he slammed the lid on what he considered weakness. Being shunted around various relatives who grudgingly took him in for a few months at a time, ignored, neglected, shouted at, was a better deal than some poor kids had, and the independence that had been forced on him at an early age had got him to where he was now. Without that early training he wouldn't have made it.

He repeated the words that had become his mantra to focus his mind on the positive as he ate, and within a minute or two he was back on an even keel. He didn't *need* anyone, he'd managed on his own for over three decades and that was the way he liked it. No, he didn't *need* anyone, but wanting physically was a different matter and entirely natural. And he wanted Willow. More and more every moment he was with her. He didn't know what it was about this defensive, wary, honey-skinned woman that made him ache with want, but whatever it was, it had knocked him for six. He admitted it. In fact it was a relief to admit it.

But it brought its own set of problems. The main one of which being he was dealing with a vulnerable young woman here, not the sort of woman he usually favoured who was capable of being as ruthless as him, in bed and out of it. Whatever had gone on with this idiot of a husband of hers, it hadn't been pleasant and the scars hadn't healed. Not by a long chalk. He had to walk away from this one. At least for a while.

Morgan's eyes narrowed but otherwise his face was impassive, displaying no emotion. This ability he had of hiding his feelings was what had made him so successful in business.

The trouble was, he didn't know if he could walk

away. A pang of desire struck, low and deep. And that left him…where? Between a rock and a hard place, as Kitty would say.

'…mine, it's pretty wonderful.'

Too late he realised Willow had spoken and he hadn't caught most of it. Pulling himself together, he said, 'Sorry?'

'I said, if your pork is as good as mine, it's pretty wonderful,' she repeated quietly, clearly slightly put out he hadn't heard her the first time. Which was understandable.

Cursing himself, he said smoothly, 'It's so good I always lose concentration for the first few mouthfuls—it's the glutton in me. Shameful, I admit it.'

She smiled, but a faint shadow remained in the green eyes. He didn't like that he'd put it there, nor the uncertainty that went with it. Which was crazy, he told himself grimly. When had he ever cared to that extent? It was further proof, if any were needed, that he had been right. He had to walk away now and stop flirting with disaster. There were plenty of Charmaines out there, nice and uncomplicated without any baggage. Why go looking for trouble?

CHAPTER EIGHT

'So you slept at his place after he'd charged in on his white horse—'

'Harley, actually. Great brute of a thing.'

'His white horse and rescued you,' Beth went on, undeterred by Willow's dry tone. 'And then the guy helps you clean the cottage, invites you back to his place for another great meal—'

'It was Kitty who invited me back, to be strictly truthful.'

'And then turns up the next evening and takes you out to dinner! And you say he's only being neighbourly? Come on, Willow, get real. From what you've told me he isn't some geek or other who's starved for female company and fastens onto the first woman he gets friendly with. The guy's a player, and hot, obviously. And don't wrinkle your nose like that.'

'Well, don't use such terminology, then. You've never even met him.' Willow stared at her sister indignantly. 'A player!'

'Does he or does he not have an active social life?'

'I guess.' She nodded. 'Yes, course he does.'

'And does he give you the impression of being celibate?'

Willow stared helplessly at her sister. Several days had passed since the last meal with Morgan and she had filled them with work, work and more work, staying late at the office and getting in to work early. Arriving home exhausted helped her sleep and prevented endless post-mortems on the hours with Morgan. 'You've got the wrong idea about this,' she said at last. 'Honestly, Beth, you've got totally the wrong idea.'

Beth surveyed her sister over the rim of her mug of hot chocolate. It was Friday lunchtime and Willow had popped in for a quick snack and a chat, although the chat had turned into the third degree for which Beth made no apology. 'So what's the right idea?' she asked, setting her mug down.

She wished she knew, Willow thought ruefully. She didn't know which end of her was up, but she couldn't very well tell Beth that. She didn't want to get involved with a man—any man—but since she'd got to know Morgan better due to the events of last weekend she couldn't get him out of her mind and it was driving her mad. Furthermore, she had been both elated and terrified when he'd turned up last Sunday, worrying all night at the pub that he was going to make a move on her when he saw her home, and then being devastated when he said goodbye with a chaste kiss on her cheek. How was that for inconsistency?

Taking a breath, she said calmly, 'I told you, Beth. Morgan's a neighbour, that's all. A friend. Someone to have a drink with.'

'Has he kissed you?' Then Beth gave a little squeal. 'He has, hasn't he? He's kissed you.'

It was useless to deny it with the flood of hot colour

staining her cheeks. 'Once, with the sort of kiss you mean, and we both agreed it was a mistake and that was the end of that.'

'Was that before or after he turned up on your doorstep and took you to the pub?' Beth asked very intensely.

'Before.' Willow's tone was wary.

'There, you see.' Beth was positively triumphant. 'He came back for more, don't you *see*? Oh, come on, Willow, you must see?'

'Beth, we went for a meal and he saw me home and kissed my cheek as if I was his maiden aunt. If that's passion, I'm a monkey,' said Willow irritably.

'Have a banana, Cheetah.' Beth grinned at her wickedly.

Willow shook her head. 'He didn't ask to see me again and if anything he seemed glad to get away. And I wasn't imagining it,' she added fiercely, as though Beth had contradicted her. 'Anyway, he knows I'm not interested in a relationship and he's not the sort of man to bang his head against a brick wall.'

'So what sort of man is he?' Beth asked gently.

Enigmatically male. Virile. Strong and gentle at the same time, which was dangerously attractive. She could go on for some time because if ever a man was complicated, Morgan was. The way he had listened to her when she'd spoken about her childhood, the hungry look in the beautiful blue eyes...

'Busy,' she said flatly. 'Very busy, with no time to waste.'

Beth cocked an eyebrow sardonically.

'Well, he is.' Willow swallowed the last of her chocolate and stood up. 'I have to be going, thanks for lunch.'

'Pleasure.' Beth reached out and took her hands. 'I'm just going to say one more thing and then I'll shut up.'

Willow eyed her sister apprehensively. She recognised the tone. Whatever Beth was going to say, she wouldn't like it.

'Piers was the biggest mistake you'd ever made in your life and you're incredibly well rid of him,' Beth said steadily. 'But what would be an even bigger mistake is to let him influence the rest of your life in a negative way by shutting yourself away from the prospect of love.' She shook Willow's hands, squeezing them tightly. 'Love might come ten years from now, but it might not. It might be tomorrow. Life isn't guaranteed to come in neat packages when we're ready for it. Just…don't close your mind to anything. That's what I'm saying. Don't miss the opportunity of something great.'

Willow stared at her sister's concerned face through misty eyes and then leant against her for a moment as Beth's arms tightened around her. Beth had spoken as their mother might have done. Then she jerked away, her gaze flashing to Beth's stomach. 'Wow, that was a kick if ever I felt one,' she said in awe. 'Does it often do that?'

'All the time,' Beth said ruefully. 'Especially when I settle down to sleep. Peter's convinced there's a world-class footballer in there. He'll be so surprised if it's a girl.'

They smiled at each other, and after a brief hug Willow left to drive back to work. Much as she loved her sister, she wasn't sorry to leave. The inquisition had been a little rigorous.

Once seated at her desk, however, Willow found melancholy had her in its grip. Feeling the vigorous power of the new life in Beth's stomach had brought home to her yet again all she was going to miss in never having a family of her own. The baby couldn't have known, of course, but it was as though it had been determined to emphasise every word its mother had spoken.

Was she letting Piers influence her even now, subtly control her decisions and her plans for the future? She had never looked at it this way before, but perhaps Beth was right.

The thought panicked her, brought the blood pounding in her ears, and she gasped as though she were drowning.

No, she couldn't risk getting it wrong again. She had thought Piers loved her, that they were going to grow old together with children and grandchildren, that he would protect and cherish her. Instead... She gulped, drawing in much-needed breaths as she willed herself to calm down. Instead she'd placed herself in a living nightmare, the culmination of which had threatened to break her. She couldn't go through that again.

She shut her eyes tightly but she could still see Piers' enraged face on the screen of her mind, hear his curses as he had sent his plate spinning to the floor with a flick of his hand. Such a small thing to signify the end of a marriage—potatoes that were slightly too hard in the centre—but if it hadn't been that it would have been something else. His control over her by that time had been obsessional and she had lived in fear of displeasing him in some way. Her confidence had gone; she'd been a shell of her former self. Piers had told her she was useless in bed and nothing to look at, stupid, dull and boring, and she had believed him. But that night something had snapped and she'd yelled back at him, telling him some home truths that had caught him on the raw.

It had been the first time he had resorted to physical abuse, and when he had hit her she had hit him back, fighting with all her might when he'd laid into her. Their neighbours had called the police and by the time they'd arrived she had been barely conscious, but lucid enough to realise that but for the police's pounding at their door his intention had been to rape her. That knowledge had been the most horrific thing of all.

The divorce had been quick and final and he hadn't even contested it, realising he had gone too far and his hold over her was finished. Her love had turned to hate and he'd known it.

She opened her eyes, staring down at the papers on her desk without seeing them, lost in her dark thoughts. How could something she had thought so good, so fine, have turned out to be so bad, a lie from start to finish? Some months after the divorce one of her friends had told her she'd heard Piers had married again. Someone from his office apparently and, her friend had murmured, the word was Piers had been seeing this girl when he was still married to Willow. She had looked her friend full in the face and told her the girl had her sympathy. And it was true. She had. No one deserved Piers.

Willow sat for a moment more and then her shoulders came back and she straightened. She had work to do. No more thinking. And anyway, Morgan hadn't asked to see her again, she reminded herself, as though that sorted everything out. Which it did, certainly for the immediate future.

She was the last one to leave her particular office at six o'clock although there were still a couple of lights on in other parts of the building when she walked out to the car park after saying goodnight to the security man. The night was windy but dry and she drove home carefully, conscious she was tired, both emotionally and physically. Tomorrow morning she had the chimney sweep coming and she couldn't wait to be able to light a fire in the sitting room again, and in the afternoon the plumber Morgan had recommended was coming to look round the cottage and give her a quote for central heating. Tonight, though, the cottage was cold and faintly damp, and it didn't do anything for her mood as she fixed herself a sandwich and a hot drink in the kitchen. The last few nights she'd gone to bed with a jumper and bedsocks over her pyjamas, and three hot-water bottles positioned at strategic parts of her body.

She went to bed early, once again cocooned like an Eskimo and fell asleep immediately, curled under the duvet like a small animal, waking just before her alarm clock went off at eight. Her nose was cold but the rest of her was as warm as toast and she stretched, willing herself to get out of bed and face the chill.

An hour later she'd washed, dressed and had breakfast and was waiting for the chimney sweep. After a gloomy, rain-filled week the weather had done one of its mercurial transformations. Bright sunshine was spilling through the cottage windows and all was golden light. Her mood, too, had changed. She was in love with her little home again and the future wasn't the black hole she had stared into the night before, but something laced with expectation and hope. Life was good and she was fortunate.

She wasn't sure if she could ever fully trust a man again or take the step Beth had spoken about yesterday, but somehow it didn't seem such an urgent obstacle today but something that would take care of itself. Shrugging at her inconsistency, she made another pot of coffee and was just taking her first sip when a knock came at the front door.

Absolutely sure it was the chimney sweep, she flung

open the door saying, 'Am I pleased to see *you*', and then felt an instant tightening in her stomach as her heart did a somersault.

'Thank you. I didn't expect such a warm welcome.' Morgan was leaning against the door post, his black hair shining in the sunlight and his blue eyes crinkled with a smile.

'I thought you were the chimney sweep,' she said weakly, knowing she'd turned beetroot red. 'I'm waiting for him.'

'Don't spoil it.'

'I— He'll be here in a—a minute.' Oh, for goodness' sake, pull yourself together, she told herself scathingly, hearing her stammer with disgust, but the knowledge had suddenly hit that part of the uplift in her mood had been because there'd been a chance of running into Morgan during the weekend. 'Come in,' she said belatedly, standing aside for him to enter and trying to ignore what the smell of his aftershave did to her senses as he walked past her. 'I've just made some coffee, if you'd like one? And there's toast and preserves in the kitchen.'

'Sounds good.'

Like before he seemed to fill the cottage; the very air seemed to crackle when he was around. Leading the way into the kitchen, she said carefully, 'The guy you recommended for the central heating is coming round this afternoon.' Keep it friendly and informal, nothing heavy, Willow. Don't ask him why he's here, much as you'd like to. 'He seemed very nice on the phone. Very helpful and friendly.'

'Jeff? Yeh, he's a good local contact,' Morgan said a trifle absently. 'He'll do a good job for you.'

'He's just had a cancellation, apparently, and thinks he'd be able to start work this coming week if we agree on a price.'

'That's fortunate. Snap him up and get the job done.'

She turned to face him, an unexpected quiver running through her as she glanced at him standing in the doorway, big and dark and tough-looking. Only somehow she didn't think he was quite as tough as he'd like people to believe, not deep inside. 'White or black?' she asked flatly, not liking the way her thoughts had gone.

'Black,' he said almost impatiently, before adding, 'Thanks.'

After pouring Morgan a coffee she picked up her own and walked over to him, intending they go and sit in the sitting room. Only he didn't move from the doorway, taking his mug but his eyes moving over her face as he murmured, 'I've thought of you all week, do you know that? I've thought of nothing but you.'

Willow stared at him. His tone had been one of self-deprecation, even annoyance, and she didn't know how to respond. Raising her chin slightly, she said, 'Do you expect me to apologise?'

There was a brief silence and then he smiled, humour briefly sparkling in his eyes. 'No, just to listen to me while I explain where I'm coming from. Will you do that?'

She was spared an answer by the real chimney sweep banging on the front door. 'I'll have to let him in.'

He stood for a moment more and then let her through. 'I'll hang around till he goes, if that's OK?'

She turned just before she opened the front door. 'Yes, that's OK,' she said quietly, blessing the fact the turmoil within wasn't evident in her voice.

The next hour was the longest of her life, but eventually Mr George—a burly, red-cheeked man with a wide smile—had removed his covers and other paraphernalia, finished his coffee and cake, and left, and all without making one spot of soot fall on her newly cleaned sitting room. He and Morgan had chatted about local goings-on while he'd worked, and between them they'd eaten most of the cherry cake she'd bought the day before. Willow found she was immensely irritated by the ease with which Morgan had conducted himself, especially because her insides had caught into a giant knot and her heart seemed determined to jump out of her chest every time she looked at him.

The moment the door had closed behind Mr George, Morgan looked straight at her and for a moment she suspected he was as nervous as she was. Then she dismissed the notion. Morgan Wright didn't have a nervous bone in his body.

'So,' he murmured softly as though the last hour hadn't happened and they were continuing their conversation in the kitchen. 'This is the problem as I see it.'

Willow found she didn't like being referred to as a problem. It gave her the strength to stare at him without betraying any emotion and keep her voice steady as she said coolly, 'Problem?'

He'd obviously read her mind and the faintly stern mouth curved upward in a crooked smile. 'Difficulty,' he amended equably. 'We're neighbours. Next-door neighbours,' he added, as though she didn't know. 'Which means the possibility of running into each other now and again is pretty high.'

She didn't agree. He made it sound as though they lived

side by side in a terrace rather than with an acre or two of his grounds separating them, not to mention a high stone wall one way and the lane the other. She opened her mouth to voice this but he didn't give her the chance.

'But that's not really the…difficulty,' he continued. 'There's an attraction between us, you know it and I know it. We enjoy each other's company.' He raised his hand as she went to speak again. 'But here's the problem. Sorry, difficulty. You've just come out of a bad relationship and aren't looking to have a man in your life. Right?'

She nodded, but now she was determined he wasn't going to have this all his own way. 'And you don't do emotional commitment beyond the short-term affair,' she said tightly. 'Which I find…cold-blooded.'

'But you didn't deny there *is* an attraction between us,' he said very quietly, his blue eyes holding hers.

No, she hadn't. She should have, but she hadn't.

He walked to where she was still standing by the front door, not touching her but so close she was enveloped in his body warmth. 'Like I said earlier, I've thought of you all week.' His jaw tensed a few times before he added, 'Awake or asleep. That's not—usual with me.'

He lifted a strand of her hair, letting it shiver through his fingers almost absent-mindedly. 'I'm in London during the week, you're in Redditch, but at the weekends we could see each other sometimes. Nothing heavy, I'm not suggesting I expect you to warm my bed, although you'd be very welcome if so inclined,' he added smokily. 'More than welcome, in fact.'

'I— That—that wouldn't be on the cards.'

He smiled, a sexy quirk that did nothing to quell her

raging hormones. 'I thought not, but bear the invitation in mind,' he murmured lazily. 'It's open-ended.'

He was flirting with her. Willow found the warm fragrance of him was making her legs tremble. And he flirted very well. Obviously plenty of practice, she told herself, danger signals going off loud and strong. 'I—I thought I'd made it clear, I don't want to date. Not after everything that's happened.'

'Oh, you did, you did. Very clear.'

She drew in a deep breath as his fingertips moved against her lower ribs, his palms cupping her sides. It wasn't an aggressive action, just the opposite, but as his strength and vitality flowed through his warm flesh she felt as panic-stricken as if he were making love to her.

'But surely there's nothing wrong in enjoying each other's company now and again?' Morgan continued in a softly cajoling voice that played havoc with her power to reason. 'I expect nothing of you and you expect nothing of me. We can just see how it goes. Take it nice and easy. What do you think?'

She couldn't *think* with him touching her. He was so tough and hard and sexy that the temptation to lay her head against his chest and agree to anything he wanted was strong. She wanted to be looked after, loved, adored, spoilt, all the things she'd made herself say goodbye to for ever long before she and Piers had split. But there was no guarantee a relationship with Morgan would be any better. Piers had been charm itself before he'd married her. She'd learnt the hard way that meant nothing.

She became aware he was studying her with narrowed eyes. 'I'm not your ex-husband,' he said quietly. 'Get that straight in your head, Willow. I like you. I'd like to make love to you, I'm not going to deny it, but I play fair. You know I don't do for ever and that won't change. If friends is all we have, then so be it. You never know, this spark between us might burn itself out in time. What do they say? Familiarity breeds contempt? Togetherness can be a two-edged sword.'

Oh, yes, and Morgan was going to change from the most sexy man on the planet to some kind of a geek, was he? When hell froze over.

She stared into the movie-star-blue eyes and for a moment allowed herself to bathe in the feeling that had been there from the second he'd spoken in the kitchen. A composite of amazement, bewilderment, gratification, delight and sheer shock that this tough, enigmatic, wealthy and intelligent man, who also happened to be deliciously attractive to boot, was interested in *her*.

'You mentioned we live next door to each other,' she said weakly. 'What if it ends badly? Wouldn't that make things awkward?'

'It won't.' He kissed the tip of her nose lightly.

'You might meet someone.' The world was full of lovely women.

'I meet people all the time, Willow,' he said gently.

'A woman, someone who's free to get involved…properly. Who wants what you want.' Even now she found it difficult to say; what would it be like if it actually happened after she'd been seeing him for a while? She shouldn't be considering this.

He didn't deny it. 'Friendship can survive worse than that.'

She couldn't think of anything worse than that right at this moment but didn't think it prudent to say so.

'Decision time.' He pulled her closer into him, but this time he took her mouth in a kiss that nipped at her lower lip before deepening into an erotic assault on her senses. Warmth spread through her as his mouth left hers and trailed over her cheek, then her throat, before returning to her lips in a swift final kiss. He stepped back a pace, letting go of her, and she felt the loss in every fibre of her being. 'So?' he said levelly, face expressionless. 'What's it to be?'

'You said no lovemaking,' she protested weakly.

'I said I didn't expect you to jump into bed with me,' he corrected gently. 'I didn't say anything about kissing or cuddling or a whole host of other…pleasant things between friends. And that's all that was, nothing heavy.'

'You kiss all your friends like that?'

His eyes were deep pools of laughter. 'Only those with honey-coloured, spicy skin, green eyes and red hair.'

There were a hundred and one reasons why she shouldn't get mixed up with Morgan Wright, be it as a 'friend' or anything else, not least because absolutely nothing could come of it and she might end up getting hurt. She stared at him, her mind racing. But guidelines *had* been drawn—albeit somewhat fuzzy ones if that kiss was anything to go by. And why shouldn't she just go out and enjoy herself sometimes with a male companion? She was still young, for goodness' sake, and free, and she knew what—and what *not*—she was getting into with Morgan. He might be able to charm the birds out of the trees, but he *had* been honest with her. She knew exactly where she stood with Morgan. Didn't she?

Willow could still smell a lingering scent of lime from his aftershave and although he hadn't ravished her mouth her lips were tingling. He was disturbingly good at this kissing business.

Could she bear to say no, to effectively wipe him out of her life for good? He wasn't the type of man to beg.

She took a deep breath. 'I see nothing wrong in us getting to know each other better. It's—it's nice to know there's a friend around if you need one,' she added primly.

'Very nice,' he agreed gravely. 'Great, in fact.'

'And the cottage is a little remote. If I need a neighbour in an emergency—'

'You can call on me, any time of the day or—' he paused briefly '—night.'

'Quite,' she said briskly, taking his words at face value and ignoring the innuendo. 'Which is reassuring for a single woman.'

His smile this time was merely a twitch, but the piercing blue eyes glimmered with laughter. She wondered if he knew how that incredible, deep, bright blueness could hold you spellbound. Then she answered herself wryly. Of course he knew. And she was going to have to be very careful to resist Morgan's particular brand of magic.

This was nothing more than a brief interlude for him, a diverting game even. She'd caught his interest more because of what she wasn't than what she was. Unwittingly her refusal to fall into bed with him had singled her out as something of a challenge; it was the age-old scenario of the thrill of the chase.

But as long as she knew all that and kept it very firmly to the forefront of her mind, she could do this. And she wanted to do it. She wanted to get to know Morgan better, to find out what made him tick. She wanted to discover more about his past, what had made him the tough, cynical man he had become. To understand his work, what motivated him. He was a fascinating individual, she admitted it. Magnetic even. He had a quality that drew people into his orbit almost in spite of themselves. And she wanted to be with him…for a while.

She had been totally straight with him; he knew she had no intention of sleeping with him. That being the case, she had nothing to lose. Nothing at all. Did she?

CHAPTER NINE

WILLOW and Morgan ate at a little restaurant tucked away in a small market town some twenty miles away that night. When he arrived at the cottage he was driving the Aston Martin and the beautiful car added to the worries that had crowded in the minute he'd left. Morgan was way, way out of her league, she told herself as he helped her into the passenger seat and shut the door quietly, the doubts that had been rampant since the morning crowding in. Seeing him like this was going against everything she'd decided for the future on breaking with Piers. How could she be so stupid, so fickle? This was such a mistake.

Contrary to her fears at the beginning of the evening, they enjoyed a night of easy talk and easy laughter, and when Morgan dropped her home he declined her offer of a nightcap and left her on the doorstep with a firm, confident kiss that kept her warm until she was in bed.

The next day Kitty cooked Sunday lunch for them and they took the dogs for a long walk in the surrounding countryside in the afternoon, talking the whole time—about his work, hers, plays and films they'd seen and books they'd read. Nothing too deep and nothing too personal.

She didn't stay for tea, saying she'd brought some work home to do, which wasn't true, and that she had to move stuff in the cottage so Jeff could start work in the morning, which was true.

By the next weekend Jeff had finished the job and the cottage was blissfully warm. Willow had never realised until the last couple of weeks what a perfectly wonderful invention radiators were, and she found herself touching them in thankfulness every time she passed. They'd transformed her home.

Beth invited herself and Peter for Saturday lunch on the excuse they wanted to drop in her housewarming present—a lovely stone birdbath for the garden—although Willow was fully aware her sister was hoping to see Morgan. She'd told Beth she was seeing Morgan occasionally—as friends, she'd emphasised—and Beth had been instantly agog but she'd resisted saying more.

She hadn't mentioned Beth's visit to Morgan when he'd phoned her in the week to invite her out to dinner on Saturday night. She didn't want him to think she was hinting he come and meet her sister, or that he stay away—depending on which way he took it—and neither did she want Beth forming an opinion about Morgan yet. If they met and Beth thought he was the bee's knees that would create one set of potential problems, and conversely if her sister and Peter didn't take to Morgan that would cause difficulty in another way. No, it was far better to maintain the status quo for the time being.

Saturday turned out to be the sort of mellow English autumn day that inspired poets to pen the odd sonnet or two, and after lunch it was warm enough to take their coffee into the garden and sit on the ancient wooden benches she'd uncovered in the midst of what had been a jungle.

The trees surrounding the garden were now clothed in a mantle of gold, bronze and orange, the sky was a bright cloudless blue and a host of birds were twittering and squabbling and enjoying the sunshine. They watched as a robin, braver than the rest of its feathered kind, explored the new bird bath, which Willow had filled earlier. He had a great time splashing around.

'This is lovely.' Beth breathed in the air, one hand resting on the swell of her stomach. 'So peaceful.'

They sat for a long time idly chatting, and when Beth dozed off with her head resting on Peter's shoulder and he whispered she'd been awake most of the night due to the baby deciding it was football practice, Willow fetched a warm throw from the house to tuck around her sister and then sat listening to Peter's plans for the baby's future, which seemed to revolve around his favourite football club.

The gentle shadows of dusk had been encroaching for some time when Willow glanced surreptitiously at her watch. Morgan was due to arrive at seven and it was getting late. She fetched Peter another coffee, making sure she was none too quiet about it, but Beth didn't stir. After another twenty minutes she threw diplomacy to the wind. 'I'm going out at seven,' she said, when Peter refused the offer of more coffee, 'and don't you think it's getting chilly out here now the light's all but gone?'

Peter smiled blithely. 'We're fine,' he said, tucking the throw more securely round his sleeping wife, 'but don't let me stop you getting ready.'

Men! She loved her brother-in-law and she couldn't

think of a better husband for Beth or father for their child, but right at that moment she could have kicked him. Somewhat helplessly, she tried again. 'I'd hate for you to get bitten. I noticed a couple of mosquitos earlier.'

'I never get bitten and there's not much of Beth visible under this rug. Besides, she needs the sleep,' he said fondly.

Great. Just great. She marched into the house.

Half an hour later she'd showered and dressed in the new, deceptively simple frock she'd bought that week, a demure, sleeveless, jade-green number, which was high-necked and slim-fitting but with a naughtily high slit up one side. Her hair, shining like silk thanks to a wickedly expensive conditioner, was looped on the back of her head and she was wearing the long jade earrings her parents had bought her for her birthday just before the accident, which were infinitely precious for that reason.

She stared at herself in the mirror. She had been so demoralised during the years with Piers, so crushed and ashamed, so angry with herself for letting him hurt her over and over again but unable to rise above the control he'd exerted, that she'd forgotten what it felt like to dress up for a man who desired her. For the first time in what seemed like aeons she was pulling out all the stops and dressing to impress.

Panic sliced through her, undoing the elusive moments of pleasure she'd felt at her reflection.

Forcing herself to breathe deeply, she shut her eyes for a few moments. The emotional claustrophobia that reared its head at the thought of involvement was a legacy of her marriage and nothing more, she told herself grimly. It wasn't even connected to Morgan, not really. It could be any man taking her out tonight and she would feel the same way. The feeling of walking into a trap, of losing her freedom and independence could be overcome. Beth had said she was letting Piers still influence her life and that had rankled ever since. Because—she opened her eyes and stared at herself again, her mouth rueful—it was true. So she had to master this feeling and herself.

'Wow! You look a million dollars.'

She hadn't heard Beth come up the stairs and now she swung round to face her sister, smiling at the expression on her face. 'It's only me,' she said with an embarrassed giggle.

'You look fantastic.' Beth was grinning like a Cheshire cat. 'Absolutely fantastic. So, this going out is a date with Morgan, I take it?' She plonked herself down happily on the bed.

Prevarication was out of the question. Willow nodded.

'And you want us to get out of your hair?'

Willow smiled. 'You're prepared to make the ultimate sacrifice?' she said lightly. 'Greater love hath no sister…'

'Grudgingly.' Beth laughed. 'What time's he coming?'

The knock at the front door was answer enough. They heard Peter open the door, the murmur of male voices and then Peter called, 'Willow? Morgan's here.'

'Sorry.' Beth's voice was apologetic but her eyes were sparkling with delight. 'Looks like it's too late to escape.'

'I won't be a minute,' Willow called down, before eyeing her sister severely. 'No third degree, OK?'

'I wouldn't dream of it.' Beth managed to look shocked.

'Course you wouldn't.' Willow sighed. Her worst nightmare.

When they entered the sitting room the two men were standing with a drink in their hands deep in conversation. Willow's heart stopped, then bounded when she caught sight of Morgan. As always, he looked bigger and tougher and sexier than she remembered. 'Hi,' she said, faintly.

'Hi, yourself,' he said very softly, intimately.

He smiled and the sun came up, or that was how it seemed. 'You've met Peter,' she said, relieved at how calm she sounded. 'And this is my sister, Beth. Beth, Morgan Wright.'

'Nice to meet you, Beth.' Morgan held out his hand and Beth took it after one swift glance at Willow, which was all too eloquent. Tasty didn't do this man justice.

OK, Willow told herself wryly. Hadn't she known all along it would be the bee's-knees reaction? What woman could resist him?

She listened to Beth gabbling that they were so-o-o sorry they'd delayed Willow, but they were leaving right now and it was so-o-o nice to have met Willow's friend, whom they'd heard so much about.

OK, Willow thought. Stop right there, Beth.

Morgan's whole face was smiling now. 'Likewise,' he said warmly, 'but do you have to rush back straight away? Why don't you join us for dinner? We'd love that, wouldn't we, Willow?'

Willow saw Beth's eyes widen. Game, set and match to Morgan, she thought resignedly. In one fell swoop he'd won her sister for ever. He was good. He was very, very good.

Beth did the 'Oh, we couldn't possibly' thing very well, but Willow could tell her sister's heart wasn't in it. Within a short while she was seated beside Morgan in the Aston Martin and Beth and Peter were following behind in their faithful old Cavalier. She sat feeling a little shell-shocked.

'You didn't mind?' Morgan asked after a moment or two.

'You inviting Beth and Peter to join us? No, not at all,' she lied smoothly. 'Why would I mind?' Why, indeed?

'Peter had mentioned they'd come for lunch and with it being seven o'clock and Beth not having eaten since, in her condition, you know…' He gave her stiff face a swift glance.

Willow flushed. The reprimand was gentle and covert, but it felt like a reprimand nonetheless. 'I said I didn't mind.'

'Good.' Another moment or two slipped by. 'You look incredible, by the way,' he said softly. 'Absolutely beautiful.'

Her flush deepened. 'Thank you.' Charmer!

'And I'd much rather have been alone with you tonight.'

In spite of the fact she knew full well she was being sweet-talked by an expert, Willow found herself melting. It took all her willpower to ignore the sensual quality to his voice and say evenly, 'With the baby coming soon Beth won't have too many opportunities for spur-of-the-moment nights out.'

'No, I guess that's right,' he replied.

'I presume wherever it is we're going can stretch a table for two to four?' she asked crisply.

'Oh, yes.' He nodded. 'They're very accommodating.'

'Good. No problem, then.' She stared out of the window.

A mile or two slipped by before he murmured, 'What, exactly, had Beth heard about me, by the way?' Laughter in his voice.

'That was just social etiquette,' she said a mite too quickly.

'Social etiquette? Ah, yes. I see.' He gave an understanding nod.

'Like your reply,' she said stiffly.

'But I *had* heard plenty about your sister, Willow,' he reminded her gently.

She supposed he had. Beth and Peter and their life

together had seemed fairly innocuous a subject on the walk last weekend. Deciding attack was the best defence, she said testily, 'Why do you always have to have the last word, Morgan Wright?'

'A definite character fault,' he agreed gravely.

She suddenly laughed; she couldn't help it. 'I've made Beth promise not to ask you if you can keep me in the manner to which I've become accustomed, but if she goes into parent mode you'll have to excuse her. Her hormones are all over the place at the moment. And being happily married she thinks that is the only way anyone can be truly happy in life.' She wrinkled her nose.

'And you? What do you think?' he said quietly.

'Me?' She had to force the laugh now. 'Like you, I think it's a recipe for disaster.'

Morgan made no comment to this. 'She's a lot like you.'

'In looks? Yes, I suppose so. And we're both like our mum.'

He glanced at her, a swift look, but said no more for some miles. It was as they drew into the grounds of a large hotel he said quietly, 'I've missed you this week. Have you missed me?'

Light words came to mind, words that could have passed off the moment without betraying anything of herself. Instead she said just as quietly, 'Yes.'

The four of them got on so well the evening flew by on wings. Willow really did think Beth would have followed them home but for Peter putting his foot down where they made their goodbye in the hotel car park. 'Say goodbye nicely,' he prompted.

'Sorry.' Beth was giggly as she whispered into Willow's ear as she hugged her goodnight. It certainly wasn't due to the sparkling water she'd consumed all night due to her condition, Willow reflected with a smile. 'But I've *so* enjoyed this evening. He's gorgeous—Morgan, I mean. And we didn't expect him to treat us, you know. The pair of you must come round for a meal soon, promise? We'd love to have you before the baby comes.'

'Peter's waiting,' Willow pointed out gently.

'Don't freeze him out, Willow.' Beth wasn't giggly any longer. 'Give it a chance. He's gorgeous, he really is.'

'Beth, neither of us want anything serious. This is just a few meals out together, a little fling, that's all.' She hugged Beth again and then stepped away from her, becoming aware as she did so that Morgan was closer than she'd thought, close enough, maybe, to hear what she'd said, even though he was talking to Peter. For a moment she felt awful, then her chin lifted. She hadn't said anything out of place. It *was* what they'd agreed. He'd been the one to suggest it, not her.

Morgan put his arm round her waist as they waved the others off. For a second the sense of déjà vu was so strong she felt sick. How many times had Piers stood with her like this, playing the devoted husband after Beth and Peter had left them after an evening together? Whispering into her hair that the meal had been a shambles, she'd laughed too much, she hadn't laughed enough, her dress was all wrong or she was putting on too much weight, and all the time disguising his poison with a tender smile.

'What's the matter? Do you feel ill?'

Morgan's voice brought her face jerking to meet his and

she saw he was looking at her with concern. Shakily she shook her head. 'I'm fine.' She attempted a smile, which didn't come off.

'You're as white as a sheet and far from fine,' he said roughly. 'What's wrong? Have I said something?'

'It's nothing to do with you—with tonight, I mean.' She took a deep breath; she was saying this all wrong. 'What I mean is, I've enjoyed tonight. I thought the four of us got on great.'

'Something reminded you of him again, didn't it?' It was as though he could read her mind at times. 'Something I did? Is that it? Tell me so I don't make the same mistake again.'

'No. Yes. Oh—' she shook her head, stepping away from him and beginning to walk to the car in a corner of the car park '—can we forget it?' She didn't want to do the Piers thing again.

He opened the car door for her and helped her in, shutting the door and walking round the bonnet with a grim face. Once he was seated, he turned to her. The muted lighting in the car park was enough for her to see he wasn't going to let the matter drop. 'Tell me,' he said very quietly. 'Please.'

'There's nothing to tell.' She felt hemmed in, trapped.

'Little fling or not, you *will* tell me, Willow, if we have to sit here all night.' He wasn't angry and his voice was soft.

So he had heard. Woodenly, she said, 'Piers used to put his arm round me like that when we said goodbye to family or friends, that's all.'

He swore softly before he said, 'And?'

'And?' she prevaricated, not wanting to say more.

'From the little you've told me about this cowboy there is definitely an and.' He reached out and lifted her chin so she was forced to meet his eyes. 'Tell me,' he said again, but this time with such tenderness she found she had to clench every muscle in her body against the urge to cry. 'I don't want to make any more mistakes that can put that look on your face.'

'I told you, it wasn't you.' She lowered her head again, smoothing her dress over her knees with small jerky movements. 'Piers was a control freak,' she whispered after a moment or two. 'I suppose the signs were there before we got married but I was too inexperienced to recognise them. Maybe we'd never have married if my parents hadn't died, I don't know.' She shrugged wearily. 'But we did marry and within a little while he'd turned into someone else. He— he built himself up by knocking me down. Not physically, at least not until the end, but he'd make me feel stupid, worthless, ugly.'

Morgan's hand covered one of hers. She could feel his anger.

'We'd stand like we stood tonight and all the time he'd keep up a litany of what I'd done wrong, how embarrassing I was, how people felt sorry for him because he was with me. It—it was just now and again at first and he said he was pointing out things for my own good, because he loved me so much. Then it got more and more—' She stopped abruptly. 'But to everyone else, even Beth, he appeared the loving husband. After I left him she said she'd known something was wrong but she thought I was still grieving for Mum and Dad.'

'You didn't confide in her?' he asked quietly. 'Not even Beth?'

She shook her head. 'I can't believe I didn't now, but at

the time…' She shook her head again. 'He made me believe I was in the wrong. He—he was very clever.'

'I can think of a better word to describe him.' He reached out and smoothed a strand of hair from her cheek. 'What made you finally break his control?'

She looked at him. Yes, that was exactly what she had done, she thought with an element of surprise. At the time she'd looked on her leaving him as an escape, a feral, self-preservation thing, but it was more than that. The night she had fought back with everything she had—spirit, soul and body—something *had* been broken. She might have been left emotionally and physically battered, but it had been her who had won. She had become herself again that night, albeit an older, wiser self.

'He went too far,' she said flatly. 'Much too far.'

'Don't tell me if you don't want to.'

She thought for a moment. Did she want to? There was an unsettling blend of tenderness and anger in the tough male face and she knew the anger wasn't directed against her. Something melted. 'He threw his dinner on the floor. It wasn't the first time but that night something in me snapped…'

She told him it all, even the fact that towards the end of their fight she'd known he intended to violate her, which had brought a strength she hadn't known she was capable of. She wasn't aware she was trembling until he leaned across and pulled her into him, one arm holding her close as he rested his chin on the silk of her hair. 'I would give all I own for five minutes alone with this man. He'd never touch another woman again.'

His voice had been soft but of a quality that brought her

head up as her eyes sought his. What she saw in his face made her say quickly, 'It's all right. *I'm* all right. I am, really.'

'Are you?' The blue eyes were piercingly direct and she found she couldn't break their hold.

She had to swallow hard before she said, 'Of course.'

'For something like this there is no "of course".'

A long pause ensued but their gazes didn't unlock. She wondered why it was that this man, a man she hadn't known until a short while ago, seemed to understand how deeply she had been affected by Piers' cruelty when most of her friends had expected her to bounce back within weeks or certainly a few months. Hesitantly, she whispered, 'I'm getting there but—'

'What?' His gaze didn't waver. 'What's the but?'

'I never want to give the control of my life over to someone else again,' she said with total honesty.

For a moment he continued to stare at her, then a slight twist of a smile touched his lips. 'It scares the hell out of me too,' he admitted huskily, his mouth falling on hers. His lips were warm and firm and as hers opened instinctively beneath them his tongue probed the corner or her mouth, teasing her, coaxing a response she was powerless to resist. The kiss changed to one of infinite hunger and she heard him groan, a half-irritated groan at the limitations within the car as he tried to move closer and was restricted by the controls.

He raised his head, faint amusement in his voice as he murmured, 'I haven't done this for years and now I re-member why. You need to be a contortionist.'

Aiming to match his tone, she said, 'You haven't kissed a girl?'

His laugh was a deep rumble. 'Made out in a car. The

idea's good but the reality is less than practical.' The blue eyes held hers. 'Coffee at your place?'

Aware that something vital had changed in the last minutes she felt a yearning that cut through all her carefully thought-out guidelines for the future. 'Yes,' she whispered. Crazy, madness even, but yes.

CHAPTER TEN

THEY said very little on the drive back from the hotel. Morgan was aware he was driving on automatic, every part of himself tuned into the woman sitting so calm and still beside him. She appeared poised and composed, dispassionate even.

The calmness was a façade. He knew it as surely as drawing in the next breath. Willow had said she didn't want a permanent relationship. Well, neither did he. Not a relationship that came with a whole load of conditions at least. So why did her honesty grate so much? And it did. Hell, it did.

She was as tense as a coiled spring behind that composed exterior. *He knew it.* He took a bend much too fast and as the tyres squealed warned himself to concentrate. The anger he felt towards the ex-husband who'd left her so painfully damaged was growing, not diminishing. He wanted to make things right for her, to convince her she was a beautiful, sexy, gorgeous woman whom any man would count himself lucky to have in his arms. That was what he wanted. Because it was true.

Oh, yeah? His conscience wouldn't let him get away

with it. So this had nothing to do with the fact he'd wanted to make love to her from the first time he'd seen her tending that damn silly bonfire, all smudged and tousled and deliciously bewildered? The gnawing hunger for her body had been with him for night after torturous night, that was the truth of it. She'd stormed into his dreams every time he'd laid his head on the pillow and resolutely stayed there no matter how many cold showers he'd taken. And he had taken plenty.

OK, OK. He made mental acknowledgement to his desire. But a good healthy sex life between a man and a woman couldn't be anything but satisfying for both of them, could it? Damn it, it was what made the world go round, after all.

And what about all his protestations of friendship and letting matters develop at their own pace? Did he genuinely think she was ready for this? Emotionally, where it counted with a woman?

His thoughts went round and round in his head and when he reached the lane leading to his house and Willow's cottage he had to admit he had no clear recollection of the journey from the hotel. He parked on the grass verge outside her garden gate, walking round the bonnet and helping her out of the car without saying a word. She looked slender and delicate, vulnerable.

'You're beautiful.' As he took her in his arms in the dark shadows the tenseness in her shoulders became apparent. He drew her closer, dropping little kisses on her hair and forehead until she slowly relaxed against him with a breath of a sigh. Her hands had been small fists against his chest but now her fingers uncurled and crept down to his waist as her body curved closer into his.

He let his mouth caress her cheeks, her nose, her ears with the same small kisses, making no demands. 'You're beautiful,' he murmured again before taking her mouth in a deeper kiss, his hands falling to her hips as he brought her softness against the hard evidence of his arousal. 'So very beautiful…'

He could feel her slowly relaxing minute by minute and for some time he contented himself with exploring the sweetness of her mouth, bringing all his control to bear to prevent himself crushing her against him. If he hadn't known she had been married he would have thought he was dealing with a virgin by the nervousness he was sensing; it was further proof of just how badly her ex-husband had hurt her.

The night was cool but not cold and the darkness was scented with the faint aroma of hedgerows and wood-smoke. Somewhere in the distance an owl hooted but Morgan's world had shrunk down to the woman in his arms. He wanted her, he thought with an ache in his loins that was painful, but he wanted more than her body. He could hardly remember this feeling; it had been a long time since Stephanie when he'd thought he'd been in love and wanted to know every little thing about a woman.

Women abounded in London, beautiful and intelligent women who were self-confident without being egotistical and who knew their way round their own needs and what they wanted from a man. They were single by choice and intended to remain that way and he had found that suited him just fine. But somehow Willow was different and he couldn't figure out why.

Then she kissed him back with an unmistakable hunger that threatened his slow and easy approach. He tugged her more securely into the cradle of his hips as her arms wound around his neck, her hands sliding into the thickness of his hair. He covered her lips with his in a kiss that held nothing back, probing, sipping, tasting as a deep hunger and explosive warmth enveloped them both. His hips ground against hers as one hand positioned itself in the small of her back, the other cupping the fullness of one breast through the soft fabric of her dress.

He heard her catch her breath as she arched against him and the evidence of her pleasure intensified his, the knowledge that she wanted him as badly as he wanted her electrifying.

This time his kiss was so demanding it was almost a kind of consummation, as though she were accepting the thrust of him inside her body and he didn't try to soften his claim. Slowly, erotically, his fingertips began a sensual rhythm on her breast until she was trembling against him, little moans escaping her throat. She felt fluid, like warm raw silk.

He could take her inside right now and do anything he wanted to her; she was his for the taking. The usual thrill of conquest was there but there was a strange feeling of something being missing. Or wrong. Yes, definitely wrong.

He lifted his head, inhaling deeply and audibly as he tried to focus on what his mind was telling him rather than the savagely strong, primal urge of his body.

If he took her to bed now he would be as guilty of manipulating her as that sick so-and-so she'd married.

He looked down at her in his arms. She was breathing raggedly, her eyes still closed and her delicious mouth half open, her swollen lips bearing evidence of their lovemaking. Desire sliced through him as viciously as the blade of a knife and he tensed against the bittersweet potency of it, even as the intensity of what he was feeling provided its own sobering check on his libido.

He was a man, not an animal. He had mastery over his physical needs, not the other way round. After what Willow had gone through she needed to be sure of what she was doing when she opened up her mind and her body to intimacy again, and he knew full well he had used his sexual experience to sweep away her defences tonight. *She was too beautiful, too special, to hurt.*

The few seconds when she kept her eyes shut enabled him to compose his features even though he felt as though he'd been punched in the stomach by the strength of that last thought. He'd been right all along—he should have listened to the small, still voice of sanity, which had told him getting involved with this woman would be a gigantic mistake. Looking back, he'd known deep inside he was falling in love with her even then. And now it was too late. He totally and irrevocably loved her.

'Morgan?'

There was bewilderment as well as desire in the green eyes when he met her gaze, and he held her close for a moment more before straightening and steadying her as he stepped back a pace. 'I'm sorry,' he said softly. 'That wasn't part of the deal, was it?' Nor had been falling in love with her.

She blinked before shaking her head, whether in affirmation of what he'd said or confusion he wasn't sure.

He stared at her, knowing he had to make one thing perfectly clear after what her ex-husband had put her through. 'I want to make love to you, Willow,' he said quietly, 'more than I've ever wanted before with anyone else. I eat, sleep, breathe you half the time and the other half I'm taking cold showers. Nothing works. I feel you're in my blood and my bones, let alone my head.'

He watched her assimilate what he'd said, her eyes searching his face as though to verify the truth of it.

'But tonight isn't the night, is it?' he continued huskily. 'It's too soon. Tomorrow you wouldn't be able to handle what'd happened and you'd be hard on yourself.'

She hooked a strand of hair behind her ear and gave a nervous half-laugh. 'I don't know what you mean.'

'I think you do.' He reached out and lightly touched her forehead as he said, 'What goes on in here is different to what your body is crying out for. The two have to agree.'

She was holding herself very straight now, her features tight as though she dared not let any expression show. 'You're very sure of yourself, aren't you?' she said, but her voice shook. 'Very sure you know what's right and wrong for me.'

'I have to be.' He kept his voice even and low. 'For your sake and mine too. I've never taken a woman who wasn't one hundred per cent sure she wanted it as much as I did, and I don't intend to start with you.' *Especially with you.* 'I don't want to hurt you, Willow. Intentionally or unintentionally, I don't want that.'

She turned her head away as though she couldn't bear to look at him. 'I'm not a child, Morgan,' she said tightly.

'Believe me, of that I am well aware.'

'And I wouldn't allow myself to be hurt by anyone again.'

He was silent until she raised her head and met his eyes again. 'That one sentence says it all,' he said softly. 'If you'd have said you are prepared to take the risk of being hurt again, that life is all about taking chances, that you were at a stage where you understood you didn't want to be standing on the touchline looking at life but entering in, I'd have felt you were ready. As it is, those barriers are still ten feet high, aren't they?'

This time the silence stretched longer. 'Who are you to talk?' she said after a full ten seconds had ticked by. 'You told me yourself you got your fingers burnt years ago and from then on decided no long-term commitment but just a series of affairs would do. You said you didn't want more than that.'

He nodded. 'Yes, I did. And the pleasure of a beautiful woman's body in bed and a mind that is stimulating and intelligent has been enough for me.' Until now. 'But you aren't like that, Willow. *You* told *me* that. So I come back to where I started and it's that you have to be sure in your head as well as your body what you want. No one can make that happen but you.'

Even in the darkness he could see her cheeks were warm. 'So why did you…?'

Her voice trailed away but the question was clear. Morgan thought about prevaricating, even lying. He didn't want to sound the final death knell on this relationship that wasn't a relationship, but having come this far… 'I wanted to sleep with you tonight because wanting you the way I do is sweet torture,' he said evenly. 'But in the final analysis I knew I couldn't look myself in the eyes when I shave tomorrow morning if I'd seduced you. You said you're not a child and you're absolutely right. You're a woman, and one who needs to know her own mind when, and if, you take that decision. If I'd continued we both know I would have been taking that away from you. Once it was over you would have regretted sleeping with me tonight. Am I right?' He stared into the green eyes steadily.

She stared back, an unreadable expression in her gaze. 'I don't know if this is a clever ploy to convince me I can trust you,' she said at last.

Anger bit. His jaw clenched and he forced himself to relax and keep his tone steady. 'That's something you'll have to work out for yourself.' He stepped backwards and away from the temptation of her. 'Kitty's expecting you for Sunday lunch. Do I tell her you're coming?' he added flatly.

A pause. She still continued to look at him, unmoving.

His heart thumped like a gong in his chest and he couldn't seem to regulate his breathing. He had no idea how she'd react.

'As friends?' she asked quietly after what seemed like a lifetime. 'We're still talking friends here?'

He looked her straight in the eyes. 'What else?'

She smiled wanly. 'If you still want me to after tonight.'

The need to take her in his arms again was fierce, but this time the desire was to comfort and protect. Softly, he said, 'Willow, I've been honest with you. I want you, you know that, but if we continue as friends and that's all there is, so be it.'

Her mouth trembled for just a second; then she turned away. 'That will be all there is,' she said with an air of finality. 'So do you still want me to come for lunch?'

He felt his temper starting to come alive again but something deep inside told him it was imperative he didn't let it show. But he wasn't going to beg. 'Like I said, that's something you'll have to work out for yourself.'

She had reached her front door and he watched her

insert the key in the lock before she turned to face him again. Before she could speak, he said, 'Goodnight, Willow. Sleep well,' and turned from the sight of her.

He was actually half in the car when she shouted, 'What time is lunch?'

Over his shoulder, he called casually, 'One or thereabouts. And bring boots and a waterproof coat; we'll be walking the dogs in the afternoon.' And without waiting for a reply he shut the car door and started the engine. By the time he had done a three-point turn there was no sign of her.

He stopped the car just before the turn into his drive and sat in the darkness, trying to get his head round what had just happened. His emotions were in turmoil and for the life of him he didn't know if he had just made the best or the worst decision of his life. One thing he did know. He loved her. And loving her he had to let her go to either love him back one day or walk away from him.

He continued to sit for a long time and when he finally started the car again, his face was damp.

CHAPTER ELEVEN

WILLOW was painfully nervous when Morgan opened the door to her the next day. He'd called her mobile phone earlier that morning to see if she was all right and the conversation had been stilted, at least on her part, she admitted miserably. Morgan had seemed his usual cool, faintly amused self. But then he probably hadn't tossed and turned the night away before finally giving up any thoughts of sleep as dawn broke. He was a man after all, she thought viciously, and they were a different species. Logical, cold, control freaks. Only Morgan wasn't like that and she knew it. Or did she? She'd thought Piers was the genuine article, hadn't she? Not exactly ten out of ten there, then.

So the arguments had gone round and round in her head until it was actually a relief when lunchtime approached and she went to face the wolf in his lair. Or that was what it felt like.

'Hi.' He was smiling with his eyes as well as his mouth as he opened the door to her, and before she could protest he'd kissed her swiftly on the mouth before taking her coat. 'Come and have a drink,' he said easily once she'd finished fussing the dogs. 'Sherry, wine or one of my famous cocktails?'

It was impossible to remain on edge for long; Morgan had a witty and slightly wicked sense of humour and within a short time she was laughing at something he'd said and the atmosphere had diffused. By the time he saw her home under a moonlit sky things were back to normal.

Or were they? Willow asked herself later that night, curled up in bed but wide awake in spite of the sleepless hours the night before. Like it or not, their relationship had gone a little deeper, moved up a gear, call it what you would. He'd kissed her warmly on the doorstep but hadn't prolonged the contact, taking the key from her fingers and opening the door for her as the kiss ended, and pushing her gently into the house as he'd blown her one last kiss before shutting the door. She had stood immobile for some moments, overwhelmed by such mixed feelings she wouldn't have been able to name any one as uppermost. Regret, longing, confusion, relief, but overall a curious kind of restlessness, which was compounded by the fact she wouldn't see Morgan for another five days.

And she wanted to see him. A rush of longing swept through her, intensifying to a physical ache as she stared into the quiet darkness. How would she feel if he suddenly said he didn't want to see *her* any more? If he'd had enough of this 'friendship'?

She clenched her muscles against the rawness of the thought, then forced herself to slowly relax. She'd cope, she'd survive. She'd got through the break-up of her marriage, hadn't she? And nothing could be worse than that.

Really? Her mind seemed determined to play devil's

advocate. Was she sure about that? Had Piers ever stirred her inner self in the way Morgan did? Piers had been like a beautifully wrapped gift that turned out to be an empty box, worthless and of no lasting value. Morgan, on the other hand, was like tough brown paper done up with string, which held something priceless inside.

The thought shocked her and she sat bolt upright in bed, telling herself she was being ridiculous. Her heart was pounding and there was a lump in her throat, the feeling that she wanted to cry uppermost. Her head was trying to tell her something.

If only he had swept her off her feet last night—literally—and carried her inside and up to bed and made love to her all night so the decision wasn't hers. That was what most men would have done in his place. Then it would have been a fait accompli. No going back.

But Morgan's dead right, isn't he? the nasty little voice pointed out. If he'd done that she would have felt terrible in the cold light of day and probably hated him as much as she loved him. *Loved* him? Where on earth had that come from?

Her body went rigid. *She didn't love him.* She hugged herself, shivering, but the chill was within. She did not love Morgan Wright. She wouldn't be so monumentally foolish as to fall in love with a man who had made it clear from the outset that he wasn't interested in permanency or for ever or anything remotely approaching it. A man who conducted his lovelife with a ruthless determination to stay clear of the trap of matrimony.

Willow sat for long minutes, her head whirling, and when she slid down under the covers again she gave a short mirthless laugh. She had to be the most stupid woman on the planet. How could she have gone from the frying pan into the fire? She had loved one man who had turned out to be so, so wrong; how could she have fallen for another who was equally wrong, if for different reasons? This couldn't be happening.

What was she going to do? She lay, fighting for composure and telling herself she was not—she was *not*—going to cry. He didn't know how she felt and she hadn't, *thank goodness*, made the fatal mistake of sleeping with him, which would have complicated things further. She was his weekend 'friend'; she had no idea what he got up to in the week and she didn't want to know. She had to face the fact she was only on the perimeter of his life and that when this desire for her body he had spoken of began to fade, most likely their weekend dates would become less and less. And that was OK, it really was. It had to be.

Over the next few weeks this resolve was tested. Morgan had taken to calling her now and again in the evenings; pleasant, warm, amiable calls, which sometimes lasted as long as an hour. He'd ask her how she was and what she'd been doing before telling her about his day, putting an amusing slant on his conversation, which often had her giggling helplessly. And the weekends—oh, the weekends… He took her to the theatre and to the cinema; dancing at a couple of nightclubs in the first big town some distance away from the cottage, and for some delicious meals out. Other times they'd dine at his home, watch TV or listen to music, and take the dogs for long walks when the weather permitted.

On her birthday in October he whisked her off to a

superb restaurant where he'd reserved a cosy table for two; presenting her with an exquisitely worked little gold and ruby brooch in the shape of a tiny fire over celebratory champagne cocktails—lest she forget how they met, he murmured with a quirk of a smile.

Willow grew to know Kitty and Jim well, discovering the couple were lovely people with hearts of gold. She was even able to distinguish each of the dogs by name after a while and appreciate their varying personalities. Although she was uncomfortably aware her love for Morgan was growing the more she got to know him, she couldn't seem to do anything about it, and he seemed determined she *did* get to know him. He shared more of his thoughts and emotions each time they met or spoke to each other on the phone during the week, but on the other hand his lovemaking was more restrained if anything, often leaving her frustrated and unhappy once they'd parted.

Monday to Friday became an eternity each week; she felt the longing for Morgan's presence like a physical pain. In spite of that she continued to ruthlessly dissect her feelings and was honest enough with herself to acknowledge part of her was relieved Morgan wasn't a for-ever type. It kept things strangely safe. He wasn't for her. And because of that she didn't have to decide whether she could trust him completely or if she was seeing the real man— all of him.

It was on the first weekend of November, a weekend which had ushered in the new month with a sudden drop in temperature and hard frosts, the glinting sparkle of spider webs and satisfying crunch of stiff white grass proclaiming it was going to be a cold winter, that things came to a head. In hindsight, Willow knew she had deliberately engineered the conversation which led to the row that followed. Seeing Morgan had become so bittersweet, her nerves were stretched as tight as a drum.

They were walking home as the sun set, the dogs gambolling in front of them in spite of having had a five-mile walk. Fleeting wisps of silver tinged the pink mother-of-pearl sky and the weather forecast had spoken of imminent snow. As they cut across a ploughed field towards the lane and home, the flash of a pheasant's iridescent plumage lit the sky as the bird rose just in front of the lead dog and flew into the air, squawking loudly in protest at being disturbed.

They stopped, and as Willow watched the pheasant disappear into a small copse some distance away, she murmured, 'Thank goodness it got away, I'd have hated for the dogs to kill it.'

Morgan nodded. 'So would I, but that's part of life in the country, I'm afraid.'

She glanced at him. 'And you would have been able to look at it like that? If the worst had happened?'

'You can't take instinct out of the dogs or the bird,' he said reasonably. 'The dogs will chase for the fun of it and the bird will flutter and excite them as it flies. They're being what they are and doing what they're programmed to do.'

'The age-old argument,' she muttered under her breath, but just loud enough for him to hear.

'I'm sorry?' He'd caught the sarcasm and as she met his gaze she saw the change in his eyes, the sudden wariness.

'The age-old argument the male population trot out to excuse all manner of things,' she said steadily, her heart thumping hard. 'You don't even realise you're doing it, do you?'

They had stopped walking and she raised her chin slightly as he studied her. 'I've never "trotted" anything out in my life, Willow. Nor do I hide behind excuses for my actions.'

'No?' She forced a disbelieving smile. 'I thought the nature thing all led up to most males' favourite theory, that it's unnatural for them to be monogamous? The old "bee gathering pollen from umpteen flowers" philosophy.'

A muscle twitched in Morgan's jaw. 'What's the matter?'

She tossed her head. 'Nothing's the matter.'

'I've obviously upset you in some way,' he said with infuriating calmness. 'I'm asking how.'

'I'm not upset. I'm just stating what is a well-known fact. Men in general are incapable of being faithful to one woman for the whole of their lives. I think it's something like eighty per cent or more will have an affair of some kind or other, even if their wife or long-term partner never finds out. And the most well-worn excuse is that they couldn't help it and it didn't mean anything, it was mere physical attraction.'

'Well, it looks as though I've learnt something more about that slimeball you married,' Morgan said coolly.

She drew in a gasp of shock. Whatever reaction she'd expected, it wasn't this. 'I don't know what you mean.'

'I think you do. Faithfulness wasn't one of his strong points.'

Willow stuffed her hands in the pockets of her coat and said overloudly, 'Every opinion I have doesn't relate back to Piers. I do actually have a mind of my own.'

The blue eyes glittered in the fading pearly light. 'Then I suggest you start using it.'

Her eyes widened. 'I beg your pardon?' she said angrily.

'You met and married one of life's emotional rejects and he put you through hell until you finished it. It was a mistake and we all make them. Deal with it and move on.'

Her life summed up Morgan-style. The anger was welcome; it provided the adrenalin needed to fight back. She glared at him. 'I don't need you to tell me how to conduct my life.'

'I think you do, because no one else can get near enough, can they? You've made sure of that. Even Beth watches what she says around you.'

'She does not!' She'd never been so furious. 'And what do you know about my relationship with my sister anyway? You've only met her once. Hardly a basis to judge anything by.'

The look on his face alerted her to the fact she'd inadvertently stumbled on something. She stared at him for a moment that seemed to stretch and swell. The dogs had gathered in a puzzled group about their legs, sensing all was not well.

'You've been talking to Beth,' she said flatly. 'Haven't you?'

He didn't deny it. 'I can talk to whomever I like.'

'You've been discussing me with my sister? How dare you, Morgan? How dare you contact Beth and talk to her about me?'

'As you have been so at pains to point out over the last little while, we're free, independent spirits, Willow,' he said with heavy sarcasm. 'That means I can do what I like, when I like and with whom. Or have I got that wrong?'

'I can't believe Beth would be so disloyal.'

'For crying out loud, will you listen to yourself?' Now he was glaring and she knew she'd pushed him beyond his limit. 'Your sister loves you very much and she's concerned about you—what's so terrible about that? Or is she now condemned to be placed with all the other untouchables that are kept on the perimeter of your life? When are you going to face the fact that you can't live as an island, Willow? Sooner or later you're going to have to let someone in.'

'That's rich, coming from you,' she tossed back with equal ferocity. 'Say as I say and not as I do. Is that your philosophy, Morgan? Because it stinks. If anyone is an island, you are, as you've made very plain from day one. No for ever for the great Morgan Wright, but if someone else dares to say the same thing it's wrong. Now what does that make you?'

'An emotional child, or at least I was,' he said, suddenly very calm. 'Until I met you. Then things changed. *I* changed. Not easily, I admit. I fought it every step of the way but I finally understood that I could no longer put my feelings and desires into neat, separate compartments any more. I don't want an affair with you, Willow. Until this very moment I hadn't realised how much I don't want that. I love you, not as a passing fancy or a temporary stopgap, but as my woman.'

'No, no, you don't.' She stepped backwards, stumbled but quickly righted herself as his arm reached out to steady her. As it fell back by his side, she said again, 'You don't. You said what you felt was physical attraction. You *said* that.'

'It is.' For a long moment he studied her face, his eyes searching hers. 'But that's only part of it.'

'No.' Panic had gripped her, she felt smothered, unable to breathe. She had done this, forced this thing that had been between them since the night he had stopped himself making love to her, out into the open. Now she couldn't pretend any more. And she had been pretending, fooling herself, lying. Instinctively she had known from that point on things were different and he hadn't been playing games. She wanted to believe in his sincerity now, to cast all doubts and fears aside and trust he was speaking the truth, that Morgan was as solid and genuine as Piers had been hollow and shallow, but it was too huge a step of faith to take. 'No, Morgan.'

'Yes,' he said. 'Yes. Whether you want to hear it or not, I love you, and it's about time I told you because something was threatening to give and it was my sanity.'

'You said we were carrying on as friends.'

'We were never friends.' There was brusqueness in his voice along with rawer emotion.

He was right. Friendship was far too tame a label. She tried to speak, failed, then cleared her throat. The air, the dogs, even the birds were still, everything—all nature—seemed suspended. She was conscious of bare-branched trees against the frosty sky and the delicate beauty hurt in view of what she was going to say.

Her throat had locked and she had to swallow hard before she could say, 'I'm sorry but I don't love you.'

She saw him flinch and for a moment the temptation to fling herself on him and take it back was strong, but what would be the outcome? Panic won and she stayed where she was, her gaze dropping from his. This had to end now, for good.

'If this was the movies or a love story I'd do the noble

thing and say it doesn't matter, that we can carry on as we are, that I've got enough love for the both of us,' Morgan said tersely. 'But it matters like hell and the last weeks have shown me my control can only be tested so far. I guess what I'm saying is that it has to be all or nothing with me, having come this close. Anything else is not an option any more.'

Struggling to match his control, Willow nodded. 'I—I can understand that.' It was like that for her too, if he did but know it. The trouble was, she didn't know if she could trust Morgan—any man—for the all. Raising her eyes, she looked into the ruggedly attractive face. He didn't deserve a nutcase like her, not after the childhood he'd endured and the knocks life had dished out. She was doing the right thing here.

Knowing she was going to howl like a banshee and make a total fool of herself, she said quickly, 'I'd better go. Th-thanks for everything. I'm sorry it's turned out this way.'

The blue eyes were boring into her soul. 'Willow—'

'It's for the best. Really, it's for the best.' She began to walk, knowing her movements were jerky but unable to do anything about it. She half expected him to walk with her and when he didn't, she waited for him to call her back. The call didn't come. She walked on but still it didn't come.

Willow reached the end of the field and stepped onto the small style that led into the lane. Then she was in the lane and walking swiftly, woodenly, aware of the cold air on her face and the smell of woodsmoke. Jim must have lit a bonfire, she thought vacantly. He often did on a Sunday afternoon.

By the time she reached the cottage the tears were streaming down her face and she fumbled with the key for what seemed like an age before the door opened. She all but fell across the threshold, pulling the door shut and then sinking down with her back against the wood as she sobbed and sobbed.

It was over. As she had wanted it to be. He thought she didn't love him and, Morgan being Morgan, that would be enough to keep him from contacting her again. No more hour-long phone calls, which had changed mediocre days into something wonderful; no more weekends filled with laughter and music and life; no more being able to watch his face as he talked and smiled; no more Morgan. What had she done? *What had she done?*

He had told her he loved her and she had flunked it big time, ruining any chance for them in the future. She couldn't have put the final seal on this relationship more effectively if she'd planned it for a lifetime, she thought sickly. She had lied to him and, in lying, sealed her fate.

Willow couldn't have said how long she sat there wallowing in misery, but by the time she dragged herself into the kitchen it was dark outside and beginning to snow. Fat, feathery flakes were falling in their millions from a laden sky. Willow wondered briefly if she was going to be able to get to work tomorrow, and then dismissed the thought just as quickly. What did work matter? What did anything matter? she asked herself wretchedly. If this was all there was, if life was going to continue to be as horrible as it had been the last few years, she might as well hibernate in the cottage and become a recluse.

After making herself a mug of hot chocolate she put a match to the fire and curled up on the sofa, staring unseeing into the burgeoning flames. Morgan said he loved her, but how could she know he wouldn't change once they were together? She didn't let herself consider marriage; togetherness was too frightening as it was. And he hadn't mentioned marriage anyway.

Piers had been the perfect boyfriend before they'd got wed: charming, amusing, loving, attentive. He hadn't put a foot wrong and she'd thought she was the luckiest girl in the world. And then they'd tied the knot and even on honeymoon he'd begun to show his true colours. How could anyone ever really know anyone else?

'They can't,' she whispered into her mug of hot chocolate, cupping her hands round its warmth. They can't, that's the truth of it. Some things had to be taken on trust and she was all out of that commodity. She couldn't, she just couldn't, take the risk.

Wiping her eyes with the back of her hand, she told herself to get a grip. She had a nice job, her own home and she was in good health. Furthermore, she had plenty of friends and was as free as a bird to do what she pleased. She was so lucky.

It didn't help. It should have, but it didn't.

After another hour or so of fruitless soul-searching she resolutely switched on the TV. The weather girl was happily warning of severe snowstorms causing major traffic problems, her hands waving like an air hostess as she pointed out the worst-hit areas. It looked worse directly where Willow lived.

Great, Willow thought. Still, she was warm and snug and had plenty of food. Even if she was kept home for a day or two it wouldn't matter. She sat gazing at the TV screen wondering if Morgan would come round to see if she was all right if they got snowed in. He might, she thought, her heart thudding, before picturing the look on his face when she'd said she didn't love him. Of course he wouldn't come. Why would he? Silly to expect it. He might go as far as sending Jim but he wouldn't come himself. Not now. He'd stay away because he thought she wanted him to.

After another bout of crying she watched an inane comedy, which even the studio audience didn't seem to find funny judging by the forced laughter, and then made herself more hot chocolate. She had just swallowed two headache pills when her mobile phone rang, causing her heart to jump into her throat.

Her hands trembling, she looked at the number and could have cried again but this time with disappointment. Beth's mobile. Likely her sister and Peter were out somewhere and checking she was safely at home in view of the weather. She was still faintly annoyed that Beth and Morgan had been having private conversations she'd known nothing about, and her voice was stiff when she said, 'Hallo, Beth?'

'It's me, Peter.'

She knew immediately something was badly wrong; she'd never heard stolid, reliable Peter's voice shake before.

'Beth's had a fall. I'm ringing on her phone because when the ambulance came I forgot mine but Beth's was in her handbag.'

Blow whose phone he was using. 'Where are you? What's happened?' she said urgently. 'Is Beth badly hurt?'

'We're at the hospital. Beth fell down the cellar steps earlier. Why the hell she went down there without telling me I don't know; apparently she wanted to sort the last of the packing cases we stored down there when we moved.

It had something in she wanted for the baby's room. The first I knew I heard her scream—' His voice broke, then he went on, 'She landed awkwardly, Willow. They—they think the baby's coming.'

A month early. Endeavouring to keep the alarm out of her voice, she said quickly, 'It might be a false labour, Peter. A reaction to the fall. Things might calm down. They often do.'

'No, we thought that at first but now they're pretty sure it's coming. Her waters have broken and everything.'

'Three or four weeks early is nothing these days,' she said reassuringly, 'and babies are tougher than you think. It'll be fine, I know it will. Beth's healthy so don't worry.'

'She's asking for you. Is there any chance of you coming to the hospital tonight? She…she needs you with her, Willow.'

She didn't have to think about it. 'Absolutely. I'll be there as soon as I can. I'll leave straight away.'

'Drive carefully though, the roads are already getting pretty bad,' Peter said worriedly. 'When you get here, go to the maternity reception and they'll direct you. OK? I'll tell them you're coming and explain so there won't be any problems.'

'That's fine. Now get back to Beth and hold her hand, and don't forget to give her my love and tell her I'm on my way.'

'Thanks, Willow.' His voice was husky. 'I appreciate it.'

She stared at the phone for a stunned moment once the call had finished, and then leapt into action. Five minutes later she was dressed in warmer clothes, the fire was banked down and the guard was in place, and everything was off that needed to be off.

When she opened the front door and the force of the wind

threatened to tear it out of her fingers, she realised how bad the storm had become. Already the snow was inches thick and it showed no signs of abating, just the opposite.

Pulling her hat more firmly over her ears, she staggered to the car, wondering if she was going to be able to get out of the lane, let alone all the way to the hospital. In the event she needn't have worried. The engine was as dead as a dodo.

She tried everything, including crying, praying and finally stamping her feet and screaming like a two-year-old. It was after this she accepted she was going nowhere in this car tonight. She would have to phone for a taxi. It was going to cost a small fortune but it wasn't the time to count the cost. Beth needed her. Whatever it took, she was going to get to that hospital. 'Hold on, Beth,' she prayed. 'I'm coming.'

CHAPTER TWELVE

MORGAN sat staring down at the papers on his desk. He'd been sitting in the same position for a while, his mind replaying for the umpteenth time the whole disastrous last conversation with Willow. In fact ever since he'd got home and immediately gone to his study, telling Kitty he had some urgent financial reports to look through, he'd been dissecting every word, every gesture, every glance they'd exchanged. It had been a relief when Kitty and Jim had turned in early due to the weather, and he'd had the house to himself. He appreciated Kitty's motherly concern for his welfare, but there was the odd occasion when he was very thankful their flat was situated over the garages and separate from the main house, and this was one of them. He couldn't stand her fussing tonight.

He scowled at the inoffensive papers. He didn't know how Kitty knew he'd fed most of his supper to the dogs, but she'd looked at the empty plate and then at him and asked him point blank if he and Willow had had an argument. He'd snapped at her then, something he felt guilty about now.

Moving restlessly, he rose to his feet and went to stand

by the fire, his back to the flames. She was a good woman, Kitty. Gentle, kind. If he'd been placed with someone like her as a boy, his childhood would have been different.

Don't start feeling sorry for yourself, for crying out loud. Self-contempt brought him straightening his shoulders before he bent to pick up another log to throw on the fire.

He'd been lucky. Overall, he'd been very lucky to get to where he was now. He'd worked hard, of course, but then so did lots of folk who never got the break he'd got. One of his friends had said he'd got the Midas touch where business was concerned, and maybe he had. It had enabled him to rise in the world, to become more wealthy and successful than he had ever dreamed of in his youth, and he had dreamed plenty.

Morgan smiled bitterly. He'd vowed every day of his childhood and teenage years that he would make something of himself, if only to show the relatives who had treated him so shamefully that he'd had the last laugh. And one by one they'd come sniffing around once he'd made his first million or two, hands held out. It had given him great satisfaction to tell them exactly where they could go.

Yes, until a few weeks ago he'd been satisfied he had everything a man could possibly wish for in life. *Until Willow.* He'd really thought he was getting somewhere with her the last little while, though; there had been something different about her since that night when he had surprised her by walking away.

He should have taken her and be damned, he told himself savagely in the next moment, spinning on his heel so sharply that the dogs—scattered about the floor—rose as one to their feet with low barks. If he had taken her that night she would probably have been in his arms right now. But he had wanted more than the pleasure of her company in bed; he still did, more fool him. He had slept with many women in his time but until Willow he hadn't wanted to make love with one, and there was a difference. Oh, yes, there was a difference.

'Enough,' he muttered as he crossed the hall. He was going to have a drink. In fact more than one. A lot more. Enough so that when he closed his eyes tonight he would sleep without thinking or dreaming. Oblivion would be sweet tonight.

The sound of the front door bell stopped him in his tracks and sent the dogs charging to perform their canine duty of repelling invaders. Morgan frowned. Who the dickens was that on a night like this? Someone who'd broken down possibly, but he had never felt less like playing the good Samaritan in his life. He could do nothing less than answer the door, though.

One sharp word of command brought the pack of dogs slinking behind him, ears pricked and eyes narrowed, as he opened the door.

'I'm so sorry, Morgan.' She was speaking before he'd even got the door properly open. 'I would never have bothered you normally but Beth's in the hospital and I have to get there and my car won't start and the taxi cabs are refusing to turn out—'

'Hey, hey, hey.' He interrupted the frantic gabble by reaching out and drawing the snow-covered figure into the warmth of the house. 'Slowly now. From the beginning, Willow.'

'Peter phoned me. Beth's had a fall and the baby's

coming early and she wants me there. I promised, Morgan, but my car won't start and no taxis are running because of the weather. I didn't know what to do…'

'Yes, you did,' he said quietly. 'You came to me and I'll sort it. The snow won't bother the Range-Rover. We'll get through. I'll get my things. Relax, it'll be all right.'

They stopped outside the garage block and Morgan explained to Jim what was happening, then they were on the road and on their way. Willow had always thought that snow was pretty, transforming even the dullest landscape into a winter wonderland. Tonight she hated it. It was a relentless enemy and unforgiving.

In spite of the powerful four by four's ability to tackle the most atrocious weather conditions, she could see Morgan was having his work cut out to keep the vehicle moving steadily forward. She sat in an agony of impatience as they passed abandoned cars every few miles; the snow was forming into great drifts in places and the roads were swiftly becoming impassable. They didn't speak; she knew Morgan needed every ounce of concentration if they were going to reach the hospital safely, but she wouldn't have known what to say anyway. She had turned up on his doorstep needing his help—yet again—and even after all that had happened that afternoon he hadn't hesitated or made her feel bad. His response had been immediate and unconditional. He was a man in a million.

She glanced at him under her eyelashes. He was hunched over the wheel, peering into the road ahead as the windscreen wipers laboured under their burden of snow, every muscle and sinew focused on the job in hand. She was cold, tired, worried and scared to death, but there was no one in the world she'd rather be with in this situation than Morgan. Ninety-nine out of a hundred men wouldn't have dreamt of turning out on a night like this for a nightmare journey, certainly not for a woman who had thrown their love back in their face only hours earlier. Piers wouldn't have put his nose out of the door for his own sister, let alone hers. She couldn't compare Morgan to Piers, or any other man if it came to it. Morgan was Morgan, a one-off. Unique. And he loved her. As she did him.

The wind was whipping the car and great swirls of snow were blasting the windows, but for the first time since she had met Morgan the storm within Willow was quietened. Any regrets she felt about the past would be nothing to what she'd feel if she lost Morgan through her own cowardice. She hadn't liked his straight talking earlier, but he was right—it was time to move on. Every word he'd said to her was true.

The Range-Rover crawled the last few miles to the hospital and they were within sight of the building when the snow finally won the battle. Two cars had slewed across the road thereby blocking it completely, and turning round wasn't an option.

'Looks like the last leg will have to be on foot.' Morgan cut the engine as he spoke, stretching his arms above his head for a moment. 'Hold on to me and we'll get there, OK?'

He had just encapsulated her thoughts for the future more neatly than he'd ever know. Quietly, she said, 'I'm sorry I dragged you out on a night like this. You seem forever destined to rescue me from one disaster or another.'

'Beth falling down the cellar steps can hardly be laid at your door.' He smiled. 'Nor the blizzard.'

She smiled back. 'Thank you,' she said softly.

A shadow passed over his face but it had gone so swiftly she thought she had imagined it. Words hovered on her lips, explanations, excuses, but then she nearly jumped out of her skin as someone tapped Morgan's window.

The police officer informed them the road ahead was impassable, as if they didn't know. 'This is not a night to be out, sir,' he added, 'and all the signs are the storm's getting worse. Have you far to go?'

Willow chimed in. 'My sister's expecting a baby and we're trying to reach the hospital. It's not far from here.'

The policeman nodded. 'You'll do that all right, but I suggest you think about staying there the night. Come morning things will be easier but any journey tonight is foolhardy. People don't realise how treacherous these sort of conditions can be. Stay in the hospital and keep warm.'

'We'll do just that, Officer,' Morgan said appeasingly.

Once the policeman had trudged off, looking more like Frosty the Snowman than anything else, Willow said again, 'I *am* sorry to have put you in this position, Morgan. Will the Range-Rover be OK to leave here until morning?'

'It'll be fine.' His tone was dismissive, even curt.

Again she told herself to *say* something but the moment—and her courage—was gone.

She watched as Morgan walked round and opened her door, helping her down into the snow, which immediately rode over the old boots she'd pulled on before leaving the cottage. The snow was blinding and she was glad of Morgan's arm around her once they began walking. Far from being the enchantingly feathery stuff of fairy tales, this snow was vicious. It stung the eyes and lashed the skin, making the several hundred yards to the hospital an ordeal. She'd never experienced snow like this.

When they reached the automatic doors leading into the maternity section of the hospital, the warmth hit them as they walked in. Willow made herself known at Reception as Peter had instructed, and the efficient hospital machine kicked in. Within a few minutes a bright, cheery little blonde nurse was standing in front of them. She explained Willow needed to be fitted with a hospital gown before she joined her sister in the delivery room, and Morgan could wait in a special area designed for that purpose close to the room where Beth and Peter were.

Willow wondered if the girl's fluttering eyelashes and bold smile had registered on Morgan, but gratifyingly she rather thought not. He'd been equally oblivious to other women's interested glances in the past too, although she'd found them irritating to say the least.

She forgot about the nurse when she walked into Beth's room, knowing she'd never forget the look on her sister's face when Beth saw her. She spent the next little while between contractions assuring Beth that *of course* the baby was fine and *lots* came early, and were happy and healthy; praying inwardly all the time it was true. Beth would never forgive herself if things went wrong.

As time went on the contractions got stronger and the minutes between them less, but Beth wouldn't hear of her leaving. It was another three hours before the baby was born. It was a boy and he was a good weight, his lusty lungs proclaiming all was well as he bellowed his way into the world.

Willow was misty-eyed and Peter was crying unashamedly, but Beth was radiant as the nurse put the baby into her arms. 'This is David Peter,' she said, glancing at Willow who nodded her understanding. David had been their father's name. As Beth glanced towards the window, she seemed to realise it was snowing for the first time. 'How did you get here?' she asked. 'You didn't drive in this, did you?'

Willow smiled at her sister. 'I came courtesy of Morgan's white horse, although it was the four by four this time, not the Harley.'

It was totally against hospital rules, the nurse murmured a little while later after she had been to see the sister, but what with the storm and all everything was topsy-turvy tonight. If Mr Wright only stayed for a minute or two the sister would turn a blind eye this once. Beth nodded and assured the nurse sixty seconds would do it. 'Go and fetch him,' she said to Willow after the nurse had left. 'I want him to feel included in this; but for him you wouldn't have got here tonight.'

It was more than that and they both knew it. Willow hugged her sister. 'I love you,' she whispered softly, marvelling at how her world—which had seemed so disastrously out of kilter when she had stumbled through the snow to Morgan's house earlier—was righting itself. If she had the courage of her convictions, that was.

The waiting room was in semi-darkness when she reached it, the subdued lighting presumably so that its occupants could grab a little sleep if they needed it. It had worked with Morgan anyway.

Willow tiptoed in. How he had managed to fall asleep on one of the so-called 'comfy' chairs in the waiting room she didn't know. The wooden arms and plastic stretched tight over lumpy stuffing would have kept a sleeping-sickness sufferer awake. But he was dead to the world, his long legs stretched out at an impossible angle and his head draped over the back of the chair.

It was the first time she had been able to study his face without fear of those piercing eyes arresting her. He looked exhausted. Her gaze stroked over the tough masculine features. But younger, more susceptible than when he was awake. How couldn't she have seen his vulnerability before?

Because she had been too hung up on the past to look beyond herself and her own feelings.

The truth was uncomfortable but then it often was. When he had spoken of his childhood and youth she hadn't pressed him for details, telling herself it was probably too painful for him to share. But that had been an excuse. She had been frightened of learning anything that would endear him further to her. The experiences he had gone through as a boy had shaped him into the complicated and enigmatic man he was today, that was for sure, but he had a capacity for love and tenderness she couldn't ignore any longer. She couldn't let him slip through her fingers.

She had to tell him how she felt and trust she hadn't ruined everything. She nodded to the thought, ignoring the panic that accompanied it. She owed him that at least.

Willow knelt down beside the chair, drinking in the sight and scent of him. He'd discarded the thick leather jacket he'd worn in the car and his sweater did little to disguise the width of his chest and muscled strength of his shoulders. His hair had got damp as they'd walked and now it curled slightly over his forehead, accentuating the suggestion of boyishness. He was a man of contradictions, impossible to fathom.

'Morgan?' She touched his arm gently, her voice little more than a whisper. 'Morgan, wake up. It's me, Willow.'

His eyelids flickered and opened slowly but he didn't move. His voice so low she could barely make out the words, he murmured, 'I was dreaming of you.'

'A good dream?' she whispered, loving him so much it hurt.

His eyes seemed bluer than she'd ever seen them before and the faint lines radiating from their corners crinkled as he smiled. 'X-rated.'

It was probably unfair to take advantage of him when he was still half asleep, but it was now or never. 'I lied to you this afternoon,' she said softly. 'I do love you. I love you like I never thought it was possible to love anyone and I've known it for a while. Can—can you forgive me?'

He didn't move, not a muscle. For what seemed an endless moment he stared at her, his face unreadable.

Willow stared back, equally immobile, holding her breath as her heart thudded so hard she was sure he must be able to hear it. Let it be all right, she prayed. Please let it be all right.

And then, as though lit from within, the hard rugged features melted in a smile that was beautiful. He opened his arms as he sat up in the chair and she scrambled into them, tilting her head back for his kiss, her mouth as hungry as his.

'I love you, I do, I do,' she murmured feverishly between kisses. 'And I'm so sorry I hurt you. I hated myself this afternoon but I was so scared, Morgan. I still am scared. I can't help it.'

'And you think I'm not?' he murmured against her lips.

'Sweetheart, this frightens me to the core. My life was all mapped out and I was doing very nicely until you came along and blew me out of the water.'

'Did I?'

'Did you what?'

'Blow you out of the water.'

'Oh, baby, did you ever.'

They kissed again, straining together in an agony of need and murmuring incoherent words of love until a sound in the corridor outside brought them back to earth. Raising his head reluctantly, Morgan said softly, 'Beth? How is she?'

'She's fine, the baby too. They've got a little boy and you're allowed to see him, just for a minute. You're not supposed to but Beth got special permission.'

'Special permission, eh?' He kissed her nose, his voice teasing to disguise the gratification he felt at being included. 'This is pure you, you know,' he said tenderly, 'finally telling me you love me in a hospital waiting room with a blizzard outside and your sister just having given birth. It should have been over an intimate meal for two with wine and candles and guitars throbbing in the background.'

Willow giggled. 'You told me you loved me in the middle of a freezing cold ploughed field when we were having a row,' she reminded him.

'Oh, boy, do we have a lot to make up for...' He took her face in his big hands, smiling shakily as he murmured, 'But in for a penny, in for a pound. This should be done with music and a ring to hand and me on one knee but I have to know. Will you marry me? Will you be my wife, to have and to hold for ever?'

Somewhere outside their room a bell was being rung impatiently; someone was clattering along with what sounded like a trolley in the corridor and the odd baby or two were crying in the background. The smell of antiseptic was strong along with that faint odour peculiar to all hospitals, which was impossible to pin down. Willow thought she had never been in such a perfect place. 'Yes,' she said, taking his lips in a kiss that was fierce. 'Yes, yes, yes.'

Beth's squeal of delight brought the nurse running when Willow gave her sister the news after she and Morgan had held David Peter for a moment or two. For such a big man, Morgan had held the tiny infant with a tender delicacy that had wrenched her heart. She'd had a vision of the future, of Morgan cradling their own baby with the same sweet gentleness, and it had reduced her to tears. Not that it mattered. Tears and smiles and laughter were flowing with abandon and had infected everyone with the same weakness.

By the time she and Morgan returned to the waiting room Willow felt dizzy with happiness. That and tiredness. It was now gone three in the morning. She felt ridiculously hungry too but the hospital restaurant and café didn't open for breakfast for another five hours. Morgan found a snack machine and returned with crisps, chocolate bars and two paper cups holding a murky brown liquid that purported to be hot chocolate.

She sat on Morgan's lap and they fed each other the food between kisses, cocooned in a couple of blankets the nurse had kindly brought them. They didn't talk about the past or the future; that could come later. They had time now, for everything. But tonight only the present mattered; being in each other's arms, able to kiss and touch and breathe the other's warmth.

If this wasn't heaven, it was close enough, Willow thought as she snuggled against his chest and shut her eyes. Thank goodness for Beth wanting her tonight, thank goodness for the snow and her car not starting and the fact it was the weekend and Morgan had been home; thank goodness that against all the odds she had found the one man who could release her from the past and make her life complete.

She settled herself more comfortably within the circle of Morgan's arms and within moments she was asleep, a half-smile on her lips and her body curled trustingly into his.

CHAPTER THIRTEEN

THEY got married on Christmas Eve at the little parish church in the village. How Morgan managed to pull everything together so quickly, Willow didn't know. It wasn't just the paperwork and legal stuff, but persuading the vicar to fit in the marriage service between the three carol concerts the church was holding that day that amazed her. She suspected a hefty donation towards the church-roof fund might have had something to do with it. Certainly the vicar seemed happy enough.

Willow wore a mermaid-style dress in pale gold guipure lace with a fake-fur-lined matching cloak and hood, and carried a Christmas bouquet. Peter was giving her away and as they reached the church and heard the organ music as they stood outside she gripped his arm tightly. 'Oh, Peter.'

'Everything's going to be fine,' he reassured her softly, 'and you look beautiful. You'll take his breath away.'

She smiled at him tremulously. She had no doubts about what she was doing but she suddenly felt so emotional as she looked at the arch of Christmas garlands hung round the church door. The December day was bitterly cold but sparkling with sunshine and the winter sky was as blue as

Morgan's eyes. She hoped her parents knew how happy she was, how happy both she and Beth were. She hoped they knew they had their first grandchild, and that she was thinking of them on this special day. She hoped…oh, lots of things.

'Ready?' Peter smiled down at her and she nodded. As they stepped into the church's tiny inner porch the music changed, announcing her arrival, and just for a second she remembered that other wedding. She'd worn a full meringue-style dress in white satin with a long veil that day and they'd had nearly three hundred guests to the reception. Piers had insisted on a very formal and grand affair and her five bridesmaids and two flower girls had been schooled by him—as had she—not to put a foot wrong. She'd felt nervous and tense all day and the dress had been too tight, the speeches too long and she'd developed a blinding headache before the day was half through. Piers, on the other hand, had been in his element.

This was so different. Their seventy guests were all close friends and family and Kitty had put on a magnificent spread at home. This was an impromptu wedding filled with love.

Slowly and gracefully she began to walk down the aisle towards the tall dark man standing beside Jim at the front of the church. Morgan turned to watch her and the blue eyes were glittering with tears as she reached him. With no respect of etiquette he bent and kissed her as he took her cold little hand in his, and immediately his warmth and love surrounded her. She smiled up at him, all her adoration in her eyes.

He kept tight hold of her hand as the minister began the service, and when the time came to say their vows his voice was strong and clear for all to hear. By then the brief poignant sadness outside the church had gone and she was glowing with happiness. She was with Morgan. Where she belonged. And she knew that, for better or worse, in sickness and in health, for richer or poorer, until death did them part, they would be there for each other, strong in their love.

When the vicar beamingly declared them man and wife Morgan lifted her off her feet and swung her round to cheers from the congregation, kissing her soundly as she clung to him, her cheeks rosy pink and her eyes shining. Beth and Kitty cried along with the rest of the women in the church, and there was even the odd male guest who had a surreptitious dab at his eyes, but Willow and Morgan were smiling as they walked down the aisle together looking radiant. Which made Beth cry still more.

A friend of Morgan's who was also a professional photographer took relaxed, natural pictures throughout the afternoon and even little David Peter beamed toothlessly into the camera. The food was delicious, the champagne flowed and everyone got a little tiddly by evening when the dancing started in the huge, heated marquee in the garden, which was decorated with Christmas garlands.

Willow felt she was floating in a dream when she and Morgan had the first dance, their guests gathered in a smiling circle around them. It had been the perfect day. She glanced at the rose-gold wedding band nestling next to the diamond engagement ring Morgan had bought her the day after he'd proposed. Her hand was resting on his shoulder and he caught her glance, his voice deep and husky when he said, 'It's there for life, sweetheart.'

'I know.' She smiled up at her brand-new husband, thinking he was the most handsome, sexy, delicious man in the world as he whirled her round the dance floor.

'Don't look at me like that,' he whispered in her ear, his warm breath tickling her cheek, 'or we won't finish this dance, let alone the rest of the evening, before I take you upstairs and rip that dress off.'

'It cost a fortune,' she protested laughingly. 'You have to undo all the little buttons down the back.'

He groaned. 'What's wrong with a good old-fashioned zip?'

'Morgan, this is a designer wedding dress,' she said with mock severity.

'Exactly.' He grinned down at her. 'And the designer should have known better.'

She touched his face with her fingertips. He had insisted they would wait until their wedding night—hence the swift arrangements and bribe to the vicar—because he wanted it to be special with her, different from all those other women he had bedded so casually. She respected him for that and understood his reasoning, but she had seen what his restraint had cost him over the last weeks. But now the time for restraint was over and she wanted him every little bit as much as he wanted her. Beneath the guipure lace she was wearing a low-cut sexy bra, positively indecent see-through briefs and stockings, her pièce de résistance a naughty little garter.

Beth's eyes had nearly popped out of her head when she'd helped her dress in her wedding finery that morning. 'Willow!' her sister had shrieked. 'You dark horse, you.'

Her cheeks scarlet, Willow had muttered, 'What is it with

you and horses, Beth? And I don't usually go for this sort of underwear,' she'd added as Beth had laboured over the host of tiny buttons at the back of the gown. 'But I wanted to surprise him. To let him know how much I want him.'

'You will. Oh, you will.'

The memory of that conversation brought her mouth turning upwards now, and as the dance finished and they were joined by other couples Morgan murmured, 'What is it?'

Feeling deliciously like a wanton hussy, she murmured back, 'I've got a surprise for you later.' She might not be able to match those other women he'd known in expertise or a knowledge of all the little tricks a woman could use to please a man of the world like Morgan, but she had something none of them had had. His love.

The first guests began to leave about eleven, and by midnight they waved the last straggler off. Kitty and Jim had retired to their flat above the garages long ago and Kitty had promised she wouldn't disturb them until she called them for Christmas Day lunch at one o'clock the next afternoon. The day after that they were flying to Hawaii for a month's honeymoon. Morgan had booked a little villa right on the beach.

They stood wrapped in each other's arms on the doorstep as the lights of the car faded down the drive. A million stars twinkled in a clear velvet sky and the frost glittered like diamond dust on the ground, thick and white. The dogs had gone out as they'd seen their guests off and now filed past them into the warmth of the house, sensing it was their bedtime at last. They'd accepted her presence in Morgan's life completely.

Morgan grinned at her. 'We've been keeping them up. I think they were ready for bed long before this.'

She turned in his arms, kissing him hungrily. 'Them and me both,' she murmured. 'I didn't think the last few would ever go.'

With a groan of longing he pulled her into him and then lifted her off her feet, carrying her over the threshold for the second time that day. Kicking the door shut behind him, he held her high against his chest as he kissed her, devouring her mouth as she yielded to his maleness, her body boneless and fluid against his. She was trembling but not with fright, and as his mouth crushed hers possessively she strained against him, wanting more, passionate and willing for all the love he had to give.

By the time they reached the bedroom they were both breathing raggedly, their faces flushed. From somewhere Morgan found the strength to slow down. This had to be so right for her after all she had been through and he didn't want to rush it. They had a thousand tomorrows and he would make sure they were all filled with happiness and fulfilment but tonight—tonight was precious, a night apart. Tonight she became his wife.

An ice-bucket with a bottle of the best champagne and two flutes, along with a huge bowl of hothouse strawberries, was standing on a small table close to the bed. He made himself walk across and pour two glasses after he had set her down on her feet, returning immediately and placing one glass in her fingers before he said, 'To us, Mrs Wright.'

She smiled up at him and touched his cheek with her palm. 'To us, Mr Wright. And you are right for me, so right.'

They drank deeply before he set the glasses down and took her in his arms again, covering her face with kisses before he turned her round and began to undo the tiny buttons, kissing and nuzzling her shoulders and the nape of her neck as he did so. He edged the dress apart, caressing the silky skin of her back, before continuing with the myriad buttons, swearing softly once or twice when a particular button resisted his efforts and making her giggle.

'Of all the dresses in all the world…'

'I wanted to look beautiful for you,' she murmured softly.

'Believe me, my darling, you don't need clothes for that.'

When the final button gave up the fight he turned her round to face him and as he did so she let the dress fall to the floor. The look of wonder on his face was all she could have wished for. 'My surprise,' she whispered, suddenly overcome with shyness at the expression on his face. 'Happy wedding day.'

'You're more beautiful than words can say,' he breathed against her skin, his hands cupping her breasts as his mouth explored her curves. He peeled off her bra and then her stockings, taking his time, using his hands and mouth with exquisitely controlled sensuality as he knelt before her. When he removed the scrap of material that was her panties, followed lastly by the garter, she tugged at his hair.

'My turn,' she murmured plaintively.

He smiled, rising to his feet and standing before her as she undressed him. Now it was she who stroked and tasted the contours of his body, the hard muscles that shivered under her fingers and the roughness of his body hair exciting her as she teased him. By the time he was naked he was hugely aroused.

He lifted her up and carried her over to the bed, placing her on the black satin sheets and lying down beside her. She had half expected that their first time would be a quick and lusty coupling born of the desire he had kept a rein on for so long, but Morgan spent a long time showing her differently. He kissed and tasted and caressed every inch of her until she was mindless beneath him and begging for the release only he could give. And still he continued to please her.

She had never dreamt her body was capable of what it was feeling, that it was possible for pleasure to reach such a pitch that it was unbearable in its intensity. He introduced her to things she'd had no idea of, things that would have made her blush in the cold light of day but which were so right in the warm womb of their room. And all the time he whispered words of love and passion, taking care not to hurt her, her pleasure his only focus.

She was sleek and wet when finally he nudged her thighs apart and entered her, moving slowly, carefully at first, conscious it had been a while for her and she would be tight. She was tight, but his ministrations had prepared her body to receive its satin-hard invader.

He filled her completely, the sensation extremely satisfying, and as he began to move with gentle thrusts to build her pleasure small rhythmic contractions began to grow deep inside, sending shivers throughout her body. And still he took his time, building passion until she no longer recognised who she was. Until she merged into him and he into her.

She knew the moment he surrendered to his own desire; suddenly he was moving faster and deeper, his voice hoarse as he groaned her name with each thrust of his body. They reached their culmination together, spiralling off into a world of colour and light and sensation that held no past and no future, just the glorious present. Morgan gave a single raw cry of fierce gratification, collapsing on top of her seconds later as he turned and drew her against him, still joined. They were both gasping for breath but slowly the frantic pounding of their hearts quietened and their eyes opened.

It was only then Willow was able to speak, her voice dazed as she whispered, 'I never knew…'

It was ample reward for his patience and restraint and he smiled, smoothing her hair back before kissing her forehead. 'You're amazing,' he murmured softly, kissing her again.

'It—it was good for you?'

He recognised the thread of doubt, the need for reassurance, and love for her made his voice husky when he said, 'It was better than good, my love. I fell off the edge of the world.'

Her voice carried laughter in it now when she said, 'That good, eh?' as she tangled her fingers in the soft hair of his chest.

He stroked her back, her waist. 'You're all I could ever have hoped for, all I could have dreamed of, and I will love you till the day I die and beyond. I would give my life for you and consider it well lost, and I will never betray your trust in me by thought or word or deed.'

She touched her fingers to his mouth, her face blazing with love. 'I know,' she said, and she did. 'Because I feel the same.' She snuggled deeper into him, feeling his body respond instantly. 'Morgan,' she whispered, 'do you realise we might have made a baby?'

His voice held amusement when he said, 'I have to admit that wasn't high on my list of priorities for tonight, but, yes, we agreed we wouldn't use precautions so I suppose it's possible from now on.'

'But we might not have done,' she said after a moment.

'No, we might not.'

She lifted her eyes to his and they were glinting with laughter. 'So we could always increase the odds, couldn't we?' She twisted her hips and heard his sharp intake of breath as she rubbed against him.

'Absolutely.'

They made love twice more before finally falling asleep in each other's arms when it was light and church bells were celebrating the birth of the Saviour. Willow's last lucid thought was that from now on she would spend her nights in this man's arms and wake up in the morning to the sound of his breathing and the promise of making love with him and feeling his arms holding her. Her body felt sensuously satisfied, her mind was at peace and she wanted to stay like this for ever. She slept.

EPILOGUE

WILLOW didn't get her wedding-night baby, but exactly twelve months to the day they married, on a snowy Christmas Eve, their twin daughters made their appearance into the world.

Willow and Morgan hadn't planned on a home birth—with it being twins and a first pregnancy they'd been advised a hospital confinement would be advisable—but the speed of the labour took everyone, including Willow, by surprise. Morgan ended up delivering the babies with Beth's help as Beth, Peter and little David had been spending the day with them.

By the time the midwife reached the house after Morgan's frantic telephone call, it was all over. Holly and Ivy were tucked up in bed with their mother having their first feed, the strains of the carol that featured their names filtering up from the kitchen below where an ecstatic Kitty was making everyone a cup of tea.

'Goodness me.' The midwife's face was a picture as she stood surveying the happy scene. 'And you say you only had your first pain a couple of hours ago? This isn't how it's normally done, believe me.'

'Oh, I do,' Beth said in heartfelt tones.

Morgan, who was sitting on the edge of the bed with his arm round Willow and one hand stroking the downy head of one of his daughters, smiled. 'We've something of a reputation for doing things our own way,' he murmured lazily. 'Isn't that right, sweetheart?'

Willow smiled back. He might have reverted to the cool, slightly laconic Morgan he liked to show the world, but a little while ago he'd been beside himself. It had certainly been a baptism of fire into parenthood. She'd had mild backache for the last twenty-four hours and had been slightly uncomfortable after lunch, but none of them had dreamed she was in labour. And now they had two daughters. She glanced down at the babies nestled against her and then looked at Morgan. The blue eyes were waiting for her and their expression touched her to the core.

Sometimes in the night he would reach for her to hold her close, not necessarily to make love but just to enfold her into him and feel her breathing and warm against him. She knew she was his world and every day she thanked God for what they had. And now they were parents and their love, like the amoeba, would metamorphose to embrace their family. And they had plans for the future, plans as yet they hadn't shared with anyone else.

This house was so big and the grounds were wonderful, and although they wanted another child of their own in the future they had discussed adopting a couple— perhaps even more—of older children who had been placed in social care through no fault of their own. Children with health problems maybe, or who were disabled in some way—children no one else wanted to adopt because it might be too much of a headache.

Morgan remembered so well how he had wanted a family and a home of his own when he had been growing up, how desperately he had tried to make his relatives love and keep him, how he had felt when eventually he had been moved on to the next place. And eventually he had stopped hoping or believing that anyone would ever want him, hiding behind toughness and autonomy and taking the world by the throat.

They had talked through the painful memories together, slowly bringing into the light the recollection of cold dark nights when a little boy had been curled up in a strange bed yet again, or standing apart from the family he happened to be with watching other children receiving gifts or sweets or a hug, and knowing there was none for him.

Their family would *be* a family, they were united on this, and their children would be loved and cared for regardless of whether they were theirs biologically or not. Kitty and Jim would be perfect grandparents and right on tap to help too, because they didn't fool themselves things would always be easy or plain sailing. Not where damaged little people were concerned. But love could move mountains and break down the most carefully constructed barricades; it had smashed those around Morgan's heart, hadn't it? Her own too.

The babies had stopped suckling, and as Beth helped the midwife check them over in their little individual Moses baskets Willow reached up and touched Morgan's cheek. 'I love you so much,' she whispered. 'And I'm so blissfully happy.'

He brought her fingers to his lips, kissing each one. 'I love you too. Thank you for our beautiful daughters.'

'Pretty personalised Christmas gift, don't you think?'

He smiled quizzically. 'What are you going to do for next year? How on earth are you going to top this?'

She dimpled up at him, and as Kitty walked in with a tray whispered, 'I'll think of something.'

'Now that, my love, I don't doubt…'

15/05

MILLS & BOON®

Why shop at millsandboon.co.uk?

Each year, thousands of romance readers find their perfect read at millsandboon.co.uk. That's because we're passionate about bringing you the very best romantic fiction. Here are some of the advantages of shopping at www.millsandboon.co.uk:

* **Get new books first**—you'll be able to buy your favourite books one month before they hit the shops

* **Get exclusive discounts**—you'll also be able to buy our specially created monthly collections, with up to 50% off the RRP

* **Find your favourite authors**—latest news, interviews and new releases for all your favourite authors and series on our website, plus ideas for what to try next

* **Join in**—once you've bought your favourite books, don't forget to register with us to rate, review and join in the discussions

Visit **www.millsandboon.co.uk**
for all this and more today!